Stray Bullet

Jay Heron

Dreamsphere Books
Winnipeg, Canada

Stray Bullet

Chapter 1
Mel—Present

Under the blue-domed sunshine, everyone in LA is thirsting for something. For the majority of Angeleenos that something is either fame, wealth or youth. Moving down the list, there are those who find their tall glass of water in security, the ability to make ends meet, or simply happiness—drug-induced or otherwise. To Detective Melvin Daniels, it was routine he was thirsting for most—especially on his drive back to work. The predictability of ordered chaos at the West LA police station was what usually kept him anchored—exactly what he needed in his current storm.

While actors in the cars around him rehearsed their lines for the next shot at their big break, Mel was having trouble focusing on his own detailed script. With his phone on the dash, Siri sashayed him through the LA traffic as if it were a crowded skiing slope in Aspen.

"Wonderful. Exquisite. Ten days felt more like ten hours. You wouldn't believe how cute she is. I didn't even mind the crying anymore after a while. I mean, how could anyone be mad at such a perfect face? She's the prettiest little girl in the northern

hemisphere. Sure, I've got pictures. I thought about becoming a stay-at-home dad full-time, but Kate wouldn't have it. Yes, I know. It's important to set the example of a good work ethic. Kate's been amazing. Such a natural. Couldn't be happier. My heart just pours over. I never wanted our special time to end, you know? But I'm glad to be back, all things considered."

Creative freedom was scarce in his lines, since nobody would want to hear about how much his paternity leave had sucked. For a while he had detected similar patterns to his college days ten years before. Sleep deprivation, cleaning up vomit, losing all sense of passing time and porn-induced masturbation sessions—all factors that had teleported him right back to those unfruitful frat days. Heavy competition between parents sharing their experiences didn't allow for such honesty, though, so he swore the details would never leave the house.

Before his daughter had turned his life upside down, getting ready for work was his sacred ritual, and his alone. Over the years he had perfected the timing of every step from jumping out of bed to pushing the start button on his Ford Explorer. Shower, ten minutes. Breakfast of fried eggs, ten minutes—five more to stuff his face. Putting on a shirt and tie, three minutes. In case he shaved, which was only once a week, he would adjust his alarm clock to ten minutes earlier. Kate often joked how she would sooner turn him on by having dinner ready at 7:00 pm sharp than putting on her see-through negligee. She wasn't wrong, although it had been a while for said turning on to have reached his pants—another joy of parenthood.

Lost in the conundrum of finding a way back to his old

routined ways, he almost hadn't noticed the maniac in the matte army-green Land Rover Defender swerving between cars—and missing them by inches. A booming honk from behind pulled his mind back to the road ahead. This asshole driver wasn't just pissing people off, he was endangering the entire S Sepulveda Boulevard, Mel included. He couldn't remember the last traffic incident he had reported, dreary as the paperwork was. Yet he found himself unable to let this one slide.

The sound of his sirens blaring through the maze of cars along the three-lane road was all Melvin needed to get back into his everyday work mood. It was like his childhood calling repossessed his every thought as he chased down the Defender burning rubber in front of him. He cursed beneath his breath when he saw the driver pull over, begrudging the end of the hero moment. It was going to be all paperwork and no thrill of the chase. *Just my luck.* He parked behind the perpetrator right next to the Maple Tree Academy.

Old habit as it was, Mel checked the magazine of his Glock just to be safe. The fancier the car around this part of town, the more unpredictable the outcome of a pull-over. Although the sight through the driver's window told him a different story.

Three taps on the window caught the guy's attention, which seemed all over the place as he clutched the steering wheel with both hands.

Drugs or booze?

After the Xerox sound of the automatic window, Mel waited for the man to speak first. More often than not, this had proved to be the best way to get a reliable first impression of the law-bending individual in these cases. Immediate questioning had a tendency to drag the scene out from the start. Hours of time on the payroll had gone to waste in Mel's early career, listening to the craziest excuses for people to misbehave on the road. Top of the list was without question the sixty-three-year-old who had claimed to be in labor.

"Good morning, Officer. My driving behavior was probably less than stellar and I apologize for my rudeness. I honestly never do this," the guy started.

Of course you don't. If I had a nickel…

"I know I must seem like a lunatic driver on whatever substance floats my boat, but it's not like that. Not at all. I just have to get home as soon as possible. Before my…," the man stopped himself and balled his fist with pursed lips. "Look, I really have to get there—now. I wish I could explain it better to you, Officer uhm—" Mel informed him of his last name, "Daniels, but I can't do that. Not now." Mel was about to correct the title to Detective, but chose to ignore the urge.

Try as he did, he couldn't get a good reading on this guy. From the blond highlights in his half-long hair, the grotesque designer black shades and the lingering s-sounds in his speech he assumed him to be one of West Hollywood's twinks in pursuit of a sugar daddy in the hills.

"I'm going to need you to step out of the vehicle, sir. And remove the sunglasses."

Like most young LA homosexuals, the man in his shorts looked like the gym was his second home, sporting toned muscle beneath tanned skin. The Sheryl Crow Threads T-shirt stood out, though. He leaned against the side of his car, arms crossed tightly as if it were winter in Colorado.

After ducking into the car's interior he handed the documentation—license and registration—over.

Colt Whittaker, twenty-six, born in Topeka, Kansas, married. Maybe his instincts about the man's situation were spot-on. Staying in his home state was not in the cards for men like him. Not even in this day and age.

"Mr. Whittaker, you were driving way past the speed limit and endangering citizens. I'll have to write it up as reckless driving."

Colt's eyes widened. He uncrossed his arms. "No. Please listen to me, Officer. I can pay in cash if you give me some time. I'll come to the station later today. Hell, I'll pay double if I have to. I know I must sound crazy, but you have to understand that my husband *cannot* catch a whiff of this. Please. I'll do anything."

Mel spotted a poker chip-sized bruise on his left cheek. Holding his palm up, Mel said "Sir, I *strongly* advise you not to say another word. You'll get a ticket in your mailbox in a few days. Standard procedure. This isn't 1960."

Colt ran his hands through his hair. "No. You don't understand. He'll… Please, I beg you. Is there any way we could do this without an official ticket?"

"This your first offense, sir?"

He nodded.

"Then you've got nothing to fear. Would you mind telling me what that bruise is about?"

To Mel's surprise the man had started weeping as he hugged himself. He wondered what his deal was. Most of his characteristics fit the LA twink profile to a tee: exuberant ride, white-trash driving behavior, sugar daddy supporting his Hollywood lifestyle. The others—the bruises on his cheek and forearms together with the breakdown over a first traffic offense—hinted at something else.

But what?

"Sir? I asked you a question. The shiner?"

"Right. Sorry. I—uhm—kissed the wrong guy last night. His boyfriend was all for it as you can see. It was nothing, it'll fade. It always does." He sniffed.

"Are you on any drugs, Mr. Whittaker?" Mel asked, grasping at straws.

He approached Mel and pointed to his pupils. This couldn't have been his first rodeo with law enforcement, that much was clear. Maybe this wasn't the guy's first offense. Black pinpoints for pupils in the morning light passed the test with flying colors.

"Look, Officer Daniels, you've got the wrong idea about me, but I don't blame you. Comes with the territory. This is all my fault. I should have known better, but I...I had to try. You're just doing what anyone in your place would have done. At least you're being polite."

As Mel repeated the issuing of the ticket, the guy stared across the street—or rather, miles beyond that point. He looked like Mel had just told him he'd have to do time in prison instead of losing petty change—to his presumed standards.

"Do you understand what I've just told you?"

"Yes, sir."

Mel sighed. He'd always been a solid people reader, but this guy seemed hell-bent on disproving that theory.

"Mr. Whittaker, is there anything else you want to tell me? You seem a little on edge. Did something happen to you?"

The man looked up at him, narrowing his eyes. "No. No, sir, but thank you for asking. I appreciate it."

Not taking the bait. Got it.

"All right then. Drive safe."

"You too, Officer Daniels."

Mel watched the man slump back into his Defender after putting his sunglasses on—to cover the bruise as best he could, Mel thought. Although the smog hadn't been as bad as last year, the air around him felt heavy with all the things left unsaid.

What a way to get back to work, baby daddy.

"I could just eat her up. Would you look at that squishy face," Rita said in a higher pitch than Mel had deemed humanly possible. Lollapalooza was nothing compared to the hearing loss he had just suffered. There was no universe in which Rita wouldn't have squealed with delight while scrolling through photos of little Rose. Though she had nothing to do with the long hours of investigative work, as the literal front lady of the station, Rita Hanson had embraced the title of West LA Mom before Mel had set foot in the premises.

Sticking to the script, Mel gave his closest colleagues

the Hallmark version of life as a new father of the past ten days. His former partner, Cam, gave him a knowing glance and sipped coffee from his *world's second best dad* mug—the backside said *Mom's always number one—at everything.*

Since he'd been in the exact same place—twice with an unexpected two-for-one deal—DEA Detective Camilo Espinoza saw through Mel's bullshit as if it were cellophane. When his son was born Cam had been exhausted, but over the moon about the whole experience of fatherhood. When the twin girls came, however, the man had aged twenty years in a fortnight. Knowing he had it three times worse than Mel himself made his shoulders relax a little. Surely it couldn't be half as bad. Besides, Cam seemed to be functioning just fine—on the outside.

"Glad to see you again and all, but I'd sooner believe you joined Jehovah's Witnesses than all that bullshit falling out of your mouth just now," he told Mel when the mob had scattered.

Mel was biting his fingernails, a habit he couldn't seem to kick. "Good to see you, too. The DEA being here can't be good, now can it?"

"All in due time, but you're starting to get it. But hey, whatever brings me back here, right?" He shrugged.

"So…any chance they bought it?" Mel asked.

"No way to be sure, but I guess parental hormones might have blocked their inner polygraphs for now. Or they just like you enough to roll with it."

"No, that can't be it. They're just afraid of Rita," Mel said.

"For once, just take the damn compliment, man."

Cam's piano-white teeth contrasted his spotless olive complexion in a way that made it hard to say no to. Back when he was Mel's wingman years ago, nine times out of ten the lady in question had gone home with him instead, leaving Mel alone in a bar with the tab. Of course his promotion to the DEA had been an allure all on its own in the dating world.

Mel stared at his feet. "Thanks, Cam. Appreciate it."

"See? Not as hard as it looks. Anyway, we need you in the meeting room in ten minutes. Our new case is splayed out over several units. Special Victims, Homicide and the DEA, all tangled up like Christmas lights in February. Looks like I'll be here for a while."

Mel nodded. He missed the days of him and Cam being partners in the Traffic Unit. How easy it had been for them to communicate in comparison to his new partner of four months who hadn't even congratulated or approached him since Rose's birth.

"By the way, I wrote someone up for reckless driving on my way here," Mel said.

"Aha. That's why you're chewing cuticles. Not your unit, but I get it—overachiever as always. Drugs or booze?"

"Neither. One of those West Hollywood gay types in a rush. Something was off about him, though." Mel recounted the events, not leaving out a single detail. He wanted his best friend's take to set his mind at ease. That look of terror in the young guy's watery marine eyes would otherwise keep poking the inside of his skull.

"You know how it is, Mel. Coming to the big city, facing rejection after rejection, barely making ends meet, hanging with the wrong crowd, breaking your moral compass in half... I bet he's got an Only Fans account netting four figures from what you're telling me. But hey, that's your area of expertise, right?" Cam said, patting him on the back before walking away with a "See you in there."

Mel found his partner in their office with her big dark eyes glued to the screen. Charlotte Weisz, the twenty-seven-year-old rookie detective of the West LA division. The wunderkind. The fastest-climbing African-American female detective the LAPD had ever seen.

If only she were human.

Rapping his knuckles against the wooden door snapped Charlotte out of her laser focus. "Mel, hi. There's a team meeting on a major case in five. I wish I had time to bring you up to speed."

Great, fatherhood's been amazing. Thanks for asking.

"That's okay. We'll play it by ear. I've gotten used to chasing my tail at home anyway." There was no way Charlotte could get out of this entrapment in their conversation. Or was there?

"Right. I can only imagine the sleep deprivation you must be dealing with. How are you holding up?" Charlotte's hair was wrapped in her signature tight bun—with no chance of loosening up.

"Fine, really. Glad to be back, but sad to be away. Parenthood's turning out to be a snake pit of dilemmas."

"Hmm, okay then. Sorry if I'm a little all over the place, but it's this case that's not letting me go. We'll talk later, okay?" Not waiting for an answer, his partner rushed to the meeting room with Mel in her wake. For all he knew, her reluctance to speak would be a blessing in disguise. Endless chitchat might have been ten times worse, especially with his new sleep pattern.

Mel was confident one day he'd learn all about his new partner's story. There had to be profound reasons for her robotic mannerisms. Given enough time and space, all kinds of people tended to open up to him. He had learned that particular wisdom early on in his life, moving back and forth between foster families and group homes. He liked to believe it made him a good detective, but at the same time it had him worried about his adequacy as a family man. How could he be good at something he had never witnessed first-hand? Maybe him questioning himself like that was what made him an excellent father. The thought had a calming effect—for now.

An hour into his shift he couldn't believe it, but he had fished his phone out of his pocket just to glance at his wallpaper: Rose sleeping with her pastel pink nightcap on. The urge was strong—primal even. So much so, he felt his cheeks twitch with a smile. He texted Kate to check up on his two girls and even added a couple of heart emojis.

Chapter 2
Mel—Present

"Glad you could all make it, and welcome back, Mel," Captain Perez said. "As you know, it's been three days since the report of the sexual assault case in Holmby Park. SV Detective Weisz will now give you the latest details on the case." She stuck out her hand to Charlotte, who remained stoic as she trod to the front desks of the meeting room in her sturdy black flats.

Charlotte cleared her throat. "Abby Fitzsimmons thirty-six, roofied and raped in broad daylight between the hours of 2 and 4pm at the northern edge of Holmby Park." She pointed out the location on the map on the slide with her laser pointer. "She doesn't remember much, but during the rape-kit protocol nurses discovered a minuscule puncture wound on her neck. Most remarkable was an initial seared into the skin of her right thigh." She paused, revealing pictures of the wounds, allowing her colleagues to wince at the sight of burnt flesh. The mark read a big C inside an uneven circle. It must have hurt like hell with every movement, Mel thought.

Charlotte flattened her black blazer with her hands.

"Our friends at the DEA's Forensics team have outdone themselves in terms of speed. Blood work showed a mix of GHB and Rohypnol. Other than that, there was no DNA evidence whatsoever on her body that could ID the perpetrator. Furthermore, there were no witnesses, no surveillance footage and, so far, no reports of strange individuals roaming the area. Besides collapsing and waking up naked in agony hours later there's nothing her initial statement has provided us to work with."

"Thank you, Charlotte." Returning to claim her throne, Captain Alana Perez eyed every single one of her underlings in the room. Together with her short, yet sturdy build, she was the kind of woman who demanded authority using her large coffee-brown eyes. Those present knew better than to interrupt or cause a disturbance. It never ceased to amaze Mel as he watched from the corner of the room—his go-to spot.

"Now, if I need to tell you why this case spans multiple units under the oversight of the DEA, then I don't see the point of paying you as detectives, am I right? But just for kicks, I'd like to hear it from you, Detectives Reynolds and Espinoza."

Gene Reynolds, the man with the tallest frame and tiniest waist in the precinct was the first to speak up. "Thank you, Chief. The branding on Mrs. Fitzsimmons's thigh— the encircled C—has been found on a total of six murder victims in the past three months. All six women had been raped, branded and strangled." Gene clicked through the crime scene images as he watched his coworkers. For a moment it looked like he was trying to emulate the Chief's methods.

"We've only caught one of the suspects so far. Miguel Gonzalez, a twenty-two-year-old with strong ties to the Cordelio cartel down in Tijuana." The mug shot showed a young Latino man with sunken cheeks, bulging eyes and greasy strands of hair plastered to his pasty forehead. It could have been a cautionary poster for schools in their anti-drug curriculum.

"Unfortunately the man killed himself in his cell using an unknown substance embedded in one of his molars. In other words, our one trail ran cold."

"And that's where the DEA comes in," Cam said as he positioned himself next to Gene. "The Cordelio cartel has rapidly overtaken every other competing drug ring in So-Cal in less than a year. Their trademark is designer drugs. Molly in the shape of unicorns or Casa de Papel masks, Adderall laced with cocaine, Vicodin with a kick of speed… In short, all popular suburban housewives's drugs, but 2.0." The pills and tablets in the slides looked more like candy to Mel. He could imagine their appeal to toddlers, a realization that made him shudder.

"Their members are not only bold enough to show force in the light of day, their leaders have the kind of money that makes all their messes vanish, too. Whenever we brought someone in for questioning, chances were high they'd reconsider and bolt before sitting down. Sadly, the only lead we've got so far is a series of sketchy high-end real-estate transactions in the Platinum Triangle of Beverly Hills, Holmby Hills and Bel Air, which would explain the bottomless financial resources for a large part. We'll have to do a lot more digging to get to the bottom of it, as you can tell."

"Thank you, detectives. I suggest you start there. As for the rest of you." Captain Perez paused with her signature move. "Special Victims, check out the neighborhood of Mrs. Fitzsimmons and possible drug habits of her family and close friends.

"Homicide, keep following those breadcrumbs of your killer. Relatives, friends, lovers, teachers, rap sheet—any stone you can turn.

"Listen everyone. I know leads are few, but we have worked with less and still kicked butt in the end. Someone in that cartel is going to get sloppy and make mistakes with a trail so clear we could hike it all the way up to bring them down. We'll reconvene once we've got more to work with, so in the meantime, look alive." After Captain Perez switched the projector off, she held a finger in the air, killing all the murmurings in the meeting's wake. "Talk to your coworkers, everyone. We're all in this together. Like white people say: sharing is caring. Thank you."

"Obvious first question, but here goes: why is Amber Fitzsimmons still alive?" Mel asked as he scribbled *WHY NOT KILLED?* on the whiteboard next to the victim's Instagram profile picture. Her straw-colored wavy hair cascading down her shoulders combined with her pearly smile felt out of place on this wall of atrocities. It was everyone's guess how long it would take before that smile would reappear on her face.

"Something could have gone wrong in the process. The perp might have had to cut things short before risking exposure. For all we know he could be waiting for things to cool down before finishing the job," Charlotte said.

"Are we having her watched?"

"Yes, but only by one officer at a time just outside her house for the time being. It's all I could accomplish before that husband of hers all but shut us down."

"He what?" Mel asked.

"Martin Fitzsimmons told us there would be no more questioning, no more snooping around. His family needs to heal and get past the tragedy, is how he put it. It's not uncommon for husbands to get all protective in rape cases, but it pisses me off nonetheless," Charlotte said, throwing her ballpoint on the desk.

Pisses me off? Mel had never heard his partner use the term before, good girl as he had her pegged. Maybe the West LA vocabulary had started to seep into her mind while he was on leave.

Good for her.

"All right, then. You coming?" he asked.

"To Holmby Hills? I'll get my camera. You're driving, right?"

"Did Hugh Hefner have fun in his caves up there? You know I'm driving."

As Mel turned onto Ohio Avenue, with its fragrant eucalyptus trees and tiny condominiums, he decided to make the most of this eleven-minute ride with his partner, who looked straight on with a creased forehead.

"You're going to get the ugliest wrinkles doing that, you know," he said.

"Doing what?"

Mel faced her with an exaggerated version of his own.

"Oh, right. Thanks, I guess," Charlotte said, then added "There has to be more to this story than a random sexual assault. Imagine the guy being a copycat of those killers, throwing us off completely. He could be having his way with another victim as we speak. Drives me mad."

Being married to the job, that's what drives you mad.

"You're right. It sucks." Mel waited until they were on the other end of the tunnel under the Nathan Shape Memorial Highway. "You know, Charlotte, I've been wondering. Have you ever been to after-work drinks at Stanley's?"

"No, I can't say I have. I'm usually the last to leave, so I've always considered it too little too late."

"You should. Take it from me, it's the best way to blow off steam in our line of work. Like the Chief said: talk to your coworkers, sharing is caring. Okay, maybe not that last line, but you get what I'm saying, don't you?"

"Yeah, I do. It's what my dad always says, too."

"Hey, look at me, killing it as a father already." He grinned, but his partner didn't budge.

Silence engulfed the Explorer once again. With the high-rise buildings of Wilshire Boulevard up ahead, Mel went for another round. "So, how are things at home?"

"Home?"

"Yes, you know, where you go after your insane hours at the precinct. The place you get your mail sent."

Jesus.

"Oh. It's fine. Nothing fancy, but it suits me for now. I don't spend a lot of time there anyway. Why do you ask?"

To break through all these layers of ice, lady. Grab something sharp and help me, will you?

"No reason. Just making conversation. It's important to talk about the smaller things in life now and then."

"We're almost there."

Mel considered his partner a true ninja in avoiding conversations that didn't involve work. Best to let it rest and try again later. At least Charlotte was now aware of her frosty people skills at the station, or so Mel hoped.

"Our victim woke up behind the public restrooms on the north side of the park…right there." Charlotte pointed toward the cream stucco structure surrounded by manicured lawns. The red terracotta roof tiles gave the impression of a Tuscan villa—even though it was a literal shit hole.

"The victim came here often for a walk in the middle of her afternoons. She lives around the bend of S Mapleton Drive, so her starting point on any day would be near these restrooms. My point is, the assailant can't have moved her far. It may have happened inside," Charlotte said.

Mel took in the surroundings in a full three-sixty. "Not a lot of hiding places around here, so I suppose you're right."

He had been there enough to know it was one of LA's best parks in terms of maintenance and surveillance—be it professional or community-related. Whoever had done this had the gall to act in plain sight. Yet nobody had witnessed anything out of the ordinary, according to Charlotte's interviews.

"What are you thinking?" he asked his partner.

"I'd like to go for another round of door-to-door questioning. Apart from it being the Chief's idea, I think it deserves a second act. It's not like we've got better things to do." She squinted at the south side of the park, holding up her arm against the sunlight.

"Sure, but let's go for lunch first. No use doing this on an empty stomach," Mel said, dreaming of the taco truck he had spotted right before he parked.

Lunch in hand, they walked back to the park to start digging into their nostril-tackling tacos on the first bench they came across—one facing the street with its back to the almost century-old lawn bowling park. Mel regretted never having tried it before and parked the idea in his list of future family outings.

As he had expected, Charlotte returned to her quiet self for the major part of their lunch break. He envied her multi-tasking talents: scrolling through her phone on the left, taking coordinated bites of her chicken burrito on her right. Seconds later, however, she spilled black beans over his shoe. *Just great. It's like I'm a father at work, too.*

"Charlotte, I don't mean to be sexist, but do you mind focusing on one thing at a time?" Mel said, pointing to his bean-bedazzled leather shoe.

"Oh, sorry. I was going through Amber's Instagram again. The woman posts her every move—well, only the happy stuff, like everyone else. There seems to have been a lot of that for her." She took another big bite, spilling lettuce shreds everywhere but on Mel's shoe.

Progress.

Never able to care less about social media, he averted his attention. Taking in the well-hidden mansions across the street, Mel was convinced Holmby Hills and its namesake park was the best part of LA. Unless people mentioned the Playboy Mansion a few blocks up the hill, no one outside of Southern California knew about the neighborhood's existence. Next to the well-trodden snaking roads of Beverly Hills and Bel Air, this hill-covered area mostly avoided unwanted attention from tourists. Historic street lights dotted the sides of the roads like all over the Platinum Triangle, but the absence of sidewalks usually stopped wanderers from feeling welcome.

"There's something odd. Three months ago Amber had a hiatus of three weeks between her posts. Before and after, she posted around the clock. Literally not a day has gone by without a selfie or some sort of teabag mantra." Charlotte showed him her screen.

"Could be anything. Plastic surgery, nasty bout of flu, psych ward, social media detox—if that's still a thing?"

"I guess so. I'll make a note of it just in case." Mel watched as she tapped the info into her Notes app. He wasn't that much older than her, yet his partner seemed to have a finer grasp on all things digital.

Mel got up and stretched out his hand to Charlotte's wrappers and Diet Coke can.

"Thank you," she said, pocketing her iPhone. *Was that a smile?* he thought as he walked to the dumpsters. Another layer of ice had been scraped off. He estimated there to be ninety-three more to go.

As he sorted every bit of waste into the corresponding bins, he noticed a familiar vehicle rushing by. A beige Land Rover Defender passed right in front of him—reminding him of his strange morning encounter. Just like Colt Whittaker, this driver handled the throttle as though it were on fire. His inability to assess the man's character didn't sit right with Mel. He tried to get the man's eyes out of his mind—devoid of hope or joy of any kind.

Going door to door meant driving up S Mapleton Drive from mansion to mansion, hoping housewives would open their gates in the middle of their Pilates workouts. Even though Charlotte had talked to the Fitzsimmons' direct neighbors before, that's where they started. Years of experience in SV had taught Mel that when it came to the delicate matter of sexual assault, people had an intuitive preference when it came to professionals' gender. Some neighbors, therefore, might be more inclined to open up to him instead of Charlotte. Whether it had to do with childhood role models or romantic inclination was one of life's many mysteries.

"Oh, she's such a sweetheart, that Amber. I don't think I've ever seen her frown—well, not until recently, I imagine. It's downright horrific what that bastard did to her. Have they caught the son of a bitch yet?" Mrs. Berg asked in her bright yoga pants. Knowing the world was still predictable in some ways brought Mel great comfort.

"Not yet, Mrs. Berg, but we're doing all we can to get to that point. How would you describe the Fitzsimmons' marriage in general?" Mel asked. The woman attempted a frown, but her botox-frozen forehead refused to let her. "In some cases rapists target failing marriages," he clarified.

"I guess they're doing all right as a couple, but you never know what goes on behind closed doors. I've never had reason to think of their relationship as failing, but I wouldn't say I know them that well." As she talked, Brianna Berg's eyes went over both detectives' outfits from head to toe as if offended to have anything less than designer clothes in her house. The three of them were sitting in the lavish living room between the sleek kitchen and the dining room featuring a table for sixteen people. The interior of the house was so white and smooth it felt more like a futuristic rehab facility than a Holmby Hills mansion.

"Have there been any signs of financial troubles in or around their home that you've been aware of? Car downgrades, fewer delivery trucks, or perhaps less frequent maintenance?" Charlotte asked.

Mel's phone buzzed. "Excuse me, I have to take this," he said after having read the station's number on the screen. He walked over to the kitchen.

"Mel, we need you back at the station ASAP," Rita said in her serious voice, which Mel hadn't heard in a while.

"I'm—we're kind of in the middle of an investigation Rita. What for?"

"Gene has a," she paused, "Colt Whittaker in custody right now. The man says he only wants to talk to Officer Daniels, so I suppose that's you, *Officer*."

His heart started pounding against his sternum. Unease threatened to clog the arteries around it.

"Tell Gene I'll be right there. Thanks, Rita." He hung up, hearing a faint *I told you so* in the back of his head. Cursing, he wondered why the guy was talking to a homicide detective. None of the reasons his mind could conjure were desirable in the slightest.

Chapter 3
Colt—Past

"I'm sorry, Gustavo, but you do realize how Grindr hookups like this work, right? In most cases we'd either be going for a second round or getting dressed at this point," Colt said, unsure how he got into this situation with the Brazilian work of art next to him on the most expensive couch that had ever hugged his butt cheeks.

Gustavo laughed, a rumbling sound that sent a tingle down Colt's spine. "This again? As a matter of fact, I do. But who ever says no to pre-coital drinks?" He put down his Old Fashioned on the marble coffee table with a clang. "Believe it or not, I get that observation a lot. It's like making conversation is scary these days. Rim jobs? Right away. Deepthroat? No problem. Listening to the other talk? Look him in the eye? Offer a compassionate smile? Run for the hills. I mean, how did we get here?" The man couldn't look more at ease with an ankle resting on his knee and both hands behind his head.

I got here by means of a Lyft driver named Hassan with a serious attention deficiency. You either sold your soul, won the lottery or B&E'd the place for the night.

The unmistakable waft of vanilla mixed with mild tobacco and sandalwood reached his nose—Amouage Memoir, one of the most expensive retail perfumes for men out there. He had never smelled it outside a store before.

Colt turned to face his date and propped his elbow on the headrest in an attempt to relax. An open, inviting body language worked wonders on his dates. "I'm not saying I mind it. I'm just surprised is all. This way it will take up more time than I had planned, for sure. But it's kind of nice. I love your voice. Go ahead. Sweet-talk me some more." Colt took a sip of his Martini—even the drink was of an intimidating quality.

He didn't just love the man's voice. His eyes kept wandering to the unbuttoned collar of his white fitted business shirt, where his chest hair seemed to deepen in color and density—something he adored in mature men like Gustavo. From the looks of the guy's forearms, Colt's imagination was running wild with anticipation of seeing the rest of his toned body. Dick pics only went so far on Grindr, and lighting could mean the difference between a sculpted chest and one having fallen victim to gravity ahead of its time—at least in Colt's filtered list of contenders.

"Don't mind if I do. So, Colt from Kansas, how are you liking the city so far?"

Colt swallowed. "Two years in, I'm still not sure. It took me ages to get my bearings and I had no idea life here would be this expensive, to be honest. And I'm among the lucky ones with a somewhat steady job."

"If it makes you feel any better, everyone I know has a

love-and-hate relationship with this town. What is it you do for a living?"

Colt smiled and exhaled through his nose. "I'm sorry, Gustavo, but it's a little early for us to be talking about personal details like that, don't you think? Next thing I know you'll come and stalk me at work, and I really can't afford to lose this job," he said, locking eyes with Gustavo. Men like him were dangerous to be this close to. That easy million-dollar smile, piercing eyes the color of Kryptonite and stylish salt-and-pepper hair nearly had him salivating.

Gustavo reached for his drink and took a sip, leaving it on the table. "I understand, and it's no big deal. You can't blame a guy for wanting to know all about a handsome specimen like yourself." As though they were trying to undress him, his eyes rolled all over Colt's body: from his tight denim shorts to his black V-neck and back. "But Colt? You should really start calling me Gus. Only *Mamãe* calls me by my full name." He inched closer and put his hand on Colt's knee, igniting sparks.

"All right then, Gus." Colt reached for the coffee table to put his drink down, hunching over. Meanwhile his date's hands had started rubbing his back, and seconds later he was in Amouage Memoir heaven with Gus's lips on his.

So far for pre-coital drinks.

It was a softer kiss than he had been accustomed to among the Los Angeles Grindr community. Gus explored every part of his lower lip with delicate strokes of his tongue, as if he were afraid to miss the tiniest detail along the way. Gentle as he was, though, his firm grip on the back of Colt's neck made it clear he was the one in the driver seat for this ride. It was exactly the way Colt liked it, even though there hadn't been any talk about consent. A risky move, considering Grindr was filled with profiles opposed to kissing of any kind.

As their kiss became hungrier and deeper, Colt found himself straddling Gus shirtless. He had no memory of how he'd climbed on top of him. Colt decided to pause their make-out session, ignoring the urge to get more of that tantalizing taste. If he hadn't pushed against Gus's rock-hard pec, Colt was sure the man would have devoured him whole—and chances were he would have let him. The room was spinning, adding to the level of surrealism that had washed over Colt the second he had entered the mansion.

"Catching your breath?" Gus whispered.

"Yes, but not only that. We have a few things to discuss before we go any further. You know, to make sure everyone has a good time. Or to avoid drama and lawsuits, if you're a glass-half-empty kind of guy."

"Fine, but you're staying where you are," Gus said, poking Colt's bare chest.

"As are you," Colt said, lowering his head to meet those sweet lips once more.

"Okay, but for real now. I take it you read my profile info?"

"I did. It's why we were a match in the first place. Please don't tell me it's all lies. That would be cruel."

Colt smiled. "Rest assured. It's all true. I need you to focus, okay? Aside from my colorful preferences there are two ground rules I need to lay down."

"Man, I really hate rules," Gus said as he caressed Colt's hips and obliques.

"Too bad, but I have to look out for myself. Anyway, number one: no props. If you feel like hurting me—and I really hope you will—only use your body. Got it?"

"Sure. It saves time in the clean-up, too."

"Second rule: respect the safe word at all times—Ferris wheel. The second I say it you're going to need to back off, no matter how close you are to finishing. Do you understand, Gus?"

"Yes, Colt. I understand. No props, Ferris wheel means stop. I doubt you're going to use your safe word, but I promise I'll respect your rules."

That voice. It was catnip to Colt's ears.

"Anything you need to tell me before we get on with it?" Colt asked, inspecting Gus's bulky traps and delts with his fingertips.

He could break me in half.

"As a matter of fact, Colt, I do have something to say. Here's what's going to happen. First I'm going to take you right here on this rug until you scream my name over and over, because you won't be able to help yourself. Then we'll go for seconds in the bedroom, where I'm going to fuck you until you're mine. Until I'm sure you'll come back for more. I intend for you to remember this night for a long time."

Colt's chest responded to the authority in Gus's voice as his heart rate climbed. It was a terrifying kind of sexy, yet he gulped down every word like oxygen, eager to surrender his mind and body to this Brazilian hunk. The primal urge was so strong he was able to drown out all the red flags he had listed since entering the mansion: too wealthy to be on Grindr, too successful to be interested in white trash like him, too smooth in his ways to be honest about everything, and too perfect to be true in this town.

Gus gripped Colt's sides and hoisted him in the air as he lifted the two of them from the couch. Sinking to his knees, he lowered Colt onto the promised rug, kissing him all the while like the physical effort was nothing. Career-chasing types like Gus usually didn't waste time during Grindr dates in Colt's experience, but it was nothing like that at all this time.

When Gus's lips had finally broken away from Colt's, he continued to explore Colt's upper body, starting with his neck and collar bone with the focus of a 3D printer. Every now and then he paused to remove another piece of Colt's clothing, unwrapping him like a present. As he stripped Colt down to his bright orange briefs—the only fancy CK pair he owned—Colt reached up for another kiss.

"No," Gus said, forcing him back down with a powerful shove of his large palm. As much as he hated the way it turned him on to be in Gus's power, there was nothing he craved more. Losing control was a dangerous drug, one that came with rules and safe words for a reason. It was why he didn't protest when Gus's one hand wrapped around his throat as the other freed him from his underwear. Gus himself remained fully clothed, making it clear to Colt that this stage in the process was all about him, and him alone.

Gustavo Carolino's mouth should have its own star on the Walk of Fame, Colt concluded after an undefinable amount of time spent on nipple teasing. He wasn't screaming the man's name yet, but it wouldn't be long. The grip around his throat intensified the moment Gus started working his magic lips on Colt's manhood, again taking his time to discover how Colt's body responded to every lick, kiss, suck, exhale and brush of his beard. Involuntary gasps, whimpers and soft moans made Colt's head feel like it was floating on the plush long-thread rug—instead of being held down.

"Gus," Colt gasped, not recognizing his own voice.

He could tell Gus was smiling, even though he couldn't see him completely.

"Now we're getting somewhere," Gus said, resuming his expedition.

Colt was suddenly close to climaxing as Gus relentlessly worked his mouth up and down and squeezed his throat a little harder. He heard himself repeat Gus's name, louder this time, making his date pull away and say, "Not now. I'll tell you when." It took all Colt's mental strength to obey, but he pulled through and tiptoed away from the ledge of sweet release.

Gus's lips found his again with a surprising amount of force, inhaling the moans that escaped Colt's throat. He pulled Colt to a seated position before he broke away again. The intense dark look in Gus's eyes should have warned him, but it didn't.

He felt his head fly to the right and held the point of impact with his left hand. There it was, the first slap across Colt's cheek he had received in years. Between the stars across his vision he saw Gus tilting his head to the side, anticipating the safe word. He couldn't say it didn't hurt, but the excitement rushing through his nervous system was too delicious to give up on. Like a scrape wound after a roller-skating fall that needed scrubbing to heal, Colt needed the sting of pain to enjoy being intimate.

Without the element of surprise, the second slap—across the same cheek—tasted even better, and the lopsided smile on Gus's face told him he wasn't the only one enjoying this new turn of events. He thought for sure the gentle phase was over when Gus pushed him back on the rug and rolled him onto his stomach. Yet, instead of more pain, soft kisses between his shoulder blades were working their way down his spine. His cheek throbbed against the soft rug, yet he savored every stinging second. Colt had no idea how much time had passed, but he was convinced this was the longest anyone had ever spent on foreplay with him.

Where some guys hesitated, Gustavo went straight for it. Parting his ass cheeks with his hands, the talents of his mouth concentrated their force on Colt's butthole—the most intimate act between men, ensuring him he welcomed every part of his body. Colt fought back the instinct to squeal and clawed at the long-threaded rug in the effort. His eyes were watering as he yelled a throaty *Gus* in response.

Gus's torso slid on top of him as he pulled Colt's hands to his sides with a firm grip on his wrists. The mind-blowing rim job continued and somehow felt better in this restrained position. It was so good Colt hadn't heard the distinct metal clinking of the handcuffs Gus was fastening around his wrists behind his back.

"Wait, what are you doing?" Colt asked in a single beat.

A second click. "Spicing things up a little. Relax, Colt, they're flimsy at best. Easy to break if need be," Gus said.

"I don't think so. We talked about this. Get them off. Now."

"Fine," Gus sighed, "if you really want to stop and order your ride home, be my guest. I just thought you were enjoying the restraining part a lot."

Colt rose to his knees after a few clumsy attempts. Looking over his shoulder, he said, "It's about trust, Gus. We had an agreement and you're breaking it. No props."

He gasped as Gus kissed his neck and caressed his shoulder. He was cradling Colt's tied wrists in both hands. "Shh. Don't get so worked up. It would be such a shame to stop now. You feel that?" He was skating a tiny piece of metal across Colt's palm. "That's the little key to these cuffs. The chain's long enough for you to reach. Try it."

Colt let out a frustrated breath and did as he was told. Gus was right: He'd be free in under thirty seconds if he wanted to. But it didn't change a thing. Gus had still broken the rules. He should up and leave before the guy did it again. What if he wouldn't respect the safe word either after this blatant breach of trust? But then again, Colt deliberated, if the foreplay was an accurate prelude to the rest of the night, it would be worth bending the rules for once. It was just one night, anyway. Tomorrow he'd go back to his shared-apartment life and probably never venture up Holmby Hills again. He might as well make the most of it.

"Okay. The handcuffs can stay. Just don't make me regret it," Colt said.

Gus responded by holding Colt back with an arm across his chest while entering him with first one, then two fingers. Colt's moans started to resemble screams, but were short-lived after Gus closed his hand over his mouth. He had never experienced this level of intimacy with anyone. It was like Gus knew what he wanted without words. Like he knew all the lines to a song he'd never heard before.

Gus only started undressing right after he had entered Colt all the way. The shivering, yet at the same time burning sensation and gritting teeth aside, the lines of Gus's torso were what really made him wince. Colt was on his back now, free of the handcuffs, and his knees resting on Gus's impressive shoulders. He was big, but not outrageously large like the types Colt had encountered around West Hollywood.

Just like before, Colt was in awe of Gus's patience. His thrusts were slow and coordinated, often retracting completely and reentering in the process. It didn't take him long to find Colt's sweet spots. Most guys didn't bother with what Gus was trying to achieve: the prostate orgasm. What Colt loved most about it was the total loss of control. His back arched. One moment his hands were trying to rip the rug apart, the next they were covering his face in a way he didn't understand. Colt screamed Gus's name as he was getting close. "Please don't stop. Gus. Please," he groaned.

"Now," Gus grunted, right before Colt felt his lower abdomen convulse a handful of times until his vision turned blank with undiluted joy.

He actually did it. I think I'm in love.

There wasn't much time for him to enjoy the moment

when he felt Gus's hand tightening around his throat. His thrusts grew methodical and powerful, like a slow-motion jackhammer, as though he were intent on destroying his body the way he had done his mind mere seconds ago.

Colt struggled to breathe against Gus's grip, unsure how long he'd be able to accommodate this treatment. He managed to say *Ferris wheel,* but Gus either didn't hear him or chose to override his protests a second time. Instead of backing off, Gus increased his grip and speed, looking him dead in the pleading eyes as Colt tried in vain to repeat the safe word, pulling and clawing at the man's wrist. He saw Gus smiling between his animalistic roars as he worked his way to his climax. Darkness crept at the edges of his vision. In a moment of desperation he felt himself give up the fight against Gus's forceful hand, succumbing to the pull of unconsciousness.

A pulsing sensation brought him back just in time as Gus was coming inside him, slowing his thrusts and loosening his grip. However, he only fully let go of Colt's throat when he was done savoring every last moment of his orgasm. As soon as he was free, Colt pushed him away and out of him, rolling to his side coughing.

"Fuck you, Gus," he said after a series of strained breaths. When he got up he moved to a safe enough distance, massaging his windpipe in an effort to make it relax.

"Colt? Hey. What's wrong?"

"Are you kidding me? What is *wrong* is you nearly killed me. I said the safe word like five times, Gus. You were supposed to back off. I thought I was going to pass out. Did you really not see me fight for air?"

"I…I…I thought that was the look of ecstasy on your face. I figured you were enjoying it, too. Not once did I hear you say it, I swear. Oh man, I'm sorry, Colt. I feel like a jerk."

"You should. Hitting me in the face is one thing, but rendering me unconscious is where I draw the line. You really couldn't tell?"

Gus ran his fingers through his hair. "No. I swear. Listen, I'm not ashamed to admit I get off on playing a little rough with guys, but I'm not a monster, Colt. Please stop looking at me like I am, because I can't take it. Not from you."

There was something endearing about how hurt he looked in that moment. The tough, controlling facade Colt had witnessed during the act had faded to a vulnerable, almost childish appearance. The intimidating features of his bright emerald eyes and square jawline no longer scared Colt as much. On the contrary, Colt wanted nothing more than to walk over and pull that face to his chest. However, that would have been against his better judgment. Tonight's situation was messy at best.

Colt put his briefs back on. "You're not a monster. I had an awesome time, up until a certain point, but I think it's best if I leave."

"Yes, I understand. I'm sorry it went down like this. I didn't mean to put you through that. I hope you believe me."

Colt put on his V-neck. "I want to believe you, but you really scared me there, Gus."

Gus exhaled and dropped his shoulders. "Man, I like it when you say my name. Tell you what? We should do this again sometime. It doesn't have to be a random Grindr rendezvous. To me, it didn't feel like that at all. There's something special about you and me, Colt. I'm going to come out and say it: I want to see you again."

You're kidding.

"Gus, I'm flattered, but that's probably the endorphins talking." He pulled his shirt down over his head. "Wait until morning and you'll be glad I'm out of your way. Straight people call it the cuddle factor." It was a standard line Colt had used a handful of times before with the clingy types across the app's fishing pond.

Gus frowned. "What happened to you, Colt? People who move to LA all have one thing in common: big dreams, waiting for their big break, their chance to shine. When did you give up on finding someone to love? Because you think it's easier this way? That's all in your head."

LA happened to me. My stepfather happened to me. Steve happened—is still happening to me.

Colt looked away. Earlier, he could tell from the too-good-to-be-true Grindr profile something had to be off about Mr. Gustavo Carolino, whom he had googled on the ride. When number one real estate magnate of Holmby Hills invites men like him to his mansion, it was a given there would be trouble. He was exactly the type of guy people had tried to warn Colt about when he moved to LA. Ironically, it had only made him want to go through with this hookup more.

This type of decisions constituted Colt's lifelong

problem. He liked trouble, or better yet, he thrived on it. To him, the presence of trouble had become his comfort zone, and not just for the sake of it. A little dose of danger lurking around the next corner had proved beneficial to his instincts over the years. *Always stay sharp. Don't let your guard down. That's how they get to you, how the strong kids label you as weak and make you their target.* Any certified therapist would label it as self-sabotage, but Colt would never go that far. In his situation he couldn't afford fancy talks in reclining chairs of any kind. At least Grindr was free of charge, and it mostly succeeded in making him feel better—for a while.

He had been staring out to the front yard through the living room window as he put on his shoes. "You know what? You're right. I'll give you my number. But only because you're really good at making me orgasm. Who knows? Maybe we'll see each other again, maybe we won't. I'll think it over." He held up a finger and added, "Only if you stick to the rules next time."

"Deal. I knew I did something right. And for what it's worth, I really couldn't tell something was wrong. See, that's why I need to see you again. To make it up to you." Gus grinned with a boyish smile Colt couldn't have imagined on the man's face fifteen minutes earlier. He was a difficult man to say no to, that much was certain. "My driver Langdon can take you home. It's the least I can do."

"Nice try, Gus." Colt ordered a Lyft with a few taps on his phone. "You'll know where I live and it's too early for that. I have trust issues."

"Well, I could always have Langdon follow you anyway."

Colt's head whipped to where Gus was seated on the white leather couch, still naked.

Gus held his palms up. "Relax. I'm not like that. Don't get me wrong, Langdon would totally go for it, but I'm too decent a person to do such things."

"Right. If you say so. I'm going to wait outside, so I don't miss my ride. Thank you for the—uhm—mostly good time tonight, Gus."

Gus got up from the couch, allowing Colt a full view of his chiseled body again. "No kiss goodnight?"

Colt's eyes rolled all over Gus's massive frame. "Fine, come get it." His blood circulation must have been focusing on the wrong parts.

With long, powerful strides Gus closed the distance between them. He pulled Colt into his arms, lifted him up against the back of the door and kissed him until Colt couldn't remember why he was leaving. His legs had automatically closed around Gus's back, as though his body didn't agree with his mind's intention to go.

As their foreheads touched after their passion had subsided, Colt marveled at how gentle Gus had become again. So many contradictions, and so many divine skills as a lover all wrapped up in a smoking hot package, and tied with a bow of intrigue. *Where have you been hiding?* As soon as the thought prompted in his head he remembered how playing with this particular fire had almost burned him to a crisp.

"Goodnight, Gus."

Gus opened the door for him. "Goodnight Colt. Oh, and if the driver looks sketchy, my offer still stands."

Colt thanked him and went outside. The driver did look sketchy, but, like always, he took his chances and added a little danger to the mix.

Chapter 4
Mel—Present

Mel was staring at Colt through the one-way window of interrogation room 1, waiting for Gene Reynolds to brief him on the events that had gone down while Mel and Charlotte were out investigating. On entering the station, Rita, the front-desk leading lady, looked shaken up.

"I've never witnessed anything like this, Mel, and I've worked here longer than any of you," she told him upon entering. Rita kept dabbing at her eyes beneath her red cat-eye glasses, which complimented her strawberry-blonde hair. She was one of those women that never changed appearances: a true staple at West Los Angeles's police station.

Someone had secured Colt's wrists with handcuffs, which couldn't be a good sign. His breathing looked strained and the bruise on his left cheek was still emitting its purple glory. By far the most unsettling feature was the look in his eyes. If it were true that eyes were the windows into one's soul, then Colt Whittaker appeared ready to die. Mel shuddered at the thought right before Gene entered the tiny space.

His coworker let out a sound that could have been either a sigh, a groan or a mix. "Thanks for coming, Mel. He was pretty adamant about only wanting to talk to you for some reason. You know him?"

"I pulled him over for reckless driving this morning."

Gene rolled his eyes. "Of course you did. Bet you wish you hadn't now."

"Tell me about it. What the hell am I walking into?"

Gene crossed his arms. "A hot mess, from what I gather." He walked Mel through the events he had missed concerning the gentleman in cuffs they were observing shoulder to shoulder. An hour ago Colt had walked up to Rita at the front desk with the same desperate look on his face. He had taken care to enunciate his words as he told her he wanted to confess to the murder of his husband. With raised hands, Colt had explained how he had left the murder weapon—a Beretta M84FS—in the front passenger seat of his car as evidence and that she was welcome to take the keys to his Defender to go check for herself.

"He got hysterical when we put the cuffs on him, but it was nothing I couldn't handle. His other cheek was already bruised, so now it kind of matches."

"You beat him?" Mel asked.

Gene's nostrils flared. "Don't give me that. I did what was in the precinct's best interests and stopped the threat. *He's* the one that put up a fight after confessing to murder. I'm not the lunatic here, okay?

"There's more," Gene continued as he mopped his brow with a handkerchief. "From the moment we closed the door of this room he was very cooperative and eloquent about how he shot his husband, Gustavo Carolino after a heated fight. The guy's some Brazilian real estate hotshot up in the hills, apparently. Now comes the kicker."

He did that thing where he savored the anticipation of the moment with a half-smile before proceeding with the last parts of the story. Mel refused to let it get to him this time and rode it out.

"Gustavo didn't die. The ER at Cedars Sinai reported him as a gunshot-wound victim half an hour ago. Looks like he's going to make it, from what the doctor on the phone could tell me. When we informed Colt here of his husband's survival the man seemed to break into a million pieces right in front of me. I've never seen anything like it. Then he refused to speak to anyone but you, so—uhm—good luck, pal." He patted Mel on the shoulder with his narrow fist.

How hard could he have hit the guy, really?

"Oh, before you go in," Gene said as he held the door handle, "I just got to say. There's something seriously off with this guy, but I can't for the life of me figure out what. It's like I can't get a good read on him, you know? I hate that. What are you smirking about?"

"This morning I told Cam the exact same thing. Glad I'm not the only one thrown by this guy."

"Well, he's all yours now." Gene threw his hands up.

Charlotte entered shortly after Gene had walked out, holding Colt Whittaker's file in one hand and her LAPD coffee mug in the other. Mel passed on the information he had just absorbed without trying to add color with personal opinions to the story. His partner deserved to get the cold hard facts. The skin at his right thumbnail felt raw, but he couldn't stop raising it to his mouth.

"It's no use jumping to conclusions, so I suggest you go talk to him ASAP."

Attagirl.

Flash moments like these made him see Charlotte Weisz as a reliable partner, despite her frigid decorum.

Mel walked into the interrogation room after a steadying deep breath. It was only when he had taken his seat that Colt's face lit up. He inhaled through his nose and seemed to relax a little. The bruise on his right cheek—in contrast with the opposing one—didn't look like it would last over twelve hours.

Instead of opening his mouth, Colt held out his cuffed wrists to him with pleading, welled-up eyes. Mel didn't react immediately, refusing to be the one to break the silence.

If he wants to talk, he should talk.

"Please," Colt said in a rushed exhale.

"Okay. I'll take those off. But first you need to tell me something. Why me? What am I doing here?"

Colt rested his hands on the table and studied them for a few seconds before he spoke. "I have a bad relationship with trust as a concept. That other detective—whose name I didn't catch—wouldn't have worked for this."

"Because he hit you?"

Colt paused. "Yeah, but not really. It was more the hatred in his eyes. I don't think he would believe a word I was going to say. Besides, he reeked of that Abercrombie cologne. You can't trust a man who still wears that."

"Okay. Thanks for the insight. This only explains why you don't want to talk to Detective Reynolds. Try again."

Colt shook his head. "Sorry. This morning, even though I wasn't acting like an upstanding citizen, you treated me like a regular person. You were level-headed and concerned about my well-being. Trustworthy, I guess. Honestly, I'm still not sure, but I bet it can't be worse than detective Reynolds. Also, your YSL L'homme is far better to endure."

Mel wrote down *fragrance expert* on his legal pad.

Colt stretched out his arms again. "Please take these off. I can't stand the feeling any longer."

"Fair enough." Mel removed the cuffs and noticed how Colt's chest rose and fell with deeper breaths than before.

"Thank you, Detective."

"Call me Mel." He knew it was a risk to get on first-name basis with this guy, but intuition overrode his rationale.

"Okay, Mel. Short for Melvin, or…?"

"That's right. Colt, what did you want to talk to me about?"

Colt's hand rose to his chin as he started rubbing his lower lip. "I'm not sure."

"You're not sure?" Mel threw his pen on the table and leaned back. "It's rather simple. You either want to talk or you don't. What's holding you back?"

"Let's see, Mel. Incarceration, endangering more lives—including yours—risking you won't believe me and send me back to hell, you giving me that pitiful look that will never go away after you hear me out? How about all of the above?" Colt counted the items off on his fingers.

Mel studied his every movement, checking for slip-ups in his body language, but hadn't found any so far. *A hot mess, indeed.*

"I have to ask. I know they read you your Miranda rights, but do you want a lawyer present? You can call one right now if you want."

"No. Absolutely not. The last thing I need is one of Gus's underlings sitting next to me for this. I can't risk it."

"All right, then. Why did you try to kill your husband?"

Colt's breaths grew shorter again. "Because it was my only way out." Tears spilled over his cheeks, but he wiped them away with quick strokes of his fingers.

Mel had an idea where this conversation was headed, but decided to give the man space. He kicked himself for not having recognized it before.

Colt cleared his throat. "Mel, if I start talking now there will be no going back. Both our lives will be in danger. I need a minute. You don't know how many times I've rehearsed this in my head, and I'm still not sure where to start."

"Take your time. Do you need anything? Coffee, water?"

"Water will do. Thank you."

Mel rose and asked Charlotte to bring in some water via the intercom.

"Who were you talking to?"

"My partner. She's a Special Victims Detective just like me."

Colt huffed. "Special Victims. Looks like I've come to the right people. She's been listening this whole time?"

"She has, yes." It was important for Mel he didn't lie to the man in this interrogation. If his gut instinct was correct, he wouldn't be the first man to betray Colt's trust. Once broken there wouldn't be any way to fix it.

"Do you trust her?"

"I do. Otherwise we wouldn't be partners." *Not a lie.*

Charlotte entered with a bottle of water and two paper cups.

"You can stay if you want to," Colt said as he watched Charlotte pour.

"Are you sure?" she asked, glancing at Mel, who couldn't believe it either.

"I'd rather you sit here with me instead of knowing you're listening to my every word behind that mirror. Nice to meet you, Detective." It wasn't exactly a smile, but Colt's mouth tried its best to resemble one.

"It's Charlotte. Charlotte Weisz." She took a seat next to Mel.

Colt took a gulp of water, then said "Okay, may the record reflect that I warned both of you of the danger we're all about to be in once I start talking."

Mel nodded, wishing at the same time Colt would get on with it and to be back home with his daughter soon.

He cleared his throat. "My husband, Gustavo Carolino, controls every aspect of my life. Every decision I make 24/7, from what to wear, what to eat, to how deeply I can breathe—or if I can breathe at all. Who I'm allowed to interact with. Where I should be at all times. How I should look, no matter the time of day. How my body should respond to his, or rather yield to his. What I should say, feel, think—everything." Colt took another sip with trembling hands. "It wasn't always like this, and I sure didn't sign up for it from one day to the next. He had staged it all so well in the background, pulling up one piece of fence at a time. Before I knew it there was no way out." He stared at the space between Charlotte and Mel as he tried to explain his situation.

"I take it you didn't kiss the wrong guy?" Mel asked as he pointed to Colt's left cheek, referring to the story Colt told him that morning.

Colt's eyes fell to his lap. He ran his fingertips over the angry bruise. "I didn't."

Mel shot a glance at his partner, feeling her eyes searching for his. It was going to be that kind of talk and they both knew it.

"How often does he hurt you?" Charlotte asked.

"Usually, whenever I disobey or break one of his many rules, but sometimes it just happens for no reason. At first it was only during sex, but it soon migrated to other times, too. This is where things get complicated, I'm afraid." He bit his lower lip.

"Complicated how?" Mel asked.

Colt took a deep breath, looking both him and his coworker in the eye alternately. "I'll put it this way. When I met Gus I was over the moon. I had finally found a man who wasn't afraid to hit me in the face. Problem is, I can't figure out how to make him stop. And believe me, I've tried all the safe words known to mankind." A chill went down Mel's spine.

"Colt, did your husband force himself onto you without consent?" Mel asked.

He swallowed hard and nodded quickly, gaze dropped to the table. Another tear ran down his cheek. "Many times," he whispered.

"You're doing great, Colt. How long have the two of you been married?" Charlotte asked.

"Come November it will be four years. Look, I know what your next question is going to be. *Why didn't I leave him if he rapes and beats me so often?* If it had been that simple I'd have left him three years ago. Like I said, in his own brilliant way Gus trapped me in his house. Leaving him would start a chain of events that would destroy me. And it wouldn't stop there."

Mel stood and faced the mirror as he held his hands behind his head, so he could think. It didn't take long for him to put two and two together about the nature of Colt's entrapment at home.

"Colt, you can trust us. There's really no need to be vague at this point. You'll feel better when you get it all out. Take your ti—" Charlotte started.

"What does he have on you?" Mel interrupted, looking at Colt's reflection.

Colt remained quiet while he studied his hands again. He raised his eyes back to Mel's. "Mel, Charlotte, do you believe me?"

"Have we got any reason not to?" Charlotte jumped in, to Mel's surprise.

More silence. Mel could feel Colt's willingness to cooperate sink. He had to act now, before it would slide further downhill. A touch of rationalization might help, he thought.

"Colt, you're in the right place. This right here is the hardest part, and you're exceptionally brave for telling us your story. You're not the first, and definitely not the last victim that seeks our help. Because of the high-strung emotions that come with cases like yours, we do our best to stay objective as detectives. That means it doesn't matter what we *believe* to be true, as it all hinges on testimonies and evidence. We'll guide you through the process of pressing sexual misconduct charges against your husband and take it from there, without letting our personal judgments taint our observations. You've got nothing to lose by talking to us."

"You don't know that, but I appreciate you saying it. Well, either way, I guess I'd better show you some evidence, then. I'm going to stand now, if that's okay?" Colt said.

The question being rhetorical, Colt rose from his seat and pulled his Sheryl Crow T-shirt over his head with a wince.

Mel struggled as he tried not to react at the sight of Colt's upper body. It resembled an elevation map of Aspen with its variety of colors across his bruised skin. Some spots looked recent—purple and red—others mid-healing process—blue and yellow. Through the damage, Mel could tell the guy had a strict workout and diet regimen—in complete accordance with the man's story so far.

He stared hard at his partner, whose jaw had dropped. It worked: she switched back to a neutral expression.

Still a lot to learn for this one.

"We're going to need to document this," she said, after which she walked back to the adjacent room.

Mel stepped closer to get a better look at the purple-colored patterns on Colt's sides.

Instinctively, the man backed away.

"Colt, listen to me. I'm not going to hurt you. I won't even so much as touch you. I promise. I'm trying to get a closer look, that's all." With his arms stretched out he might as well have approached a wild horse.

"No offense, but I'd rather you wait until your partner gets back."

Mel felt like an idiot. From Colt's perspective the optics were far from good. Alone in a tiny room with a strange man inching closer when he was most vulnerable. He could only imagine what the guy had been through for his self-preservation instincts to be this powerful.

"As you wish. No problem."

Charlotte reappeared with her camera handy. As Charlotte started taking photos, Mel recognized the pattern on Colt's sides. "Are those—?"

"Imprints of his hands, yes. My husband has a very powerful grip. It'll make sense when you see him."

Shit.

He was able to count fingers on Colt's obliques. They couldn't have been the result of a quick fuck. Marks like these, no matter how strong a person's arms, required long-term contact—as in hours.

"It happened yesterday, together with the ones on my back. The ones right here," he indicated the yellowing spots right below his midriff, "are from last week. He thought I'd been rude to his business partner. Said I should be more inviting when we have guests." Mel watched his Adam's apple bob down in a hard swallow. Colt looked away and wiped his dampened right cheek with his palm.

After Charlotte had taken pictures from every angle, Colt got dressed again and reclaimed his seat at the table. Mel and Charlotte stepped out to confer. "We need to tell the Chief about this. Make it an official case," Charlotte said, browsing through the shots on her camera's screen.

"You're right. But maybe we should wait until we get a little more out of him. There's a library of information in that room we're still clueless about. And I don't like it."

She zoomed in on a photograph. "Holy shit."

Without warning she stormed back inside the interrogation room, startling their already jumpy victim.

"Colt, can you show us the tattoo on your hip?"

He stood and lowered the elastic waistband of his gym shorts. "You mean this? The damn thing was a wedding anniversary gift. One Gus insisted on, of course. It's a letter C, a customized tramp stamp. It wasn't worth another beating, so I went along with it."

Don't react. Do not react. Don't do it.

Charlotte's hand flew to her gaping mouth. *Fuck.* This was going to require a corrective talk with her. Granted, she was still new to the job, but her reaction was unprofessional to say the least. He could see Colt's distress amplify tenfold.

"What's wrong?" Colt asked.

"That's not what that sign stands for, Colt," Mel said, then to Charlotte, "We need the Chief. Now."

Chapter 5
Colt—Past

"Gustavo Carolino, if you make me come one more time I swear I'll go blind. Just like those abstinence advocates warned us about in high school," Colt said, panting.

Gus chuckled. "I'll try to resist. It won't be easy, though. The way your body responds to mine is addictive to say the least. I'd do this all day if you let me."

Easy, tiger.

Exactly one week after their first hookup, Colt found himself lying next to Gus in his magnanimous bedroom. Days of relentless texts, audio and video messages—dirty or not—and one FaceTime session had overridden all of Colt's objections to a repeat performance after his not-so-happy end the last time. His mind couldn't stop replaying the spectacular scenes of their encounter over and over. That low, breathy voice, the commanding touch, dominance radiating from that giant, sculpted-to-perfection physique—until he remembered the part where he could have died. Colt knew deep down he shouldn't allow a controlling type like Gus anywhere near him again, but that only made him want it more. As far as he was concerned, it trumped spending another night in the same apartment as Steve and his homophobic bitch of a girlfriend.

Speaking of that horrific moment of near-successful asphyxiation, Colt feared it had forever ruined that side of their interactions, which explained the frown on his face as he stared at the air-conditioning vent hidden in the ceiling.

What if I scared him off? The sex was amazing, but it could have been so much more enticing. Should I cut my losses and move on?

"Hey, Gus?"

"Yes, Colt?"

"Is everything okay?"

"Well, in case you can't tell, I'm ecstatic. I just got lucky with who I think is my favorite guy in town. What's on your mind?" Gus rolled to his side to face him, with his head resting on the swell of his bicep.

I'm your favorite?

Colt looked around to take in the in-your-face beauty of Gus's bedroom for what he considered the last time. Stepping inside an hour ago, he half-expected there to be a mirror on the ceiling, but that wouldn't have matched the rest of the oasis of calm surrounding him. Two cream leather armchairs with their Chesterfield padding identical to the headboard stood near the opposing wall—ideal for reading, especially because of the wide fireplace behind them. A TV screen bigger than the dining room table in his apartment hung over it on a black granite wall—the only interruption of the downtown views.

"It's just...you didn't...*hurt* me this time."

Gus sighed and rolled on his back. "You sound disappointed."

"I am, a little. I thought you were okay with all of my odd requests." He stretched out his arm. "Hello sir. My name is Colt Whittaker and I prefer men who get rough with me." Smiling at Colt's attempt to defuse the tension, Gus shook his hand. "To tell you the truth, I've been masturbating to the memory of you hitting me in the face all week. Maybe that's why I'm about to go blind."

Gus sat upright against the headboard. "Really? You masturbated to me? Same here." He started twirling Colt's smooth hair in his fingers. "Colt, I'll be honest, too. I got spooked last time, so when I felt the urge, I didn't dare to hit you. Trust me, I wanted to, but I didn't want our date to end that way again. So I dialed it down for you—tamed the beast, so to speak."

He said date.

"Beast. Now there's one way to describe you." As he pushed on his arms to sit up, Gus did the same and pulled him against his massive chest. He didn't resist and leaned back, surprised at how comfortable the position was.

"Seriously though, Gus. I understand what you're saying, but promise you won't kill that beast inside you. I kind of want to get to know him better. I'll teach him some manners."

Gus kissed the top of his head. "Promise. He's looking forward to it, or so I hear," Gus whispered in his ear.

Colt smiled. "By the way, were my ears playing tricks on me or do you think we've upgraded to a real date this time?"

"Busted. I'm not sure, but I really want us to get acquired…acquainted, I mean. To get to know each other." Gus shook his head. "Sorry. It's a second language."

"Second. So you actually grew up in Brazil? I thought that was just your ancestry."

Colt felt a new tension in Gus's body.

"How do you know I'm Brazilian?"

Crap.

"I—uhm—kind of googled you on the way here last week."

"Shit. I probably shouldn't have given you my full name. Rookie mistake, I guess."

Colt jerked up and faced him. "Please tell me I didn't take your Grindr virginity."

Gus laughed. "That you did not. But you're in a tight league, if you must know."

And just like that Colt saw all the puzzle pieces fitting together. "Oh my God. You're the escort type, aren't you?"

"Man, it's like you see right through me."

His interest piquing, Colt got up and started pacing the length of the bed. "So it's true. Fuck. It makes *so* much sense. Eligible bachelor in Holmby Hills in need of discreet dates who look like supermodels on his arm at business events. You must have spent a fortune."

Gus hummed as though he had a number in mind.

"Why did you graduate to Grindr?"

"Now look who's fishing for personal life details. I thought that was against your rules during hookups?"

"Good thing this is not a hookup, then. Like you said," he jerked his eyebrows up, "we're on a date."

What the hell am I doing?

Gus bared his Hollywood-perfect teeth in a grin that took hold of his entire face. Colt needed to look away in fear of what it would do to his pounding chest.

"All right then. Let's get dressed. I'm buying you dinner," Gus said.

"Now? It's 3 pm."

Gus got out of bed and closed the distance between the two of them. Towering over Colt, he cupped his face. "Which ensures we'll be back to see if another orgasm will really make you go blind."

He pushed his forehead against Gus's and inhaled as if he wanted to get high on his scent. The intimacy he had been experiencing since entering the house a second time was overwhelming. He wondered if it was a mistake to let his guard down like this, but ignored the thought as soon as Gus kissed him with his signature patient passion.

Upon arrival, the maître d' of the Guzman restaurant in Westwood ushered them to their private table overlooking both the city and the Pacific Ocean through floor-to-ceiling windows. The table was private indeed, as there was no one inside except for the maître d', Gus and Colt. It was bad enough for Colt to be confronted with his date's outrageous Holmby Hills mansion, now he got to feel even more out of place in an empty restaurant that reminded him of the Great Gatsby movie.

Gus picked up on his sentiment and said, "They

opened early at my request over the phone. I know it's a little weird, but you're all the company I want, anyway."

"Oh, it's weird all right." He suspected there were ulterior motives to this arrangement of Gus, but decided not to say anything about it—not yet, at least.

Gus pulled out his chair for him, which was the very first time someone had done that for Colt. He had entered a whole new world, one where maybe not all guys he went out with were self-absorbed Instagram-addicted jerks. Going to dinner on actual dates in LA so far had proved to be a landmine-infested no-man's land. Ordering food could be more complicated than learning German. Every dish either had to be gluten-free, organic, lactose-free, sugar-free, free-range, fair-trade, homegrown, low-carb, high-protein or fresh from the vine. He remembered thinking *we're not in Kansas anymore, Toto* many times.

"I kind of have one rule for dinner dates," Gus started.

"Oh, do you? Is this payback for the other night?"

"God, no. Hear me out. No phones during dinner. It's rude, doesn't bode well for your personality and shows a massive lack of restraint. I don't care for any of those characteristics, do you?"

"No. Not at all. Consider it done."

Much like the sensation of Gus's skin against Colt's an hour ago, conversation was smooth between the two. After the mild shock of learning Gus was exactly twice his age—forty-four to his twenty-two—even though he didn't look a day over thirty, Colt could shake the nerves completely and began to ask bolder questions. He discovered Gus had moved to the US with his parents when he was five during

LA's golden 80s and that his folks had moved back to São Paulo in 2014. That's when Gus had taken over his parents' real estate business, which explained his stunning home even more.

When the maître d'—Bruno—came back, Gus talked to him in Brazilian Portuguese, rendering Colt mesmerized by the juicy sounds and intonation Gus's voice had taken on.

"Wow. You should do that more often around me. What was that all about?"

"Nothing. I just ordered our food."

"But…how do you know I'll like it? You didn't even ask about allergies or intolerances."

Gus shrugged. "I'm taking my chances. If any food could kill you, I figured you would have told me."

You have to stop trying to kill me.

Gus moved on. "So how about your family? Are they still in Topeka?"

"My mom is, yes. My brother, Dave, moved to New York a few years ago."

Gus nodded slowly. "I'm guessing that means there's no father in the family pictures?"

Colt took a slow breath. "There isn't. My dad died in Afghanistan a year after I was born. I do have a very colorful sort of stepdad, but I'm afraid he's the reason I moved to LA faster than planned. I don't want to get into the whole thing right now, if you don't mind."

"I'm sorry about your dad, Colt. We won't talk about things you're not comfortable with. I promise."

Bruno returned with a wine bottle and made a show of

its introduction: showing them the label, pouring an inch into a glass. After whirling the clear liquid around, Gus tasted it, smacked his lips in a sexual way and relayed his approval with an *obrigado*. Colt took a sip from his own glass of the Moscato, not having a clue whether it was as good as the theatrics had proclaimed.

"Thanks for understanding, Gus. Also for not acknowledging the obvious cliché."

Gus turned his head to the side and frowned.

Colt looked down at the folded napkin on his bread plate. "Daddy issues."

"Don't do that to yourself, Colt. Listen to me," Gus waited until Colt met his eyes again, "if that part of your upbringing contributed to the fantastic person sitting across from me, then I don't care. And neither should you. If that asshole stepfather is what led you here, then I think I should go thank the guy personally."

Mayday. Shields are down.

Two waiters set down plates smelling better than Gus's Amouage perfume, but Colt wasn't paying attention to their explanations at all.

He is really into me, and…could it be?

Colt allowed himself to wonder if it could be true, if there was a chance the two of them would ever be able to call each other boyfriend. Or perhaps more.

Colt's inner soliloquy had prevented him from hearing a word of the introduction of the dish in front of him: clay pots holding mostly prawns and cream with a side of rice.

"I'm sorry, what is this exactly?"

"Moqueca, traditional Brazilian fish stew. Try it."

While Colt was in creamy fish heaven, he couldn't hold back the question in his head any longer.

"So, what's the deal with your escort habit? I've been a very patient man up until now. This is really good, by the way."

Gus dipped a piece of bread in the concoction as he spoke. "There's not much to tell, really. Through a discreet agency I used to order good-looking men to attend business dinners and other events at my side. Afterward, I, uhm, got my money's worth in hotel rooms. It was a very professional experience, and, more often than not, cold and distant once I saw through the act those guys put on."

"Let me guess. They couldn't handle the beast?"

Gus huffed. "Some could, others not at all. The ones that couldn't always did the same thing. They pretended they were up for it until they got a real taste. But that wasn't the biggest problem."

Colt's eyes went wide. "Oh my God. One of them made you believe it was real, didn't he?"

"Fuck. How do you do that? If we were in business together I'd lose millions to you in negotiations."

"Maybe I'm your Kryptonite, Clark." Colt winked.

"Who knows? Anyway, one of them was a sublime actor who strung me along for months. That's when I retired from that kind of dating. I wanted a chance at something real. Something honest. And so, I ended up taking my chances on Grindr. And here I am, experiencing honesty for the first time in years."

Colt absolutely felt like an honest guy in that moment as he became painfully aware of the differences between the two of them. Gus on one side, sitting there 100% at ease in this fancy restaurant, looking mighty fine in his army-green customized Polo Ralph Lauren polo shirt with matching jeans and squeaky-clean white Chanel sneakers. As if the Amouage wasn't intimidating enough, his golden Rolex and black Dior sunglasses from earlier practically spouted dollar bills from across the table. Colt himself, on the other end, was having trouble breathing in the air-conditioned universe of the restaurant that charged his weekly paycheck for certain champagne bottles. He couldn't blame himself for not having dressed up for this impromptu dinner date, yet his navy Gap T-shirt, loungewear shorts and worn-out sneakers with nineties-style socks made him regret his outfit nonetheless.

The waiters collected their plates, giving Colt time to collect courage and speak his mind. "Well, I'm glad we met—I'll say that much. But there's something bothering me, Gus. We're very different people, you and me. I don't know if you can tell, but I'm sweating like crazy."

"Interesting. Was it the Moqueca? It can have that effect on people."

Colt shook his head. "No. It was delicious, really. Allow me to explain." He leaned back. "Look around this place, Gus. See anything out of place? Well, I do: me. I don't belong in this world of yours. It's like I'm on the wrong deck of the Titanic, waiting for the crew to notice and cuff me to a lead pipe. I'm afraid it's only a matter of time before you wake up and realize it, too. Please don't take this the wrong way, but all this luxury is very intimidating if you're not used to it. One moment I can't get enough and the next I'm loathing it. You may have guessed it, but I'll tell you anyway. I make minimum wage trying to sell fragrances and cosmetics to millennials who, by the way, order everything online the minute they walk out the store. I know I'm rambling, but I'm not done." He held up his hand, not allowing interruptions.

"I share a run-down apartment in Koreatown with an asshole roommate. I own eight shirts and four pairs of pants. You see these shoes? As of yesterday, they are the only ones I own besides my flip-flops. If I take a bad fall on my way out of this place, I could end up homeless, seeing as I don't have any insurance. I could buy some if I stopped eating altogether, of course.

"Gus, you can be honest about your little stunt now. We're here by ourselves at this hour, because you don't want to be seen with someone as white-trash as me. Because you can't risk your reputation. I understand your reasoning behind it and I don't blame you, but at least be truthful about it. See, this is why I don't date hot, rich men like you."

Colt lowered his head between his propped-up elbows and massaged his temples. Gus broke his right hand away and held it like porcelain.

"Are you done freaking out? Good. Now I'm going to ignore the fact that you believe me to be as superficial as you think I am for a minute, okay? Why wouldn't you belong here, Colt? What I see when I look at you is a hard-working man who didn't take any shortcuts coming to this high-paced town. Someone who's never taken anything for granted, because he knows how unpredictable this world can be. There's nothing fake or self-serving about the man holding my hand right now, and I don't know about you, but in my experience that is a rare commodity in Los Angeles.

"What I also see is someone who's scared to ask for help or even accept occasional kindness from others, because he's afraid to trust good deeds. And sadly—sorry to do this—someone who no longer believes he's allowed to have nice things in life. Maybe because they used to lead to disappointment in your childhood."

No. Stop it. Don't let him see it.

A tear rolled down Colt's cheek, making him look away toward the view of the Pacific.

"It's okay, Colt. I'm not mad, but you have to believe me when I say Bruno is just doing me a favor because of our poor timing."

Colt felt his anger drown in those green eyes. Gus's hand in his didn't feel weird at all. If anything, it felt right, safe, and so hot his palm had turned even more sweaty. After putting up a show like Colt had, his date should have been running for the hills—or down from these hills—yet here he was, unbothered by any of his theatrics.

This could really work.

"I'm sorry. Man, I feel like a real jerk. I am not used to hearing praise, especially coming from someone like you. I got to say, it feels rather good." He raised his eyebrows, "I can really bring the drama when I'm feeling it, right?"

"No problem. But if you've really felt that way all along, why did it take you so long to freak out about it? Why not tell me at the house or on the way here?"

Colt couldn't help but smile. He looked down at their

gathered hands and said, "There's a reason I freaked out only now. I just discovered I have feelings for you—and not just in my pants. It's scary as fuck, but that's the way it is. There, happy?" When Colt looked Gus in the eye again, he could swear he saw the man's eyes fill with emotion. It was better than any view money could buy in this part of town.

"Very."

Chapter 6
Mel—Present

When he was sure rookie Officer Ryder was going to keep an eye on Colt, Mel headed for Captain Perez's office together with his partner to follow the chain of command for this white whale of a case.

"What was all that about following procedure? Looking at the facts instead of believing? Instead of mansplaining it to him, you could have just said we believed him, Mel."

"I didn't want to lie to him or get his hopes up. The man has the worst imaginable trust issues, Charlotte. He deserves to know what will happen. It worked, didn't it?"

"We'll have to wait and see."

She's reprimanding me *now?*

"By the way, you should keep your face in check next time a victim shows their wounds."

Charlotte froze and stopped walking, forcing Mel to look over his shoulder. "I know. I screwed up. I'm sorry."

He dismissed it with a wave if his hand. Truth was he was kind of proud at how level-headed she had remained in the interrogation room.

"Come in, you two. I've just received a call from Officer

Dmitrov. Get this: Gustavo Carolino is not pressing charges against his husband for armed assault or attempted murder," Captain Perez said as soon as Mel opened the door.

Even though there were two guest chairs in the Chief's office, he doubted anyone had ever sat on them for longer than ten minutes.

"He isn't? So Colt's a free man... That's good, but there's a lot more to say about him, Chief," Mel said as he started filling his boss in on Colt's interview so far.

When Charlotte showed her the photographs on her camera screen, the leading lady of the West LA Division couldn't control her language any longer.

"Goddamn bastard. I got to take this to the DA ASAP. Damn it, your guy should have been a better shot. Don't repeat this outside this office, because I'll deny having said it. Hold on. Is that—?"

"A similar tattoo as the other victims connected to the Cordelio cartel," Charlotte said.

The Chief shifted frowned glances from Mel to Charlotte and back. "This is huge. That can't be a coincidence, can it?"

"He said it was a wedding anniversary gift," Mel said.

"Like hell it is. Until we get to the bottom of this, your guy's not going anywhere. He could be our star witness for all we know. The key to bringing down the Cordelio cartel, or at least its grip on this city. Man, I could use a drink." She mopped her brow with a tissue from a chrome box on her desk.

"Right, but let's not get ahead of ourselves. He's

holding back information out of fear. With good reason, I assume," Mel said, thinking about Colt's reaction when he had tried to approach him alone.

Captain Perez instructed Mel and Charlotte to arrange a stay at a safe house for Colt as a special victim. As it was growing late in the afternoon, she promised to plan a new meeting with all involved divisions the next day. While Charlotte was making calls to safe houses, the Chief took the opportunity to walk back alongside Mel to introduce herself to Colt.

"Thank you for waiting, Colt. This is the head of LAPD's West LA precinct, Captain Alana Perez. We've just discussed your case, which will be reported to the District Attorney shortly. She wanted to meet you in person, and I couldn't have stopped her if I'd tried," Mel said.

The two of them shook hands.

"Nice to meet you, Colt. Can I say Colt?"

"Well, given you've probably seen dozens of half-naked pictures of me, I guess you can." Colt narrowed his eyes, "Ange Ou Démon, Givenchy. Bold choice."

Impressed at his apparent gift once more, Mel made a mental note to bring it up in later conversations. Getting Colt to open up about everything concerning his abusive husband was going to be tricky to say the least. He was going to need all the ammo he could forage.

"O-kay then. Thank you, I guess. Anyway, I've got good news. Your husband is not pressing charges at this moment, so you are no longer under arrest."

Mel watched his reaction closely. Instead of the

expected relief, Colt remains stoic. Then a slight frown worked his way down his brow. "Of course he isn't. He wants to be the one doing the punishing, and he can't do that with me in jail." Colt's eyes were fixed on the table while he was speaking, mostly to himself.

"I'm sorry this has been happening to you, Colt," the Captain continued.

Colt's eyes shot to Mel. "Why is she really here?"

He opened his mouth, but his boss held up her manicured hand without making eye contact, commanding in her non-verbal ways as always.

"Colt, your case is now part of our biggest investigation. That tattoo on your hip? The one you think was an innocent anniversary gift? I'm sorry to tell you it's much more than that."

"Yes, Mel here also hinted at that earlier. What the fuck are you getting at?"

"Our detectives have found this particular mark on six murder victims and one sexual assault victim," Mel said, taking over the conversation again. He half-expected the Chief to stop him, but was relieved she didn't. This was about winning Colt's trust, and right now his odds were better than hers.

Colt's face went pale as his hand traveled to the tattoo's spot on his right hip.

"All of those crimes are related to the Mexican Cordelio cartel that has been gaining ground in the city these last years. All I can tell you is they're ruthless, wealthy and smart. Worse than we've seen here at LAPD."

Mel was vaguely aware of his boss eyeing him from his

left, assessing his performance. He couldn't care less. This wasn't about his competence as an SV detective, this was all about doing right by Colt, to make sure he felt as safe as possible under the circumstances. Fatherhood had intensified the urge to protect people, which he saw as a lucky byproduct to the whole experience.

Colt's hands covered his face. "Dear God. That explains so much. Why haven't I considered this before?"

Mel blinked hard. When he looked at the Chief, she was every bit as perplexed. "Explains what, Colt?" he asked.

"Everything. The sketchy improvised meetings at wicked hours, the constant need to please his business partners, the Latino men appearing at our house. The extent of Gus's power over people."

"Colt, would you recognize those men?" Captain Perez asked.

"Maybe. Gus kept me away from them as much as possible. Sent me upstairs whenever they paid unannounced visits. There's one of them I would definitely be able to pick out of a lineup, though."

"Why is that?" Mel asked, suspecting something sinister. One minute the guy was singing like a canary, the next he shut off completely. It was exhausting, but he kept trying to push the right buttons.

"One morning, I got to the kitchen after working out and ran into a man named Alejandro Suarez. I had met him before on a business dinner date with his now ex-husband Jonathan—I forget his last name. Anyway, Gus was in his office doing whatever, so we were alone. He started telling me about his divorce and how he envied our marriage. Next thing I knew he had me pinned to the floor and…" Colt paused and searched Mel's eyes, "If it hadn't been for Gus I don't know how the scene would have ended. It was the last I saw of that guy, fortunately. Gus really went ballistic on him. Broke his nose. Wait—" Colt looked down at his hip.

"What are you thinking?" Mel asked.

"I'm not sure, but I think it was a week or two before I got this tattoo. I remember it well, as it was the first time Gus had looked scared. Fuck. Mel, what do you think this mark means?"

"We don't know," Mel said, which wasn't a lie despite the dark theories that were springing to life in his head.

"Well, it can't be good, can it? Seeing as the others were either raped or killed. My God, how is this my life now?"

Colt's hairdo had come undone from running his hands through it. Blond strands of it were rebelling against his meticulous parting. Aware of his own retreating hairline, Mel felt a little more self-conscious.

"Please tell me you're planning on keeping me safe."

"Colt, we are going to do everything within our power to protect you from both your husband and the cartel. You have my word," the Chief said.

The door flew open before Colt had a chance to thank her. "Mel, Chief, a word?" Charlotte asked.

Once outside, she shook her head and started speaking. "I just finished my calls to the safe houses in the vicinity." She huffed, "There's no room for Colt anywhere at the moment."

The Chief cursed in Spanish.

"The lady on the phone from the one in McLaughlin

infuriated me to my core. Listen to this. They do have rooms available, more than one, but they won't accept Colt as a resident. She gave me a whole speech about how a male presence could trigger the other residents. When I explained he was not a threat to any woman on earth at all, she said it didn't make any difference. She needed to protect the women in her house at all costs." Charlotte's otherwise perfect dark skin now looked pasty—the toll of all the long hours she put in on average.

"I really need to go see about that drink," the Chief said after taking off her glasses to pinch the bridge of her nose.

"Didn't the one in West Adams burn down a while ago?" Mel asked, remembering the images on the news.

"It did, which is why there's a shortage," Charlotte said.

His boss promising Colt she'd keep him safe echoed in his mind. Beside safe houses there weren't many options for victims like Colt. Sexism in LA institutions—he never thought he'd see the day.

"Chief, we can't lock him up here, he's too traumatized," he said.

"You think I don't know that? Then what do you suggest? From where I'm standing it's our only option."

"There's an alternative, but it's out-of-the-box thinking. Chief, I live three blocks from here in an apartment all by myself. He could stay with me until we find a better solution. It takes four minutes to get back here if need be," Charlotte said.

Captain Perez looked up at her like she'd never laid eyes on the woman before.

"Chief? She's got a point. Granted, it's unorthodox, but it's the best we can—"

A raised hand shushed him. "I'm trying to think of a way I could possibly explain this up the LAPD food chain." She held her chin between her thumb and index fingers, studying the tiles on the floor. After a long sigh she said "I'm going to regret this."

Mel explained the new living situation to Colt while Charlotte was out getting more supplies for her new guest. He imagined she needed to buy pretty much everything imaginable, since she never spent more time than needed at her place herself. Maybe this was a good thing for her, too. To finally be able to relax a little. He had never known a more lonely detective in his career.

"Any word on how Gus is doing?" Colt asked.

The question threw him, but only a little. Domestic abuse victims mostly had a deeply rooted affection for their assailants. One that was hard to let go of.

"Not that I know. I can make a call later if you want."

He used the opportunity to ask his next, overdue question. "Is that why you chose to stay all those years? Because at the end of the day you still love him? It's okay, I won't judge."

Colt ran his thumb over his bottom lip. "I don't know. I loved the man he pretended to be in the beginning more than the real him. It's like I said, he trapped me on all sides. I had no choice."

"Yeah, you keep saying that. But how?"

"For one, he'll hurt my family. My mom in Kansas and my brother in New York City. I've been meaning to ask, Mel. Can I use a phone? I need to warn them. I just hope they'll believe me after everything that went down."

He crossed his arms and gave Colt a sidelong glance, fed up with the half answers the guy had been giving him. "This isn't going to work if you keep holding back on me, Colt. At some point you're going to have to trust me."

"I can't, Mel. Not yet. I've already said too much. You don't know him like I do. What he's capable of. What he would do to make me pay for shooting him and running away. You think I look beaten up now? You should have seen me after I tried to escape last time."

A text from Charlotte buzzed through his Apple Watch.

Charlotte: All set. You can drop him off.

He rose from his seat and said, "Time to go. You can call your relatives from Charlotte's place."

Years in foster care had taught Mel one thing. Spelling out boundaries from the get-go goes a long way. Everyone feels safer once they know where the lines are. His wife Kate always made fun of his car rules, breaking a rule or two whenever she felt like challenging him.

"Before I start the engine, I have a few rules in my car. One: no smoking. Two: the volume on the radio only goes up to 4. Three: no touching. The fourth one is about the shotgun seat passenger being responsible for the backseat, but that doesn't apply here now. Do you understand?"

"Sure, Mel. Whatever you say. I've got plenty of

experience following another man's rules, thank you," Colt said, sounding more and more drained by the minute.

Sheryl Crow's *All I Wanna Do* was playing from the radio, prompting Mel's next question. "Is that a random T-shirt or do you really like her music?"

Colt frowned. "Of course I like her. How can you not? The woman's a genre on her own."

Mel smiled. "That's what *I* always say about her. I'm not claiming I've heard all of her songs, but her big hits sure are something."

He could feel Colt's eyes on him, even though his passenger remained silent.

Charlotte had been waiting for them on the sidewalk, so Mel drove right up to where she was standing.

"Okay, Colt. I'll see you tomorrow. I know it won't be easy, but try to get some sleep. That's really all I can say."

"Thanks for the ride, Mel. I'll try." Colt didn't meet his eyes.

Mel secretly hoped there was an extra advantage to Charlotte's apartment serving as Colt's safe house. Maybe when the formal, fate-deciding environment of the West LA station disappeared from view he would be more forthcoming. Best case scenario, he'd share some of the details of his life with his real-estate mogul husband—and perhaps his ties to the cartel.

It would have to wait anyway, since he was finally headed home to his personal safe house, where sleep was a valuable commodity, just like in Colt's.

Chapter 7
Colt—Past

Not yet. God, no, not yet. Keep it together. You got this.

During the last six months sex with Gus had become more extreme, more painful, more frightening even—at times—and all the more addictive. The one time he had to say *Ferris wheel* was about a month ago when Gus had applied his powerful grip on his throat again. When he did, Gus had complied without further ado and backed down like a big puppy. Their arrangement seemed to be working, which is why Colt chose to trust him at times like these, when he saw the limits of his pain tolerance closing in at the horizon.

He was blindfolded on the bed, lying flat on his stomach with every inch of Gus's cock inside of him. It was a playful punishment for having woken up Gus the way he had. Roughly half an hour earlier, Colt had used his stealthiest moves to dive below the soft sheets, lower the waistband of Gus's Emporio Armani briefs and slurp all over his dozing boyfriend's manhood. It was his way of turning the tables, with him being the one in control for a change. The expression on Gus's face looking down under the sheets alone had been worth it.

As always, Gus was taking his time riding him. After a few series of rhythmic thrusts he paused for a while, allowing Colt to go crazy with anticipation.

Just when he was about to beg Gus to keep going, Colt felt a hand slide up his spine. Gus pulled him up by the hair with a violent jerk, making him cry out. Holding him in place, Gus lowered his mouth to his ear and whispered "This is what you get for waking me up on a Sunday. I hope it was worth it, because I'm not even close to done. I need to teach you a lesson Mr. Whittaker." His sinister tone only added to Colt's satisfaction. No matter how soft Gus whispered, the sound made Colt ignite.

Colt gasped as Gus started licking his way up from the base of his backbone all the way to his shoulder blades, lapping up every drop of sweat along the way. Once he reached Colt's face he continued to his cheek and temple. It could have been the heightened sensation of his tongue over his body making him shiver. Or maybe it was the contrast between his commanding words and the pleasing nature of the follow-up act. Either way, Colt couldn't get enough of Gus claiming his body like this.

Still holding his head up by his hair, Gus resumed his forceful thrusts. As he built up speed, he pushed Colt's head down hard into the mattress. He grabbed Colt by the wrist and yanked it toward the middle of his back, causing his shoulder tendons to burn.

When Colt's arm was free again, Gus's hands focused their force on his sides, pulling Colt back to meet his pulsating hips. As though he was still not satisfied with his show of power, Gus squeezed Colt's obliques harder and upped the ante on his rhythm once more. Colt's jaw tensed as he winced. *Please don't make me say it.*

Whether it was the insane amount of stimulus of his prostate or the rocking back and forth over the mattress, was something Colt didn't know for sure, but he couldn't have cared less. "I'm going to come. God, Gus."

"Come all you want, baby. You're not going anywhere…until I'm done," Gus said, not slowing down one bit. If it hadn't been for the blindfold, Colt would have seen the room coming in and out of focus from the sheer strength of his orgasm. It was his favorite kind: handsfree, his boyfriend raging into him from behind as he surrendered every last ounce of control to the dominance of Gus's body and mind.

Nearing his own climax, Gus slowed down and loosened his hold. He rested the full weight of his impressive body resting on Colt's back in the final throes. Just as warm convulsions hit Colt's center—they had stopped using condoms a month ago—a stinging pain originated from his left shoulder, making him scream the safe word.

Taking off his blindfold, the sight of teeth marks confirmed his suspicion.

"Shit. I'm sorry, baby. I don't know what came over me. Are you okay? You're not bleeding, are you?"

"Damn. A little, yeah. I guess that counts as my *punishment*, right?"

"Don't say that. I was just playing. You know that,

right?" Gus kissed the sore spot gently, then moved on to Colt's lips. "You have to admit, though, it was hot as fuck," he said, slowly rubbing his fingertips over his own teeth marks as if he were banking the memory.

"It kind of was, but now I won't be wearing tank tops for a whole week from the looks of it."

"Why not? It would be nice to be able to show people you're mine. Maybe you should get that as a tattoo."

"Not happening, honey. Not. Happening."

As Gus tried to move back, Colt stopped him. "Wait, Gus, stop. Stay for a while. You know, on top of me, inside me. I…don't want you to leave yet." He had never requested it before, but felt an inexplicable need to hold onto their physical connection a while longer.

A rush of air brushed his back. "Sure, baby. Whatever you need." Gus rested his head on Colt's shoulder.

After getting lost in those sated kryptonite eyes, Colt said, "I love you, Gus." He had been planning it for a week, but hadn't found the right moment. Not that this was a perfect one, but he couldn't help himself.

"I love you too, Colt. Don't make fun of me, okay? I think I've loved you from the moment you freaked out at the restaurant on our first date."

Colt pushed his face to the mattress. "Oh God. I'm never hearing the end of that, am I?"

Gus laughed. "I'm serious. It was hot. *We're very different people, you and me,*" he said, mimicking Colt's voice before laughing even harder.

• • •

Post-coital showering had become a sacred ritual for Colt and Gus. Commanding and rough as his boyfriend could be between the sheets, he was every bit as sweet under the double shower heads of the ensuite bathroom. Soaping each other up, tasting each other's wet lips, massaging aching muscles… Colt came to think of it as a more intimate act than any of their love-making could ever achieve.

When Colt stared back at his reflection in the mirror, he gasped. He had expected to see the teeth marks on his left shoulder, but not the red and purple blooms on his right wrist and both his obliques. He knew Gus wasn't afraid to use physical strength on him, but hadn't considered how his body might suffer in the process. *He could break me in half.* He remembered the thought going through his head all those months ago.

Stepping out of the bathroom, he heard his phone chime on the nightstand. Upon inspecting it, he groaned and rolled his eyes.

Steve: I know you're hanging out at your rich boyfriend's house again, but would you mind your responsibilities in our apartment in the future? It was your turn to clean.

"Crap. I knew I'd forgotten something."

"What was that?" Gus asked. He walked back inside from the terrace, wearing gray gym shorts and sneakers, chest bare—looking yummy as ever to Colt, who had trouble focusing.

"Uhm. Nothing, Steve's sort of harassing me about clean-up duty."

Colt: I totally forgot and I'm sorry. I was in a hurry to get to Gus last night after work. I'll make it up to you and head home in time.

Steve: Never mind, Colt. Diana's done it already. You're not scoring any points with her, to be frank. I'll try my best to put in a good word for you, but you're not making it easy with your new lifestyle.

"The fuck? That bitch." Colt had as much affection for Steve's girlfriend Diana as he had for politicians in Uganda. He remembered their introduction so vividly, he couldn't help but travel down that particular lane in his mind.

He would have preferred waterboarding to the rude set of questions the *bitch* had asked him during their first dinner with the three of them. *Aren't you afraid to catch a disease, like HIV or monkey pox? How can you have sex with someone you don't know? So you never see them again after? Don't you want to get married some day? You know, you are allowed to have kids these days. But do you think that would be a good idea at all? How's your mother doing? She must be worried sick about you all the time. Does she have more children? Otherwise she'd be missing out on so much in her life. Grandkids for starters. This all must be tough on her, I'm sure. Don't take this the wrong way, Colt, I just tell it like it is.*

Instead of giving into the urge to gouge her eyes out using a fork doused in Sriracha sauce, Colt gave her a smile and said *I bet it's tough to be a cishet white female in this world. I mean, who can you possibly trust when everyone's immediate reaction is to smile when they see you? At least I usually know from the start who's about to stab me in the eye. You must be living in constant fear. I am in awe, truly.*

"Hand it to me," Gus said, stretching out his palm.

"Please don't text him back, okay?" Colt gave up his phone without further thought.

"New lifestyle. What is that supposed to mean? Passive-aggressive much? I got to say, baby, that roommate of yours is a real jerk to you most of the time. It pisses me off, the way he talks to you. Why do you put up with him?"

Colt scoffed. "We talked about this, honey. Because I can't afford an apartment on my own and I don't want a new roommate on the other side of town who turns out to be a toenail-collecting creep. Steve has not been ideal these last few months, but at least I know him. You know I have a hard time trusting people. So I'll suck it up and stay with him for the time being. He's not a bad person."

Gus looked at him with full-blown green intensity, then shook his head. "He doesn't deserve you, baby. I thought you said you were friends? What happened?"

Crap.

Since they'd said I love you to each other, Colt figured he'd better start sharing more about his personal life. "I'll tell you, but I need you to sit down for this, honey."

With Gus hanging on his every word Colt started telling him all about his former best friend Steve Blake. Two and a half years prior, Colt had lucked out when Steve's original roommate had been arrested on a drug charge, after which his ad popped up on Craigslist. Not hesitating, especially not after having checked the shared rent amount, Colt dialed the number. Exactly two days later he moved in.

"We kind of hit it off right away. We laughed at the memes of living in LA—the Instagram version versus reality—and kept sending them back and forth. Soon we were sharing everything about our personal lives. We started waiting for the other to watch some show on Netflix. Before I knew it we were going out together, too. At first it was all about making sure nothing sketchy would happen on the way back late at night, but I have to admit we had a good time. It felt amazing to be best friends with him, and it made the crappy apartment feel like a real home." Colt started fidgeting with his hands in his lap, unsure how to tell the next part.

"Then one night we got back home after Friday night drinks around the corner in one of those trending Tofu restaurants. I could say we'd been drinking too much, but I…I don't think that was it."

"I don't like where this is going," Gus said, rubbing his chin.

"That's why you need to sit. Anyway, Steve kept getting closer as we mounted the stairs up to our apartment. He did that thing where you guide someone you like inside your apartment with your hand on their lower back. It was odd, but kind of nice, too."

Colt went on to tell how he had plopped onto the bed, having no idea Steve had followed suit next to him. Exhausted from work and a few stiff drinks in his system, it hadn't taken him long to doze off with his face buried in the sheets. "He was rubbing my back when I woke up. I think I even moaned in response. When I asked him what he was doing, he said he was curious about how it would feel. And then I joked in response, *one way to find out.*"

Gus covered his face. "Oh my God. Please tell me he didn't fuck you."

"He did. It was extremely awkward from that first kiss to the point of removing his condom. All in all he was surprisingly interested. I'm ashamed to admit it kind of turned me on in the moment, too, to be his first gay experience. Sorry if that sounds messed-up."

As he saw Gus trying his best to control the building rage inside, Colt ended his story by telling him all about the cold shoulder he had received left and right starting the next morning. They never talked about what had happened in depth, as Steve kept referring to it as *that one drunk night*, whenever he chose to acknowledge it at all. Their friendship had ripped in half, especially after Diana had entered the stage two weeks later.

When Colt's story had concluded Gus jumped up from the bed. He cursed twice in Portuguese, shouting at the top of his lungs. Then he raised his fists and punched a hole in the formerly perfect white wall next to the bathroom door.

"Gus. What the fuck? What were you thinking? You can't just go around punching walls."

Gus winced as he held his right fist. "Well, baby, I was *thinking* I want to kill that Steve guy. But seeing as that would land me in prison, this was the next best thing. Man, that hurt."

"Honey, you're bleeding. Let me have a look." He turned Gus's big hand over in his own, feeling his shock regress into love. "It's swelling, too. Follow me."

Colt took him by the undamaged hand and guided him downstairs to the kitchen. Deep down, he wanted to be able to take care of Gus like this all the time, instead of just on the weekends or late at night.

If Colt had to choose one place in the mansion to be his favorite it was a no-brainer: the kitchen. He led Gus to one of the white leather bar stools standing at the center stage of the room: the marble island with a built-in sink on the far side and a matte gold faucet. Behind that, an eight-pitted black gas-fired stove with six oven compartments stood proud inside the gleaming white cupboard wall. A secret door connected to the pantry space in the adjacent room. It was a dream come to life—bigger than his Koreatown place.

Gus winced when Colt dabbed antiseptic gel on the spots where his skin had broken.

"I'm just going to throw it out there. I never want to be on the business end of your punches. You should call someone to fix that hole before I end up taking a wrong step and disappear in it. It's *that* big, honey."

Looking up, Colt saw the sheepish smile on his lover's face staring back at him. "I can't promise that. I love you so much, there's no telling what I'd do if you break my heart at this point."

Colt tilted his head at him. "How is it that it sounds like a threat, but still has a romantic touch to it?"

Gus shrugged. "It's a gift."

Colt finished putting bandages on Gus's wounds and fastened an ice pack over the top of his hand. "There. Good to go."

"*Obrigado*, baby. I love you." He planted a quick kiss on Colt's lips.

"Love you too. So glad I said it."

Gus sighed. "We're not done on the subject of Steve, Colt."

"Gus…"

"You shouldn't have to go back there."

"I already told you, honey, It's not ideal, but it'll have to do for now."

"Not ideal? That asshole literally fucks you over, denies his actions and then treats you like dirt. And you still go back to him? Just because you're afraid to take a chance and start over? I love you, Colt, but I can't stand by and do nothing."

Colt studied his bare feet. He knew Gus was making a hell of a point, but didn't see a quick solution to his problem. Their relationship was far too fresh out of the box for them to be living together, and he didn't feel comfortable forcing the man he loved into a situation they both weren't ready for. He enjoyed going through the milestones and didn't want to skip any. "I know. You're right. It won't be easy finding a new place, though. Craigslist, here I come."

Gus stood and walked over to caress the side of Colt's face with his free hand as he loomed over him. "Tomorrow's our anniversary—well, our sexual one, at least, but still. The last six months have been wonderful, Colt. You're such a good-hearted man. I'm so glad I found you after all these years, I don't ever want to let you go. I've never felt this way before, it's…amazing. The way we take care of each other, the way every moment we share feels too short, how our bodies fit together perfectly. How, despite our differences, we understand each other in a way no one else could. In my job I see a lot of couples when I show them houses in

Hollywood and when I watch them interact I feel pity. You know why? Because I realize they could never have our kind of connection."

Don't stop. Keep talking.

Colt was vaguely aware of his gaping mouth, but couldn't care less. He was glad to be able to hold onto the island counter, since he no longer trusted his knees.

Two emeralds were shining at Colt and turned liquid when Gus's mouth opened again. "Marry me, Colt."

He took two steps back, still resting one palm on the counter while the other flew up. "Hold on, right there. You must be losing too much blood."

Gus kept staring at him, unwavering in his intent.

Colt gasped. "You're serious."

"I am. I love you. I want you to live here with me. As my husband. So, will you marry me, Colt Whittaker?"

"Jesus. I—I don't know what to say. Isn't it too soon? Shouldn't we, like, try to live together first? Take this for— I don't know—a test drive? Sorry, I'm not up to date on the correct order of things."

Gus snickered, keeping that boyish smile plastered on his face. "Neither am I, which is why it shouldn't matter. Why would I spend more time not calling you my husband? I've kind of been doing it in my head lately, anyway."

He took another step back. "You have? Really? *Hi, I'm Colt and this is my husband Gustavo. But you can call him Gus.* It does have a nice ring to it."

"Ring. Fuck. I did not think this through." Gus runs a hand through his silver-streaked hair, still smiling with flushed cheeks.

"Wow, I feel so special," Colt said, smirking. "I'm kidding, doofus. I don't need a ring, Gus. I've got you—all six feet six of you. Wedding rings I get, but engagement rings, no. That's just a waste of money."

"You do realize you'd be marrying a millionaire, right baby?"

"I do, and that scares the shit out of me. Dear God, I'm sweating again. Why do you keep doing that? Anyway, I assume you didn't become a millionaire throwing cash out the window, *right baby?*"

Gus enveloped him in a strong embrace, careful not to use his bandaged hand. "Touché. You want to hear something creepy? I really love your sweat. The way it tastes off your soft skin," he whistles, "does things to my head. So sweat all you want."

Fuck me.

He lowered his face to the side of Colt's neck and licked it all the way to his ear, repeating the move from earlier.

"All right, all right, enough. Please let me focus for a minute, Gus," he managed between giggles. He pushed a hand against his lover's firm chest. "Look, I don't think we should be pushing our luck right now and jump into something we might not be ready for. I need to think it over. Will you allow me to do that?"

He saw Gus's eyes drop to the floor and prayed he hadn't scared him off.

"I guess that's fair. I'll give you exactly one week. You either want to be with me, or you don't. I don't want to waste time with this boyfriend bullshit any longer. I've gotten too old for it."

There it was, that three-letter-word Colt had been trying to avoid at all times since they got together. "I understand. Thank you. I swear this has nothing to do with my inferiority issues. I just want to be careful going forward. There are days I still can't believe you're my lover." Colt gave into his need for another hug and closed the distance between them. Gus's heart beating against his cheek was the best drug in the world, and in that moment of insecurity Colt downed big gulps of it.

"Gus, can I stay the night? I don't want to deal with Steve at home."

Gus kissed the top of his head and said, "Nothing would make me happier. Langdon will drive you to work tomorrow. Now before you start protesting like you always do, let me tell you this: I won't have it any other way. It's time you got used to your future life right here."

Colt nodded. Gus may have pushed him into a corner he didn't particularly like, but he decided to be okay with it for the time being. Hearing his boyfriend pour his heart out had turned him mellow and stupidly happy. So what if it came with a limited set of options?

The next morning, Gus had already left at 6:00 am, leaving Colt to doze on with a soft, lingering kiss and a whispered *I love you*. After getting ready for work, Colt met Hannah Reid, Gus's personal chef on weekdays, in the kitchen. It was the first time he saw any of the house's staff other than Langdon, adding to the discomfort of having stayed over on a weeknight.

"Good morning, Mr. Whittaker, have a seat. What do you want for breakfast?" Dressed up as a fancy restaurant chef in slate-colored slacks and matching chef beanie, Hannah's presence was like a ray of sunlight.

"Good morning, Hannah. I usually have coffee and oatmeal at home, but I can go with cereal if that's too much to ask."

"Coming right up. What kind of milk do you like?" She was already opening and shutting drawers to fish out the right size among the copper pans.

"Skimmed will do, thank you."

"No eggs?"

Colt thought for a second. Gus wanted him to adjust to his house's luxuries, so he might as well start putting in some effort to please his possible future husband.

"Mr. Whittaker?"

He shook his head. "Sorry. Do you happen to make one of those egg-white omelets?"

"Sure. I'll add a little fresh spinach and tomato if you don't mind?"

"Sounds terrific. Thank you."

"You don't have to thank me, Mr. Whittaker. It's my job. Nice meeting you, by the way."

Colt ate his breakfast all by himself after Hannah had retreated to the pantry. Though it was the best he had ever eaten, it was weird to be sitting there without Gus. Maybe tying the knot was indeed the right move for their relationship. However, from what he could tell from watching married couples from behind the counter at Sephora in FIGat7th, he suspected marriage would complicate things in ways his young mind couldn't imagine. His love for Gus already ran deep, but he feared the destructive powers of a serious commitment. All he was certain of after breakfast was he needed more time to ponder on the matter.

"What kind of music do you like?" Langdon asked once he closed the door in the car. The privacy screen had sunken into the Bentley's interior as though this were a James Bond movie.

"Music? Uhm, country and rock. Preferably nineties and early 2000s. Oh, and Sheryl Crow is always a safe bet."

Langdon smiled. "That's what I'm talking about." As soon as he raised the screen again Colt heard the first notes of Deana Carter's *Strawberry Wine* and decided to sing along.

I could get used to this.

On entering the store through the front, Sophia waved him over to the counter. Over two years ago he had impressed the shop's manager so much she couldn't have refused his application if her life had depended on it. It was his expertise in the world of fragrances and perfumes that had done her in after their interview. They'd been semi-friends ever since, gushing about their favorite luxury perfume houses.

"Colt, we need to talk. My office," the tall blonde in a soft cream pantsuit whispered.

Promotion?

In actuality the term *my office* referred to the break

room/inventory space behind the actual store's square footage. They sat on opposite sides of a neat desk holding one square-shaped computer screen. Ominous tension translated into Sophia's pinched eyebrows. This wasn't going to be a happy, champagne-popping promotion talk.

"Colt, there's no easy way to break this to you, but we're letting you go."

Colt rose. "What? Why?"

"I got a call from corporate about our store's online reviews on Yelp, Google Maps and other platforms. You should see for yourself." She handed Colt her iPad.

He couldn't register what he was reading, so he simply kept scrolling to see if this were all one big prank. After five swipes over the screen, he knew it wasn't. Dozens of reviews on Colt's performance as a salesman had appeared online, and none of them were remotely good.

Meghan O: 0 stars—I have never been this humiliated. That Colt guy kept flirting with my husband while completely ignoring me. I'm never setting foot inside that store again.

Cindy Perkins: 1 star—Stay away from Colt, and perhaps the entire store. Being yelled at is not okay. It's not my fault they can't meet my standards.

Oscar R: 0 stars—Worst shopping experience ever. The salesman by the name of Colt wouldn't sell me anything until he got my number. Management didn't seem to notice at all.

Bert Conrad: 1 star—These people don't know their products. This one guy, Colt, kept steering me to their most expensive products. The dude went ballistic when I called his bullshit. Never stepping foot inside again.

It went on and on. With every review Colt's chest

tightened a little more. His hand flew to his opened mouth once the scope of this blatant assault on his person hit him. His name was in every review he had read.

"If it's any consolation, I don't believe any of them personally. It breaks my heart to see you go, Colt. You're the one we all turn to when we're out of fragrance suggestions. Your level of expertise is off the charts, and even better, you're passionate about it."

"This is such bullshit, Sophia. I'm the best you've got. Do you know what this means for me? Do you? I will never get a job in retail ever again. I'll lose my apartment, my life here in LA, my reputation, everything. The internet is forever. Please do something." His throat felt raw, but he wasn't going to accept his fate quietly.

"Colt, calm down. I told management firing you would be an epic mistake, seeing as we've hit all of our sales targets since hiring you. I'm sorry I couldn't change their minds. They are terminating you as of today and there is going to be a statement on all platforms as a corrective measure. Again, Colt, I am so sorry it had to go down like this. There's no notice, but we're paying for the next two weeks as severance. I wasn't going to budge on that demand and they knew it." Through the Botox-frozen features of his former boss Colt could see genuine compassion.

"Thank you for that, I suppose. Not that it will help in the least. I worked my butt off at this place, Sophia. I never even took a sick day or anything." He ran his hand through his hair. "God, it just seems so aggressive and personal. Who would do this? Who did I piss off so much they would charge at me from a distance?"

She shook her head. "I don't know. I can't wrap my head around it either. It could be our competitors or some influencer who really doesn't like you for personal reasons. Whoever it was, I hope Karma's on their tail."

Sophia reached over for a parting hug, but Colt wouldn't allow it. Instead they shook hands in accordance with the corporate nature of this financial tragedy for Colt's future. Walking back into the store—for the last time, he figured—he wondered if he should say something to his now former coworkers. Their astonished high-school drama faces, however, had quickly made the decision for him. Once outside he started hyperventilating and found a bench to lower himself onto just in time. All he could think through the heaving breaths was *What the fuck am I going to do?* He unlocked his phone, went to his favorite contacts and tapped Gus's name.

Chapter 8
Mel—Present

"Mel? Mel, hello? Hey!" Kate snapped her fingers in front of his eyes, waking Mel from his daze. "God, what is up with you? You haven't said three words since you got home. Stop biting your fingernails."

She wasn't wrong. Mel had indeed been quieter than usual after the seemingly longest day at the station. First thing he had done was check on Rose to watch her belly rise and fall like the waves of the Pacific. He had been craving the sight ever since sitting down across Colt in the interrogation room, in dire need to witness innocence. Kate was a saint for going easy on him, seeing as he had all but ignored her for the past hour. Even their *welcome-home* kiss had been half-assed on his side.

"I'm sorry, darling. It's been quite a day."

"Apparently. You missed her, and that's only natural. It's okay, honey. I'm sure I'm rambling. I've just been cooped up in here all day, waiting for an adult to interact with. Let's try this again. How's your steak?"

"It's good, thanks," he lied. There was no room for bad food comments at his dining table tonight. *Yeah, to be frank it's both charred and raw at the same time, so I'll hit Chipotle in an hour* wouldn't have gone over well.

"Oh, you should have seen what Rose did this morning. I swear it was the cutest thing I've ever seen. So I was upstairs on the bed with her and all of a sudden she looked up to me with those perfect little blue eyes—you know how she gets that twinkle in them. Anyway, so there I was, not really paying attention or anything and…"

Mel zoned out at the words *blue eyes* and thought back to those of Colt widening as he tried to approach him when they had been alone in the room. That broken, wretched look was all he could see as he fake-listened to his wife's ramblings, nodding occasionally.

"…it was so funny. I swear our daughter's going to be intelligent. There's no other explanation for it. UCLA, here we come."

"That's great, darling. Sorry I missed it."

They stuffed their faces in silence, until Mel couldn't drown out his worrisome thoughts anymore. "Kate? Do you ever wonder if we did the right thing, bringing a child into this world?"

Kate swallowed wrong and started coughing, reaching for her water glass. A few chest knocks and throat massages later she said, "Whoa. Way to kill the mood of blissful parenting, Mel," in a hoarse voice. Her green eyes now looked wet and frightened. "Of course we did the right thing. How can you say that about your own daughter? Where is this coming from? What the hell happened at the station? You were doing fine this morning." She tugged strands of her copper hair back behind her ears.

Mel let out a long breath. He couldn't flat-out tell Kate every single detail of what had transpired at the station with Colt today. When it came to spouses, lines got blurry about how much detectives could share with them about ongoing cases. He trusted Kate more than anyone in the world, yet he knew his wife to be a chatterbox in her own social circles—physical, digital or mixed. It might have been against his better judgment, but a little voice in his head told him she wasn't going to let him off easy on this bombshell question. Besides, it didn't feel right to keep this supernova blaze of a case all to himself—not with him becoming a responsible father trying to set an example. "What I'm about to tell you cannot leave this house. Promise me that."

After Kate's hurried confirmation, Mel told her all he could without using names or other direct details about Colt's case. He referred to Colt as John, to Holmby Hills as Disneyland and to the drug cartel as the thieves. It felt good letting her in on what he had been going through all day. He and Charlotte hadn't reached that point in their partnership where they could lean on each other at times like these. He hoped they would get there soon for his wife's sake. Dragging her into this jackpot of misery on a regular basis wasn't fair.

After checking on Rose's crib, allowing the information to sink in, he figured, Kate reclaimed her seat and said, "So this John person. I'll admit it was an odd move, but I understand why he'd ask for you. You know, considering Gene's elegant—*uhuhm*—ways as opposed to your natural charm. But why would he hold back information on you? How could that possibly benefit him right now?"

Mel smiled at his wife. Within minutes they were on the same page and he loved her all the more for it. "I don't know, but whatever the reason, it can't be good."

"God. Now I understand your question from earlier." Kate started to push around the creamed broccoli on her plate. "Be careful, Mel. I know you. You're going to move mountains to try and save this guy—I can see it in your eyes. I made you a promise, so now you're going to make me one. Don't go out there doing anything stupid for this John to endanger your own life or your family's. Promise me you'll think twice before you act."

"Fair enough. I promise. I love you."

"I love you, too. You have got to stop pulling people over in traffic. You get too attached to them afterward. By the way, should I be jealous?" Kate said with a naughty grin, referring to how they first met.

Mel chuckled. "The things your mind goes to."

Almost eight years ago, while he was still in the Traffic unit, Mel had pulled over a silver Suburban filled with singing drunk ladies in their twenties. Kate was the designated driver to her sister's bachelorette party, and the first face Mel saw after having tapped on the window. Encouraged by her liquid-bravado-fueled companions, Kate asked him out on the spot, wildly embarrassed by her friends' cackles and shrieks. The memory was priceless to both and would no doubt serve as a lesson about driving under the influence for Rose one day.

After dinner Mel passed out on the couch trying to watch CNN's news. As a member of law enforcement he had learned to dread watching news of any kind. You never knew who was going to leak anything to those vultures of the press about ongoing cases. The Chief was an expert on tearing her whole team a new one whenever it happened, which had made him like her even more.

Kate shook him awake with his phone in her hand. "Honey, it's the station. They need you."

He arrived at the scene, adding one more LAPD vehicle to the three already parked in the street. Charlotte's apartment was part of a complex of at least fifty residences, making it impossible to get a good view of the place. A bunch of nosy neighbors were giving into their curiosity in front of the building, some hugging their robes. An ambulance was struggling to get closer to the entrance in the middle of the building's facade.

Cam walked up to Mel's car.

"What the hell happened?" Mel asked.

"Calm down. There was an attack on Charlotte and Colt about an hour ago. They're not sure what happened exactly, but all signs point to the cartel, which is why I'm here." Cam sighed and scratched his head. "It's not pretty, man."

His best friend didn't need to tell him the last phrase, as his face alone conveyed enough. The ambulance had finally made it to the entrance, but it would take another few minutes before the crowd would disperse, despite the officers trying their best to maintain order.

"By the way," Cam started, "I didn't catch you earlier to tell you something about your guy. I thought I recognized him from somewhere, so I did a little digging. A few years back, he was a person of interest on one of my murder cases. Steve Blake, his former roommate."

Cam had been in Homicide at the time, but migrated to the Gang and Narcotics Division after about a year of dealing with drug-related cases. Showing high potential to the DEA on several cases, they had groomed Cam to join them last year.

"Did you interrogate him?"

"Yes, but he was never a real suspect. We paid him a visit at his mansion to ask him some routine questions. Guess who cut us short?"

"His loving husband."

"Yup. Made all kinds of legal threats and asked us to leave his husband alone. Colt had actually been very cooperative until then. That Gustavo's a real charmer, I'll tell you that." Cam's eyes widened at his last phrase.

Mel parked the information in the file in his head, sensing he'd be needing it at some point. The entrance doors swung open wide, revealing a paramedic walking backward. Mel ran past the crowd to Charlotte as soon as he saw her on the gurney with a heavy bandage across her waist.

Fuck, no.

"Sir, you need to give her space," the slender paramedic with blond spiky hair said. Up close, Charlotte's face looked drenched in sweat.

"Charlotte, what happened?" Mel said, ignoring him.

"Sir, are you hearing me? She's heavily sedated. I need you to back away." He enunciated the last words.

Charlotte's eyes fluttered while she remained oblivious to Mel's presence.

As they wheeled her into the ambulance Cam accompanied Mel upstairs to her apartment, struggling to keep up with him.

"Mr. Whittaker? I'm talking to you. Colt? You have to tell us what happened. Do you want to spend the night at the station or what?" an officer barked at Colt, who sat on the floor against the kitchen wall hugging his knees.

"That's enough, Alex. Step away from him," Mel said.

"Not until I get his statement, Mel. Good to see you, too," Alex said, with a deep frown on his puffed face. All those years of polishing the LAPD's public image still couldn't prevent the occasional donut-munching stereotypes roaming the city. "The paramedic just cleared him for questioning, so there's nothing wrong with him."

"Alex, look at him. You're not going to get his statement tonight. I appreciate you wanting to complete your job here, but it's a rather sensitive and complicated case you've walked in on just now. Go home to your family. I'll take it from here."

Alex sighed, threw up both hands and started walking back to the stairwell.

Charlotte's apartment looked sterile just as Mel had imagined it to be. Stray plates and pans cluttered the sink, which meant she had made an effort to present Colt with a homemade meal—a sight that filled him with pride. The place was as nice as the outside of the building had promised: modern, functional and light with those uninterrupted large windows to one side, covered with sleek black roll-down curtains.

"What is that smell?" Mel asked.

"Burnt flesh," Cam answered. A moment of eye contact between the two conveyed the rest of the information on the subject, causing Mel to rub his forehead, craving his retired vaping pen with a vigor.

As Mel took in the remnants of whatever violent scene had taken place around the dining table, his eyes kept wandering to Colt. Knocked-over chairs and broken glass scattered on the floor aside, Colt seemed unharmed—on the outside.

Mel lowered to his haunches in front of him, trying to meet his eyes that looked right through him. From his new vantage point he spotted a new bruise on the side of Colt's neck, and possibly one on his forearm, if memory served him right.

"Colt, I know you're terrified and that's okay. If you don't want to talk, I won't force you to. No one is going to force you to do anything."

There was no reaction. He just kept staring, blinking occasionally, while holding his knees against his chest with white knuckles.

"Nothing?" Cam asked from the doorway.

Mel shook his head. Captain Perez walked into the apartment, scrunching her nose the same way Mel had seen Cam do.

"What the hell happened here?"

Cam filled her in on the details—or lack thereof—

while the Chief studied the interior and Colt's sunken figure.

After taking in the details of the scene around her, she said, "I guess we'll have to take him back, then."

Mel jumped right in, "Chief, no. We can't do that, Not if we ever want him to talk to us again. Look at him, the guy's catatonic. He's got new bruises, too."

Captain Perez looked him dead in the eye, widening her eyes. "No, Mel. If you're about to suggest what I think, then no. You've got a family to think about. What is Kate going to say? Whoever did this to Charlotte knew what they were doing. They hurt one of our own without alarming neighbors, bypassing our surveillance. That reminds me I have to add something to my to-do list for tomorrow. Like I haven't yelled enough in my career."

"Chief, hear me out. What are the odds of a repeat performance? We'll double surveillance efforts to be sure, but these thugs have already accomplished their main objective here: scaring the shit out of Colt and our Division. They'd be stupid to risk doing it again. Besides, and I don't need to tell you this, there's no safe house for Colt anywhere near the station."

The Chief groaned with her eyes covered. "God, I hate it when you make sense. You got to stop doing that." She shook her head. "Fine, take him. But he's your responsibility now, and you better get him to talk while you're at it. Man, I'm going to be in deep shit with the people upstairs."

Cam turned to his team of CSIs filing in. "Listen up, I want this place turned over with a fine-tooth comb. The finest. They can't get away with this. Am I making myself clear?"

Instead of a response, the hazmat-suited investigators went to work with equal parts of focus and speed. *Got to love the DEA's federal budget.*

Mel approached Colt and carefully put his hand on his forearm to draw his attention, talking about what he was going to do before doing so the whole time. To his surprise Colt didn't flinch at his touch. Step by step, with Colt staring into a void, they managed to get down to the street. Most of the neighbors had gone back home save for a few thrill seekers on the curb. He only touched Colt on that same spot on his forearm, not daring to push his luck as he guided him into his Explorer. Not fastening Colt's seatbelt was a chance he was happy to take for the drive home.

Much as he tried, talking wasn't in the cards that evening. Not on the ride home, nor on meeting Kate or when he showed him the guest bedroom. Mel had ignored the worried look on his wife's face for as long as he could, but she didn't wait for him to cave.

"So, it's Colt instead of John. Fucking hell, Mel. You need to start telling me what happened. Now," she spat.

Mel's inner debating skills were uncooperative to say the least. After a few hesitant moments in which he felt his mouth open and close several times, he ended up reasoning she was going to be mad about his decision either way. He might as well take the medicine at once. "Look. All I can tell you is there was an attack. Charlotte got hurt, but her life is not in danger. We found Colt at the scene like this."

"And you brought him here? To our daughter?"

"Keep your voice down. Darling, I—"

She raised her finger at him. "No, no, no. You don't get to *darling* me right now. You promised not to endanger our family like this, Mel. But here we are, hours later with you breaking said promise. You really outdid yourself this time."

"What I promised was to think twice before acting, which I did," Mel started, but none of his semantic reasonings made any difference in their fight. He chose to believe Kate would come around and see it from his perspective, that he couldn't allow Colt to be locked in a holding cell after the added trauma of tonight's events.

"You're sleeping on the couch. We'll talk about it tomorrow. I can't believe you did this, Mel."

He stopped himself from protesting just in time. Quick-tempered as Kate could be, it was that kind of—literally—red-headed passion that attracted him more than her perfect hour-glass silhouette ever could.

In the early hours, as his restless frustration on the lumpy old couch got the better of him, Mel heard soft singing coming from upstairs.

Kate? He immediately dismissed the thought. His wife had many talents, none of which involved her vocal cords. Truth be told, she couldn't hold a note if her life depended on it, but he'd never tell that to her face.

Then the other option hit him.

He shot up from the couch, cursing his aching back muscles, and dashed upstairs to the nursery. In between the singing he could hear Rose's distinct cooing sounds.

As Mel held his breath and listened to the soothing voice, he neared the doorframe trying his best not to make a sound. The soft moonlight breaching the thin curtains made the scene even more magical.

Colt's voice roared softly as he sang *Wayfaring Stranger* the Emmylou Harris way, croaking and whispering some of the words to Rose's apparent delight, who looked up at him from inside her crib, as dumbfounded as Mel himself.

When the chorus came to a close, he rapped the doorframe lightly with his knuckles, signaling for Colt to meet him in the hallway. Backing away from the crib, the latter repeated the last part of the chorus.

"What?" Colt whispered. The tartan pajamas Kate had provided him with hung over him like a tablecloth over a Christmas tree. Mel signaled again to follow him downstairs.

"I swear I was only trying to calm her down. She got fussy and neither of you reacted, so I thought it couldn't hurt. I'm sorry, Mel, I should've asked." Colt was sitting at the dining room table with one leg tucked under this knee.

Mel stared at him while he gathered water bottles from the fridge in the kitchen. A tiny smile forced its way up his mouth and he couldn't suppress it.

Colt looked away toward the couch on the other end of the open-plan space, then back to Mel with an arched eyebrow.

"Why am I getting the feeling it's a good thing your wife didn't see me hover over your daughter just now?"

Mel took a seat opposite him and slid a bottle to Colt's

side. "Don't worry about that. Momma bear took hold of her. She'll come around before you know it."

Colt twisted the cap off and took a swig.

"I'm glad to hear you talk again, Colt. You got me worried for a moment. I thought whatever had gone down at the apartment had broken you for good, to be honest."

"I've been broken like that a few times now. That state of shock always passes. Thanks for getting me out of there, Mel. And for taking me in."

"You're welcome. There are a few rules in my house I'm going to need you to abide by."

"Sure."

"One, say thank you and please. Two, dinner's at 7:00 pm or close to that. Three, lights out at 10 pm, which means no noise after that. Four, customized for you, stay inside. Don't go near windows or the backyard."

"That'll work. It's the least I can do."

Mel eyed him and nodded, doing his best to resist ruining his fingernails further. "Colt, would you mind telling me what happened?"

Colt leaned forward and pressed his mouth to his clasped hands. He released a shuddered breath. "They made me watch. Said they'd do both sides if I didn't. One of them held me down while the other two handled Charlotte." His eyes welled up as he looked Mel in the eye again.

I really need to start vaping again.

"So there were three of them?"

Colt nodded. "They used the delivery guy as a decoy to get inside. Charlotte had ordered pizza after a failed attempt at a homemade dinner. It all happened so fast. And it's all my fault, Mel. If I hadn't…"

As was so often the case with special victims like Colt, they ended up blaming themselves for all the bad things happening around them. It was part of the mental side of the abuse, but they could rarely see it that way themselves.

"Colt, what you did today was a brave thing. Even if you had killed your husband, you would have faced the consequences head-on. Talking about your husband's abusive ways might have been even more courageous than that. There's no way you could have known about your husband's involvement with the Cordelio cartel, so that is not on you. What happened to Charlotte is a clear sign we need to stop them from hurting others."

"What if you or your family are next?"

Mel repeated what he had told Captain Perez at Charlotte's apartment hours ago, how it wouldn't be a smart move on the cartel's side.

After Mel had found his laptop, he urged Colt to continue his statement. The three men entering Charlotte's place had come prepared. Wearing ski masks, long clothing and gloves, they hadn't lost time in their endeavor to scare Colt out of his mind. With Colt pinned to the floor they had forced Charlotte on the dining table. Working together like professionals, they had fastened her wrists with plastic cuffs, taped her mouth shut and taken off her lounge shorts. Using the stove, they had heated a branding iron until red-hot. While two of them had been holding Charlotte in place, the other had seared the cartel's symbol into her skin. When Mel asked Colt if he'd noticed anything special about the assailants, all he said was they had addressed one another in Spanish. "I would have known if it were Portuguese."

While typing the scene's details into the file, Mel felt his stomach turn. One thing he was sure of was he could never tell Kate about the attack. He looked at Colt, thinking how remarkable his shift in demeanor was. Hours ago the guy seemed ready for a psychiatric ward, yet now he was as cooperative as he could have wished for. He closed his laptop.

"Did you call your family?" Mel asked.

"I did, yes. I don't think they believed a word I said. Charlotte called them back and told them it was serious, so I hope they'll do as she said."

Nice work, my partner.

"That's why you couldn't get out. He'd hurt your family."

Colt nodded. "It's more complicated than that, but yes. I threatened to leave early in our marriage when I had figured out what our life together was going to be like. The next day my brother got beaten into the ER in the subway in the Bronx. That's how it works: I make a run for it, they pay the price. Gus forced me to break all ties with them so they wouldn't believe me in situations like this. I haven't seen my mom since our engagement." He sniffed and wiped at his eyes with his finger.

"Thank you for telling me, Colt. I won't push you any further tonight. We'll continue this tomorrow. Get some rest. I'll tell you this, though. You've got a solid voice. Feel free to use it again. I really love that song and I bet Rose does, too."

Colt smiled at Mel for the first time that day. The expression reached all the way to the wrinkles around his exhausted eyes. This was how he was going to gain ground in earning Colt's trust: music.

"Emmylou Harris's version is my favorite. The song always does the trick. In one of my group homes there was this kid I was close to with anxiety issues. He'd ask me to sing it whenever he got worked up. It's a tougher song than it looks. Took me weeks to get it right."

"It shows. For what it's worth, I was in the system, too."

Colt's head tilted to the side. "Really?"

Mel nodded.

"Good night, Mel."

"Good night, Colt."

Mel toyed with the idea of telling Colt about his planned visit to the hospital tomorrow, but quickly decided against it. Knowing Mel would be interviewing Gustavo in a few hours wasn't going to help Colt get some much-needed rest.

Chapter 9
Colt—Past

With the last of his tears drying, Colt was sitting at the kitchen island, trying to make sense of his professional demise. In between the waves of despair he came to understand it wasn't so much the loss of income he was mourning. Sure, LA life as he had known it was forever ruined because of the brutal digital assault, but that's not what had caused his heart to break. Knowing he'd never be able to match a customer to that one fragrance on the shelves—that not only amplified their character traits, but complemented their natural scent—was what truly devastated him. The world had fucked him over once again. When would the giving part of his life slow down enough for the taking to enter the stage?

"Langdon, you don't have to sit with me. I'll be okay."

"Sorry, Mr. Whittaker. Mr. Carolino was adamant about not leaving your side until he gets here. Can I say something personal?" the driver asked. Always in the background, it was easy to forget he was around. His signature dark formal clothing aside, there was not one physical feature about the man that stood out from the rest.

Average build and height, light brown short hair, brown eyes and pale skin—cookie-cutter as could be.

"Sure. Please do."

"I'm sorry about your job."

Of course Langdon had put two and two together after having to pick Colt back up from his workplace so soon. Crying all over the car's interior hadn't concealed much either.

"Thank you for saying that."

Langdon gave him a pressed-lips smile and resumed his staring contest with his phone. Colt had an idea and rolled with it.

"Langdon, I'm going to say something personal, too. That Spicebomb fragrance from Viktor&Rolf isn't doing you any favors. First of all, it's way too aggressive for a guy like you. And second, it doesn't play well with your skin's natural scent. I can almost hear the notes fighting."

He frowned. "How did you—"

"Trust me. You should try Dior's Fahrenheit. The cologne version, not the perfume. I guarantee you'll like it."

Colt repeated the name as Langdon entered it into his phone. The slight smile on his face was priceless and served Colt with another slice of grief cake over his job.

He heard Gus's black Mercedes G-Class on the driveway. Gus had once explained to him how some clients needed to see him drive for himself while others required him to arrive with Langdon in his Bentley.

Removing his aviator Prada sunglasses, Gus entered the front door, approached the kitchen island and put his arms around Colt. "It's going to be okay, baby. I'm here."

Gus turned to Langdon and added, "Thanks," sending him off.

"It's so unfair, Gus. I'm ruined." Colt conveyed the details of his termination while Gus made espressos, causing Colt to pause when the grinding process of the machine became too loud. Then they sat next to each other in silence for a while, sipping their shots.

"What are you going to do?"

"I don't know. I could start waiting tables or look for some shitty fast-food job, I guess. Not the best options, and certainly not where I thought I was headed in life until this morning. Imagine introducing me to one of your business relations as *my boyfriend who works at McDonalds.*"

Gus worked his jaw before he spoke. "Colt, I want you to listen to me." At hearing that first phrase he knew exactly what would be coming out of his mouth. His heart rate sky-rocketed. It's not like he hadn't been thinking about it since leaving Sophia's makeshift office. Where it had been the question yesterday, now his possible answer terrified him.

"There's an obvious solution to your problem right here. I know I promised you could think it over for six more days, but it appears the universe doesn't play by our rules." He lowered to one knee. "On the condition that you move in today, will you marry me, Colt Whittaker?"

Out of options, Colt decided then and there it was time for that taking in life to get a jump start and accepted Gus's hand in what was soon to become *their* gorgeous kitchen.

• • •

Steve: You're letting some driver pick up your stuff? Man, you've changed. I guess I should say have a nice life, Mr. Carolino?

Colt: I'm actually keeping Dad's name. Fuck you, Steve. See how YOU like it.

"You really sent that?" Gus asked after seeing it on Colt's phone, shaking with laughter.

"I'm not sorry. The asshole deserves it—pun intended."

"Hey, come here. I'm proud of you, my gorgeous fiancé." He kissed Colt the way he had done when they first met, building from exploring to devouring tongue swirls, lifting Colt from the floor onto the counter.

"I can't wait for *my* fiancé to fuck me," Colt whispered, making Gus growl into his ear.

"You're lucky Tommy will be here any minute, or you'd be taking it right here. Do you think he'd mind? We could teach him a thing or two." Gus pushed Colt's back to the marble surface, an ocean of cool against his spine. After grabbing hold of his thighs Gus started grinding his erection against Colt's denim-encased crotch.

Colt got back up, pushing against Gus's tight abs. "You really are insatiable. Just like I always dreamed my husband to be."

Minutes later Tommy Silveira—really Tomé, but no American had succeeded in pronouncing it correctly—walked into the kitchen chatting away with Gus in their native language. Hearing his fiancé speak Portuguese always put a smile on Colt's face as Gus seemed a little more at ease while doing so. It was like catching a glimpse of the man's younger years.

Tommy was there for one purpose only: getting Colt to

sign the prenup his fiancé had already requested over the weekend. However, Gus assured him the meeting was mostly about helping Colt understand all the legalese in the lengthy document. He confirmed his intentions by giving the two space after retreating to his office with an *I love you.*

It was challenging to keep up with Tommy as he either slung legal terms left and right or mansplained the basics in such a way that irritated the hell out of Colt. What he fathomed after a few pages were Gus's motives behind the arrangement. As a wealthy man, he needed to protect his assets in case their marriage wouldn't go as planned—aka end in brutal divorce. He guessed it also had to do with their age difference to a certain degree, which he feared would always play a part in their lives somehow.

"Gus told me you intend to keep your last name and not change it to Carolino? I have to say, Colt Carolino sounds like a badass."

Colt met his smile. "I know, but I can't do that. My father's name is all I have left from him. He died when I was one."

"I'm sorry. Must've been tough. Now, there's one more thing to discuss, Colt, and then we're done. It's about what happens in the event of Gus's death."

Gus had introduced Tommy to him when they had been dating for two months. Apart from his lawyer, Colt considered the man Gus's best friend, as he didn't know any other contestants for the position. With his short hair the color of wildfire, freckled skin combined with dark eyes and a remarkable V-shaped torso, the man could turn a number of heads. Apart from his looks, his fast tongue and quick draw in court had made him a force to be reckoned with in the cutthroat legal realm of LA, if half the stories were true.

"I'm not going to like this part, am I?" Colt asked.

"Oh, I think you are. In truth, it's never a smooth conversation between lovers of any kind, but what Gus had me draw up on this page really speaks to his feelings for you."

Colt read the paragraph-length sentence over three times, then stared at Tommy in disbelief. "I must be reading this wrong. Is temporary dyslexia a thing?"

Tommy smiled, baring thousands of dollars worth of dental investments. "In short, if Gus's death precedes yours you will inherit every last one of his assets. The real estate, the business, cars, everything. It goes without saying, but this is not the case if you're responsible for his death. There's a whole clause about that in there, too."

He couldn't believe his ears. Six months before he had come here looking for a night of pleasure with no strings attached, not planning on seeing Gus ever again after, like he had done countless times before. What he had never dared to dream was becoming reality fast. Finding out Gus had been planning to look after him even after his death left him speechless. All he could do, in spite of Tommy's frown, was run to Gus's office.

As soon as he got there he wrapped his arms around his fiancé's back. "Hey, what's wrong?" Gus asked. He did his best to hide it, but Colt loved seeing him wear his reading glasses. Gus swiveled his chair around and pulled Colt onto his lap. The central glass-topped desk faced the uninterrupted windows so that the views of the Pacific would always be a lift of the head away from his work. To the back of the white leather desk chair stood a wall of bookcases with a ladder attached on a railing spanning the entire width. Plush silver rugs added warmth.

"Honey, about that prenup. You can't be serious. What about your family in Brazil? This is too much. I'm not after your money. How many times do I need to say that?"

"Baby, listen to me. It's not a big deal. If we should divorce for some reason you don't get anything. I think we can agree on that being reasonable. But if I die I want you to be comfortable. Let's face it, Colt. I know neither of us likes to talk about it, but I'm twice your age. What that means in our marriage is I'll likely be the first to check out. It's not a sexy conversation topic, but in all likelihood that's the way it will be for us. And I can't stand the thought of you out on the street the minute I take my last breath."

Colt started tracing Gus's chest with his fingertips to avoid eye contact. "I really hate the thought of you dying before me, Gus. Sorry if I'm crying, but it breaks my heart knowing I'll have to do this without you. Man, there goes our party mood."

Gus rearranged a strand of Colt's hair. "You'll just have to keep me alive, then."

"I'll try. It won't be easy if our sex life keeps escalating at its current rate. We have to start considering your heart next time. That's it. No more all-nighters. I'm thinking only Sundays and federal holidays, just to be safe."

Gus pinched Colt's side, making him yelp. "You clearly didn't read all parts of the prenup. It clearly states your body is now my official property to use as I see fit. I'm seeing a *property of Carolino* tattoo in your future."

He rolled his eyes. "In your dreams."

Gus smirked. "We'll see. Oh, and before I forget. There's a surprise for you on Wednesday, so don't make any plans."

Practically jumping from Gus's lap, Colt faced him. "Yeah, I'll try my best to clear my schedule for the day. Won't be easy with all the balls I've got up in the air these days."

Gus's eyes widened. "Baby, I'm sorry, that's not what I meant. I'm an idiot."

Colt's hands were propped on his sides as he felt the hurt subside. "You're not. It's okay, honey. It's not you I'm mad at. So this surprise, is it a dirty one?" he asked, arching a brow.

Gus pantomimed zipping his mouth shut and swiveled back to work.

Two mornings later Colt nearly choked on his oatmeal the moment he recognized the voice behind him. With Gus working from home and Hannah having left only minutes ago, he wondered if the sound had been imaginary. On turning around he couldn't believe his eyes.

"Collie," his mother shrieked, jumping up and down in her typical tan raincoat and denim combo.

Fuck.

"Mom? What are you... How did you get here?"

"Surprise," Gus said, making his way to the kitchen.

"Well, sweetie, your gorgeous fiancé has just flown me in with his private jet. Can you fucking believe it? Me in a private jet? I'm still shaking." Her volume had grown intolerable in seconds, and it was only morning. "Now give your mom a kiss already."

Hugging his mother, taking in her familiar warmth and perfume, he mouthed words of gratitude to his grinning fiancé. It was an off-the-charts gesture only days after their engagement, but he wasn't sure it was the right move given his mother's track record with celebrating his good news.

"Are my nostrils playing tricks on me or is my baby wearing Amouage Interlude?" his mother asked when she released him. Colt had found the lavish perfume in a box next to his pillow when he woke up and was wearing it for the first time.

"That's right. Gus got it for me as an engagement gift. While we're on the subject, you've gone back to Lancôme's Poême. Should I be worried?"

The world of fragrances was perhaps the only place on earth where Colt and his mom knew how to interact without fighting. Going to the Sephora store at Kohl's in Topeka had been their sacred ritual as mother and son for as long as Colt could remember. They'd always start off on their own on the respective His and Hers sides of the store spraying their favorites on paper testers or their wrists. Armed with more foreign vocabulary than they would otherwise have known, they'd meet in the middle aisle and turn it into a guessing game. Where the salespeople at first had asked them to leave politely, they soon ended up joining in, marveling at their combined expertise of names and notes. The no-purchase rule his mother had imposed on nine out of every ten trips to the store on average had often saddened Colt when he was too young to understand the financial side of single parenthood.

"No, sweetie. Relax, I know it cost me a fortune, but I don't wear it every single day. I'm going for quality, not quantity. My God, look at this place. I can't believe this is where you live. How are you not jumping up and down all the time? Both of you?"

"Thank you, Anna. Please make yourself at home," Gus said.

"Was that a personal chef I ran into outside? I don't think I can take any more of this, you guys." Her palm was now plastered to her forehead. The handles of her tan suede handbag kept getting tangled from all the gesticulation.

"Sit down, mom. I'll make you some coffee. I'm glad you're here." He waited for the machine to stop burring, then continued, "I know I should have told you sooner about Gus and me, but I didn't want you to worry. I planned on calling you today, if that makes things better?"

"Please. You had me at private jet." She winked. Although her complexion didn't look as healthy as any other woman's her age, Colt could tell she was doing all right at home. She would never be the glowing woman from Colt's earliest memories again, but at least she was trying her best not to make things worse. It made him breathe easier knowing that.

Colt handed her the mug holding an Americano with two sugars, no cream. Bitter and sweet, just like her.

"Gustavo—I mean Gus, could you leave us alone to talk

for a few minutes, please? You know, mother to son and all that?"

Uh-oh. Not good.

"Sure. I'll be in my office."

Take the knives with you.

Stirring her mug, his mother waited for Gus's heavy footsteps to drown out completely before she spoke. Colt knew all too well what that clinking sound of her spoon was really stirring up between them.

"Collie," she started, "I'm sorry to ask, but am I right in my assumption that your fiancé is about my age?"

Jumping right in.

In need of something stronger, Colt turned back to the coffeemaker, selected the tiniest cup he could find in the cupboard and pressed the ristretto button, hoping the grinding process to take a full five minutes at least. "Yes, mother, Gus will be forty-five in two months, just like you. Why do you ask?"

"I'm asking because I'm worried, sweetie. Don't get me wrong, he's insanely good-looking and I totally see why you're into him besides all of this," she flung her arms wide to indicate the house and all of its luxury, "but I'm not sure he's what you need right now. You're still so young and finding your way.

"I'm sorry to sound harsh, but think of it from Gus's perspective. Why would a rich and successful man like him take in someone like you? Why not date guys his own age? Looking like that, he probably has to fight them off left and right when he's out there. My head is spinning trying to figure it out, and frankly, two words keep flashing in my mind. Sugar daddy."

After downing the strong ristretto in one gulp, Colt banged the cup on the counter. "You just can't help yourself, can you? I can't believe this. First chance you get, you go out of your way to make me feel worthless like you always do. You know, Gus told me this before. He calls it my inferiority complex. It's why I often don't believe I deserve good things in life and therefore have trouble accepting them. Guess who made me that way—no, who's still making me that way?" He was being loud, but didn't care.

His mother sighed and said, "Here we go." Her sapphire eyes widened briefly as she fixed her gaze on her mug, ready to take blows.

"Yes, here we go. Believe what you want, but Gus accepts every single part of me. You think I haven't had my doubts about our relationship? I freaked out a lot at the beginning. At our very first date I was doing a really good job at pushing him away the minute I feared it could be real, that a man like him would want anything to do with white trash like me. That's how messed up I was, Mom. And I'm sorry to tell you this, but that's on you and that broke-ass man of yours. I love Gus. And for reasons beyond any of our understanding he loves me back. Shouldn't that be enough for you?"

She held up her palm. "Collie, sweetie. I am only human. At some point you're going to have to stop blaming me for all the bad things in your life. I am trying to be here for you. I'm just concerned for my son. Isn't that my right? What kind of mother would I be if I didn't express those feelings to you? I don't want anyone taking advantage of my baby." She stood and reached for his shoulder, but Colt took a step back.

They'd never acknowledge it in their fights, but deep down both knew their tug-of-war relationship had its roots in Anna's drug abuse that had started when Colt was eight and lasted until he was fourteen. It was during that time Colt had grown accustomed to instability in life, as he traveled between his mother's apartment, foster families and several group homes—separated from his older brother, Dave, most of the time. The intermittent abandonment he had experienced through those years had left deep scars in his heart. In the tempestuous ocean of his life, where Colt needed his mother to be an anchor, she'd been a wayward sail instead.

"It's a little late for your concern. Contrary to what you think, Mom, parenting is not seasonal work. Excuse me." Striding off, Colt ran into Gus near the couch, who whispered *I'll talk to her, don't worry* as they shared a quick embrace.

The rest of the day, after both Colt and his mother had calmed down enough to apologize and be civil again, the three of them spent a few hours exploring the greatest assets of the City of Angels he knew his mother would enjoy: the Playboy Mansion, The Griffith Observatory, Rodeo Drive, The Grove, Hollywood Boulevard's Walk of Fame and the Paramount Pictures Studios, with a private tour after a quick call from Gus. He loved how phone calls from his fiancé had the power to bend people to his will.

All through their sightseeing his mother played the

part of the enthusiastic school girl, taking selfies with or without the happy couple and gasping at the views of the ocean and downtown. For the first time in years he was having an enjoyable, argument-free time with his mom that didn't involve a single perfume bottle.

At their late lunch, Gus informed him about his conversation with his mother in the kitchen after he had stormed off in the heat of their fight. They had chosen the Guzman restaurant again, liberating another round of *oohs* and *aahs* from his mother upon arrival. Her puzzled look at Gus speaking his native language as he chatted away with Bruno was worth the traffic-congested drive.

"Colt. My dear fiancé. Earlier your mom and I discussed our wedding, among other things. She told me she supports our decision of doing a small intimate wedding. You know, like you and I talked about a few days ago."

Colt eyed his mother, who nodded from across the table of four, eyes welling up as she rested her chin on her hands.

"It was supposed to be another surprise, but I guess I'll make it official. Four weeks from now you and I are getting married in Rio de Janeiro. It will be only you and me, just the way we want."

Instead of using words, Colt thanked his fiancé with a not-so-chaste kiss as he leaned toward his left. Anna applauded in the background, then reached for her son's hand.

"Go live your life, Collie. You don't need me to do that.

Honestly, I don't think you ever did." She walked over and wrapped her arms around him, the way only she could.

Tearing up at the truest words he had ever heard his mother utter, he squeezed her tight, inhaling every last drop of her Poême, making a mental note to send her at least three bottles when he got home.

Colt and Anne repeated the scene at home when she was about to leave. Watching Langdon drive her off, Colt wondered when he'd see her again. He didn't know if he wanted that moment to be sooner or later. Not that he didn't love her, but there would always be an impending outburst of drama lurking around the corner whenever they were together. Maybe that's why he wanted her to be part of his new life, needing that little dose of trouble on the horizon to keep him on edge. Shrugging the idea off, he counted his blessings and headed inside, feeling at home more than he had ever done.

Chapter 10
Mel—Present

Not having slept more than a few half-hour stretches on his damned couch, Mel hadn't had the clarity of mind to pick up takeaway coffee. When he had kissed Kate goodbye in bed, she had only mumbled unintelligible syllables in return. Understanding one of them as *love you too* he had taken the win. It would only be a matter of time before they'd be on the same page again. There had been a moment of hesitation to open the door to the guest room, but he had decided against it, allowing Colt his privacy.

Swirling the last of what the vending machine called cappuccino in a styrofoam cup, he prayed his protesting stomach would accept it. Divulging details of the attack on his partner to Gene hadn't exactly encouraged his intestines. His coworker looked at him intently, waiting for him to finish his drink. When he finally dared to ask about Mel's rash decision to babysit another child, Mel couldn't maintain professional demeanor any longer.

"Look, Gene, it's far from ideal, but it's the best I could do for Colt. He's got round-the-clock chaperoning in a safe neighborhood. It sure beats punching him in the face, wouldn't you agree?"

Gene planted his fists on his sides. "Good. I was wondering when you were going to throw that in my face. Now we can put it behind us." He patted Mel on the shoulder and started walking toward the elevators. He didn't always see eye to eye with Gene Reynolds, but he respected him as a detective and was grateful he let him tag along for this interview.

There were few things Melvin hated more than hospitals. It was the combination of the smell of antiseptic, sweat and urine, the tube lighting, the sallow-faced people rolling IV-bags along in robes—which were not fulfilling their sole duty adequately—and the incessant coughing that drove Mel nuts every time he set foot inside a facility like Cedars-Sinai. In the elevator he waited for Gene to hit the seventh-floor button, so he wouldn't have to make contact with the obvious nuke of germs it represented in his mind.

"Scared of hospitals, huh?" Gene asked.

"More disgusted. Anyway, what do you think we're walking into up there?" he asked, hoping more conversation would distract him from the sensory assault.

Gene's narrow chest expanded with another deep breath. "I really can't tell. His husband tries to kill him, yet he doesn't press charges. He either loves the guy so much he can't bear the thought of him going to prison, or—"

"Or Colt is right about him being a controlling monster," Mel says.

"That's right. I don't want to get mixed up in your unit, but this case has the potential to become the most complicated our station has ever stumbled on. Somehow one person now stands at the center of our biggest current investigation." Gene paused until they exited the elevator. "Do you believe him? Colt, I mean?"

"Right now, I think I do. You saw the bruising patterns too, right? Combine that with his instinctive jumpiness and that broken expression in his eyes, and it becomes hard not to take it for truth."

"I hope you're right."

With Mel breathing through his mouth the entire time, they headed for Gus's private room. The air-conditioning blasted from all corners, making him glad he had put on his suit jacket. A chipper nurse bounced out of the room they were aiming for, smiling just a little too much to be treating a gunshot-wound victim. Mel imagined her getting her hopes up with the rich patient under her care. Was everyone in LA these days this desperate to hook a rich husband?

Everything about Gustavo Carolino looked too big for this hospital room. One of his legs stuck out dangling over the bed's edge while he had his other pulled up below the covers. His impressive torso, widening into bulging shoulders, was partially wrapped in gauze and bandages. Gus was sitting up in an angle that looked just comfortable enough to have conversations without straining his neck. Colt had been right about one thing so far—the man staring back at Mel was more than capable of inflicting all kinds of bruises.

"Detectives, I can't get hold of my husband. Where is he? Is he okay? Is someone with him? He shouldn't be alone right now," Gus said right after their introductions. Fixed by his side, his attorney, Tommy Silveira, watched the detectives' every move, ready to slap them on the proverbial wrist the second a question didn't sit right with him.

"Colt is somewhere safe and in good company. That's all you need to know. Mr. Carolino, just so you know why we're here, Detective Daniels and I are trying to get a better understanding of the nature of your relationship, given yesterday's events. Does your decision not to press charges still stand?" Gene asked.

The red-haired suit said something to his client in Portuguese. It had Mel wishing Cam had gone with him instead, figuring he'd catch some of the vocabulary.

"That's correct, yes. It was more an accident than a real attempt at my life. At least that's what I think." As if on cue, Gus grimaced and held his left side. Bags beneath his eyes and sunken cheeks drew the attention away from his otherwise chiseled jawline. He still managed to give off an unmistakably intimidating air, even in his compromised situation.

"Why do you think it was an accident?" Mel asked.

"Colt wasn't in his right mind when he shot me. I should have seen it in the days before. I've learned to watch for the signs, but I guess I'd been too caught up in work. I hope he's okay now. He must be scared."

Mel watched the man's facial expressions like a hawk spotting a rat on a hillside. He had considered Colt a difficult man to read, but his husband was possibly worse in that area. Maybe it was the pain medication the guy was on that blocked out some expressions.

"Could you elaborate on your husband's mental health?" Gene asked.

Gus thought for a moment before answering, his eyes shooting from Mel to Gene and back. "Sorry to ask, detectives, but what has he been telling you about me?"

"Sir, I was going to wait until my coworker completed his side of the interview, but since you're asking, I'll tell you about the second reason I'm here," Mel said. "Your husband filed an unrestricted report of sexual misconduct yesterday."

Gus's eyes fell to the bedsheets. "So that's the story he's rolling with. That I'm the abusive husband. Man, he's really gone off the rails this time." He looked out the window after his last phrase. Mel took the opportunity to ask the harder questions.

"Mr. Carolino, can you explain the extensive bruising we've discovered on your husband's body?" Mel handed him his phone to show him the photographs Charlotte had taken the day before.

Gus's breathing was steady as he took his time swiping through the images. His attorney started talking, but Gus shushed the man with a hand in the air.

"I can explain, yes. When my husband and I are intimate, we like it…rough—more so than most couples. I don't need to justify our preferences to you, but that's the way it is. Always has been from the moment we met. What those pictures show you is the result of our recent escalation in bed. For some reason Colt keeps pushing me, begging me to hurt him worse every time. I don't fully understand it, but I can't say no to him. Then I guess I got carried away and really went for it. Right after I always feel bad about it.

It keeps me up at night. I would never hurt him intentionally like that, or beat him black and blue. I know how it looks, but that's not how it happened."

Gus showed all the signs of a worried husband Mel had studied for his detective exam: downcast eyes, miniature frown, restless hands, calm speech and an eagerness to make eye contact. Whenever two items on that list weren't present in the demeanor of a victim's spouse something was likely off. Could this man, who looked a good ten years younger than his age, be that great an actor?

Gene stepped in, "Sir, you've hinted at your husband's mental health twice now. Do you mind telling us more about that?"

"I can tell you he's not well, Detective. I can give you his psychiatrist's number, Dr. Erik Petersen. The thing you need to know about Colt is that he has a self-sabotaging tendency. Every time something good happens in his life he doesn't trust how it feels and ends up doing something stupid. He'd been miserable for so long before we met that he has trouble adjusting to a happy marriage."

"You can send the contact info to us, thank you," Gene said, shooting a glance at Mel that must have conveyed the thought *what the fuck*.

"Just so we're covering all bases, did you ever have sex without your husband's consent?" Mel asked.

Gus and his attorney gave each other a knowing look, as if they'd been expecting the question.

"In spite of what he may have told you, our sexual relations are always consensual. I know what you're thinking. It's what everyone thinks when they see us. Meanassed sugar daddy taking advantage of his trophy boy husband, beating the shit out of him as some sort of stress-relieving mechanism. I can assure you it's nothing like that with me and Colt."

"Do you respect your husband's limits during your recent escalations? In other words, do you stop when he asks you to—perhaps with some agreed-upon code words?"

"This is clear speculation, Detective Daniels. You're better than—" Gus interrupted his lawyer again.

"It's okay. I'll be honest with you. There have been times when I was so absorbed in the moment I hadn't responded to our safe word. It wasn't intentional or anything and it scared the hell out of me when he gave me grief about it. After a while we worked out a better system, so it wouldn't repeat itself."

"Detectives, my client needs to get some rest. I believe he's given you the answers you were seeking," his attorney said.

"One more thing," Mel said. "What can you tell us about the tattoo on Colt's hip?"

"What about it?" Gus asked, jumping at the question a little too soon to Mel's liking. It was the first off-beat sign he'd received from the guy.

"What's the story behind it? A letter C in a circle doesn't exactly speak for itself unless someone has an affinity with copyright symbols."

"He got it last year. I was never for it, but Colt thought it was a romantic way of combining our initials for our third anniversary. He'd always wanted one, so I went along with his crazy idea. Anything to make him happy. It obviously meant more to him than it did to me."

"Okay, that's enough, Detectives. We've been very cooperative, but now I really must insist on seeing you out," Silveira said, playing his part.

"Detective Daniels, wait. I need your help. If I send some of Colt's belongings to the station, will you bring them to him? Wherever he is, he needs his own clothes, toiletries and other trinkets. It's just...I'll sleep better knowing he's comfortable," Gus said.

Mel had to exercise a ton of mental strength not to allow his jaw to drop. Green eyes slowly misting over were staring at him, angling for approval. There were, again, no visible deception cues about Gustavo Carolino during his request.

Maybe they fit together well because they're both extremely good actors?

He dismissed the thought almost immediately and nodded in response.

"You're here," Charlotte said, having just closed the laptop she was balancing on her lap.

"Of course I'm here, Charlotte. We're partners," Mel said, kissing the top of her head. It was the first sign of affection they had shared other than a handshake since their partnership. Besides looking twice as exhausted as himself, Charlotte seemed calm and collected. Her room was less fancy than Gus's in the other wing, but provided everything she needed—except for a desk, a whiteboard and black markers in her case. Six bouquets of flowers crowded the surfaces: two gaudy ones on the table, two white ones on both chairs, a soft-pink one on her bedside table and one more on the window sill on the far side with sunflowers. The salmon privacy curtain screamed the word hospital.

Gene remained quiet after acknowledging how happy he was to know she was safe and that he hoped she would be back soon. Awkwardness flushed his cheeks.

"Should you be working right now?" Mel asked, pointing his chin at the closed computer.

Charlotte explained that Rita had been the culprit who had brought her laptop from their office an hour before. "When she called at the crack of dawn she flat-out asked what would make me feel better in the next five minutes. I said work, and next thing I knew she came bearing gifts."

She was wearing a navy LAPD sweatshirt and pajama pants, layers of white bandages peeping from and thickening the waistband.

"Sounds like Rita," Gene said, smiling.

"Don't tell the Chief, okay?"

Mel was glad to be talking about work instead of addressing the elephant in the room. Charlotte was not an easy woman to talk to under normal circumstances, let alone now.

"Are you in pain?" he asked, having rephrased the *how are you feeling* question right before he spoke.

"It's fine."

"What did the doctors say about the mark? Is it permanent?" Gene asked.

Charlotte glanced down at the point of injury and said

"They told me last night it needed to heal properly first. Because of the debridement procedure it's too early to tell how big the scar is going to be. Next step involves skin grafts, but I'm not sure I heard them correctly. It sounded complicated."

Charlotte's knack for sucking out all the emotion in her speech was a clear souvenir from her adoptive father, criminal judge, Weisz. Although it served as a strong coping mechanism at times like these, he knew it could be malignant to her psychological recovery in the long run.

She asked him about Colt and exhaled for a long time after hearing about his new living situation, like a weight had lifted from her shoulders. It reminded Mel of her intention to make a homemade dinner for Colt. Even though she knew cooking wasn't her strong suit, she jumped into the deep end just to make her new guest feel better.

"Looks like someone's popular," Gene said, fumbling with a card attached to one of the white bouquets.

"Yeah, I haven't been alone for five minutes. I suspect you guys are taking shifts keeping me company."

"Of course we are. You're one of us," Mel said.

She cocked an eyebrow. "Am I? Don't get me wrong, I'm glad, but how come I'm only feeling the love now that I've been brutalized? Where was all this before?"

"Gene, would you give us a minute?" Mel asked. Gene raised his arms and obeyed with a "Take care, Charlotte."

"Charlotte. You're still fairly new to the team. You can be a little intense and work insane hours, yes. But that doesn't mean your good work goes unnoticed. At least not to me or the Chief. If the rest of us didn't respect you they wouldn't be here. Not in this capacity at least."

"I'll try to look at it that way. It's nice knowing something good is resulting from all this."

"Do you want to go over what happened? I got Colt to give a statement last night—well, a few hours ago. It took him a while to snap out of his shock."

She looked away from Mel and pretended to rub her right temple to conceal the first droplets of tears. "Can we not? I already gave my statement to Anderson an hour ago. I want to focus on Colt's case instead."

"Absolutely. Whatever you want."

Mel told her about his discoveries from talking to both Colt and his husband and how their responses couldn't have been any more different. He noticed how Charlotte's distress morphed back into her usual analytic drive.

"Of course, he would want to appear like the wounded, forgiving husband right now. It could be a ploy to put the spotlight back on Colt."

"There is one other possible explanation to keep in mind," Mel said.

"Colt could be lying to us. Man, that would be a kick in the groin. Do you really think it's possible?"

Mel rubbed his forehead. "I don't. But we can't rule it out. Not until we get more proof. Either way, one of those two men is one hell of an actor."

"What can I do?" Charlotte asked.

"All right," he said, passing her the laptop. "There's still a lot we don't know. Do some digging into both gentlemen's pasts. Jobs, business associates, family, friends, social media—your expertise. I'm questioning the staff of Gus's house starting tomorrow. There's no way nobody knows what went on between them. I'll email you a list of names, so you can keep busy if you want to. In the meantime I'll keep talking with Colt."

"On it. Thanks for enabling my compulsion, Mel."

"Promise me you'll take naps in between. This conversation never happened."

"Got it." Her eyes went wide. "Dad?"

Judge Weisz entered, looking like someone stole his meatball sub from his chambers. After hugging and kissing his daughter, he turned to the only target for his anger in the room. "This happened on your watch. I understand it wasn't an intentional error, but you failed to keep my girl safe. I'd appreciate it if you left."

"He wasn't on surveillance duty last night, Dad. Don't take it out on him. Mel's been—"

"On behalf of the West LA station I apologize, sir. I'll leave you two alone," Mel interrupted before stepping outside with a wink to his partner. He respected the judge too much to add to his concerns. Lord knows he would have used fists instead of words in the man's place. When he hopped into his car in the hospital's carpark he made a silent vow never to allow Rose to go into law enforcement.

An hour into his morning paperwork session, Rita's waving hand pulled Mel from his trance. Colt's and Gustavo's voices had been fighting for airtime in his tired mind. As

Gus had told him, the driver named Langdon had dropped off a brown Louis Vuitton leather suitcase for Colt.

"There are no bombs in it. I checked. Can't be too careful. Fancy stuff, if you ask me. He's that shooter guy from yesterday, right? Talk about a plot twist." Rita said, pushing her red glasses back up her nose.

Mel thanked her and took Colt's stuff to his desk, planning on typing up statements from the married couple. It's the one task any officer of the law hated about the job, yet Mel had always considered a handful of admin work to have a therapeutic effect during a troubling investigation. Sometimes he needed to see his thoughts on screen to get the bigger picture or watch sudden connections form. Staying anchored to facts was a strong survival mechanism in life. *Don't start dreaming when there's still work to do.* It had helped him through foster care, especially in the years he had come to understand there wouldn't be any adoption for him in the cards.

Satisfied with his reports, he made phone calls to set up interviews with Gus's home staff: driver Langdon Bryan and the private chef, Hannah Reid. Natalee Prescott, Gus's only business associate at Carolino Real Estate, was the last phone call he made. It was going to be a busy day tomorrow, that much was certain.

When he walked to the Chief's office to give her an update, Officer Ryder—the surveillance guy—crossed his path with downcast eyes. The man had been crying at his own failure, and rightfully so. He probably hadn't done anything wrong, but Mel was sure he didn't see it that way.

Someone should tell him to do better the next day. And then repeat the process for the rest of his career.

To his surprise, Colt was helping out with dinner when Mel got home. He was cutting up zucchini at the dining table while Kate was frying garlicky onions on the stove. The promise of an Italian-style pasta hung in the air. His daughter was sleeping on her cot in the corner next to the couch. The only word prompting in Mel's head was *how*. He wondered if it were a trick of the mind.

"Hi, Mel," Colt said, not looking up from his cutting board. Mel's eyes fixed on his bruises for a moment. Colt was wearing a black tank top he vaguely recognized.

He kissed his wife, then rolled the suitcase to Colt's end of the table. "Your husband sent you some of your stuff."

Colt dropped the knife to the floor, making Kate jump at the clattering sound.

"I'm sorry," he said, "Why would he do this?"

"He said he wanted you to be comfortable. It would help him sleep better at night."

Colt's eyes went saucer-wide. "You talked to him?"

Mel nodded. "It's standard procedure. I went to see Charlotte, too."

"How was she?"

Mel hung his coat on the wooden rack next to the front door. "Not great, but okay, I guess. She's distracting herself with work as we speak."

"Good. I wish I could see her, but I'm not going

anywhere near that hospital. So what did my husband tell you?"

Mel didn't respond right away, not knowing where to begin. Before he could speak, Colt jumped from his chair, covering his face. "Oh my God, no. He got to you. Played you like a fiddle with his lies and manipulation. This can't be happening." He started pacing and swaying his arms. "I trusted you, Mel. How could you fall for his tricks? I told you this is what he does. I can't believe I misjudged you."

"Hey. Calm down. I'm trying to help in case you haven't noticed. Let me do my job, okay? Now sit down and hear me out."

"Please don't yell at me," Colt said, taking a step back.

He hadn't realized it, but one glance at Kate told him Colt was right. Rose started to get fussy, so Kate took her out of the cot, shooting daggers out of her eyes in passing.

Colt reclaimed his seat, surrounded by cut-up zucchini once more.

"I'm sorry. I get mad when people question my integrity, I suppose. So, this is what I've learned from your husband's interview." As he told him about his husband's interview, all color drained from Colt's face. "It's his word against yours, as I expected. During the line of questions he hinted at your mental health issues twice. Have you been to a professional for counseling of some sort?"

Colt let his head sink between his arms on the table. Contrastively, Mel's heart leaped when he noticed the couch behind Colt had been cleared.

"Shortly after I realized Gus had fenced me in, I suffered from depression. He urged me to have an appointment with Dr. Petersen—I think—so I went. We started talking about my mom, my time in the system and how I lost my job, which was kind of nice. But then he kept asking if everything was all right in my marriage. He assured me I could tell him anything given doctor-patient confidentiality, like three times. I got so scared I cut the session short. Knowing Gus, I was sure it was a set-up." He sighed. "This is not helping my case, is it?"

Kate's footfalls traveled down the stairs with a half-asleep Rose. "Not really. I'll talk to that doctor when I get the chance. In the meantime I need you to write us a letter of consent to disclose medical information. On a different note, did Gus have any meaningful past relationships?"

Colt scoffed. "From what he's told me, he only got interested in the romantic side of relationships about five years ago. He used to bring escorts to business dinners and other events that required a plus one. One of them had tricked him into thinking they were more than just a business transaction. It's all I know."

"We'll do some digging on that. I can't believe I'm saying this, but I hope he got rough with them, too."

"You can count on it, but he's too smart to have left a trail for you there. My guess is he paid double, or triple after each violent episode."

"We'll see." Mel cocked his head. "Are you wearing my wife's clothes?"

"My bad," Kate said from the kitchen. "It was the only thing that fit."

She's heard every word.

"I suggest you go unpack, Colt. Dinner will be ready when you get back down," she said.

"Thank you, Kate."

Mel walked up to his wife and hugged her from behind, taking in the scent from her neck. "Does that empty couch mean you forgive me?"

He could almost feel the roll of her eyes. "If you help me out with dinner then yes. Go gather up Colt's mess for starters."

While Mel was stirring the marinara, Kate was boiling noodles, twirling them with a fork every now and then.

"I've been talking to him, Mel. It wasn't easy on either of us, but I think I understand why you're letting him stay here. I heard him cry this morning when I passed his door, so I invited him to breakfast. He didn't give me specifics, but it's clear he's been through a lot, Mel. It makes me mad someone would do this to him. By the way, did you know he can sing? He soothed Rose in thirty seconds flat with that voice."

"You don't say," Mel said, smirking.

"I still don't like him being here, given what happened at Charlotte's, but it's better than the idea of him being in some holding cell. Also, I think I know why he trusts you."

"You do?" Mel lowered the flame in fear of splatters.

"He spent time in foster care just like you. By the way, we kind of made fun of your obsessive car and house rules." With a wink she broke down Mel's last emotional barriers.

"I love you, honey," he said, beaming at her.

"Love you too. Come on, let's eat. Will you call—"

A crash upstairs cut Kate's question short. Mel rushed

to Colt's room, taking the stairs two at a time. Kate wasn't far behind, judging from the sound.

Hyperventilating on the floor, Colt was trying to get as far away from the bed as possible with his legs pushing him to the opposite wall.

"Colt? Colt? What is it?"

"He needs a bag," Kate said, dashing down the landing. She returned with a brown paper lunch bag and handed it to Mel. He knelt beside Colt and instructed him to breathe in the bag for a while, adjusting the fit over his mouth. Five breaths later Colt's panic subsided. Sweat prickled his forehead, plastering a lock of his blond hair to it.

"Uhm, Mel? You should take a look at this." Kate said.

The Louis Vuitton suitcase lay on the bed, half-emptied of its contents. In between the folded clothes and Dopp kits, a black leather muzzle revealed itself, stacked between shirts. It featured a complete cover for the lower part of a person's face, which could be fastened around the neck. Twin metal-studded straps converging at the forehead could be pulled all the way over the top of the head and connect to the neck piece on the backside. When Mel turned it over in his hands, the red built-in ball gag made him shiver.

Chapter 11
Colt—Past

"Ready for our wedding night, Mr. Carolino?"

"I know you think it's hot, but that's not my name."

"It's *so* hot," Gus said, spinning Colt so they both faced Copacabana from their suite at the Flor Da Madrugada by Marriott. The last of the golden light brushed the top of the Pão de Açúcar—or Sugar Loaf—basaltic cone in the distance, while the beach looked calmer than it had since they got there. High up on the sixteenth floor, the views were spectacular any time of day.

Colt knew undressing was going to take a while, since Gus had splurged on custom-designed wedding tuxedos by Diane Von Furstenberg. With Gus in white and Colt in gold, the details such as cufflinks, necklaces, wristbands, sunglasses and shoes complimented the other's. Their ties, as well as the lining on the inside of all garments had G&C printing all over. Combined with their Amouage perfumes, Colt had been feeling like a million dollars all day.

"It's so beautiful here. This is the best day of my life, Gus."

Gus started kissing his neck ever so gently until he hit

the collar of Colt's shirt and growled. "I got to get you out of this."

"It's going to take like an hour. You do realize that, right?"

Gus shrugged. "Foreplay it is, then. You feel that?" He pushed his erection against Colt's backside, holding his hands over Colt's chest. "Your husband needs you."

Colt turned around and kissed him, guiding his husband to the bed while stripping away their suit jackets. The giant suite was perfect for their wedding night needs: a kingsize bed facing two large windows in both corners of the wall on one side, and a massive shower cubicle on the other—perfect for their post-coital ritual. Everything was white or beech-wood, almost matching their outfits.

The moment of panic Colt had experienced the day before was long-forgotten as soon as he set foot inside the lavish junior suite. Before setting off to Rio, Gus and Colt had paid the Carolinos a visit in São Paulo. The wedding planning had gone at such a cosmic speed Colt hadn't even considered meeting his fiancé's parents. Only ever having known his mom and off-and-on stepdad, Colt found the concept of parents one of life's enigmas. Try as he might, he would never understand family dynamics, especially not between fathers and sons. Groggy from the spicy little mile-high adventure in Gus's private jet, he clutched his fiancé's hand during the drive up to his future in-laws' house in Velho Brooklin, one of the fanciest neighborhoods in town.

The Carolino residence's facade was made of one big

white stucco wall. A large black double garage door with golden details and a similarly designed front door stood in contrast with the rest of the wall, which was topped with black metal bar fencing with golden tips. Behind said fence the front patio started, leading to the elevated white villa with a red-tile roof and modest windows. *Los Angeles, but make it Prison Break.*

Pedro Carolino opened the front door and waved with the same kind of smile Colt had woken up to for a month now. As he shut the car door Colt saw father and son sharing a warm embrace. Pedro broke free and patted Gus's abs, saying something that might have been about Gus not eating well enough in the US.

"*Papai*, I'd like you to meet my fiancé, Colt Whittaker."

"Nice to meet you, Colt," Pedro said, giving Colt the same treatment he had given his son.

"Likewise, Mr. Carolino."

"Call me Pedro or *Papai*. Anything else won't do."

Gus's father was about Colt's height, not tall nor short. Despite the age-appropriate belly fat barely hidden underneath the light-blue polo shirt, he was rather handsome. He still had a full head of light gray hair and clear blue eyes that gave him an intelligent spark.

"Where's *Mamãe*?" Gus asked.

"Back porch. Let's go find her. Come on, Colt."

Colt swallowed hard as he approached his future mother-in-law, who sat on a lawn chair next to the pool with her cane and butterfly sunglasses. Gus had told him on the flight his mother didn't speak English anymore out of principle. She had never really been happy in LA, so she and her husband had cut a deal in life: raising their son in the US and making enough money for retirement, then moving back to São Paulo to reap her rewards. In short, Gus had confessed, the woman hated everything American.

The game of making Dilma Carolino approve of him as her son's husband seemed rigged from the start. Stretching out his hand to her, he parroted Gus's phrase they had been practicing on the drive. "Boa tarde, senhora Carolino. Prazer em conheçer você."

Dilma removed her sunglasses and stared at Colt's hand, then looked him up and down. She had Gus's kryptonite-colored eyes, although her version of it seemed meaner. Colt dropped his hand and looked at Gus.

She mumbled something to her son, who sighed in return. What followed was a three-party argument in Portuguese. Words like *nunca, casamento, vida, Americano* and *passar* flew around. None of those combinations sounded like a peaceful exchange of thoughts.

Gus cupped Colt's face in both hands and said, "I'm taking her for a walk. She's being impossible, but I know how to handle her. Don't worry, this is not your fault. It's going to be fine."

"Thanks. Is there something I can do?"

"No, I got this. I love you."

"Love you too."

A slow kiss later, Gus disappeared with his mother clinging to his elbow with one arm and working her cane with the other. The sound of the metal tip was the only thing Colt could hear until it drowned out completely. A gnawing sensation at the back of his head had sprung to life as he understood what Dilma's rejection really stood for: him not belonging in Gus's world. These were people who had helped build LA's neighborhoods into the coveted lifestyle the whole world gawked at in movies. A legacy so intimidating, the thought of it alone made him short of breath. By comparison, all Colt had to show for his life was a prematurely nuked retail career and a soon-to-be rich husband who loved him for reasons he often struggled to understand.

"Sit with me, son," Pedro said, patting the lawn chair next to his. "We might as well have a little chat of our own. It'll help you loosen that tension between your shoulders, if nothing else."

Colt did as he said after rolling his shoulders. He hadn't been aware of the strain himself. The maid brought them espressos, a forty-something latino lady with a gray uniform and a warm smile.

"*Obrigado*, Maia. So Colt, how was your flight?"

"Quite comfortable, thank you. By the way, you have a beautiful home."

"Thanks, son. You're very polite. It was your first flight, wasn't it?"

Colt's jaw tensed. "How did you—?"

"Educated guess. Colt, forgive me for saying this, but Dilma and I never expected Gus to end up marrying someone like you. If I know my wife half as well as I think, then she's trying to change Gus's mind about your wedding as we speak. You have to forgive her, she's stuck in her old ways. It's nothing personal, it's the way she's always been.

"As his father I envy the strong bond Gus and his

mother share. No matter how much they differ in opinions, they always find their way back to each other. He wasn't an easy kid for her to raise, I can tell you that. Gus's coming out was anything but easy on her. She cried for days and only relented when Gus threatened to leave the house for good. So, long story short, she accepted his lifestyle because she was forced to.

"Now, I'm going to be frank with you, Colt: you're very young, never went to college, don't have a steady job and don't come from a solid family like ours. There's not a lot of reasons for me to root for you based on that information."

A smack in the face would have hurt less.

Colt wished Gus would come back soon—preferably without Dilma. Did this woman really used to live in Los Angeles? One of the most liberal cities in the USA? He couldn't for the life of him imagine running into her at The Grove. Colt knocked back his espresso to push down the urge to throw dear *Papai* in the pool next to him.

"However. That being said, I don't think I've ever seen my son in love like this. You're the first one he's ever introduced. You seem to bring out a side of him I can't say I've seen a lot. It's like he wants to protect you from the rest of the world at all costs from the way he looks at you. I'm hoping it's a good sign, for your sake. While I'm at it, I'll do you one better: I think you're just what he needs right now."

Say what now?

"You're shitting me. Was it your plan all along to tear me down and then praise me all the way to heaven? Is that some sort of realtor trick?"

Pedro chuckled, showing his remarkably white teeth—

the key to looking young at his age. "You got me. But it worked, didn't it? Let's make a deal. I'll handle my wife, like I've done since I can't remember when, and you take care of our Gustavo. Love him, be by his side in this crazy business he's chosen and forgive him for his shortcomings. I know he's far from perfect, so you're definitely in for a bumpy ride."

By the time Gus and his mother had returned, Colt and his *papai* had covered an array of stories on Gus's childhood, the changes in LA real estate and the rivalry between the cities of São Paulo and Rio de Janeiro. Dilma continued to ignore him all through the rest of their time, but had lost her hostility toward him—all in all a better outcome than he could have hoped for.

"No. Leave your tie on."

Colt had stripped down to his golden pants and dropped the shirt on the chair beside the room's desk. He readjusted his tie—as per Gus's instructions—and returned to the bed. There wasn't much he wouldn't do when Gus bossed him around with that deep voice. Colt's eager obedience scared him sometimes. After all, trusting someone the way he did Gus was not for everyone. It empowered him, made him feel all the more special.

"On your knees." Gus was standing beside the bed with his hands on his hips, still fully clothed.

He reached for Colt's tie and pulled him against his crotch. Colt started to unbuckle Gus's belt and unzip his pants, happy to give into his husband's requests.

Gus's left hand cupped his cheek, then stroked his hair a few times. The soft gesture transformed into a rough one in a split second as Gus tugged at a fistful of his hair, making Colt wince. "Take it. All of it."

Colt didn't need three seconds to get started. He took Gus in and out of his mouth over and over again, taking pleasure in the satisfied moans he heard—and felt—as he went to work. He stopped and played with the tip, teasing it with his tongue, after which he licked the length of his husband's manhood down to his balls. He vowed to make it the best head he'd ever given.

Gus yanked his head back again. "Uh-uh. Teasing won't do."

He slapped Colt right across his left cheek. As he caught his breath and shook his head, Colt's chest constricted with delight. He craved this delicious kind of fear, and Gus seemed more than willing to feed him. No hesitation, no warning—pleasure with an edge.

Gus graduated to pushing himself into Colt's mouth and throat, still holding him in place. The thrusts came faster as Gus's groans grew louder. His jaw and palate burning, Colt was now gagging, unable to breathe for large stretches of time. He had to force his head to the side to recuperate. Every time he did, Gus slapped him again. Although he was into it, it was rapidly turning into their most extreme domination game to date. He'd be needing to say *Ferris wheel* soon.

It was as though Gus had sensed it. After a last round of driving in and out of Colt's throat he pulled back. Colt dropped forward onto his palms, gasping and coughing.

Next thing he knew Gus took him by the hands and pulled him into a soft embrace.

"Are you okay? That was a little too rough, perhaps," he said, pressing their foreheads together.

"I'm fine. It was…intense, yes."

"You did good. I'm proud of you." He caressed the side of Colt's head and kissed him on the temple. "Now let's see what I can do to return the favor."

"Wait," Colt said, "I have a surprise for you." He stripped off his pants to make Gus's face light up with a dirty grin.

"You didn't."

"I did." Underneath his tuxedo Colt was wearing a golden jockstrap with a black see-through front and sparkling golden linings.

Gus growled as Colt allowed him to explore the length of the straps around his butt cheeks with his fingers, making them snap every now and then. Colt was smiling again. Rough and dominant as his husband could be, Colt knew how to entice him in his own way.

"On the bed. Face down," Gus whispered.

As Colt felt his husband's kisses and licks work their way south of the golden strap on his back, he knew wearing the jockstrap all through their wedding day had been worth it. A little sand in between the straps wouldn't have surprised him.

For the ceremony, Gus had negotiated with the city council to have the Praia Vermelha beach closed off for two hours to make sure their wedding was theirs, and theirs alone. Colt's jaw dropped when he saw the *acesso proibido* signs with their G&C logo printed beneath the words.

Praia Vermelha, or Red beach, was far more private than Copacabana. Tucked in a narrow bay only about a hundred yards wide, it sat in the shadow of the Sugar Loaf mountain cone and its cable car traffic. Beyond the rolling waves the landscape gave out to more green hills rising from the Atlantic—like bubbles breaching the surface. The heavy buzz from the city with its recurring sirens, though close, seemed like a distant dream. Colt had to cover his gaping mouth as he wondered how on earth Gus had accomplished all of this. It made him go weak in the knees.

"You like it?"

"It's too much, Gus. I need a minute." Gus held him through the overwhelming moment.

Colt broke away. "How?"

"Pulled a few strings. You know me." Gus shrugged like he had just made a dentist appointment instead of barricading an entire beach. He really was the most beautiful man on earth as he stood there in front of Colt, who admired his figure-hugging white tuxedo through glazed-over eyes, in the middle of this breathtaking bay. The spectacular greenery topping the surrounding volcanic hills couldn't hold a candle to Gus's eyes. Colt loved him so much it made his chest feel too small to contain the emotion.

A golden carpet led the way to the officiant lady under a white tent structure—an intricate design of several Nike-disc wings in the shape of a swan. *Quem Me Dera* by Mariza played from white Sonos speakers on both sides of the tent, a song Colt had picked after a week of studying the Portuguese fado genre. The soft guitar strumming and emotion-tinted voice was the last perfect addition to the ceremony. When he could, he sang along, doing his best not to butcher the language.

After the exchange of white gold rings and a tear-stained kiss neither gentleman could get enough of, Gus and Colt walked into the ocean barefoot with their pant legs rolled up, splashing, laughing and kissing like there was no one else around—which was more than accurate.

They didn't need to share their moment of bliss with anyone else. There was no need for approval, pretend happiness or nauseating platitudes like *love is love, in whatever size or shape* from outsiders. It was only while posing for the hired photographer that Colt gave his mom a fleeting thought. What would it have been like if she'd been there beside him? Yet, one look at his fresh-from-the-field husband moved the thought to the back of the line again.

When they returned to the tent they celebrated eating fresh Moqueca, like they had done on their first date, followed by a steak dinner that was so tender it might as well have melted through the tines of Colt's fork. The sexual tension intensified after a few glasses of red wine and several satisfied moans had escaped their mouths. They had barely finished their *brigadeiros*—fudge truffle balls— and Pave—chocolate trifle—dishes when they could no longer wait to get back to their suite.

• • •

Colt was squirming on the mattress from his husband's relentless efforts in his rim job, unable to control his limbs or voice after each jolt of pleasure coursed from his prostate through his spinal cord and back. It wasn't enough, though. He needed more, and was ready to do anything to make it happen. Only Gus held the power to unlock this animalistic yearning in his mind.

"Fuck me, Gus. Please."

Gus grabbed Colt's waist and pulled him up against his wide chest, cradling him, both of them on their knees now.

"Someone's impatient tonight," Gus said, kissing Colt's neck in just the right spot.

"And whose fault is that?" Colt said, stroking his husband's cock behind his back.

"Wait. I—uhm—also have a surprise for us tonight. You're going to love it," Gus whispered.

He reached underneath the bed as Colt admired the flex in his left deltoid. When he got back up and hid the precious item behind his back, Colt couldn't quite place the grin on his face. Something had changed in the curl of his lip on one side, deepening the dimple in his cheek Colt had often kissed.

"Now, baby, I want you to keep an open mind. Promise?"

Colt lay back, propped up on his elbows. "O-kay, I guess?"

At first glance Colt had a hard time figuring out the purpose of the mysterious gift. He understood the attraction to leather and adored the smell of it, but he couldn't tell what the thing in his hands was supposed to add to their wedding night experience. Not until he turned it over.

"You want me to wear this—whatever this is?"

"It's a muzzle. Comes with a gag and everything as you can see. Perfect for power plays like the ones we enjoy. And yes, I'd be stoked to have you wear it," Gus said, rubbing Colt's thigh.

A hint of fear prickled the hairs on Colt's neck. "I don't know, Gus. It seems a little over the top. Can't we just enjoy ourselves without any more bells and whistles? It's our wedding night. Our very first time as husbands."

Gus pulled the jockstrap's fabric to the side with both hands to uncover Colt's cock. "I know. That's why I wanted it to be special. Trust me, it'll feel amazing once you put it on. You know you like being dominated that way. This will enhance everything in ways you couldn't imagine. For both of us."

In the middle of his plea Gus had started to handle his husband's shaft with slow, almost tantric strokes, making it difficult for Colt to stay focused. And then he switched to giving head, blocking Colt's rational thinking.

"But, honey," Colt moaned, "I won't be able to say the safe word."

Gus stopped with a plop of his lips. "I can't believe this." He rose from the bed. "You still don't trust me after all this time. Baby, tell me something. Since we've been together, how many times have you actually needed to say your safe word?"

Colt thought for a second. "Two, maybe three times? But that's not the poi—"

"Listen to me, my dear husband." Gus made a steeple with his hands. "I know you better than anyone, maybe even yourself. I know your limits. I would never go too far, because I've learned how to interpret every one of your moans, grunts, screams and gasps. I've studied the way your body reacts to mine like a science. Why do you think I'm so good at making you orgasm?"

Colt hated how much sense he was making. Gus lowered onto the mattress again, sitting on his knees like before. "Come on, baby. We got this. Think of it as the ultimate loss of control. Total surrender. The deepest trust in your husband. What could be more intimate or romantic than that? I promise I'll be patient and observant throughout. Nothing bad is going to happen. The second it feels wrong, I'll stop." He flicked his eyebrows at Colt. "Just thinking about it has got me harder than ever."

Gus's pitch intrigued Colt, making his heart pound in his chest. *Total surrender, loss of control.* Concepts he'd advertised on his Grindr profile for years. His husband really did know him like no one else. Ever since their first hookup all those months ago Gus had come a long way. Despite having come close to saying Ferris wheel a few times, Colt couldn't remember actually having said it. The byproduct of mind-blowing orgasms: memory lapses. Gus would never disrespect his boundaries. He loved him too much. No doubt about it.

More than once, Colt had needed to apply concealer on his arms, face and neck to cover up some of the bruises he had suffered during sex. However, Colt had enjoyed every second of it.

The childlike glee in Gus's Christmas morning eyes tipped the scales.

"Fine. But stick to your promise, okay? It won't exactly be easy for me to stop you," Colt said.

"Best day of my life. I love you." He leaned in for a kiss.

"I love you too. Now help me get this on."

"Wait. Let me kiss you again first."

As soon as Colt had put it on with his husband's help, he saw Gus's eyes go darker. Breathing wasn't easy, but manageable thanks to the space the ball gag provided. The studded straps leading to his forehead made his vision partially obstructed, but it was nothing he couldn't handle. Or so he kept telling himself.

What the hell am I doing?

Admittedly, the new tingle of submission combined with the feel and scent of the fabric hit that sweet spot in his mind like a military-grade sniper. The idea that his mind and body now belonged to his husband for him to use as he pleased had made him eject tendrils of precome on the sheets. It could only mean one thing: he was into it.

It's going to be okay.

"Oh, baby. Beast is going to love this."

As Colt lay on his back, Gus pulled him to the edge of the mattress with a growl. He knelt in front of the bed and teased Colt's butt hole with his finger before inserting it completely, making his back arch up as he hooked it in all the right spots. Colt moaned, but all that passed through the fabric were muffled grunts. He heard the bottle of lube snap open and braced.

Lubed up and ready, Gus entered him slowly, waiting

for Colt to widen and accept him completely. Gus had been right when he said he could read all of his signs during sex. Watching him closely, he could pinpoint exactly when Colt's pain and discomfort would stop to make way for pleasure.

It'll be fine. Trust him.

Gus's thrusts gained momentum as he drove in and out of Colt with the enthusiasm of a teenager. Colt's muted moans put an evil grin on Gus's face.

When his eyes locked onto Colt's the grin disappeared. His hand reached over Colt's chest to his throat and covered the neck strap of the muzzle. He squeezed.

Colt shook his head and groaned through the fabric, reaching for Gus's hand. It took him right back to their first time in his head, springing the terror of that moment back to life.

"Easy, baby. I got this," Gus said, removing his hand as he kissed Colt's chest. He then targeted Colt's nipples and washed away all of his defenses. The tiny stings left in the trail of Gus's teeth shot right to his neck as he shivered, surrendering to whatever Gus had planned for him next.

"Like reading a book. You're going to love the next part. I promise." He turned Colt onto his stomach and pulled the jockstrap off. With his palm against Colt's lower back he pressed Colt down to the mattress, pinning him in place. The next thing Colt felt was his husband reentering him in one go with a powerful thrust. He gasped from the impact.

Gus pushed Colt's head down into the mattress, almost blocking his view completely. His husband's hips clapped against his butt cheeks with every impact. Never before had Gus fucked him so hard, so fast. Every now and then he would stop for about five seconds, only to resume the action with deepened vigor. Colt was trembling all over, never knowing what would come next. How much more was he prepared to take?

Gus's fist exploded on his back as Colt felt the wind leave his lungs. He struggled to breathe from both the muzzle's tight fabric and the blows his back was absorbing. Another followed. And another. The mattress jerked back up with him after each impact. This would have been the point where he'd say the safe word, but it wasn't an option. He attempted to scream, but Gus didn't hear him.

Gus's groans had grown feral. Colt pushed on his hands to get up, but every attempt led to another beating and more coughing inside the muzzle. The aggressive thrusts had become painful. He tried to get up one more time, but Gus put his full weight on him.

"Stop it. You're going to lie here and take it. Got it?" Gus shouted, too close to Colt's ear. It was no longer sexy in any way. Colt wanted to break free, but Gus was now restraining his wrists behind his back. He tried to shout for him to stop, but it was no use.

Gus was right. He had to lie there and take it until it was over. He was out of options.

In between the punches and yanking at his hands and hair he wondered how much time had passed, and how much longer the torture would go on for. He felt tears stinging his eyes and the hot dampness of sobs against the leather around his face.

This time Gus had forced him past his mental and physical limits, broken his body and mind. Terror ran through his veins, cold and itchy. Since it didn't help him at all, he stopped fighting and went limp from head to toe. It was like he was watching it all happen from the ceiling, like it was someone else trapped on the bed at his husband's mercy.

Please get it over with.

Gus climaxed in five raging spasms, his screams so loud the entire floor must have heard. He pulled away almost immediately and rolled next to Colt, catching his breath. "Wow, baby. That was amazing. I told you it'd be worth it."

After about a minute Colt snapped out of his subdued state and started clawing at the muzzle with frantic arm movements.

"Colt. Wait, I'll help. Jesus, stay still."

As soon as he was free he took big gulps of air, rose from the bed and walked as far away from Gus as possible, stumbling over shoes.

"Baby?"

Satisfied with the amount of distance, he rested his back against the glass shower wall and sank to the floor, hugging his knees. The pressure against his bruised back was painful, but nothing compared to what he had just gone through.

"Colt. What's wrong? Hey." Gus started in his direction.

"No. Stay back," Colt said, aiming his palm at his husband. His breathing came in uncontrollable heaves.

"Colt, talk to me." He took another step forward.

"I said stay back. Don't you dare come closer. You hear me?" Colt shouted, making Gus flinch.

"I don't understand. What did I… Oh no. Baby, I… Oh my God." Gus's face lost all color. He had to sit, running his hand through his hair. "I'm so sorry. I didn't—"

"Don't give me that. There's no way you didn't notice something was wrong, Gus. I was screaming for you to stop, trying to get away every chance I got. I was crying near the end and you still didn't care. You knew it was too much and decided to go on anyway. Just like you did our first time."

Gus's bottom lip quivered. He looked like he had crashed a brand-new Maserati on its maiden ride home from the dealership.

"Colt," his voice scraped, "please let me make it up to you. I love you."

Colt huffed. "Make it up to me? How? You can't buy your way out of this. You *violated* me, Gus. On our fucking wedding night. I trusted you and you just went on to do whatever you wanted. Just because you could. I'm sorry, but I don't see how we can get back from this." Colt broke down again, burying his face in his forearms.

Gus paced between the door and the bed. "No no no. This can't be happening. I'm not a beast. I'm a monster. I destroyed what we had because of…because of my sick urges. What the fuck is wrong with me? Oh my God. I screwed up our marriage before it even started. You're right. You need to get away from me. I could have killed you just now. I need help. Be locked up. I can't breathe. I…I can't breathe." Gus started hyperventilating: eyes bulging, hand grabbing his chest, skin reddening.

"Gus. Gus! Calm down. You're going to pass out," Colt said, to no avail as his husband's heaves grew more and more strained.

"Fucking hell." Colt stood and walked over to his suitcase. He found a cloth shoe bag and passed it to Gus. "Breathe in this. Come on."

Gus eyed him as he obeyed. His breathing became calmer, more controlled after a while.

"Thank you," he wheezed.

"Yeah. I'm taking a shower. Don't join me," Colt said, pointing.

Gus's gaze dropped. Colt could almost sense the disappointment emanating from his husband. Showering together was a ritual he could no longer sustain. Not then, and perhaps not ever again.

It was the longest shower he had ever taken. When standing had become too strenuous for his aching legs he tried to find the least painful seating position on the tiles. He wished the hot water would wash away all the pain his body had endured, even though he soon realized the water wouldn't reach his heart. He mourned Gus's loving touch from before their married life and wondered if it would ever return. How could it when all he'd be thinking about was this wedding night from hell? Would he ever be able to forgive him?

A knock on the glass stopped his train of thoughts.

"Colt? It's been over forty minutes. I'm worried. Please tell me you're alive."

Forty minutes?

"I am. I need five more minutes."

Gus opened the door and stepped inside.

"Gus, you can't be in here. You just can't."

Gus started sobbing with renewed strength and joined Colt on the floor, grabbing him in a fierce hug, pushing Colt's head against his shoulder with both arms. "I'm sorry."

"Gus, let go of me. You're hurting me. I can't fucking do this right now." Colt tried to squirm free, but much like before couldn't. Gus was, and always would be, stronger than him.

"Please don't leave me. I'm so sorry. I love you. I need you. Don't walk out on me. I promise I'll be better to you. You're all I have."

Colt stopped protesting as he listened to his husband's repetitive phrases between sobs.

"Please don't leave me. I'm sorry. Please don't leave me. I love you. I need you. Don't walk out on me. I promise I'll do better. You're all I have. I can't lose you. Please don't leave me. You're my everything. Don't walk out on me. Give me another chance. Please stay. I'm so sorry. I love you."

Water splashed every which way off their joined bodies resting against the steamy wall as Colt allowed Gus to rock him in his arms. Hot droplets that could have been tears ran down his and Gus's faces. He couldn't find it in his heart to speak yet—not knowing where to start—but eventually reciprocated the hug. If someone had told him that morning this was how he'd spend the last fleeting minutes of the most beautiful day of his life, he wouldn't have believed them for one second.

Chapter 12
Mel—Present

Mel woke to his daughter's cries from the other room. He got to his feet, shook the numbed shoulder he had been sleeping on and shuffled over to his beautiful girl, who sure could be a screamer from time to time.

"There there. Daddy's here, Buttercup." He held her against his chest and rubbed her back with his thumb. It wasn't a foolproof soothing method, but it worked this time. Cries turned to cooing and soft sighs in minutes. Afraid she'd start again if he stopped, he sat on the wicker rocking chair by the window, leaning back with Rose's head on his shoulder. Maybe it was more for his benefit than his daughter's, as he couldn't get enough of that intoxicating baby head smell.

As he was taking in the heavenly scent with deeper, steadier breaths, his mind wandered. He thought of Rose's future and hoped the world wouldn't go to shit at the rate it had been doing those days. There were so many dangers out there. Even if he'd go out of his way to keep Rose safe from the tiniest threats imaginable, chances were she'd still get hurt. His reasoning likely originated from his encounter with judge Weisz when he visited his partner at the hospital. He couldn't help but wonder what he'd do if someone attacked his daughter one day.

No matter what the future would bring, Rose was luckier than he had been himself. As his blinks became longer he thought about how blessed he was with the people around him. Never having had a real family, Mel had always figured out ways to keep people that mattered close. Cam and his loud family, the Chief's leadership and guidance, Rita's warm heart, and even Charlotte with all her clumsiness. He maintained contact with a few fellow foster kids in his last group home, but it was limited to birthday wishes and random likes on Facebook.

Next thing he knew, Kate took Rose in her arms in the now very bright nursery. Shades of pastel pink seemed intent on gouging his eyes out.

"Good morning to you too, sleepyhead," she said, kissing her daughter's plump cheek.

"What time is it?"

"Almost 7:30. Have you been here all night?"

"Sort of. It was nice." He yawned and stretched before he got up. "How's Colt?"

"I don't know. His door is still closed. You think he'll be okay?" Kate switched Rose to her other arm.

"It depends on your definition of okay."

Mel got dressed while Colt's reaction to the muzzle last night kept hitting replay in his mind. It was so intense he hadn't eaten after. Whatever the muzzle signified, slipping it between Colt's clothes for him to unpack in his safe space had been beyond cruel. What other sick games had Gustavo subjected his husband to?

"Oh, Mel? That driver guy is waiting for you in room 2," Rita said as Mel passed her desk, "Langdon Bryan?"

"Yeah, that's him. Thanks, Rita."

Cam was waiting for him outside the interrogation room to the left in the hallway. Gene wished them both a good morning as he strode inside the opposite room, where Gus's chef, Hannah Reid, had been waiting. The three detectives joined forces to get to the bottom of Gustavo Carolino's ties to the Cordelio cartel. It was the Chief's plan to dig for more information under the guise of Colt's sexual misconduct investigation.

He was watching Gus's driver through the one-sided window as he filled Cam in on the affair with the surprise gift in Colt's suitcase. As he went into detail, he wondered if the driver had been the one doing the packing the day before.

Mel's phone buzzed.

"Charlotte?"

"Good morning, Mel. Ready for interrogations?"

Rita. Of course.

"Yes. How are you?"

"Fine. Listen, Mel, I've found something on Colt's premarital life you may find interesting. Four weeks before their wedding he lost his job as a salesman at Sephora. I talked to his former boss on the phone."

Colt had mentioned something about losing his job

yesterday, before his panic attack. "Four weeks before the wedding... Why was he fired?"

"A landslide of toxic online customer reviews pretty much nuked his reputation. Sephora got rid of him the next day. That manager lady was still heartbroken about it. Said he was the best employee she ever had. You've heard him talk about fragrances, right? I can imagine he's the guy Sephora would want to keep around."

"Thanks Charlotte. What do you make of all this?" Mel asked, testing her to see if his hunch was a stretch.

"Right now I'm thinking Colt's termination and his wedding happened too close after each other not to be suspicious."

Mel smiled. "Come back soon, partner. Sounds like we need you." He hung up and caught himself biting on his thumbnail again.

"Come on, Let's see if he sings," Cam said, and inside they went. Both of them faced Langdon head-on in front of the one-sided mirror.

"Thank you for being here on time, Mr. Bryan. I'd like to inform you right away that this is a recorded session."

"No problem." Langdon had his elbows on the table and played with his thumbs. Just like his outfit, his facial expression was as neutral as could be. Black denim pants, navy button-up and black suit jacket. Nothing about Langdon's looks stood out. His ability to blend into any background seemed more than deliberate.

"I'm Detective Melvin Daniels and this is special agent Camilo Espinoza. Since you already know the reason you're here I'd like to save time and move along."

"Sure. Go ahead."

"Mr. Bryan, how would you describe the nature of your employer's marriage to Colt Whittaker?"

"Well, they've been married for over three years now, although it might not last given what happened. I don't know, I guess their marriage is in many ways similar to any other out there. They're about as different as two people can get, but I do believe their love is real. More real than anyone I've seen Gustavo with these last ten years, at least. They have their highs and their lows, but I always thought they were a good fit."

"Have you ever witnessed violence between them?"

He shook his head. "Not really, no. I often heard them being—you know—intimate from their bedroom in the mornings while I waited outside in the driveway. There have been times where I thought they were hurting each other, seeing as they were so loud—especially Colt. However, they always seemed fine as soon as they were having breakfast. Sweet, even. I remember envying their relationship on some level in those glimpses of moments, to be honest with you."

"Did you ever notice bruises or other wounds on Colt?"

He nodded. "Sometimes, yes. On his wrists and neck. I once stared at him for too long because of it and he explained it as the result of his bedroom preferences. I didn't pry, obviously." Langdon's eyes widened at the memory.

Cam took over. "Mr. Bryan, as the driver you've had ample opportunity to observe, and maybe talk to, both men over the years. Did you notice any changes in Colt's behavior during that time? Was there a build-up toward the shooting incident, in your opinion?"

Good one, Cam.

Langdon's finger toyed with his bottom lip. "Uhm, I don't know. You could look at it that way, I suppose. In the beginning of their relationship Colt was eager to talk to me whenever I needed to drive him someplace. He was unemployed and struggled to kill time. When he was alone or bored he'd invite me for coffee, which was nice. I don't know if you've talked to him a lot, but he's a pretty great conversationalist."

Cam shot Mel the *what the fuck* look.

"Colt's specialty is fragrances, so he soon steered me toward Dior Fahrenheit. Three years later I'm still wearing it, actually. Anyway, that's the way it was the first years he lived in Gustavo's house. For reasons unknown to me he grew more and more distant. Eventually he stopped inviting me for coffee, and in the end he barely acknowledged my existence in passing."

Mel noticed a small deception cue as Langdon's answers lengthened. Every time the guy paused his nostrils flared just a little. Adding to his suspicions was the heavy amount of detail in his ramblings. The key to a good lie, in other words. This driver was holding back, but why? Mel switched gears.

"Would you call Gustavo's real estate business successful?"

"I think so, yes."

"What makes you say that?"

"Well, for one, he closes several deals a week. No

matter how reluctant the sellers sometimes seem, by the end of the week they're all on board with Gustavo's plans. He has a way with people. Makes them see it from a buyer's point of view. I once witnessed an old man shouting obscenities at him from his front porch—you know, with a cane and everything. By the end of the day I had to drive back there to have him sign the papers. You should have seen the smile on Gustavo's face."

Has a way with people. Mel scribbled it on his legal pad. Something about the phrase rubbed him the wrong way.

When Mel asked Langdon who had packed Colt's suitcase, he confirmed Mel's suspicion and said he had done it himself. Mel then pulled up a photo on his phone and handed it to Langdon.

"Mr. Bryan, what can you tell us about this item?"

Langdon squinted. "I don't know. What is it?"

"Take a closer look. There are three pictures of it, so feel free to swipe."

The picture of the ball gag inside the muzzle brought the man's face even closer to the screen. "Is it some kind of sex toy?"

"It is, yes. A human muzzle for sexual purposes."

"I can't say I've seen it before. Looks extreme."

Mel shrugged. "To each their own. I could have you guess where we've found this item, but I don't enjoy wasting time. It was hidden in Colt's suitcase. The one you packed. Care to explain how that happened?"

Langdon's eyes shot from the screen to Cam, to Mel and back before he answered. He scooted back against the back of the chair to sit up straighter. "Are you sure?"

Mel nodded. "Saw it for myself."

Langdon looked to his left for a moment, his memory trying to retrace his steps while packing, perhaps. He did that nostril flare again. "Look, I don't know what to tell you. Gustavo asked me to pack basic items from Colt's suitcase for a whole week. Underwear, socks, pants, shorts, T-shirts, tank tops in case he'd want to work out, and his complete bathroom cabinet. I packed everything myself. Maybe it was stuck between two shirts or something? Or maybe someone of your own around here put it in there? I really wouldn't know."

Really, the most deceptive quantifier. Gus seemed to have a lot of power over this guy somehow. The way the muzzle had been hidden wasn't exactly inconspicuous. This interrogation wouldn't lead anywhere, so Mel and Cam thanked the guy and advised him to stay in town.

When they were alone, Cam agreed with Mel's observations about Langdon being under Gus's thumb. They watched Hannah Reid walk out a few minutes later, followed by Gene's signature pissed-off expression.

"That was a waste of time," Raymond Mercer, Gene's partner said. Pornstache Ray was how the LAPD knew him best, yet never to his face. He wasn't the kind of guy anyone wanted to piss off.

Even worse than Langdon, the chef hadn't been any help at all. She had kept her answers short and irrefutable, claiming she had never witnessed anything other than a happily married couple at the house. In her profession she preferred to keep a healthy distance from her employers, so she kept her head down at all times and steered clear of conversations that went beyond *good morning, more coffee* and *how do you like your filet mignon?*

Finally giving into his vaping urge in the parking lot, Mel called Charlotte to give her the digest version of both events.

"So you think he was lying? Why would he do that?"

"My money's on Gus having instructed him to do so. I don't know, but if Colt's right about his husband's controlling methods, it wouldn't be so strange." The nicotine rush was better than sex, he was sure of it.

"I know it looks like a mess, but we'll get there, Mel. Oh, I called Abby Fitzsimmons about an hour ago. She and her husband sold their house and are moving to Montana, to her family. Guess who they sold it through?"

"No way."

"Yes way. Carolino Real Estate. I called the IT guys from the DEA to look into it some more."

Of course you did.

"Charlotte, promise me you'll take a long nap after this call. It's like you've never left with the way you're outdoing yourself."

"Sure. Just a few more things to check off my list and then I'll be out like a light. They said I could leave tomorrow morning. Too early for skin grafts, so there's nothing they can do for me here in the meantime."

"Good. I'm glad to hear it, partner. By the way, how were things with your father?"

She sighed. "Not great. He really wants to go after Oliver for not doing his job that night. Let me try to talk him out of it some more. Don't tell anyone, okay?"

It made sense for the judge to follow his father instincts and demand people to be held accountable for their mistakes. From what Mel had witnessed at the scene and on the young officer's face, though, he hoped Charlotte would succeed in her efforts. These were not everyday criminals attacking people randomly. What they had done to her followed a set of meticulously prepared guidelines only organized mobsters could execute without hesitation.

After lunch it was time for Natalee Prescott's interview, Gus's business partner at his firm. While Mel was still sipping the last of his coffee, Cam showed him his homework on Miss Prescott. With raised eyebrows Mel suggested his friend take the lead this time.

"Glad you found time to be here, Miss," Cam said. The lovely Miss Prescott with the tight blond ponytail and bigger-than-life black square glasses possessed many talents. Punctuality, however, hadn't made the list.

She scoffed, bouncing her foot over crossed knees. "I can't believe I had to cancel meetings with prospective clients for this. I must look like an idiot." Instead of making apologies or blaming her tardiness on traffic, she seemed honest.

"Meetings for Carolino Real Estate. You've worked there for, what, eight years now?"

"I'm sorry, was that a question? You'll have to do better, agent Esteban." Eye roll right on cue.

Mel suppressed a smile.

"Espinoza. Okay then. Since we're on the subject of

your job, explain this to me. Before partnering up with Gustavo you had been unable to keep any job for longer than a few months. It's quite a list my colleagues have found. Intern at Google, manager of a hair salon, private insurance secretary, English teacher at Venice High, and some more secretary jobs. So what's your story?"

"My *story* is I enjoyed trying out a few job titles. Along the way to my current position under Gus I got to discover what I wanted from my career—and more importantly, what I didn't. I highly recommend the course I've taken professionally." Annoyance beamed through her answers as she studied her manicure.

Mel jumped in. "So you could tell after three weeks at Google it wasn't for you? In total honesty, miss, I still figure out new sides to being a detective every day, and I've been doing this for nine years now."

"I bet you do. And I like to believe I could, yes. I simply had the balls to cut my losses earlier than most people would."

"How would you describe your relationship with Gustavo?" Cam asked.

"The first thing you need to know is that Gus and I have a strictly professional relationship. At the office we only ever discuss business, which is a simple, yet effective, rule for both of us. Once every month we have breakfast at his house to talk about lighter subjects, but that's it. Realtors in Hollywood are all pricks, no matter how friendly and understanding we may seem at first. It's a cutthroat business steeped in millions of dollars. The more distracted we would become, the more our business would suffer from our competitors.

"Our arrangement works. Gus is very dependable as a partner and has people skills I could only dream of. He closes so many deals, I don't even try to beat him anymore in that area. Apart from his dazzling looks, he's charming as fuck. Maybe he lays it on a little too thick sometimes, but it works with, like, 80% of all clients."

"When you were at his house for your breakfast dates, did you see his husband, Colt, as well?" Mel asked.

"Yes, I did. He'd often sit with us for a while until he got bored and went on with his life of leisure."

Life of leisure. Passive-aggressive much?

"Did you ever witness any physical or verbal violence between Gustavo and Colt?"

"I knew you were going to ask that. Gus was right." Natalee leaned forward on her elbows and held an invisible bowling ball with her hands as she spoke. "Look, Detectives, I'm his *business* partner. We're not friends. We're not even that close. I don't even know his birthday, okay? Did I see them together often? Yes. Did Colt look roughed up or depressed sometimes? Absolutely. But it wasn't my concern. I was there as part of my job. I knew better than to ask questions that would have jeopardized my career. So I stayed out of their way. You never know the ins and outs of anyone's marriage, anyway. Only a fool makes assumptions."

Rage crawled up Mel's throat. She knew—she fucking knew about Gus's abuse and had chosen to look the other way on multiple occasions. This was the kind of danger that had made him question wanting kids a little over a year ago. There would always be troubled individuals roaming the planet and he had accepted that in his profession. What he had been failing to stomach, however, was that people like Natalee Prescott, sitting here in front of him with those ridiculous glasses, would keep enabling those individuals as long as they benefited from them.

"Miss Prescott, how many deals does Gustavo close on average?" Cam asked while Mel struggled to focus.

"Like I said, he's a machine. I'd say he sells five properties a month, give or take."

Mel and Cam exchanged a look. They had talked about Charlotte's findings over lunch. Something over at Carolino Real Estate was fishy. Fishy enough to concentrate their next steps on.

They soon got rid of Natalee Prescott after asking more questions about her personal contributions to the company. She took great pride in her night-time house showings in the Hills and complained about how certain eligible Hollywood bachelors would string her along to go from house to house without ever buying one just to spend time with her. When she was out of sight, Cam pantomimed barfing in the trash can.

"That's what you get for not bringing your A game, agent *Esteban*." Mel's impersonation had both men howling in the hallway.

"Cam, so good to see you. How's Penelope?" Kate asked as

Mel kissed his daughter in her cot in the living room. Had she grown since that morning?

"Like every mother of three, she's great, yet exhausted. Perhaps more than me. Be glad you're not outnumbered. Yet," Cam said with a wink. "How've you been?"

Kate gave him the digest version of all things motherhood and went on to say how badly she needed to invite them all over for dinner. However, between their newborn and their guest, Mel knew it wasn't in the cards for the time being. Speaking of which, Colt was nowhere in sight as Mel's eyes searched for his presence.

Inviting Cam to his house that afternoon had a twofold purpose for the investigation. On one hand, Mel thought it would be good to have another set of eyes in the room— beside Kate's—when he questioned Colt some more. Getting all the details out of him about his abuse-ridden existence at Gus's house was like uncovering a dinosaur fossil. He never knew how far certain bones would stretch or how fragile the cartilage would be once he started. On the other, the unsolved murder of Colt's former roommate had been tickling his curiosity. Since Cam had questioned Colt at Gus's house before, it would be an interesting throwback, if nothing else.

"He's upstairs. Resting, I think," Kate said. Mel hadn't needed to ask. She knew how to read him after eight years. He heard his wife batter his friend's eardrums some more about her Zumba class on Thursday nights. She needed to get out of the house more, he realized as he mounted the stairs.

Mel knocked and waited for an answer outside the

guest room. A sweaty version of Colt in a black tank top and shorts waited on the other side as the door swung open. "Yes?"

"Hi. I was wondering if we could talk downstairs. Everything all right in here?" Mel looked him up and down, then scanned the room quickly. The blue comforter had been thrown on the floor and looked flattened.

"Sure. I was just working out a little. Got to stay strong. Mind if I take a quick shower first?" He took off his shirt, revealing the bruises again, which were now more blue and yellow than before.

"Not at all. Meet me downstairs after, okay?"

Before Mel reached the bottom step of the staircase he heard the first verse of Sheryl Crow's *Favorite Mistake* coming from the bathroom. It made him smile. Despite the traces of violence—some more permanent than others—Colt still sang under the shower. That part of him hadn't been broken in spite of all those years of suppression.

When he came down the stairs and saw Cam holding Rose, he froze—his right foot in midair. His hair was towel dry and combed back. Comfortable as he looked with his V-neck and gym shorts, his posture was anything but. A soft crease ran across his forehead as he seemed to flip through his memory.

"Colt, this is special agent Camilo Espinoza from the DEA, and my best friend. He helped me out with the interrogations today. Him being my best friend means I trust him through and through."

Kate took Rose upstairs, crossing Colt's path and

patting his shoulder as she went. Colt defrosted and walked to his seat. "Right. Nice to meet you, special agent."

Cam told him he could use his first name while Colt kept eyeing him with his lips pressed together tightly.

"Like I said, we wanted to ask you some more questions about your life with Gus, if you don't mind," Mel said.

With Kate having brewed a fresh pot of coffee, Mel took out mugs and started filling them while he talked about the investigation in general. How they were talking to a lot of people to get a bigger picture, that it was mostly Gus's personal staff, that Charlotte was working from her hospital bed. Cam helped him carry the mugs, cream and sugar back to the table. His two guests were seated kitty-corner at the oval oaken table, while Mel took the seat at the narrow edge.

"I could have told you most of their information, Mel. I don't know how he did it, but every single person who works for Gus is beyond loyal to him. They'd lie for him without questioning themselves. I begged them for help many times, but neither of them did a damned thing," Colt said after hearing about the interrogations.

After starting the recording device Mel went through the mandatory mentioning of names, case number, date and time of their interview. He took a scalding sip of black coffee, then asked the question he had been dreading most all day. "Colt, you had quite a reaction to the muzzle in your suitcase last night. Can you explain its significance?"

Colt exhaled through his nose and studied his hands on the table as though he'd find the words he needed in them. He looked at Cam for a long time, then his eyes went back to Mel. Colt started shifting in his seat, his hands clenching and unclenching.

"You can trust him. He's just like me," Mel said.

"You don't know that. He's been at the house before a few years back. This is all Gus's doing. He's still fucking with my head like always." His breathing grew louder.

"Colt, please. I've known him for ten years. Longer than Kate." He turned to his friend. "Show him your badge, Cam."

Cam obeyed and slid his wallet over to Colt. He examined both his DEA badge and ID before folding it closed and returning it in a similar fashion.

"I'm sorry, guys, it's just... You don't know what it's like to have the world turn against you."

"It's okay, Colt. You're a wise man for double-checking," Cam said.

"Go on," Mel said, sensing the gravity of what he was about to hear.

After a few deep breaths, Colt said, "That muzzle. That...that awful thing. You want to know what it really represents? The end of my happiness. The end of enjoying sex. The end of my freedom, of my body belonging to no one else but me. It was Gus's idea. On our wedding night in Rio, he talked me into wearing it, and I...I played along, eager to please my husband. Soon after I put it on things got too rough for me, but I couldn't call out our safe word. He promised he'd take it easy, but he didn't. I screamed, cried, tried to fight him off, but it only made him beat me harder." Colt paused and looked away, fighting tears. "It went on and on. And I just laid there and took it. You want to hear something fucked-up? *I* was the one soothing *him* right after. Like he was the one who'd gotten abused. He cried like a child as he apologized. And I fucking fell for it." Colt buried his face in his palms. His shoulders jerked with every breath between sobs.

Mel noticed a glistening in Cam's eyes as they shared a glance. Neither of them dared to speak.

Cam walked to the kitchen to grab a box of tissues for Colt. He put it down in front of him and laid a hand on his shoulder.

Colt flinched, then sighed. "Sorry. I'm so messed up." He took a tissue and started dabbing his eyes.

"Thank you for telling us. You're very brave," Mel said. Colt stared into the void, much like during his catatonic state two days before. His fists were clenched on the table again, knuckles turning white.

"Colt, do you remember why my partner and I came to your house all those years ago?" Cam asked.

"I do. Steve Blake, my former roommate. You never found his killer, did you?"

"Sadly, we didn't, no. Colt, I hate to ask, but is there something you know about his murder? Something you couldn't tell us back then because of your husband's interruption? You seemed to know him pretty well."

Colt went stock still and kept his eyes on Cam. Mel sensed this was going to be a big bone in uncovering the fossil of this case. Perhaps the biggest one yet. He was in awe of Cam's interrogation skills.

"I know a lot, but I can't tell you on the record."

"Why not, Colt?" Mel asked.

"Please stop the recording."

Mel sighed and slammed his mug on the table. "No. I can't do that. This is all part of our case."

"Mel, I'm begging you to trust me. Otherwise I'm going to have to keep withholding information, and I don't want to do that to you. Not after all you've done."

Mel stopped the machine and crossed his arms.

Chapter 13
Colt—Past

Colt was enjoying the late afternoon sun in his lounge chair by the diamond-shaped pool on the back deck of Gus's house. On his golden MacBook—one of the surprise gifts Gus had showered him with when they had returned from their shortened honeymoon—he was preparing content as an aspiring influencer in the fragrance world. His last three posts—all pictures of his own collection of bottles, plus a few extra from Gus's shopping spree—had been mildly successful, with one accumulating over fifty likes. The video he had been assembling would really set things off. It was high time someone lamented the endless parade of so-called summer fragrances. Calling a fragrance *l'eau* or *eau fraîche* in reality meant nothing more than a regular eau de toilette diluted with water, yet people still fell for it in swarms.

After the horror of their wedding night, Gus and Colt had sat down to discuss proceedings in the hotel lobby—Colt had wanted people around. The first thing they decided on was not to have sex for a full month at least. Second on the list was returning home that same day, cutting their honeymoon short by seven days. And the third agreement they had made was not making any rash decisions about their future as a married couple.

Focusing on what could be his next career kept Colt's mind from exploring the darkest corners of his imagination, so that's what he did. Eight days after returning home he still hadn't slept longer than three hours at a stretch. He repeatedly woke to the sensation of wearing the muzzle, screaming for Gus to stop as his voice thundered through the house. Occasionally he still recoiled at Gus's touch, putting that sorrowful look on his husband's face time after time. Even though Colt tried to hug that look away, it was safe to say they were not in a good place.

Until yesterday, Gus had spent three days in Monterrey, Mexico on a business trip, leaving Colt on his own in the house for the first time. Overprotective as he was, Gus had instructed Colt to defend himself if he needed to. "You won't be on your own a lot, but I still don't like you being defenseless here. Follow me," Gus said, walking to the Rio De Janeiro watercolor painting in the den— depicting the view of Cristo Redentor over the city. He slid it aside to reveal a stainless steel vault with a turning knob in the center.

"The code is 2343, the coordinates to Praia Vermelha. I changed it this morning." He entered the code and pulled the door open.

"Gus, I don't think this is a good idea. I've never fired one in my life," Colt said as he perused the contents: a silver-topped handgun lay in the center among a few manila folders and a wad of cash.

"Really? I just assumed, you know? With you growing

up in Kansas and all." He winked. "Seriously though. That right there is a Desert Eagle .44 Magnum. One shot should put any intruder through hell, no matter where you hit them. Now, I don't have the time to show you how to use it, but I suggest you take it in your hand. Then at least your muscle memory will imprint its weight and shape. Go on." He stepped aside.

Colt picked up the gun like it was glazed with poison and turned it over in his hand. He lifted it with both hands and aimed for the TV, closing one eye like he had seen in movies.

"Don't forget to unlock the safety, okay? It's at the back end of the barrel. Red means bad, as you could have guessed. Now put it back. You don't want to get me killed." Gus's gaze dropped, "Or maybe you do."

"Jesus, Gus. Is that what you think of me?" He put the Desert Eagle back where it belonged.

"I can't say I'd blame you. What I did to you was awful, Colt. I'd happily take a bullet if I knew it'd make you feel better about us."

"Gus…" Colt wrapped his arms around his husband and pressed his cheek to his chest. "We just need time. To heal and find our way back to each other."

"I know, baby. I just hope you stop flinching whenever we touch someday soon. It breaks my heart."

Thinking about how hard Gus had been trying to make up for his unspeakable behavior on their wedding night, Colt closed his laptop and breathed in the balmy Californian air, wishing time was indeed the key to resolving the aching rupture in his marriage. While he went over the list of things he needed for his video tomorrow he succumbed to the sunlight on his face and dozed off.

"Colt?" Someone nudged his bare shoulder. He jumped and stumbled over the reclining chair's legs, scraping his knee on the rough sandstone tiles.

"Fuck. What the hell, Langdon? What's with you?"

"I'm sorry. Are you okay?" Langdon's eyes were saucer-wide, his palms up as he backed away from Colt's wild-animal reaction. "I assumed you were getting ready upstairs."

Getting ready? Oh no.

"What time is it?"

"Seven. You better hurry."

Colt had to attend a business dinner at 7:30 at the Bomb Soir restaurant in West Hollywood. Gus would be waiting there for him after sightings with high-maintenance clients in need of wining and dining.

"Langdon, I need your help."

With Langdon as his assistant Colt got dressed in a lightning blue suit with a crisp white shirt. While Colt buttoned his shirt, Langdon had procured a bandaid and some antiseptic gel from the kitchen for Colt's knee. He skipped the tie, fished out the silver TAGHeuer Gus had bought him the week before and had Langdon search for his silver python Floris Van Bommel shoes. Five minutes later the driver had also found the matching belt. Colt kissed him on the cheek, turning it scarlet when he pulled away. With no time to fix his pool-frizzed hair, Colt sprayed on an extra coat of Amouage Interlude to mask the pool scent and raced to the car.

If traffic had been more like Topeka instead of West LA rush hour on a Friday night, they would have made it in time. Colt texted Gus their ETA after the car hadn't moved for five whole minutes.

Colt: Honey, I'm going to be over ten minutes late. Traffic is insane. xx

Gus: Please tell me you're kidding.

Colt: I wish I were. I'm sorry. xx

Gus: Fuck. Just get here.

Colt saw dots move, but no more messages came through. He couldn't shake the feeling that something about Gus's responses was off. There was no *baby*, no *love you*, no kisses like he had been used to. Their marriage being in the shape it was, double-dating could very well be a mistake. He shifted in his seat, suddenly too hot from either his sunbathing glow or the accumulating unease.

"Looks like they're moving again up ahead. Are you okay, Colt?" Langdon asked. The privacy screen hadn't been up.

"I'm fine, Langdon. Thank you for helping me."

"No problem. I've stocked up on some Sheryl Crow on Spotify if you want?"

Colt smiled. "Sure. Knock yourself out."

"Could you—uhm. Could you sing along? I haven't heard you do that in a while. Think of it as an extra tip for my help. What do you say?"

I haven't had any reason to.

"Not tonight, Langdon. Maybe next time."

Langdon dropped Colt off at 7:50. Gus met him by the

door in his double-breasted ink-black suit and golden tie, rendering him twice as intimidating in the fading light.

"Hello, gorgeous." He planted a peck on Colt's lips.

"Sorry I'm late, Gus."

"It's fine. What happened to your hair?"

Fuck.

"Long story."

"Come on, they're dying to meet you." Gus took him by the hand and led him to their table in the back of the restaurant. The firmer than necessary grip of Gus's hand brought back the events of their wedding night in short, bright flashes. The numbing of his fingertips as Gus restrained his wrists behind his back. The hot tears stinging his eyes. Gus yelling him into submission. Blow after blow from his giant fists. The moment he gave up fighting.

His breathing became labored.

I can't do this.

Colt pulled at Gus's wrist. "Gus, stop."

"What is it?"

"I need to go to the bathroom. I'll be right there."

Gus sighed and looked away. "Stop embarrassing me, Colt. This doesn't look great for business."

"I need two minutes, damn it," Colt said, louder than intended. After checking the turned faces near them, Gus nodded.

Colt splashed watering his face, gripped the sides of the enamel sink with golden faucets and took a few steadying breaths.

When will this get better? Will it ever?

The restroom attendant asked him if everything was all

right. Colt declined the offer to be spritzed with l'Occitane eau de toilette by raising an eyebrow.

The restaurant's interior was trying too hard to resemble a French chateau. So much so that it was more a Renaissance Fair meets Mexico type of situation. Pointed arches separated the foyer from two dining halls: one for group dinners, one with a more intimate setting. Black shiny square tiles merged into red carpeting in the latter space, which is where Gus and his two guests were waiting. Castle-like, wrought-iron chandeliers bathed the room in artificial candlelight. The bar was in the other room, together with eighty percent of the noise. Intimate, in other words, could easily transgress into awkward and self-conscious.

"There he is, the man of the hour," Mark Fitzsimmons said as he watched Colt approach.

"I'm sorry for being late. You got to love rush hour in Hollywood, am I right? Nice to meet you. I'm Colt. Colt Whittaker."

"With the way Gus has been praising you to the moon and back, I think the pleasure is all ours. I'm Abby, by the way."

What Colt immediately liked about Abby was how she, too, was at least a decade younger than her husband. She tucked a strand of her honey-blonde hair behind her ear as she sipped her white wine. A single drop threatening to travel down her chin met its end through a quick sweep of her index finger.

"I believe congratulations are in order, Colt. Somehow

you've brought this giant of a man to his knees in under a year. I got to ask. How did you do it?" Mark asked.

By letting him rape me on my wedding night, Mark.

Heat rose to his temples as Colt tried to build sentences in his mind. He ordered the same wine as Abby by pointing to her glass at the nearest waiter.

"Well, that's one way to start a conversation, Mark. Let's see. When I met Gus I was living in a dingy apartment in Koreatown working at Sephora. It was a commission salary, so I basically had to choose between health insurance and food. Where I saw failure in myself trying to make it in LA, Gus saw perseverance, strength and authenticity. Before him, no one had ever been able to see those things in me, because I wouldn't let them. I had a habit of keeping people at a distance. Gus, however, broke right through all of my barriers and saved me from my self-sabotaging ways, even after I tried to push him away."

Gus covered his hand with his on the table, making Colt's arm tense, but not flinch.

"That's beautiful," Abby said, bleary-eyed with her hand on her chest. Then she turned to her husband. "You could never say things like that about me."

"Gee, thanks Colt. Way to make the rest of us look bad," Mark said. He scratched the back of his head and winked. Apart from bright blue eyes, nothing was attractive about Mark. To Colt he was just another rich graying, beer-belly type that bought suits with labels such as *comfort fit*.

Colt shrugged. "You asked. Anyway, Gus tells me you are looking to move here. Tell me all about it and don't leave anything out."

Mark started answering the question, but Abby soon couldn't contain her enthusiasm and took over, laying a hand on his shoulder. Mark had grown up in a mansion in the Flats as a child and had followed in his father's footsteps as a heart surgeon. At a conference in Helena, Montana, he fell in love with his wife after taking the seat of her blind date that had stood her up. Completely mesmerized by his younger girlfriend, he took a position at Saint Peter's Hospital just to stay close. After a year of dating around his surgery schedule they'd sealed the deal. "Then we visited LA after our wedding and it really seemed to fit our new lifestyle better than Montana. I thought it'd take much more convincing for me to leave home, but LA does all that for you, doesn't it?"

After ordering hors d'œuvres, entrées and main courses, Colt relaxed a little more and applied his go-to party trick.

"Abby, now that you're going to live here, I've got a little advice. You should quit wearing Chanel Number Five. It's edgy on your natural scent and doesn't fit your sweet personality. Try to go with something playful, like Insolence by Guerlain or Manifesto by Yves Saint Laurent. I'll go shopping with you if you want."

Abby was about to take another sip of wine, but her glass stopped halfway up to her mouth after hearing Colt's comment. She put it back down. "That's very, uhm, forward of you, Colt." A cough of nervous laughter escaped her mouth. "It's funny. Mark has been buying it for me since we started dating. I've never strayed from Number Five. He really loves it on me, don't you sweetie?" She had turned to Mark, whose face reddened.

"I do, I guess. In all honesty, sometimes I think it's a little over the top, and in my face. It's not bad, but I figured it made you happy, so I kept buying it for you," Mark said.

"For real? So you buying it over and over again was more convenient than anything else? Interesting." She squinted at her husband.

Colt cursed his perfume talents for the very first time in his life. It usually had the power to bring people closer, not uncover white lies.

"You have to forgive Colt, Abby, he's kind of obsessed. He's trying to become an influencer on Instagram these days, so he's experimenting with giving people recommendations. It's nothing personal. Just his hobby gone haywire. I'm sure it smells great on you. Not to worry, he doesn't get it right every time."

He wouldn't look Colt in the eye. If he had, he would have seen the daggers waiting for their *bombs away*. Colt's situation dawned on him. There he was, sitting in one of the most expensive restaurants in Hollywood, entertaining clients for Gus's job while the latter criticized his professional talent for his own benefit.

I always get it right.

Gus knew how important this part of Colt's life was. Knew how it tethered Colt to his mother.

Colt remained quiet for the rest of the dinner and only gave brief answers to questions about his family and home state. Gus had instructed him not to mention his foster care history to clients, adding another blow to Colt's self-esteem. He felt a trickle of sweat run down his back.

As Abby talked across from him, Colt's mind

wandered. This woman was about to leave her old life behind to chase that Hollywood housewife dream. Was she making a mistake? Did people like Abby and him always have to pay some kind of price for the Hollywood lifestyle? Was it only fair if they did?

Unwilling to give into the lurking despair of the evening, Colt brushed his knee against Gus's, forcing him to meet his gaze. Those sparkling greens somehow filled his heart with a single ounce of hope again. It could have been the memories of their early dating days or the wine in his bloodstream that made him decide to be somewhat optimistic again.

After the mandatory *so glad we met you guys* and *we should do this again sometime*, Colt drove home with Gus in the Mercedes. When they were alone in the confines of the car, Colt started debriefing. "I liked them. She's not very LA yet, but she'll get there. It seems like she could use a little sunshine in her life, don't you think? Have they made any offers yet?"

Gus had a frown on his face that could have split his face in half. "Not yet. Colt, I have a headache, so I'd like to focus on the road if you don't mind."

"Sure. Whatever you need," he said, touching Gus's thigh. Colt took out his phone to check his Instagram account's insights. As the palm trees of Sunset Boulevard passed by he wished things would soon get better between them. Maybe couples counseling could help speed things along toward a healthy relationship—emotionally and physically. It would be challenging, but everyone in LA seemed to do it, so why not? Colt made a mental note to bring it up in the morning.

Once inside he poured himself a tall glass of water—an old habit from his partying days in Koreatown. His nightly escapades with Steve seemed like a lifetime ago. When he put the Fiji bottle back in the fridge and closed the door Gus was standing next to him.

"Feeling better?" Colt asked.

"A little, yeah." His eyes fluttered up and down Colt's unbuttoned shirt. "I was looking for some medicine, and I think I've found just the right one." He put his arms around Colt's waist and leaned closer.

Colt's breath caught, but he didn't flinch. Instinctively, his hands found the back of Gus's neck. All he could see were his husband's lips craving his. Next thing he knew they got what they had come for.

They hadn't kissed this way in a long time. Colt hadn't realized how much he'd missed it. The chills running down his spine, the devouring qualities of Gus's tongue, the hungry growl swallowing his soft moan, allowing Gus to move him back against the wall of cupboards, pinning him in place with his gentle, yet commanding hands.

Wait.

Colt turned his head away. He felt his heart beat faster from an odd mix of desire and dread. Gus targeted his neck and earlobe next, but his efforts were no match for Colt's apprehension.

"Honey?" Gus hummed in response while his lips stayed glued to Colt's skin. "Gus, could we talk about this for a minute? Please?"

Gus complied, but groaned with an eye roll. He put his hands on either side of Colt, leaning closer as he looked him in the eye—so close Colt didn't know which one of those gorgeous eyes to focus on. "Fine. You want to talk? Let's talk. You're not going to like this part very much, but have it your way," he started, firing so fast Colt couldn't object. "Colt, you embarrassed me tonight. For starters you were late. Even though you've got nothing to do all day—nothing at all—you somehow managed to show up late when I really needed you." His eyes were devoid of light in a way Colt had only seen once before.

"I'm sorry. I lost track and hurt my knee when—"

Two simultaneous bangs near his ears cut his attempt at an explanation short. Colt tensed up as his breathing became unsteady.

"Let me finish. On top of being late and making me look like a fool you just couldn't help yourself and acted like a total snob. That perfume comment struck a nerve, Colt. And then you completely withdrew from conversations for the rest of the night. How am I supposed to impress these people if they think my husband's a deranged egotistic fragrance queen?" He enunciated the last four words.

Colt fought back tears. This was uncalled for and he wasn't going to lie down and take it—not this time. "That's not fair, Gus. You know we're not in a good place right now. You can't expect me to be all smiles and rainbows on dinner dates. If you're looking for someone to blame, find yourself a mirror. *You* caused this rift between us, not me."

Gus's nostrils flared as steam seemed to be coming from them. He backed away from Colt and straightened.

Colt lived through the next seconds in slow motion. Gus took a quick breath. His right hand jerked back and launched forward with a turn of his torso, striking Colt's ribs with full force. Pain exploded from the point of impact all the way to his shoulder.

He collapsed to his knees, panting as his hand clung to his midsection. When he tried to check for broken bones he groaned. His temples throbbed while he was looking up at his husband, the one who was supposed to love and protect him.

Gus's hands were trembling as he paced the room. He had untucked his shirt, which now hung in flaps over his belt. "Colt, you really shouldn't challenge me like that when I'm wound up. Now look what you made me do." His voice was unsteady, like he was on the verge of a breakdown.

Colt shifted so he sat up against the cupboards, wincing when he pulled his legs from underneath him—too stunned to speak.

"Oh my God, what have I done?" Gus approached Colt again, who held up his elbow in front of his face to fence him off. "I'm so sorry. I didn't mean to. I couldn't help it. You were being so…goddamn stubborn. I just lost it." He lowered to his knees.

"Stay away from me," Colt said in the middle of a sob, trying hard to find a steady tone himself. He cleared his throat, still shaking. "You need to listen to me, Gus. I can't do this anymore. I thought I could overlook our wedding night as an isolated incident far away from our home. I've been spending all my time trying to do that, and I think I could have succeeded. But this," he gestured between the two of them with his right arm, "changes everything. This is not healthy. You need help to deal with your issues. And until you figure that out, I can't be here. I will not become your abused husband." He took another shuddering breath and wiped his cheeks with his shirtsleeves. "Here's what I'm going to do, Gus. I'm going to be sleeping in the guest room from now on. Starting tomorrow, I'm going to look for a job and a place of my own. I'm not giving up on you, but you and I can't live under the same roof."

Fear flashed across Gus's pale features. "No. You can't leave me. You're my husband. I don't know what I'd do without you. I can't...I can't let you go. I love you. I'll be better to you. I promise. Please, baby."

"Gus, you can't keep doing this to me. Beat me up and then ask for forgiveness. It may have worked on our wedding night, but I'm not falling for this again. I love you too, and I probably always will, but if I stay here, our marriage is going to destroy me. *You* are going to destroy me."

"Colt, don't say that. I love you." Gus broke down in a sobbing heap on the floor in a fetal position. Through his own tears and Gus's wails, Colt managed to get up and made his way to the guest room upstairs. His heart was breaking, and a painful shard detached as he had to maneuver away from Gus reaching for him in passing.

The lay-out of the guest room, though identical to the master suite across the hall, made Colt feel somewhat safe that night. As he undressed he examined the angry purple bruise over his ribs in the ensuite bathroom mirror. He held a cold wet towel against it and grimaced. Looking at his reflection, he realized the pain on his ribs was nothing compared to the damage on the inside.

I married a monster. I told him it turned me on when he hurt me. Told him I craved his beast side. Urged him to dominate me. Did I cause this? Where will I go? Is my marriage over?

Sleep was out of the question. Every time he floated toward oblivion it was either the bruise or the endless worrisome thoughts pulling him off the ledge. At some point in the early hours he had almost dialed his mother's number. Maybe this was why she had second-guessed his engagement at the time. After a series of conflicting thoughts he decided on giving her a call the next day, starting with an apology about the way he had treated her last time. For the first time in his life, he wanted her help.

Chapter 14
Colt—Past

Colt jerked awake when he felt Gus's hand on his shoulder. He got up and moved as far away as he could—until his elbow hit the window.

"Baby, I'm sorry to wake you, but there are two detectives downstairs. Said they needed to talk to you."

Colt rubbed his crusted eyes. "Detectives? Talk about what? What time is it?"

"10:40. They didn't say."

He put on gym shorts and a hoodie as quickly as his bruised ribs allowed and went downstairs barefoot. Hannah had already left, but he wasn't hungry anyway.

"Good morning, Detectives. I'm Colt Whittaker."

"Good morning to you, too, Mr. Whittaker. Apologies for waking you. I promise this won't take long," the older one said. He looked more than ready for retirement in Colt's eyes. A bald head with gray tufts on the sides was his first clue. The other appeared far younger and had an attractive olive glow like Gus. Their names, Colt learned in the next phase, were Parsons and Espinoza. For some reason they needed to talk to him about Steve. Sharing their crappy apartment with him felt like years ago.

Colt made himself an espresso and asked if the detectives wanted some after firing up the machine. They both declined, so Colt took a seat at the island after a first sip. As he settled in his chair he tried not to wince. For some reason he didn't want the detectives to know about Gus's aggressive ways. Maybe he wasn't ready to be victimized, but he couldn't tell for sure that was it.

"I'm not sure you're at the right address, gentlemen. I haven't seen or talked to Steve in over two months." He took another sip, wishing for the caffeine to wake him up faster.

"Sir, you were his roommate for a long time. That makes you his longest-lasting acquaintance in town. His girlfriend Diana Ortega told us about your current living situation, which brought us here," the younger one said.

"I'm sorry, Detectives, but it feels like I'm missing something. Where is Steve now? What has he done to involve you guys?"

Parsons shot his colleague a glance and said, "Mr. Whittaker, we're sorry for your loss. Steve Blake is dead. He was shot in his apartment five days ago,"

Colt's heart rate climbed. "Steve was murdered? No, that can't be right. Are you sure?"

"Sadly we are. I'm sorry to ask you this, but where were you on the night of April 26 between 8:00 and 10:30 pm?" Espinoza said.

Colt could hear the words and saw lips moving, but failed to register any information. He thought he had buried his feelings for Steve deep down after moving in with Gus, but right now they came flooding back. The way he liked his coffee—two sugars—the light in his eyes as he talked about his screenplay writer dream, his Chanel Égoïste cologne that he had recommended. Their bond had once meant everything to Colt, right until that night he allowed—and perhaps encouraged—Steve inside of him. Why did sex always make things worse in his life? Tears blurred his vision. No matter what, Steve was family.

"Mr. Whittaker?"

"Sorry. I—uhm—I was here, working on my social media exposure and watching Netflix. I think I hit the pool, too."

"Can anyone testify to you having been here between those hours? We're just trying to turn over every stone."

"Uhm, yes. Hannah, our chef, was here until…9:00 pm, I think. Oh, and Langdon was here, too—our driver. He went home after 11:00 or something. My husband was on a business trip and he had asked Langdon to keep an eye on me after his hours."

"All right. Mr. Whittaker, we found a confusing text from you on Steve's phone. Allow me to read it for you," the older detective cleared his throat. *I'm actually keeping my name. Fuck you, Steve. See how YOU like it.* The *you* was in caps. Care to explain?"

Colt sighed, then explained how Diana had caused a rift between him and Steve as his new girlfriend. It wasn't the entire story behind the text, but Colt didn't consider it a good idea to throw Steve's bisexual experiment into this interrogation. "I was just so mad at him for cutting me out of his life piece by piece. It was either him pushing me away every chance he got, or me taking control and moving out from one day to the next. I chose the latter and went to live with my fiancé. Diana was always awful to me and he never stopped her from making the most passive aggressive comments about my sex life—I was rather active on Grindr at the time. It ruined our friendship, so I texted him in a way that reflected my lifestyle of, you know, getting fucked."

Gus walked in and said, "Okay, Detectives, I think it's time for you to go. Somehow you've turned this into a full-on interrogation when all you wanted to do was talk to my husband. We've been very cooperative, so I'd appreciate it if you left this instant. Any further questions can be dealt with through our attorney."

With a *thank you for your time* and a *sorry again for your loss* the detectives were out the door. Steve's murder didn't make sense. Colt couldn't believe anyone would want to kill him. Of course, he didn't know a whole lot about Steve's life before LA, so there might have been a side of him Colt knew nothing about. If there was one thing Colt had learned in Hollywood it was that every individual was essentially a diamond. Some were still rough, others polished to perfection. The key to becoming shimmeringly successful was all about catching the light in such a way that it reflected only your good sides. Fake it 'til you make it, in other words.

"I'm sorry about Steve," Gus said, taking a seat next to him. "Can I get you some breakfast?"

"No, I'm not hungry."

"I understand. Listen, I really am sorry about last night. Can we please talk?"

It was hard to align Gus's kind eyes today with the aggressive, dark ones he had gazed into twelve hours before. He nodded. "I think we should, yes. Difficult as this will be, we really need to discuss further steps."

"So, you still intend to get away from me?" Gus looked away like he was afraid of Colt's answer.

"Yes, Gus. I do. It's what's best for us, and you know it. I wish I didn't have to, but I can't live through another night like that. I meant what I said. You need professional help to deal with your personal issues. It's the only way you and I stand a chance to survive."

Gus made a clicking sound with his tongue. "Yeah, I was afraid you were going to say that." He got to his feet, towering over Colt, closer than comfortable. Intuition guided Colt's hand to his bruise.

"Colt, my sweet, darling husband. I need you to listen to what I have to say. You're not going anywhere. Not today. Not next week. Not ever if I have a say in it. You don't get to just quit and walk away. You knew about my aggressive tendency from day one. Deep down that's what attracts you most. Face it, baby. You need someone to boss you around, to dictate your every move. It's why we work so well as a couple." His voice sounded almost robotic, sending a chill straight to Colt's heart. Even in his most commanding tone, Gus's voice used to emanate a kind of warmth.

"I can't believe this," Colt whispered, running his hand through his hair. Then he faced Gus and found his voice.

"Are you out of your mind? Me wanting you to hurt me a little and give me dirty commands, and you holding me down and beating the crap out of me are two completely different things, Gus. One's called liking it rough, the other sexual abuse. I'm leaving. Today."

"No, you're not."

Colt stood, but didn't get far after Gus gripped his wrist, squeezing hard.

"Let go of me. You're hurting me."

"I'm not letting you go."

"You can't stop me."

"I won't need to. You're going to want to stay with me of your own volition." He let go of Colt's wrist—another bruise in the making.

"Gus, you're delusional. I am so out of here." Colt hastened toward the staircase.

"Fine. Then I guess I'll have to call those detectives for a repeat visit. This time I think I'll show them your gun. If that won't pique their interest, then I don't know what will." Gus took a seat at the kitchen island, relaxed as ever.

Colt stopped and turned, taking a few steps back to the kitchen. "Gun? What are you talking about?"

"You know, the gun you used to kill Steve. Don't you remember? You put it in my safe right after. How else would you explain your fingerprints all over it? It's missing two bullets, too. One pierced his stomach, the other made his head look like the dark side of the moon. We all know your alibi for that night sucks. Oh, and when I tell them about Steve's little bicurious experiment, I bet they'll be all ears about why you left that part out just now."

Colt forced himself to blink after a few seconds of hoping Gus's evil smirk would turn back to normal. "But I didn't... I was here. Langdon was here."

"Langdon will do as I say, like he always does. He and I go way back, actually. Loyalty like that can't be bought."

Looking at Gus sitting at the kitchen island of his dreams, Colt failed to recognize the man he had fallen in love with half a year before. Where he once saw an overly protective, kind and reliable man, he now witnessed a deranged, manipulative and violent individual.

"Gus, I don't understand. What happened? Why are you doing this?" He moved three steps closer.

Gus cocked his head. "Come on, baby. You know why. You were threatening to leave me. I love you, Colt Whittaker. There's no way I'm letting you go. Ever. Now come sit so we can talk some more."

Colt didn't move. "So your idea of a reason to make me stay is the threat of going to prison? Frame me for murder? That's crazy. Sounds like I'll be in prison whether I stay or go. You know what? Do what you got to do, Gus. I'm not staying."

"I said sit," Gus shouted. It was the same voice he had used the night before with its thundering echo.

With wobbly knees Colt walked to the left side of the island and moved the stool back until Gus corrected him. "No. Closer." Colt pulled the one next to him back, his heart racing.

"That's better. Now I'm going to put my arm around you like I used to and you're going to let me. Understand?"

Colt nodded and swallowed the first sob. As he sensed

Gus's palm on his hip he looked away in an attempt to hide his tears. "Gus, please don't do this."

Gus leaned close to Colt's ear, "There's nothing strange about a man wanting to hold his husband. I love you. I missed you." Then he pulled his face away and said, "Okay. Objectively speaking, you going to prison would benefit neither of us. That's why the next part is crucial." He fished his phone out of his pocket and laid it on the countertop. "You're going to sit here and make some calls to your family. If you value the lives of your mom and your brother you'll do as I say."

Colt's head was spinning. He was too stunned to ask what Gus was talking about.

Gus unlocked his phone and browsed through his photos app. He tilted the screen to landscape and said, "I've got something to show you. Here's your mother's apartment—a real shit hole. This is her at the supermarket. And yes, this is her again at Sephora. Next up is your brother. On a packed subway. In the OR in his scrubs. In line at Starbucks. Accidents happen, Colt." Colt swiped back and forth between the images a few times, ice water running through his veins.

"It's time for you to let them go and say your goodbyes. I'll be your family."

"What? W-why?" Colt blinked hard.

"Colt, you're smarter than this. In case you'd run out on me, I want them to hate you so much they won't believe a word you say. When you try to warn them about the danger they're in, I want them to laugh in your face." The evil smirk had returned.

"But what would I even say to them?" Gus's hand tensed on Colt's hip.

"Easy. Holmby Hills changed you. Wealth changed you. You want a fresh start in life without any baggage. Your memories are too painful. You've never really forgiven your mother's decisions in life. Hell, you could even tell them you joined Scientology or some other cult. As long as you infuriate them I'll be okay with whatever. Your brother never calls you anyway, so you can simply tell him to go fuck himself."

Colt could almost smell his mother's Poême thinking about her warm embrace. He wept without sound, scared of what Gus's reaction would be. "I can't do it. They'll know something is off when they hear me crying." He sniffled.

Gus scoffed, making Colt's skin crawl. "You still don't get it, do you, baby? You've got two options. One, you stay here with me, do as I say and nothing bad will happen to either you or your family. Two, you leave, end up in prison and become responsible for their deaths. Now, I'll be upstairs. If you decide to stay and make those calls later, I'll be needing you in my bed. You've got thirty minutes to figure out the kind of life you want to live."

Chapter 15
Mel—Present

"Colt, you need to start talking," Cam said.

"Cam, don't rush him. He'll get there." Mel turned to Colt and added, "What's worrying you?"

Colt jutted his chin to Cam. "He is. I can't go to prison. He'll get to me."

"All right. Listen to me. No one is locking you up, Colt," Cam said, a little too quickly.

"You don't know that. I know how it's going to sound to you. It was *your* case, remember?"

The hair on Mel's neck stood erect. The stopping of the recording, the fear of incarceration, it all made sense—though he wished it didn't.

"Please tell me you didn't kill Steve," Mel said.

"Of course I didn't kill him, Mel. But it might look that way once LAPD gets their hands on the gun in Gus's safe." Colt explained how Gus had tricked him into touching the Glock in his safe under the guise of being able to defend himself when he was alone in the house. Later, after Cam and Gunnar had interrogated him at home, his husband pointed out that it was the same gun that had shot and killed

Steve Blake. "Langdon is my alibi for that night, and he'd sooner die than disobey Gus. I don't know who murdered Steve, but somehow that gun ended up in our house as a constant motivator. Together with the threats to my mom and Dave, it guaranteed me becoming a slave to Gus indefinitely. His master plan unfolded in the days after our wedding. As his fear of losing me got the better of him, he took action and overachieved like always."

Mel's coffee had gone cold, but he knew he wouldn't have enjoyed it anyway. With Gus's alleged ties to the Cordelio cartel, he'd have had plenty of options when it came to ordering a hit on a random guy in Koreatown, in addition to shadowing Colt's relatives. The question was what he'd given the cartel in return for this outrageous favor.

Cam jumped from his chair and started swearing in Spanish.

Kate appeared at the top of the stairs, carrying her daughter on her arm. "You guys, I'm sorry to interrupt, but I have to take Rose on her stroll before dinner. I have Zumba class tonight."

"That's fine, honey," Mel said. He asked if she needed help with the stroller, but she declined.

"Cam? Say something," Colt said.

Cam sighed and eyed Colt for a long time. Neither of them broke their stare, which was a good sign. Mel had seen his friend use this unorthodox method countless times. *Liars always look away, Mel.*

Cam got back on his chair and put both palms on the table. "Colt, I'm going to tell you what I told Gunnar Parsons after our visit. You're no killer. That reaction to

Steve's death, even though your friendship had soured, was both appropriate and genuine. Personally I don't believe you killed him, but if we take the evidence and your flimsy alibi into account, it puts you in a tight spot. You're lucky you don't have a clear motive."

Kate closed the door behind her, trying not to make any sound.

Colt bit his lower lip. "Yeah, about that. There's one more thing you need to know. Steve and I had sex one time after going out. It was awful and ended up burning our friendship to the ground. His girlfriend hating my guts was just the final straw. I don't think Steve ever told anyone," Colt paused, "but Gus knows." Colt turned to Mel. "This is why I couldn't tell you before, Mel. You would have arrested me without another thought."

The blood in Mel's face evacuated. After the attempted murder on Gus, there was no way anyone would believe Colt hadn't killed Steve five years ago. *Kansas lowlife kills ex-boyfriend and shoots sugar daddy.* The media would eat that right up. He'd hit national news as the detective that housed a killer. Gus having murdered Steve with the help of the biggest drug cartel in LA was far harder for the public to believe. They needed a connection between the two, and they needed it fast. Colt's tattoo was a good start, but worthless on its own.

"What's taking him so long to reveal the gun to LAPD?" Mel asked.

Cam answered, "As long as he's in the hospital he'd be complicit. He'd have to admit he knew about the gun. Once he gets home, he can stumble upon it and claim he hasn't used the safe in years."

Colt excused himself and went upstairs to the bathroom, allowing Cam and Mel to discuss further steps. Just like the old days, they were immediately on the same page. They decided to make a bold move the next morning. Mel prayed Captain Perez would wake up in a good mood.

"Good morning, Mel. Who's your—oh," Rita's mouth made a perfect lipstick-red O as she saw Colt striding along next to him.

"Good morning, Rita. You remember Colt?" Mel said, smiling.

"Oh, I do. Does the Chief know about this?"

Mel didn't answer. In time-sensitive cases like this he'd rather ask for forgiveness than permission.

The squeaky sounds of their footsteps on the gray linoleum floors added to the disruption of bringing Colt back to this place. As he watched him take in the various rooms, he noticed many of his colleagues looking up from their desks. The several rooms were all pretty much alike with their uniform desks and fake-leather chairs. Apart from the recent addition of white notary-style desk lights, the offices looked about as fashionable as the J. Edgar Hoover building in DC.

Through the large office space most officers used in the middle of the building he guided Colt into the kitchen area and poured him an LAPD mug of coffee—black, as he had learned. The Special Victims office he shared with

Charlotte was at the back of the sea of desks. The hallway on the other side of the kitchen led to interrogation and conference rooms, and the Chief's office. Working at this West LA station often meant moving back and forth through the kitchen a hundred times a day.

"Hey, Mel, what the hell is he doing here?" Gene asked, his eyes fixed on Colt as he spoke.

"Good morning to you, too, Gene. Colt's here to help on one of your cold cases, actually. Well, sort of. It's a long story."

"Does the Chief know about this? We've got team meeting in like half an hour," Gene said.

"She doesn't. There were new developments last night. Whether she likes it or not, Gene, this couldn't wait. Colt's essential to our case."

"Okay, sure. It's your funeral. By the way, Charlotte's back. She's in your office." Gene gave Colt another look before he disappeared.

Of course she's here.

Mel smiled and nodded at Colt to follow him to their office. If Colt were a magnet, the officers' eyes were iron shreds. Both of them stood in the doorway as they watched Charlotte put up a printed page on the wall for Abby Fitzsimmons's case—an image of her mansion from Carolino Real Estate's website. She dropped a pin when she saw them.

As she got back up, Mel hugged her immediately. "Good to have you back," he whispered.

"I'm not *back* back yet, but they listed me as a visitor for today, with Rita's powers of persuasion. I'm one psych eval away from being your awkward partner again."

When they pulled away, Charlotte's smile vanished as she looked at Colt. They stared at each other for a long time, both reliving the horror of the attack in her apartment, or so it seemed.

"Charlotte, I brought Colt because of a new turn in his case. I'll fill you in on the details in a min—"

Charlotte didn't hear him. She approached Colt and pulled him into her arms. Colt closed his eyes, letting one tear spill over his cheek. Charlotte being only an inch or so shorter, the sight was heart-warming. Mel couldn't hear what Charlotte was saying, but there was no need. What happened wasn't Colt's fault and he needed to hear it from her.

Mel had experienced Colt's need for kind, untainted human touch himself last night. With Kate out on her Zumba class and subsequent after-workout drinks with her classmates, Mel was on his own to take care of Rose for the first time. It had taken him half an hour before he got lost in self-doubt as a parent and looked to Colt for help.

"How are you so bad at this, Mel? She's your daughter. Unless she was an accident, you wanted this, right?" Colt asked with Rose on his arm.

Mel's future opera singer daughter had been screaming intermittently since Kate left. He had tried everything his parenthood ammo provided: bottle, warmer bottle, mobile, rocking, physical disorientation—swaying her around—

pacifier, checking her diaper, dangling with keys. He had laid her down in her crib on her back, then turned her on her stomach for a few minutes until he panicked, failing to remember whether it was still an advisable thing to do.

"Of course she wasn't an accident. It's just that I'm not sure how to do this. Be a father. Take care of her without Kate to fall back on. I know it sounds awful."

"Mel, babies are like sponges, meaning they absorb all of your emotions. If you keep getting worked-up about your insecurities as a father, your anxiety is going to project on her like it has done just now. Sit down and relax, take a few deep breaths and try again. Don't they teach you this stuff in Lamaze classes or whatever they call them?" Rose was digging into Colt's side, making him wince. He switched arms like a pro.

"That's easy for you to say. Look at you, you're a natural. And, you've got that voice to get her to sleep if all else fails. This game feels rigged."

Colt gave him a lopsided smile and started singing. It was a song Mel didn't recognize, but the pain of loss shimmered throughout Colt's voice. It was about how one of two lovers was fine walking away, leaving the other heartbroken. The song, though dark in its nature, lit up the pastel-pink room. Rose quieted down almost instantly, only adding heaps to Mel's anxiety about fatherhood.

"Are you calm?" Colt whispered to him.

Mel nodded, after which Colt handed him his daughter. Humming the song's melody, Mel laid Rose in her crib and kissed her forehead. After checking the monitor he turned on the mobile with the merry-go-round painted horses and backed away trying not to make a sound.

Once downstairs Colt fell into the couch in the living room, pulling his legs to his side.

"It worked. Thank you, Colt. I didn't mean to drag you into this." Mel lowered himself onto the couch next to Colt, making sure not to sit too close.

"It's fine, Mel. It's kind of fucked-up if you think about it. Two foster kids playing house. She's a lot luckier than us. You know, being here kind of feels like a group home. But nicer, of course. Far nicer."

Mel cocked his head. "I'm going to choose to take that as a compliment for now." He looked around at the dining room and kitchen and realized they needed remodeling in the next five years. Group home was not the look and feel he had been going for. Rose and Kate deserved better. When he looked back at Colt he allowed his curiosity to get the better of him. "Colt, do you ever want kids yourself? Sorry if that's a weird question."

"It's not. There was a time I thought I did. When Gus proposed I thought anything was possible, like I had finally found a steady foundation in life. I had never even considered starting a family before. Anyway, soon after our wedding there was no way my future was going to have kids in it. I'm really too damaged to be a parent, and I know what it's like to be raised by someone like that."

Mel looked away and nodded, then decided to think out loud. "I wish I could say something to make you feel better, but I can't. What happened to you is awful. I really hope you can get that fresh start in your life. You want a beer?"

"Thanks, Mel. Me too. Beer actually sounds great."

When Mel got back from the kitchen with two longnecks he paused mid-stride as he heard himself hum again. He asked about the song when he sat down again.

"You don't know it? You can't be serious. Allison Krauss. *That Makes One of Us*. It's from her first—and best—album."

"I know her, but vaguely. I'm not really into bluegrass."

Colt scoffed. "It's more a country album, really."

Mel stared at him for a while. "I have to say, Colt, your taste in music is quite unexpected. In a good way, don't get me wrong. Not a lot of people your age even know about the songs I've heard you sing."

Colt narrowed his eyes. "Yeah, Mel, I'm going to let that subtle stereotypical comment slide. If you must know, my taste in music originates from my father. You know he died in Afghanistan before I turned one, right? I have no memories of him, but I did find a box full of CDs when I was fifteen. He was really passionate about country, rock and bluegrass. I used to stare at his framed picture on my nightstand while I listened to John Hiatt, Dolly, Emmylou Harris, Sheryl Crow, Keith Whitley, Del McCoury, The Judds and other big names. I imagined him singing along, so that's what I did, too."

They talked about music a lot from that point on, about certain niche artists and albums they both liked and advised the other to listen to. Mel steered Colt toward more Fleetwood Mac albums, while Colt returned the favor and insisted he listened to Emmylou Harris's *Wrecking Ball* album. The TV turned out to be the most useless device in the room. Rose hadn't given them any trouble at all in their conversation that lasted for over two hours.

At the end of the night Colt's gaze dropped to the carpet. "I didn't realize how much I miss this. Talking just for the sake of it, without any painful topics."

Mel gave him a sympathetic smile. He had enjoyed their chat just as much, if not more. It was one of those September nights he was fond of: warm, balmy air that cooled down just enough to be comfortable long after dusk.

"Mel, could you do me a favor?"

"Sure. It's the least I can do after your help with my daughter."

"Sorry if it's weird, but would you—uhm—hold me? It's just…I haven't been held by someone who doesn't want to control me in a very long time. It scares me, but I need to start trusting people again." Colt spoke while he studied his hands in his lap. Only at the end did he dare glance in Mel's direction.

Every last bit of info from his training days went through his head as Mel pondered the request. It was considered unethical for many reasons. Getting attached to a victim was a sure-fire way to cloud a detective's judgment and could therefore jeopardize the entire investigation or trial. But then again, he thought, having Colt in his house and sing to his daughter had already been two steps in the wrong direction. He was way past the point of getting attached to Colt on a personal level, so he didn't see the harm in indulging a broken man in some well-deserved kindness. If he could add a modicum of strength to Colt's frail heart, then why the hell not?

He stood and held out his arms. Colt was a foot shorter, so he wrapped his arms around Mel's waist while Mel held his shoulders. All in all, their embrace lasted about half a minute. Just as he felt Colt's breathing slow down—and anxiety ebb—Kate walked through the front door. He held up his palms with Colt still clinging to his midsection, yet it didn't erase her wide-eyed surprise.

"Wait. Is that Abby Fitzsimmons?" Colt asked, bringing Mel's mind back to the present.

"You know her?" Mel and Charlotte asked in unison.

Colt nodded. "She and her husband were Gus's clients when they were moving to Hollywood. We had dinner with them several times. What happened to her?"

Neither Mel or Charlotte dared answer right away, so one looked at the other for a while until Colt put two and two together.

"Oh. Special Victims. Was it Mark?"

"No, we don't think he did it. She was drugged and raped in broad daylight, then woke up with…that." Mel pointed at the photo of the branding on Abby's right hip.

"Just like in my case, we believe it was the Cordelio cartel. Colt, is there anything you can tell us about Gus's ties to them? Anything at all?" Charlotte asked. Mel marveled at her mental strength. *My case,* like it had happened to someone else.

"You know, I've been thinking about it ever since you

hinted at my tattoo's real significance. Gus had mood swings every now and then. He'd get so worked up sometimes, mostly when he needed me to come to one of his business dinners like we had with the Fitzsimmons. If I recall correctly, Gus was most abusive right after those dinner outings. It would often start as soon as we were in the car." Colt started rubbing his left shoulder.

A lightbulb flashed in Mel's mind. Bringing Colt might have been the most brilliant move he'd done in this investigation.

"Colt, follow me. I've got an idea. Charlotte?"

"Give me a few minutes. I got to go check something with IT."

He started toward the conference room that held all pictures of the cartel's alleged victims. Gene and his partner Raymond Mercer were discussing their side of the case in the room in preparation of the team meeting. The Chief was staring at the wall of evidence. Together with her wide eyes, her mouth opened of its own volition as soon as she recognized Colt.

Uh-oh.

"Detective Daniels, what is the meaning of this?"

"Chief, I can explain. There were new developments last night that are time-sensitive. We also may have a breakthrough in the connection between Carolino Real Estate and the Cordelio cartel." He liked his choice of words.

"O-kay, I think I hear you. Nevertheless, he can't be in here, Mel."

"Just one minute. He may know the other victims."

Captain Perez leaned in with her mouth next to his ear. "I've given you a lot of leeway with this guy. You and I need to talk after our meeting. One minute, then he's out. Officer Ryder can babysit. Can someone call him?" in a louder voice.

Mel gestured for Colt to come closer with a tilt of his head. Gene and Ray made room, eyeing him like he was going to pull a gun on them.

Colt looked at his own pictures for a second, then moved on. The room went quiet and suddenly the air changed as Colt took slow steps back from the wall.

"Colt?" Mel could hear him breathing now.

"Except for the first one, I've met these people. They were all in business with Gus. All of them." Colt had turned to Mel and seemed to be only talking to him. He put a hand on his right hip. Mel watched terror make its way to Colt's face, which was rapidly losing color. "Some bought a place in Hollywood, others in Beverly Hills or Holmby Hills. We had dinner with all of these people before they sealed the deal. What the fuck does this mean for me?" Before Mel could say anything, Gene swooped in with all of his tact.

"Okay, time for you to go, Mr. Whittaker. Officer Ryder will escort you back to the kitchen." He put his hand on Colt's shoulder, making the latter jerk away.

"Keep your fucking hands off him, Gene," Mel shouted. Everyone around him seemed frozen, Colt included.

Gene raised his hands and said, "Jesus, Mel. I'm sorry. I—uhm—I didn't mean to."

The Chief cut in. "All right. That's enough, you two.

Colt, that right there is Officer Oliver Ryder, who will stay with you until this meeting is over." She pointed to Oliver near the door. "Thank you for your cooperation."

Colt and Mel exchanged glances and nodded. Mel wasn't sure if it was a *thank you for standing up for me* or a *do you trust this guy?* It could have been both. Mel hoped Colt didn't remember him as the failing surveillance cop.

Captain Perez started her intro to the team meeting and addressed all the basics. Today was about the ongoing events in every unit connected to the hunt on the Cordelio cartel. When Cam held the floor for the DEA, he described the arrest of a minor drug ring of former juvenile delinquents in and around Beverly Gardens Park. So far, they hadn't been able to connect the youngsters to any significant bigger players in the outstretched hierarchy of the cartel. "The product most definitely came from Cordelio, but every one of the five dealers was more willing to go to jail for intent rather than rat anyone out. They were, as usual, broke records."

When Charlotte arrived, Mel raised his hand to be the next one to present their findings. Charlotte's sparkling brown eyes told him she had just found out something big. *Playing it by ear it is*, he thought as he stepped to the front.

He walked the team through his interrogations with Gus and his staff members at the house, and pointed out how futile the entire operation had been. "Cam and I were confident afterward that his driver, Langdon Bryan, was lying to us the entire time. Gustavo Carolino appears to have left no loose ends when it came to enslaving Colt." He moved on to the muzzle in the suitcase, paused for reactions, and segued into his conversations with Colt at home. Captain Perez's crossed arms and stern expression told him the conversation she had planned for him after wouldn't be enjoyable in the least.

"Last night Cam and I found out the true nature of Colt's entrapment in Gustavo's house. It's good that you're sitting down for this, especially Gene and Ray."

After he had explained the details of Steve Blake's murder weapon, Gene jumped from his seat and buried his face in his hands. A groan and a half later he said, "That little miss Perfect Girlfriend of his still harasses us every few months to ask for new discoveries. If Gustavo indeed walks through that door and brings us that gun, we'll have no choice, Mel. He'll go down for this. With him shooting his husband I'm a little inclined to believe it. Goddammit."

"Hold on. Why is he telling you this now?" The Chief asked.

"Chief, if I may?" Cam asked. "I interrogated Colt together with Gunnar at the time. Colt said he hadn't known about the gun back then, and frankly, I believe him. His grief over his best friend, even though he hadn't seen him in months, was authentic. You can't fake the loss of someone close to you like that, trust me.

"Now, Mel and I thought it best to perform a polygraph test on Colt, conducted by Homicide, of course. That way, if the gun should turn up, we'll at least have something as a counterweight. It's not ideal, but nothing about this major investigation has been a walk in the park so far."

"Detective Reynolds?" Captain Perez asked, swiveling her chair to him.

"Sure, I guess. It won't hold up in court, especially not with lawyers like that Silveira guy Gus hired, but it couldn't hurt. It's the only thing we can do."

Swiveling back, the Chief said, "Okay, Mel. Consider it done. Now, I think that's all for this—"

"I'm sorry, Chief, but there's more," Charlotte said, rising from her chair with a manila binder in her hand. Captain Perez gave her a pointed stare as though she were deliberating whether to allow Charlotte's presence or not. Interrupting the Chief was not something anyone in this room took lightly, with or without good reason. Mel was certain there was going to be one-sided yelling, but instead the Chief gestured for Charlotte to speak up.

As he watched Charlotte, he noticed how slender she had become over the span of a few days. She seemed okay, but was she really? Could anyone in her place be okay this soon after having lived through a brutal assault? He vowed to keep a closer eye on her for now. Just another ball in the air for him to juggle around.

"…were very reluctant to cooperate after the initial questioning at the hospital, especially the husband, Mark. These people bought their Holmby Hills house for thirty million dollars, but…they sold it yesterday for twenty-two. Guess who their realtor was on both occasions. That's right: Gustavo. The guys at IT did a little digging and found real estate deals with every single one of the victims. Get this. Every widower in the list sold their house below market value through Gustavo's business not long after the murders. I don't know how long you guys have lived in this side of town, but home prices around here don't exactly drop like that.

"Now comes the kicker. I should really buy Tim and Rosalie at IT a drink one of these days. Every house was sold to a private holding with the name of Dahlia Rubia LTD. The sole shareholder on the official deed of this—presumed—shell company is no other than Colt Whittaker."

Chapter 16
Colt—Past

"That's it, baby. I'm so proud of you," Gus said, his breath brushing Colt's inner thigh. Then he continued licking Colt's scrotum with his shoulders tucked under Colt's legs. Powerless against Gus's intent to make him orgasm, Colt heard himself moan with misplaced pleasure. It shouldn't, but it felt so good. If only his imagination had been a little more powerful, his mind would have been able to go back to their dating days to fully enjoy Gus's crafty bedroom skills. Flares of ecstasy met a nauseating sense of shame somewhere between his heart and underbelly. He couldn't tell whether he wanted Gus to stop or keep going. Everything about their new *arrangement* had his head spinning.

It had been a week since Colt's new reality had dawned on him, even though it felt like more time had passed. It was hard to tell the days apart in a world as lonely as his, in which every dreadful minute carried the risk of more abuse. When he walked into Gus's bedroom that afternoon, sealing his fate as his husband's slave once and for all, he was shaking all over, fighting back tears.

"Oh, please don't be scared, baby. Come here. I won't hurt you, I just need you in my arms. From here on out we'll take it slow, I promise," Gus said in the sweet voice Colt had come to cherish.

When Colt approached him, Gus stopped him by holding up his palm. "Wait. No more clothes in bed. New rule."

New rule aside, Gus had kept his promise. Instead of forcing him to succumb to Gus's every wish between the sheets like he had expected, his husband only hugged him tight, enveloping him in his wide shoulders. They didn't talk at all, but kept holding onto each other. Somehow it unnerved Colt even more as realization hit him that this calm before the storm wouldn't last.

Much like this morning, the little sex they'd had all week entirely focused on Colt's supposed needs. Scared to refuse his husband's desires, he had played along. He'd grown suspicious of Gus's endeavors. It was like he was trying to rehabilitate Colt's sex drive one orgasm at a time. But then again, it might have been a unique kind of torture, having his personal prison ward please him when he was in no position to say no.

Colt's back arched from the relentless stimulation of his strongest erogenous zones. He pulled a pillow over his eyes out of instinct. Another shameful climax was on its way, no doubt with the power to deepen his self-loathing.

"You're so beautiful right now. You're close, aren't you? Time to bring you home," Gus said.

Colt's eyes opened wide when Gus put two wet fingers inside of him. The pillow had flown to the side, past the mattress. He struggled to breathe. It was the first time any part of Gus had entered him since that awful night. Not that it was in any way painful, but it made his reality all the more real. Gus would always be in control, doing to his body whatever he chose to, at any given time. He didn't even need permission, or consent. He'd just take whatever he needed from Colt's body—and in time, his mind. Colt would never have a say in any of it again.

Something in the look of his eyes must have changed while the epiphany emerged in his thoughts.

"Is something wrong?"

"No, honey. You're just really good at this. It's hard to keep up." As the words escaped his mouth he knew it sounded like an act. Though he tried to stop it, every time Gus brushed his prostate a twitch exploded from his hips. An ominous grin spread over his husband's face.

Gus sat on his knees and retracted. "I've got one more trick up my sleeve for today. I think it's time we fully reconnected. What do you say?"

It's sort of impossible for me to say no, remember?

Unable to say the words, Colt nodded. The alternative could have been ten times worse, he reasoned.

Slick with lube, Gus pushed inside—or invaded—him. Colt was still on his back, watching Gus ease into him with laser focus as his hips gained ground. He bit his lower lip against the discomfort, struggling to maintain his arousal.

"You're doing great, baby. God, I missed this. You're mine, Colt. Inside and out. Just the way it was always meant to be. I love you so much." He leaned in for a kiss as he bottomed out. Colt had swallowed down so many sobs his throat was now aching from the effort. He was afraid Gus would notice in the next few moans.

The thrusts accelerated and clearly targeted Colt's sweet spots. Ashamed to admit it as he was, Gus's tactics had been working. His uncontrollable gasps deepened, but he couldn't find joy in any of it. Colt kept his eyes on Gus, waiting for any sign of animalistic behavior in his features. He feared the *beast* would soon take over.

Gus halted. "You need to listen to me, baby. I need you to come. Do you understand?" he said with his growling voice.

"Gus, I….I don't think I can. I'm sorry."

Gus brushed the back of his hand over Colt's cheek. "Either you come, or I will. We both know you're going to like the first option a lot better. I don't want to hurt you, but don't think I won't."

Later, when they were in the middle of their post-sex shower ritual, Colt tried his best to wash away the disgust he felt at his sexual urges. Gus commanding him to climax and threatening with violence had sadly worked like a charm. It was the same reason he had returned to Gus's doorstep after that horrible first Grindr hookup: the irresistible hint of danger at the horizon calling out to him. Now that he was analyzing his sexual behavior under the hot water stream, he discovered he craved the prospect of violence, but not the concept itself. Maybe he wasn't as fucked up as he had always thought himself to be.

Gus was so gentle with him in the shower that it was

screwing with his mind. On one hand he welcomed the massages, the warmth of his embrace and the familiar scents of Gus's handpicked products. On the other, however, he cursed himself for not having learned his lesson after his first wedding night. If only he had walked away then and there. Life on the streets in Rio couldn't have been that much worse.

Gus stood behind him in the billowing steam, tracing every inch of his skin with his fingertips as though he were inspecting his property—which, in a way, he was. The bruise on his ribs had almost healed completely. As Gus's finger ran over it Colt wondered how long it would be before a new one would take its place.

When he tried to leave Gus's arms, the latter tightened his grip. "No. Not yet. I'm not ready to miss you. I wish we could stay here like this forever."

Colt relaxed as much as he could and said, "Me too," without needing to lie.

Eventually he got downstairs first, happy to see Langdon sitting at the kitchen island. It meant Gus would be out on business for the largest part of the day. Relief flooding his veins, his chest filled with deeper breaths.

"Good morning, Colt," Langdon said, raising his thermos at him.

"Good morning, Langdon. Where's Hannah?" Colt's eyes rolled over Langdon's usual dark outfit. He'd seen the off-brand pinstripe suit vest at least three times in one week.

How much had Gus been paying him all this time? *You can't buy loyalty like that.*

"She's at the farmers' market at The Grove. You've just missed her." Colt knew Hannah hated waiting for a late breakfast, especially without notice.

"Is everything all right?" Simple enough a question as it was, Colt contemplated his options. Just how far would Langdon's loyalty to Gus go? Was there any chance he would help him out? He glanced over his shoulder to check the staircase and started talking.

"No. Not at all. I need to talk to you about Gus, but I can't do that right now. Come find me at a better time." Just when he had pronounced the last hasted word he walked around the island to the stove and uncovered the cooled oatmeal Hannah had prepared for him.

"Good morning, Langdon. Tell me, isn't my husband the most beautiful creature you've seen in this house?" He was wearing the dark forest-green three-piece that made his eyes pop like emeralds.

"Good morning. I'm sure he is, Gustavo." Langdon's thin smile made Colt's heart sink. Of course he'd parrot anything Gus would tell him.

Putting a bowl of oatmeal into the microwave, Colt decided to make a bold move. "I don't know, honey. You might surpass me today in that gorgeous suit. I'm not sure I can let you leave like that."

Gus closed the distance between them, hoisted him onto the worktop and kissed him as if there were no Langdon watching them. The kiss went on longer than expected, leaving Colt out of breath.

"You should be punished for talking to me like that. We might get to that later," he said, raising his eyebrows. Then he looked over his shoulder and told Langdon to go start the car.

When they were alone, Gus took a step back and started rubbing the stubble on his chin.

"No breakfast?" Colt asked.

"Colt, cut the bullshit. What did you say to him?"

Fuck.

"Gus, I..." Colt started, "Look, I understand the workings of our new arrangement. I'm not stupid. Langdon's on your side. You've made that perfectly clear."

Gus's eyes traveled from his own feet to Colt's eyes in slow-motion. "Baby, I promise you'll get used to all of this soon. Just try not to do anything foolish. You won't like the consequences. Do you understand?"

Still seated on the island, Colt nodded and averted his eyes, unaware of his mistake.

Gus moved in, grabbed hold of Colt's chin with a tight squeeze and forced him to meet his eyes. "Answer me," he growled.

"I underst—understand," Colt said in a strained voice.

"Good." Gus planted another kiss on his lips. "I love you. See you at dinner tonight."

Having learned his lesson, Colt reciprocated the three words this time. As soon as Gus let go of him, he released the breath he'd been holding.

In the doorway, Gus turned around. "Oh, and be sure to do some workouts while I'm away. It's time you got back in shape."

"Will do." It took all of his strength not to cry until he was sure Gus was inside the car. The crying itself, however, did nothing to alleviate his hurt. Breathing became harder and he was rapidly turning light-headed. Black spots gathered all over his vision as he felt himself sway. Before they completely eclipsed the light of day, a blissful falling sensation took over.

"Colt! Colt! Please wake up. Fuck! You got to wake up. He'll blame this on me. Come on. Open your eyes for both our sakes, dammit," a familiar voice said as Colt struggled to open his eyes.

"Oh, thank God." A woman picked him up and held him around his waist. He'd been face down, which explained the peculiar point of view. The slate embroidered uniform was all he needed for identification.

"Hannah?"

"I'm here, Colt. Let's get you on this stool."

Colt marveled at the slender woman's strength as she hoisted him on the stool. His knees were still wobbly, but it was a relief to be vertical again.

Colt explained what had happened in the seconds before he had hit the ground after he had been left alone. Hannah nodded and inspected Colt's chin.

"I think you've had a panic attack. Have you had them before?"

"No, I don't think so." His brain started working again, so he added, "Don't tell Gus about this, okay?"

She looked outside the window as if she were checking

something. "Colt, you didn't hurt your chin when you collapsed, did you?"

A spark of hope made his breath catch. "I didn't, no. I need your help." He swallowed hard. "Gus. He, uhm—"

Hannah's hands flew up. "Stop. Don't say another word, Colt. Everything you tell me will go back to him. It's part of our arrangement. That also means I'll have to tell Gustavo you collapsed. I'm sorry, but I can't help you."

Blinking furiously, Colt asked her to repeat herself. On hearing it a second time, he got up from his chair and started pacing. "He always wins, doesn't he? There is no way out. There is no fucking way out. He's just going to take everything he needs from me until there's nothing left. Until either my mind or body is broken beyond repair. Every day he'll be killing me in what will go down as the slowest murder in recorded history." His breathing had turned into heaves again. "And now you're telling me you can't help me. So…what? You're just going to watch me suffer? Count my bruises while you're poaching eggs? You're a monster just like him, you know that?" The black spots were making a comeback as the room started spinning. Luckily Hannah was there to catch him this time.

"Colt, stay in your seat." He heard her rummaging through drawers in the kitchen.

"Breathe in this." Familiar with the technique, he held on tight to the paper bag from the farmers' market, which smelled of clementines.

"I really am sorry I can't help you out, Colt. I wish I could tell you why, but Gustavo's power over me and my career is indestructible." Her brown eyes pleaded for him to understand.

Colt wanted to tell her many things in response. Topping that list was expressing how badly she should go to hell. He further thought about asking more questions about her side of the arrangement, and lastly, he wanted to tell her how strength lay in numbers—that together with Langdon they could team up and find a way out of Gus's talons once and for all. However, he remained stoic as a nun of a silent order. Colt had been disappointed in people way too many times to still believe in HBO-type dramatic plot twists like that.

When it came down to it, no one was going to help anyone but themselves in this life—in this town. Colt didn't have much to offer when it came to changing Hannah's mind. What got him out of the dreadful kitchen was the hope that he might be able to persuade her one day. One thing he was sure of: he wasn't planning on giving up any time soon. He vowed to play the part of Gus's perfect trophy boy husband in the meantime, and headed to the gym room downstairs.

Chapter 17
Mel—Present

While Oliver Ryder guided Colt to interrogation room 2 for his polygraph test, Mel stayed behind in the conference room to wait for the Chief to finish her conversation with Cam. It was still odd to see his best friend in cahoots with the boss like this. Technically he outranked her, but from their respective body language no one would have been able to tell. To Mel it resembled running into high school teachers long after graduation. Just like with those teachers, he'd never heard Cam call the Chief by her first name.

He knew how the talk would go, as he had heard a preview the night before with Kate. When heading off to bed, she had cornered him in their bathroom, demanding an explanation to the scene she had walked into on her return from Zumba class.

"Honey, I know it may have looked weird, but trust me when I say it was the right thing to do. That was his first non-manipulative hug in years, Kate. Years."

"Mel, I'm not questioning your judgment. I was surprised, is all. It's not like you to get this close to one of the victims in your cases. I want you to be careful, honey.

There's a reason detectives don't usually open their houses to persons of interest. Don't get me wrong, I like Colt—it's hard not to—but I'm starting to think you're in over your head."

His marriage was so strong that Kate was often able to see things he himself couldn't. Therefore, he had learned, she was mostly right about her observations. The late-night discussion had ended in Mel making another promise to her. He wouldn't allow Colt to become closer than he already was to him. On the plus side of the argument, Kate had initiated sex almost right after, which had been long overdue. It could have been the after-Zumba drinks, but he couldn't have cared less.

Sitting in front of Captain Perez's mahogany desk reminded him of his group home years. He had once been summoned to the school principal, Mrs. Petrelli's, office after having beaten up a few bullies. The group of five teenagers had been harassing the new kid that week, Damien. Mel had intervened after watching them push the kid to the ground over and over again calling him names like *fuckface*, because of the kid's walnut-sized birthmark on his forehead. In hindsight, Mrs. Petrelli should have been more lenient to his good-hearted actions—especially since she herself had a neon-flashing wart on her chin. It was all Mel could look at during the reprimand while hearing how she would take away two weeks of TV privileges.

"So, Mel. This is new for me. In all the seven years I've never had to call you in here once on your job performance. What do you think is different this time?" the Chief asked.

Her legs were crossed at the knees while her hands made a steeple in her lap.

Mel sighed and had to restrain an eye roll. "It's because Colt has gotten too close to me or the other way around, I assume."

"You assume correctly, Detective, though assuming won't get you far. Make no mistake, Mel, I'm glad to see Colt trusts you. This could work miracles for our project with the DEA. But I have to warn you. Your integrity might be compromised without you realizing it. Somehow both of my SV detectives are now in too deep with this case. Take good care of Charlotte, Mel. The full scope of her trauma hasn't hit her yet."

He stared at her for a long time while his mind worked through a set of comebacks at the accusation the Chief had laid on him so elegantly. *How dare you question my integrity after all those years of case-solving magic on my side? I'm doing this to save lives and make this City of Angels live up to its name again.* His last thought, though he would never share it with anyone, was *you could never understand what it's like for foster kids like Colt and me in this world. Your parents never discarded you that way.*

Instead of venting those thoughts, he bit his tongue, then said "Okay, Chief. I understand your concern. What do you want me to do?" Maybe Mrs. Petrelli had taught him some things after all.

"I knew you would. You're an excellent detective, Mel. Just watch your back. Him trusting you doesn't mean you should trust *him* completely. There might be more to Colt than meets the eye. He's been through years of torture in any shape and size. That means his moral compass could be off-kilter. No one would blame him, but the last thing I want is for you to get in trouble."

After leaving the Chief's office Mel knocked on the opened door to his own, where Charlotte's eyes were scanning her laptop screen.

"Partner, we're going to lunch. Chief's orders."

"Okay, as long as we'll be back before Colt's polygraph ends." He wanted to high-five her then and there.

Mel agreed and drove Charlotte to ArmaDylan's Diner on Santa Monica Boulevard. Apart from their no-nonsense, anti-gluten-free policy, Mel could never resist their brioche French toast. The day he'd been having so far had the words French toast written all over it—in a bacon font. The square booths stood facing each other in two neat rows, which made it ideal for quick lunch breaks. The fake moss-green leather didn't allow people to sit for longer than half an hour, anyway—not if they didn't want to peel themselves off the seats. What the service staff in pastel yellow uniforms lacked in kindness, they made up for in speed.

While he was gathering courage to tell Charlotte what she needed to hear, he talked about their case until their order arrived with a refill of their coffee mugs.

"So, Charlotte. There's a reason I took you to lunch. One, I hope you won't be mad for. Well, even if you do start to yell, I won't mind. As long as you'll feel better, I'll handle everything you throw at me. But maybe not the French toast. That'd be a waste. Now tell me how you're feeling. And don't give me that bullshit about how work is pulling you through the trauma like some magic savior. We're not leaving this place until you tell me what's really going on."

Charlotte waited, then said, "Are you done?"

Mel nodded.

"Mel, I…" Her gaze dropped to the lower side of her plate. "Okay, fine. I'm not doing great. I can't sleep. I can't eat, I can't get close to anyone physically, not even Dad. I am never setting foot in that apartment again. It keeps replaying in my head whenever I pause for too long, so I try to stay busy." She looked right at Mel again. "We've seen our share of victims—well, you've seen a lot more of them—but it didn't prepare me in the slightest. The physical pain is nothing compared to the terror that comes with it.

"They used me to get to Colt. It wasn't even personal. I was just a prop to their show. A means to an end. Wrong place, wrong time. Simple as that. I wasn't their target, but I had to let them hold me down and attack me all the same. That makes it even more fucked-up somehow." Her welled-up eyes started overflowing, so Mel handed her a napkin from the chrome dispenser.

Mel couldn't help but smile at her. Showing emotions was hard on Charlotte, and this counted as the first time she had really allowed Mel into her head. Four months of partnership during which he had been patient as a primary school special needs teacher had finally paid off.

"I'm proud of you, partner. That must have been hard. I know you prefer to hide your emotions. Thank you for letting me in. We should do this more often. Well, without another assault, of course."

A tiny smile met his gaze across the table for a fleeting

second. "Definitely. I've also decided on something. After this case I'm taking some time off. I'm not leaving until there's justice, but after that, I need to reassess my life. There's got to be more than work out there. If I hadn't been so diligent and over-the-top, trying to move our case forward, then none of this would have happened. It's a cruel wake-up call, but maybe it leads to a better, more balanced future for me. If I ever get to leave Dad's house, that is. Don't get me wrong, I love him, but he's just as intense at home as he is in court. Perhaps more."

"I'd be in even worse shape if I were him right now. Your father has every right to be furious with the world. Do you want me to go talk to him?"

"No. He has trouble opening up to people he doesn't know that well." She smiled and said, "I guess that part of him kind of rubbed off on me."

Mel pantomimed zipping his mouth shut.

Her phone rang. After checking the screen she said "Speaking of the devil."

Mel listened to the one end of the conversation while he chewed his maple-syrup-injected toast. Five mono-syllabic responses later she hung up and broke the good news to Mel about the warrant coming through for tomorrow's raid on Gus's house and offices.

After completing their meals Mel got up and waited for Charlotte. Her phone rang again, so he turned to start in the direction of the register.

Charlotte answered and pulled at Mel's wrist to stop him.

"Yes, I think so. I'm the one you talked to earlier."

Still holding his wrist, Charlotte's eyes went wide as she faced him.

"Ma'am, do you want your son to call you back? I can do that in half an hour or less." After the other person stopped she said, "Are you sure?" She let go of his wrist and ended the call with, "I understand. I'll tell him. Sorry for your loss, ma'am."

When they walked back into the kitchen of the station Colt was talking to Oliver Ryder, his designated babysitter for the day. Mel tried to avoid eye contact and focused on Oliver, who seemed to take his job rather seriously. If Mel had to guess, it was all part of falling into the Chief's good graces again. She could be forgiving, if she wanted to be.

"We'll take it from here, Ol," Mel said.

"Okay. I could stay close if you want. Colt, it was nice meeting you."

Colt nodded with a thin smile, and watched him leave. "Is it just me or did that boss lady assign the rookie cop to my care?"

"You guessed it," Mel said. Charlotte had closed the door to the hallway. They had shared one glance too many.

"Mel? What's going on?" Colt asked.

Taking a seat in front of him, Mel forced himself to make eye contact. On their way back Charlotte had agreed he'd be the one to tell him. Hard as it would be, he wouldn't have had it any other way.

He swallowed and said, "Your brother is dead. I'm so sorry." Delivering bad news wasn't something Mel had to do often in the Special Victims Division, but he had paid attention in his training. Most people on the receiving end were only able to register the first six words. Any further information would dissolve in the shock of the moment.

Colt blinked as his forehead creased in slow-motion. "What? No. Why would you say that?" His eyes landed on Charlotte, then shot back to Mel. "It's got to be Gus playing more of his sick games on us. Where did you even get this shit?"

"Colt, listen to me. Your mother called Charlotte and asked us to break the news to you. She's not ready to talk to you. Not yet," Mel said in a soft voice.

Mel watched his eyebrows lift as acceptance closed in on Colt's mind. "Tell me it's not true… Please? Oh my God, Dave." He collapsed in on himself with his head hovering over his knees, his voice building to a low wail—in perfect pitch. In the other room heads rose from their seats through the glass walls. While Colt's body gave way to his grief, the Chief briefly appeared at the door to check out the disturbance.

"Tell me what happened," Colt finally said, sniffling.

Charlotte jumped in and recounted his mother's phone call half an hour before. "Your brother died in a subway accident. He fell on the tracks somewhere in the Bronx and hit the back of his head."

Charlotte handed him a water bottle from the fridge. He turned to Mel after a long swig. "There's no way what happened to Dave was an accident. It's literally what Gus threatened to do to punish me. My brother is dead because of me—because I got away. He'll never stop until he gets what he wants. Until he gets me back in that house. Maybe I should just go. I'm putting you all in danger. Everyone here. Mom's probably next."

Mel rose and knelt before him. "Colt, don't say that. Gus enables all the cartel's crimes here in LA. All the rapes, the murders, the extortions, all of it. More lives will be destroyed if you allow him to go on. You can't give up. I won't let you. Are you hearing me?"

When he resumed sobbing Colt flung his arms around Mel and shed tears on his shoulder. He knew there wasn't any harm in the gesture—not that he really had a choice this time—but he was glad the Chief hadn't seen it all the same.

Before Mel took Colt home he talked to Gene about the polygraph test while Charlotte went off to her psychological evaluation downtown. In general, Colt had passed the test with flying colors. The first few baseline questions had been hard to read according to Gene. "He seemed awfully anxious to be alone with me in that room. You'll be glad to hear I apologized for hitting him. Go ahead and gloat, Mel. Anyway, from that point on it was smooth sailing." Try as he did, Mel couldn't stop the smirk on his face.

There was one thing that had bothered Gene during the interview. When asked about the nature of his relationship with Steve Blake, Colt's polygraph readings had shown irregularities. "See these tremors here?" Gene pointed to the uneven scribblings of Colt's vitals. "They're not strong enough to constitute a lie, especially not since it's the only slip-up in the whole test. Like I said, this won't hold up in court once this shit show goes to trial. If they find that gun tomorrow and all the forensics line up to point in his direction, I'm not sure we'll be able to stop the ball from rolling."

Chapter 18
Colt—Past

When Colt awoke he couldn't move. He lay on his right side as the little spoon with his husband's right arm under his pillow and the other resting on his abdomen. Not that he was physically unable to, he just couldn't risk waking Gus before the alarm of his Apple Watch would start buzzing. Two months after the fallout of his new situation, Colt was still waiting for Gus to explode with anger like before. The unpredictability had kept him on edge.

It had almost felt too easy to obey Gus's wishes during those eight weeks. He had worked out more hours than in the whole of last year, had made all the right food decisions, hadn't strayed from the house…and had been able to push the terror down long enough to satisfy Gus's sexual urges. In return, his husband had showered him with more gifts and weekend outings across town. Colt had even experienced a few moments when he had almost forgotten about his enslavement altogether.

The buzzing alarm had Gus squeezing Colt's naked body harder. "Good morning, beautiful." He dropped two kisses on Colt's neck. "You were spectacular last night. I'm hard just thinking about it." Gus pushed his erection between Colt's thighs. "And you're so tight. That gym time has really paid off. I mean, look at you. I'm so lucky to call you mine."

Yes, so fucking lucky.

Colt had indeed outdone himself when it came to sculpting his body, and not just because of his husband's lowly comment about him being out of shape. The purpose to his spartan workout routines was threefold. One, it kept him in Gus's good graces to show him how he would obey his every word. Two, it made him strong so that he'd be able to defend himself should Gus's violent side take over again. Three, it helped stave off the downward helix of thoughts.

When he stepped out of the shower, Colt noticed a new bruise on his left bicep. It was so distinct he could count Gus's fingers on his skin. As he touched it he couldn't help but see it as a bad omen for worse things to come. Tension had been building in the last couple of days, ever since Gus had announced a new business dinner he needed Colt to attend. His body had gone rigid on hearing those two words, as though he were enduring an aftershock of the horror of the previous one. When Gus looked at him, he detected a change in the shade of his eyes. It was a darker and somehow colder green than the week before.

Throughout the day Colt had only one goal in mind: doing everything in his power to make the dinner a success—avoiding repeat mistakes at all costs. He kept an eye on his watch and planned to get dressed at least an hour in advance. He made a list of conversation topics and rehearsed stories about his marriage in front of the dressing mirror. And to leave no stone unturned, he had asked Gus to have their hairdresser come over.

November in LA being one of those unpredictable months temperature-wise, Colt had agreed on a plain black suit, a cream business shirt with a band collar and his new cashmere and silk Hermès scarf with orange pops of color–very Holmby Hills. More money than he had ever earned in a year was hanging from his admirable physique. Colt had come a long way from Koreatown, though he never would have been able to imagine the price he'd have to pay. He shook the thought from his mind and pulled his black leather Prada loafers out of the drawer. They would surely seal the deal for the look he was going for—or so he thought.

"Is that what you'll be wearing?" Gus said behind him, his tone colder than before.

"Uhm, yes. You don't like it?"

"Keep the scarf, but change the shirt. Oh, and make sure you wear a tie, too. Something classy."

Colt changed into a plain white shirt and picked out a black tie with an orange floral pattern, careful to match the scarf's color. Gus had just put on his suit pants and walked over bare-chested.

"No, no no. You got it all wrong. By the way, what is up with those hideous shoes?"

Something was definitely off. Colt's breaths came faster as he undressed again in the shadow of Gus's intimidating figure. He stared into those eyes quietly for a moment too long.

"What are you waiting for? We're not going to be late, so hurry up."

In the softest voice he could summon, Colt said, "Honey, can you just pick something for me? I'm not sure what it is you want me to do here, and we're running out of time."

Gus sighed and pinched the bridge of his nose. "You've got to be kidding me. Okay, fine." He went through drawers and racks with the grace of a grizzly bear, throwing clothes to the floor in the process. The outfit he had chosen was a navy blue suit and tie, a light-blue patterned shirt, a cream and gold Hermès scarf and suede loafers with a golden buckle. Colt was finally able to relax again when Gus nodded his approval. He didn't allow his mind to travel down the road of what-ifs, because if he had imagined other outcomes to this scene, he would have started trembling for sure.

On their way to the Blanc Nez de Provence restaurant on Melrose Avenue Gus hadn't said a word since shutting his car door. The privacy screen in the Bentley made it even more awkward than last time. When Colt complimented Gus's outfit, he had only grunted in return, so he gave up on small talk and hoped Langdon would do the same.

Colt's mental strength was no match for the flood of recollections from the last business dinner he had to attend with Gus. His left wrist stung when he remembered the phone call to his mother two days after. Painful as it had been, he knew it was the only way to keep her and his brother safe.

"I'm not sure, Gus. She'll see right through this," he said after scribbling down his speech on Gus's legal pad. They were sitting at Gus's home desk.

"Don't worry. I've got a back-up plan in case she doesn't believe you right away. You got this."

"Is there any other way we can do this? I won't run, I promise. You win. Can't that be enough for you?"

Gus held his wrist tightly as he said, "Make the call."

Colt dialed the number and desperately tried to control his breathing while the connection was established.

"Anna Whittaker, who is this?"

"Mom, it's me."

"Collie! I'm so glad to hear your voice. When are you boys coming to Kansas? I've missed you."

Colt swallowed hard and took a deep breath, scanning his notes. "Mom, listen to me. I need to tell you something. The reason I'm calling is to say goodbye."

A beat passed. "Goodbye? Collie, what are you talking about?"

"Let me explain. Since our wedding I've been very happy here in LA. It made me realize how…toxic you've been in my life. Mom, I can't keep trying to turn you into something you're not. I want to live a good, healthy life, and I don't think you can contribute to that. Too much has happened between us."

"I don't…I can't… Where the hell is this coming from?

What's wrong? What happened? Is someone threatening you or something? Colt, this isn't you. Is it Gus? Is he doing this?"

Fuck.

"No, Mom. This is all me. You'll be better off without me, anyway. Look at it this way. Now you'll be able to focus on Gerald and Dave. Conflict-free, just like you always wanted."

A sharp inhale followed by a stuttering sob boomed through the speaker. Colt's eyes misted over, but Gus's grip on his wrist kept him focused.

His mother coughed to steady herself, then gave into her rage. "You can't be serious. I'm not giving up on my son, you hear me? I love you, Colt. I'm your mother. I don't understand any of this. We were good last time I saw you. I respected your wish to elope. Even though I wanted to be there with you, I sacrificed my wish for your happiness. That's what parents do, Colt. You don't get to discard me now that you're rich. Are you hearing me?" Her final phrase was a hysterical shout, every word stabbing and clawing its way into Colt's mind.

His throat felt blocked. This was exactly what he had feared would happen. Gus handed him a note that made his blood run cold—colder than the glass of the desk. He shook his head, but an encouraging show of force targeting his wrist once more had him grimacing, and talking again.

"Mom, if you don't leave me alone, I will sue you for child abuse. Gus's lawyer will take you for all you have. I'll get the group home counselors to testify against you."

Anna seemed stunned in the silence that followed.

"What the fuck? You wouldn't. Collie, we were good. Why would you do such a thing?"

"That's the deal, *Anna*. I'm sorry. I love you. Goodbye."

Gus had complimented him on his ingenuity to use his mother's first name, but Colt had been too busy crumbling down to the floor to register it. The pain of his bruised ribs had been nothing compared to the hollowness in his chest.

Thinking about his mom right then wasn't going to help Colt turn this night into a personal victory in his imprisoned state, so he took Gus's hand and smiled at his husband saying "I love you." Gus smiled and said it back. *So far so good. I can do this.*

Once inside the packed restaurant Gus didn't let go of his hand and flashed his Hollywood smile at everyone around him. Since they had arrived half an hour early, the maître d' led them to their dinner dates who had already been sitting at the bar.

"Gustavo, glad you made it. We always arrive early, too. Great minds and all that, am I right?" the Latino man said.

"Alejandro, good to see you, too," Gus said, shaking the man's hand. "Colt, this is Alejandro Suarez, and his husband, Jonathan Greer. Gentlemen, this is Colt, my greatest achievement."

When Jonathan was done sipping his Martini, he turned to shake Colt's hand. Just like Colt's, his eyes went wide.

No way. No fucking way.

"Nice to meet you, Alejandro and Jonathan," he said,

wishing Jonathan would play along. If only his eyes could have sent him the message.

"Colt? I thought that was you. Come here, you," Jonathan said, pulling Colt in for a hug and a kiss on his cheek. Colt's heart jackhammered. There was no way Gus would be okay with this—especially not today.

"My God. How long has it been since our little, uhm, rendezvous? Two, maybe three years? But hey, look at us now, married to these gorgeous men. I'll drink to that."

The innocent lights appearing in those blue eyes jogged Colt's memory. "I think it was two years ago. You were living in that house in, uhm, Faircrest Heights or something?"

"Yes, wow, you really do remember me," he said, then turned to Gus with his palms up. "Don't worry, Gustavo, he's all yours. Your husband and I had one encounter. I didn't even know his last name, I swear. Please don't hurt me," Jonathan said. He covered his face, then chuckled at his joke.

Little does he know.

Gus's expression was hard to read. He seemed undecided between a polite smile and a dagger-shooting stare. Then the million-dollar smile took over, allowing Colt to breathe again.

Blanc Nez de Provence, except for being yet another French-wannabe restaurant, specialized in seafood dishes and had accumulated pristine reviews. Looking around the place, everything about the interior screamed the word *ocean*. The light fixtures were white paper fishnets in billowing shapes, while the teal walls were covered in haphazard patterns of seashell clusters. The amuse-bouches sat on columns in the shape of seagull legs—a comical sight that lightened the mood.

Sitting at their table and having ordered a second round of drinks, Colt remembered all too well why Jonathan had been so unforgettable as a Grindr hookup.

"I'm telling you, this time next year Ale and I will be the owners of the number one Andalusian horse farm in all of Southern California. I know how it sounds, but we've been making some clever investments in the sperm trade, making sure only the best of the best ended up in our hands—and our mares' uteruses, obviously. But it really is only one part of the whole industry. Do you want to know why our fawns grow up to become million-dollar prize winners at shows? We feed them the best organic food on the planet. Not one fiber in their meals has been compromised by human interference. I'm sorry, I've been rambling on and on, haven't I?"

The guy never shut up. Despite the question at the end, Colt knew the incessant chatter would just keep flooding their table. It was too bad, really, considering his angelic looks. Focusing on that carved square jaw and shiny straw-colored hair—which he knew was even softer to the touch—made it a little easier to pretend to be listening to the guy. Alejandro must have been head over heels for his husband by the way he looked at him.

Alejandro's intense dark-eyed stare landed on Colt when he asked, "Colt, your accent is a little hard to place. Where are you from, originally?"

"Topeka, Kansas, if you can believe it," Colt said, thickening his accent like he had practiced in the mirror.

"Wow, must have been quite the adjustment. I got to say, California seems to agree with you. Nice tan, healthy complexion. It appears you've gone all in with the LA gym lifestyle, too. Good for you," Alejandro said, raising his glass at Colt. The man's eyes rolled down Colt's chest, which was getting increasingly uncomfortable. He was good-looking, but in an intimidating way with his thick immaculately kept beard and buzz-cut. A little too smooth in his ways, to Colt's liking.

Exactly my type, sadly.

"Thank you for noticing. You're very kind." Roughly translated: *stay away from me, you don't want to find out what my husband would do to you.*

"I, for one, can't wait to live here in Hollywood Hills myself. Tell me, Colt, what's it like?" Jonathan asked.

Colt took another sip of his Strawberry Daiquiri before he answered. "If I'm being honest, it's far better than anyone from the outside thinks. Whenever you hear people bitch about their rich snobbish neighbors, the filthy smog hanging over the city or the impossible traffic between the hills and downtown, they're just raining on your parade. Those views of both the Pacific with its Santa Monica Pier and downtown LA with those gleaming skyscrapers never get old. You wouldn't believe how quiet it can get up there. It really is the best place to live, no matter how you look at it. I'm so lucky Gus took me in. You have no idea." He grabbed Gus's hand and kissed it. At least the last phrase was true. Gus was leaning his elbow on the back of his chair, and gazed at him the way he had done on their first date. Colt felt a pang of bittersweet longing.

After their main courses—salmon filets, smoked halibut and almond-crusted swordfish—the subject of Alejandro's job as a hedge fund manager arose. Jonathan once again failed to keep his trap shut, to his husband's dismay. "It's so secretive you'd think he's with the FBI or CIA or something. I stopped asking questions a while ago. I really don't care where the money comes from, as long as it maintains a steady flow."

"Maybe take it easy with the drinks, honey," Alejandro said with a not-so-loving scowl on his face, then he explained how it's just a consequence of him working for very private people in business and politics. Colt decided then and there the guy couldn't be trusted.

"If you'll excuse me, I need to go use the restroom," Colt said, throwing his napkin on the table.

"Me too, actually," Gus said. "I'm sure you guys will understand." He winked at Jonathan and Alejandro and took hold of Colt's hand again on their way.

While Colt was going about his business in the stall, he heard Gus whisper to the other men in the room, after which they disappeared one by one.

"Thank you, Carlos. Twenty minutes. I'll make it worth your while," Gus told the bathroom attendant.

As Colt walked out of the stall to the sinks, he saw Gus lock the door. "Honey, is everything okay?"

"Sure, I just wanted a little privacy, is all. I don't know about you, but if I hear about horse breeding one more time I'm going to gag."

Colt snickered as he soaped his hands. "Maybe it's all the action they got this week."

Gus chuckled, baring his teeth. "No, that can't be it. I bet it's the only way to shut Jonathan up."

Colt howled with laughter. It being the first time in months, his stomach hurt with the best kind of pain. It felt oddly normal to unwind with Gus like this. It allowed Colt a glimpse into the life they could have led. He hated how that beautiful smile on his husband's face still did things to his head he couldn't put into words.

"Anyway. So how are you liking them so far?" Gus asked.

"They're nice. Jonathan indeed talks way too much, but other than that he's nice enough. Alejandro, on the other hand, can be a little unnerving. What do you think?" Colt was drying his hands, not wanting to meet Gus's eyes right away as he spoke. He didn't have a clue what this private moment would really be about. Instead he studied the matte black taps and bowl-shaped sinks.

Gus walked up to him and leaned his backside against the sink, folding his arms. "Nice enough, huh?"

The elephant in the room made Colt forget about the laughter they had just shared. "Gus, look, I'm sorry about that. It was only one time, way before we met. He told me his name was Nate back then. Besides, you know I was on Grindr for quite some time." Before going down the apology road too far, Colt switched gears. "If it makes you feel better, the guy can't hold a candle to you, honey," he said, putting his hand on Gus's elbow.

"Glad to hear it. I'm going to need more than just your

word, though. We've got twenty minutes." The dark shade in his eyes had returned as they bore into Colt's.

Colt's heart was pounding. The locked door, the tip to the attendant.

Please let me be wrong about this.

Gus started unbuckling his belt. "I need you to give me some kind of assurance that you'll remember who it is you belong to. You're going to suck me off, Colt." The matter-of-fact tone of his voice made Colt's heart sink.

"Gus. You can't be serious. They'll know something is wrong if we stay here too long."

Gus licked his lips. "They'll understand. I'm pretty sure they're into this kind of thing. I can practically see Alejandro salivating in my mind."

Colt froze from head to toe. He didn't dare speak his mind, not with such darkness staring back at him.

If I screamed, would anyone come to my rescue?

He immediately saw the futility of his thought and remained silent.

"Come on, then. Get to it. It's not a big deal. You've done this dozens of times before and enjoyed yourself plenty. It's kind of hot in this public space, isn't it?"

Colt still hadn't moved, praying for a knock on the door.

"Baby," Gus continued, "I hate to say it, but you won't like the second option here. People slip and fall in bathrooms all the time."

Left with no more options, Colt forced his legs to move and got to his knees before his husband. His hands struggled when he freed Gus's impossibly hard cock from its confinements. The threats had turned him on, which made Colt sick to his stomach, knowing it would always be like this. Luckily he knew how Gus liked it: no teasing, hard and fast, and a lot of appreciative sounds.

Gus loved every second and looked down at him with a sated grin. When he couldn't help himself anymore, he held Colt's head on both sides and started thrusting. Colt gagged, coughed and wept, gasping for breath. When he finally came, he instructed Colt to swallow and only pulled out of him when he was sure Colt had obeyed.

Then he cupped Colt's jaw in both hands and said, "I love you, baby. You're the best. Sorry if I got a little rough." He ran his thumb across Colt's cheek, catching a tear. "Now clean yourself up. I'll go back to our table and explain. Oh, but don't keep us waiting for too long, okay?"

Not waiting for an answer, he kissed Colt deeply, taking his time to savor his own taste. Satisfied in more ways than one, he unlocked the door and walked away. Colt didn't dare to look at his reflection in the mirror, at what he had become. He was afraid he'd never stop screaming if he did.

Chapter 19
Mel—Present

Mel didn't understand what was happening. One minute he was balls-deep into his ex-girlfriend Amber Bondarenko, cupping her breasts as she begged for more, the next his head was pounding from the rude awakening rocking his shoulder. *Rose?* Unless he had been sleeping for four years it couldn't have been his daughter.

"Mel, please wake up."

He groaned and felt a hand cover his mouth.

"You'll wake her. Sorry, but I really need you," Colt whispered, breaking all kinds of boundaries again.

He sat upright and waited for his circulation to resolve the situation in his pants, to Colt's gesturing frustration. Mel sure wasn't planning on explaining it to Colt, of all people—not in these loose pajama pants. Kate stirred next to him.

Once downstairs he had finally rubbed away his blurred vision. Colt had turned the light on the sideboard at the dinner table on and sat on the far chair with his hands gathered on the table.

"Needed a little time to fix the wooden situation?"

Mel's eyes went wide, so much so it hurt.

"Sorry. Don't answer that. Apologies for waking you. And for overstepping once more."

Mel sat opposite him. "It's all right. What's on your mind?"

Colt looked down at his hands and said, "Is it at all possible for me to attend Dave's funeral?"

Hard as the answer would be for Colt to stomach, he needed to hear it. "No, Colt. It is not. It's too dangerous for you to be out in the open like that. You're the only connection between Gus and the cartel we've found. If something happened to you, getting justice for all those faces you saw on the whiteboard yesterday would become next to impossible. I'm sorry, but that's the way it has to be."

Colt's eyes filled. "I knew you were going to say that, but I had to try. I just wish Dave didn't hate me as much as I think he did. He didn't deserve to die like that. Not while he was doing okay for the first time in his life."

There was no way Mel could leave Colt on his own like this. As a young father, what harm would another sleepless night do in the grand scheme of things, anyway?

"Tell me about your brother. Was he in the system too?"

Colt nodded. "He was. Although, he had it worse than me. In our first group home we got separated the minute we got there. Because of my continuous screaming for my mom, they took me to the back room of the house while he was shipped off to a foster family. I don't need to tell you how quickly I toughened up after that first day."

Mel took a strained breath at the memory of his own

first days in group homes. The pecking order between kids of all sizes kicked in right away, no matter how hard anyone cried upon arrival, or who brought them in. Without realizing the extent of the hurt, children could be extremely rough on one another in places like that.

"When the foster family had kicked him out after a few months he was forever changed. We both looked roughed up, but his wounds ran a lot deeper than mine. His cheeks had sunken, his eyes were staring at nothing in particular and he barely acknowledged me at times. That's when he got mad and started blaming me for being the luckier one. Dave never opened up about his experiences with that family, so I'll never know what that they did to him."

Colt went on to talk about the troubled teenager Dave was—a kid that steered to drugs and booze whenever he wanted to escape his memories or the reality of his forever scarred youth. When he aged out of the system he took his chances under the bright lights of New York City instead of going back to their mother. "The guilt often got too much for our mom, so she would send him money whenever she could. Even though we were sure he'd snort or drink every last cent, she did it to help her sleep at night." Two years before Colt's wedding Dave had gotten clean and completed his nursing school degree at the Borough of Manhattan Community College. The last thing Colt had heard of his brother was that he had started working at North General Hospital as an OR scrub nurse.

Footsteps on the staircase turned both their heads in their direction. Kate's silver silk nightgown shimmered as she made her way to the table.

"You guys, it's really late—or early, I suppose. What's going on?" She leaned into Mel, who wrapped an arm around her waist. He really loved the way the material curved over his wife's hips. As if she'd read his thoughts, she tugged at the hem of her gown to pull it down.

"Oh God, this is not an official interrogation or anything, is it?" she asked.

"No, Kate, feel free to join us. I was just telling Mel a little about my brother. Turns out I'm not even going to be at his funeral service."

Kate took the chair next to Mel, still holding his hand. "I'm sorry, Colt. If there's anything I can do, please let me know. I hate how this brings you down on top of everything else. It's not fair." It could have been the nightgown clouding his judgment, but Mel's heart melted hearing Kate's kind words. Rose was lucky to be her daughter.

"You've done plenty for me, Kate. But thanks for asking." Colt's smile didn't reach his eyes.

Mel noticed Colt's foot bouncing under the table. Aside from his apparent grief, there was another layer to his edginess tonight.

"Colt, are you nervous for tomorrow?" Mel asked.

Colt nodded slowly. "Is it that obvious? I've been trying not to think about it, but once they find that gun everything will change, right? Just like Gus intended."

Kate gave him a puzzled look, but remained silent.

"Even though you aced the polygraph test, you might get arrested, yes. They'll have to report it to the District Attorney, so it will take some strong-arming from both Cam and the Chief to stop it," Mel said.

"I understand—I think. Well, in case they come for me tomorrow, I want to thank you both for taking me in. I hope someday I'll be able to repay you. Mel, you're the first man I've trusted in a long time. You're going to be a great dad. You know, some day." He winked at Mel, who snickered at the jab. This was going to take a lot of explaining to Kate after this conversation. "Kate, I know you weren't on board that first night, so thank you for letting me stay. It was the singing to Rose that did it, right?"

"Absolutely. If it were up to me, I wouldn't let you out of this house until she's eight," Kate said and soon regretted her comeback. With her palm against her forehead she said, "Oh my God, I'm so sorry. I don't know why I said that. I didn't mean anything by it."

Colt smiled and said, "It's okay, Kate. A little soon to joke about it, though." He suppressed a yawn and said, "You know what I hate about all of this, Mel? Gus is too fucking smart to leave breadcrumbs, so even though it's a raid on his house, I'll be the one going down. Like I said, he always wins. If only there were a way to get him, to lock him out of my life and throw away the key."

Colt stared at his hands on the table, then inhaled sharply. "Hold on. That's it. There's a way." His eyes widened. "You're not going to like it, Mel, but there's one way to ensure Gus will step out of line long enough for you to catch him. One way to make him lose control like you can't imagine."

By the end of Colt's wild suggestion, Mel was almost screaming in his opposition to the idea. Kate had gone upstairs to Rose just in time to avoid hearing the worst of it.

Softening toward the end of the discussion, Mel promised he'd think about it, no matter how insane the idea sounded.

The next day Gus answered the intercom at the gate of his mansion after three buzzes. "Who is this? What do you want?"

"This is DEA special agent Espinoza. I have a warrant to search your house and your offices," Cam said, holding out the printed document in front of the camera in his Kevlar vest. Waiting to be buzzed through, Mel counted four cars driving by—four cars filled with neighbors gobbling up the sight for future gossip. He hated how Kevlar vests always made his shirt cling to his skin.

Once through the gate, the team of ten DEA agents wasted no time approaching the front door, where Gus stood waiting for them, espresso cup in hand.

"Good morning. Make yourselves at home. Where do you want me?" Gus asked, looking a lot healthier than he had three days before. Of course, a pristine white business shirt with rolled-up sleeves on top of pinstripe suit pants would have ameliorated any Cedars Sinai patient's looks.

After handing him a copy of the warrant—stating all places the DEA was about to turn inside out in the house—Cam and Mel took him to the back deck next to the pool. Downtown, Gene and Ray were searching the Carolino Real Estate offices at the same time. On informing Gus, he mentioned Natalee Prescott would be dealing with things on that end.

Gus sat on one of the lounge chairs with a wince as he clenched his left side.

"How are your wounds healing, Mr. Carolino?" Mel asked.

Faster than Colt's?

"It's getting there. Shouldn't be long before I'm all up and running again. Thank you for asking, Detective Daniels."

"Sir, if there's anything you need to tell us right now, it will be on the record. It might help your case when it goes to trial," Cam said.

"You mean *if* it goes to trial. No, I don't think so. Honestly, except for maybe some colorful porn on my computer, I've got nothing to be afraid of. Search all you want."

"You'll have to come to the station for an official interrogation once we've conducted a thorough investigation of your files," Cam said.

"I understand. FYI, my attorney's on his way. But on a different note, how's my husband?"

A man and a woman wearing white hazmat suits stepped out. The man whispered something to Cam, after which he gave his approval.

"Your husband is doing fine, given the circumstances. We're keeping him safe for the time being," Mel said.

"That's good to know. I wish he were here. The place is not the same without him. *I* am not the same without him."

Was it all part of his act or was there truth to his words?

Mel couldn't tell. He imagined Gus really did love Colt on some level, in his own possessive and controlling way.

"Agent Espinoza, we've located the safe," another hazmat man announced from the doorstep.

"Mr. Carolino, can you open your office safe? We'll open it anyway, but you might not want it back once we're through the process," Cam said.

Gus shrugged. "Sure. Like I said, I've got nothing to be afraid of." He stood, steadied himself with a small step back, and headed into his office with Cam and Mel close behind. Looking over his shoulder, Mel took in the diamond-shaped pool surrounded by a mahogany deck all around, with views of both the Pacific and Downtown. Mel marveled at the sight, and wondered if it helped crooks like Gus sleep at night.

The Rio De Janeiro painting had been slid to the left to reveal the vault's stainless steel door. Gus fumbled with the wheel, holding his right ear out to hear the satisfying clicks of the combination lock. Mel's heartbeat was ringing in his ears as he waited for the moment of truth that had kept both him and Colt awake.

Time seemed to stand still as two hazmat people rummaged through the small space, blocking the view. One of them turned around and shook his head. No gun. A handful of Manila binders aside, there was nothing in the secure space.

Mel's head whipped in Gus's direction just in time to see the hint of a smirk flash across his mouth before he put on his poker face again.

He knew. He fucking knew.

Back at the station, Mel reported back to Charlotte in their office. Her pressed red blazer told him the psych evaluation had been a breeze. He had already texted Kate to inform Colt about the missing gun. Undecided whether it was good or bad news, he was dying to get some good detective work done as they waited for the IT department of the DEA to do their job.

"Man, just when you think this case is headed in one direction it just boomerangs back in our faces. If this is indeed an elaborate scheme to discredit Colt, then he's doing a hell of a job at it," Charlotte said.

"We'll just have to trust the process and cover more ground in the meantime. Ready to take this show on the road?" Mel asked.

Dr. Erik Petersen's private practice in Brentwood Park was only a ten-minute drive from the West LA station. South Bristol Avenue, known for its roundabouts in between majestic palm-tree parks, looked as though it were part of the therapist experience all on its own. Long before anyone would step into Dr. Petersen's home office, their anxiety levels would have halved from the surrounding scenery alone. The doctor's white Mexican-inspired house with a round tower in the middle featured a golden plaque reading his title on the front gate. Apparently the man specialized in medical psychotherapy. With Colt's written letter of consent in hand, Mel and Charlotte rang the doorbell.

As the good doctor scrutinized the document with his tiny rounded glasses, Mel took in the vibe of the place and decided he didn't like it one bit. A glass-topped coffee table and matching desk with a metallic monstrosity as its foot gave off a chilly mood, while the black leather reclining chair—a cliché Mel couldn't believe still existed—looked about as comfortable as a dentist's chair. A silver rug had every intention to warm the place up, but was no match to the rest of the furniture. Especially not with the three chrome bookcases behind the desk.

"Well, I suppose this will do. May I ask why Mr. Whittaker's mental health is of any concern to the LAPD?" Dr. Petersen asked.

Charlotte answered, "Colt is a person of interest to us in an ongoing case. This interview is all about covering as many tracks as we can."

"Person of interest. I see," the doctor said, rubbing the white beard on his chin. "Let me guess. You want to make sure some cocky lawyer doesn't destroy Colt's testimony in court on the grounds of mental health issues." The framed Ivy League degrees on the right wall near the door had paid off.

"Sure, let's go with that. So, what can you tell us about Colt?" Mel asked.

Dr. Petersen folded his Harry Potter glasses into the breast pocket of his powder-blue checkered button-down. His beady brown eyes teetered between Charlotte and Mel before he spoke. "I had to review my notes last night, given that it's been a few years since I last talked to him. It's my process, as it fires all the right neurons in my brain during sleep—much like students reviewing everything one last time before heading off to bed."

Great. Of course a man like him loves to talk.

"Colt Whittaker may be one of those cases you see as a psychiatrist that stay with you long after you part ways. We only had one long session after which it all ended, and quite abruptly. His husband had arranged the appointment out of growing concerns about Colt's general state of mind and mood swings. It is my professional opinion that Mr. Carolino was onto something and had made the correct call sending him here." The doctor's Mid-Atlantic accent was getting harder to endure by the minute. It reminded Mel of his most belligerent Ethics professor, Fonseca, in college.

"For all intents and purposes, I did not believe Colt to be in danger of harming himself or others, if that's the information you're after. My notes will tell you the same thing should you send a subpoena for them in the future.

"Now, you may be familiar with the details of his upbringing, so I'll give you the gist. He had a rough shake, both as a kid and as an adult before his marriage to Gustavo. It had made it so that it took Colt about an hour to open up to me as his therapist. Trust never comes naturally to former foster kids, but Colt had it particularly bad. We started covering the absence of a father figure, the addictions of his mother and the estrangement from his sister. When he talked about his mother, I started noticing a pattern in her behavior that seemed to echo through Colt's general demeanor."

Mel interrupted, "I'm sorry, doctor, but did you say sister? You mean brother, right?"

Out came Dr. Petersen's spectacles. He hunched over the pages of notes on the coffee table between them. "No, it says so right here. Amelia, five years his senior. She moved to New York City after aging out of the foster system. She's a recovering alcoholic who worked as a nurse at the time in some big hospital in Manhattan."

Mel and Charlotte shared a glance with crooked eyebrows, then aimed for the doctor's eyes. He handed over the page. There it was: *Older sister Amelia* in the doctor's elegant longhand, right between the info about Anna Whittaker and her lover Gerald.

"Doctor, in your professional opinion, did Colt suffer from mental illness?" Charlotte asked.

The doctor exhaled through his large fuzzy nostrils and said, "I can't be conclusive due to the lack of extensive data, but at the time I believed there were strong indicators for bipolar disorder in Colt's case. But like I said, this is not an official diagnosis and shouldn't be seen as such in your current investigations."

"One more question, Doctor. Did you prescribe Colt any medications?" Mel asked.

"Yes, I did." He scanned the pages again. "Zoloft, to take the edge off his depressive thoughts. It's a fairly basic antidepressant. I further recommended him to come in at least twice a week, but he never came back here. He was acting quite paranoid before he left. The whole affair reminded me of one of my other bipolar patients, to be honest. I remember wondering if I should have gone with mood stabilizers instead, but that would have been unethical without an official diagnosis."

While Charlotte was thanking Petersen for his time, Mel thought about Kate's regular appointments with her therapist, Dr. Stevens. Along with her white privileged life her parents had always invested in her mental health. It sure was a fancy way to ship your daughter off to a shrink to avoid dealing with the hard questions as a parent, Mel thought in his self-made ways.

With both doors shut in Mel's Ford Explorer, exhaustion caught up with his determination. While he was resting his head on the wheel's soft leather, Charlotte made the obvious observations he was too tired to verbalize.

"I hate to say it, Mel, but I don't think Dr. Petersen was lying. Maybe Colt got scared of him being in cahoots with Gus and ended up referring to a made-up sister instead of Dave. You know, to protect his brother or something? What are you making of all this?"

"I don't know. I'll have to confront Colt. This case really is taking a lot more turns than I'm at all comfortable with. I keep thinking Colt is holding back. It's like we're constantly missing some key piece of information that ties everything together."

"I really hope you're wrong, but I understand the feeling. Have you ever wondered how striking it is that he's so clever in spite of his upbringing? He barely finished high school, but when you hear him talk you'd believe him to have some white-trash degree in English or History or something."

Mel scoffed. "I'll be damned, Charlotte. That's what the Chief told me. Except for the white-trash part, of course."

As he started the car and drove back to the precinct Mel went on to explain how Captain Perez was worried he'd grown too close to Colt to maintain objectivity. Charlotte agreed, but told him it was fairly impossible not to get close to a victim living under the same roof. "We're only human, Mel. The fact that we realize it could endanger our investigation probably says enough on its own."

When they approached the station on the north side, Mel noticed something odd enough to make him pull over to the side. A black Rivian R2 came from the other side at a remarkably low speed, but then accelerated and took a sharp turn to its left side, crashing into the white-painted cement poles in front of the station's entrance with a metallic thud. Mel parked his car on the curb and hurried to check out the fuss. His first thought was just another day drinker making all the wrong decisions.

Rita, together with a few uniformed officers emerged to check out the disturbance. Hands flew over gaping mouths as they watched the interior. Rita turned back inside to get help. That help, however, would not do in this particular instance, Mel concluded as he took a look for himself. The two people in the front seats showed gaping dark holes in their foreheads. Plastered against the inside window was a single page that made Mel's blood run cold when his retinas had translated the message to his brain.

The page featured a photograph with the message *next* in red lettering. When he recognized the scene depicted in the photograph, he looked over his shoulder to make sure Charlotte wouldn't have to see it. He held up his arm and told her to keep her distance. In the picture, a man covered in black clothing was holding Colt down to the floor in Charlotte's apartment. There was no mistaking who had sent this message or why.

Chapter 20
Colt—Past

Colt was brushing his teeth with such a vigor his gums had started to bleed. It was the last of his worries, as his sole priority was scrubbing away the foul taste of his new reality. What had made him feel even worse after the episode in the restaurant's bathroom was the way Alejandro and Jonathan smiled at him after he had returned to their table. Much as he wondered what Gus had told them, he didn't ask and tried his best to remain civil for the rest of the night—with mild success, if he had to say so himself.

His phone buzzed on the edge of the wide double sink.

Gus: Meet me in my office in three.

After another quiet ride home during which Gus had been on his phone mostly, he had retreated to his office right away when they got home. Colt had undressed and changed to nothing but shorts, so he put on a tank top and headed downstairs. The last thing he wanted was to be late for Gus's request. It wasn't lost on him that he was now nothing more than his husband's private hooker, forever at his beck and call. Every step down seemed to launch a new question in his mind.

Is he going to apologize in tears? Does he feel bad about it? Is he looking for a repeat performance? Does he need to go all the way just to make his point once more?

Barefoot, he approached Gus's office as he tried to shake the building dread inside. Like he had described over dinner, Holmby Hills could indeed be quiet at night—too quiet. The arched glow of the silver designer desk light was the only thing piercing the darkness. Gus was standing behind his desk, still fully clothed save for his tie, gazing at the lights of the Santa Monica Pier in the distance.

"Honey?"

"Right on time, baby," Gus said, eyeing Colt through the window's reflection. The distinct sound of clinking ice caught his attention. He had never seen Gus drink anything other than wine with his dinner.

"There are some things we need to discuss. Come here." He turned around and took another sip. His Adam's apple bobbed.

Colt took a few steps closer. His heart thumped as if it were a caged mountain lion, but there was no alternative. What frightened him most was the addition of hard liquor to the mix.

Gus closed the distance and connected his forehead to Colt's. The burning waft of bourbon or whiskey filled Colt's nostrils and reminded him of Dave at his worst.

"Colt, do you love me?"

"Of course I do. You know that."

"Do I?" Gus took a step back. "Then why do you need so much fucking convincing when I tell you to go down on me? I thought you understood our arrangement."

Colt swallowed his initial reaction, took a deep breath and said, "Gus, I love you. I always have and always will. Our arrangement doesn't change that. You just...you caught me off-guard tonight."

"It was really hot, though. Did you like it, too?"

This time Colt wasn't able to put on a show—it had been enough for one night. "Gus, what do you want me to say here? I did everything you told me tonight so that your important dinner would go well, which I think it did. I gave into your request in the bathroom because I knew it would make you happy. So, I guess I enjoyed it because of that. You know I'll do anything to please you. It's part of our arrangement." As soon as the last phrase escaped his mouth he knew he had gone too far.

Gus downed the last of his glass and put it on his desk with a bang that made Colt jump. For some reason Gus thought his husband's reaction was hilarious, as he started chuckling. "Colt, are you scared?" Colt remained quiet, unwilling to give him the satisfaction. "Well, from where I'm standing you're not scared enough. Otherwise you wouldn't talk back to me like this, or insult me. You make it sound like you're some escort that only pleases me for their own benefit. If satisfying me is what you want, then you won't mind me doing this."

He swung his long arm out and slapped Colt hard in the face. The tingle of arousal was nowhere to be found this time. He held his heated cheek and staggered backward, yet not fast enough.

"Or this." Gus wrapped his hand around Colt's throat and pushed him back into the wall next to the door to the living room. "Oh, come on, baby. You know this is what you want. See? You're enjoying this more than I am."

Gus squeezed, making Colt gag for the second time that night. Struggling for breath, Colt knew there was no way he'd be able to fight him off. Playing along and taking it was all he could do. What had once been the pleasure of submission and loss of control had turned into powerlessness and blind fear.

"You're so beautiful. So pretty it hurts," Gus said as he relaxed his grip, only to bang Colt's head against the wall, pulling it back and forth twice. Pain screamed from the back of his skull. Black spots danced around his vision, making him dizzy.

Before Colt had time to recover Gus punched his other cheek with a closed fist, sending him flying to his left. As he stumbled to his knees he sensed the sting of a cut, together with the tangy metallic taste of blood in his mouth. Gus's wedding band had grazed his cheek, the symbol of their troubled marriage.

"Gus, please, no."

As if Colt's cries urged him on, Gus pushed him off balance with his foot and followed the motion up with a hard kick in Colt's stomach. He gasped and coughed, praying for the blows to stop coming. As he broke down in tears in a fetal position Gus pulled his head up by the hair, grinning down at him.

"Stop, Gus. Please don't kill me." His head fell back down again. Refusing to believe his pleading had worked, he covered his head in his arms to prevent further beating. He shivered uncontrollably in between sobs. His breath caught when he felt Gus's hand stroking up and down his back. When Colt looked over his shoulder Gus was weeping now, too. He had knelt beside him on the floor and waited, afraid to touch Colt again.

"Get away from me, Gus, I—"

Gus cut him off and whispered "Shh. It's over. No talking. I can't."

Gus lifted Colt from the floor and carried him to the kitchen, cradling him in his arms as he pushed his head against Colt's. The tears on their cheeks mixed, which would have been beautiful in any other circumstance.

Once they reached the island, Gus sat Colt down on a stool. He walked around to the First Aid cabinet and pulled out gauze, antiseptic gel, bandaids and scissors. Colt didn't dare to open his mouth. He figured it would be a long time before he'd be inclined to disobey his husband again. Backtalk, he had learned, would result in violence.

With both of them not uttering so much as a word, Gus got to work to fix the damage he had done to Colt's face— or limit, rather. Even though Colt had dialed down the volume on his sobs, the tears kept coming. The dangerous man before him loved him more than anyone ever had. If only the price were fair. Colt tried to imagine his life with Gus in this wonderful house without the violence and entrapment, but it was too painful on top of everything else on his plate tonight.

Every now and then their eyes would meet, making it hard for Gus to focus on his tasks. When he applied antiseptic to the cut on Colt's cheek with a piece of gauze, his hands started trembling. His husband's wince seemed too much for him to handle. Colt grabbed his wrist and steadied it as he brought it to the intended place on his skin. Whether it was because he still loved him, or because he wanted to get it over with was a question he couldn't have answered.

After putting all the materials back in the cabinet, Gus carried Colt up the stairs and laid him on the bed. Right before they went to sleep, Gus caressed the side of Colt's head and planted a soft kiss on his lips. Colt dozed off that night wondering about many things. Was every business dinner he'd need to attend in the future going to end in violence? What was the point of obeying every command when he would get beat up anyway? How much more of this could he take before going mad? Was a life filled with fear and pain worth living at all?

In the morning Colt was unable to react to anything from outside his own body and mind. He was vaguely aware of Gus trying to communicate, yelling next to the bed, but he couldn't focus on his words, or his face long enough to register information. It was as though his spiraling thoughts had rendered him constricted and closed off from everything around him. The only sensation it came close to was being underwater.

Somehow he had made it to the breakfast table. How much time had passed between the two scenes was unclear. He had changed clothes, but that was the only clue he could find. This time it was Hannah who was trying to get through to him, sliding a bowl of cinnamon oatmeal to his side of the counter. On some level he realized Hannah was trying to get him to eat, but he couldn't bring himself to comply. Hunger was a distant memory in his dazed state. It just didn't matter. Flashes of the previous night kept troubling his senses.

So pretty it hurts.

The phrase kept replaying in his head every time he tried to resurface to reality.

It was only when Gus wrapped him in his arms that Colt was able to react. He jumped from his chair and nearly tripped over his feet. As he stretched his torso the bruise on his stomach turned angry.

"No. Don't, Gus. Stay back."

"Hannah, go be somewhere else," Gus said, keeping his eyes on Colt. She complied instantly.

"Sit down, baby. I'm not going to hurt you. You just scared me, is all. What was with you?"

I scared you? Are you serious?

Colt did as he was told. "I don't know. I just sort of zoned out for a few hours. Can you really blame me, Gus?" Surprised at his bravado, Colt's shoulders tensed.

Gus studied his hands on the counter. "You won't believe me, but I really am sorry for hurting you—again. I want to say I didn't mean to, but that would be a lie."

Before Colt could say anything, Natalee Prescott walked in, Gus's business partner. Colt despised the woman. She barely acknowledged his existence whenever they crossed paths and when she did, it was like she couldn't wait to get as far away from him as possible. Colt imagined her thinking he was after the company's money. Her black-

and-white striped pantsuit and cascade-collared white shirt would have looked great on any woman her age. On her, Colt thought, it made her look like a clown with her excessive makeup. Gus told her to wait in his office, so off she went, gluing her face to her phone.

With one more witness in the house, Colt saw an opportunity and took it. "Gus, I've been wondering about your parents. Meeting your mother was no picnic for me, if you recall it the way I do. Honey, did she ever hurt you as a kid?"

Gus slowly turned his head in Colt's direction, his eyes boring into Colt's with a flash of hatred so dark it made his heart skip a beat. With a swift arc of his arm he slapped Colt in the face with a hard smacking sound, reviving the sting from last night.

"Don't you ever, *ever* talk about *Mamãe* again. Do you hear me?" Gus shouted with his deep, rumbling voice. His headache made the sound worse than the actual slap. From the home office Natalee looked right at Colt, but quickly fixed her eyes back to her screen.

That bitch.

"I understand," Colt said.

"Good. Make sure to remember this, because I won't stop the next time you bring her up." Gus put a hand on his shoulder and said, "You should stop infuriating me like this. Nothing good can come of it," in a lower voice. "All right. Now, I need to discuss some things with Natalee and after that we're off to spot new listings with Langdon. I'll be home early, so we can have some fun together. Try to get more sleep in the meantime, okay? I love you." He kissed Colt's burning cheek like he had forgotten about the slap.

Of course Dilma Carolino had done a number on her son when he was a kid. It made so much sense with him being an only child. He thought back to the phrase Gus's father had told him. *Knowing my son, it's going to be a bumpy ride.* The son of a bitch knew all about Gus's violent inclination. He had probably nourished it together with his basket-case wife.

"Colt? Are you okay? What happened?" Langdon had walked through the front door, looking like a lab whose owner had taken away his favorite tennis ball.

Colt sniffed and said, "Nothing. I'm just… It's nothing, Langdon."

Langdon looked around to the office and whispered, "I'm sorry I can't help you, Colt. I really wish I could. You don't deserve this. It's exactly what I feared would happen eventually. Gus and I have an—"

"An arrangement. Yeah, it seems to be a theme around here. He's got you hog-tied and you're too chicken-shit to do anything about it."

"That's right. I hate myself for it, if it's any consolation."

Colt stared at him for a while. Bad as his headache was, he wasn't going to let the driver off easy.

"You know, I really want you to, Langdon. Chances are he's going to kill me one day, so for your sake, I hope this is all worth it. You might as well be the one beating me up, because standing by and looking the other way is so much worse."

Langdon was the one that looked slapped now. "Colt, you don't know what he'll do if I help you. You have no idea."

Colt huffed. "No idea? Tell me something, Langdon. What will he do? Will he rape you? Make you pretend you enjoy it? Make you say *I love you* like you mean it? Make you go down on him in a public bathroom? Beat you up despite doing everything he asked? Beat you up because you're too fucking pretty?"

Langdon remained silent and looked at a random spot near his shoes.

"Yeah, I didn't think so." Colt walked away from a watery-eyed Langdon and headed upstairs. Maybe a hot bath would conjure up a long-term plan to survive Gus's aggressive streak—or help find a reason to keep on living.

Chapter 21
Mel—Present

Colt got in the car on the passenger side after Mel had started the engine. He was wearing the big black sunglasses from when Mel had pulled him over. Thinking back, Mel couldn't help but wonder how odd it was that he hadn't been able to identify Colt as a special victims case. The tough act, the hurt in his eyes, the hopelessness in his posture. Parenthood had really been screwing with his head at the time.

Those characteristics were now making a comeback in Colt's features, shrouded in silence. He had been like that ever since he had heard about the threats against his life the night before. On entering his home the night before, Mel had witnessed the beautiful vulnerability of Colt's voice once more. He had been singing *The Boxer* while holding Rose against his chest in the living room.

His voice cracked a little more than usual. It looked like he needed the comfort of Rose's warmth more than she needed his singing. He hadn't heard Mel approach him.

"Great song, Colt."

Colt turned around, revealing his tears. "Hi Mel. I know, right?" He handed him his daughter.

Mel kissed his daughter and sniffed her head.

"Great, now she smells like your fancy perfume."

"I'm sorry." Colt looked away and chewed his lower lip, then said, "I always envision Dave as the character in that song. You know, when he had just moved to New York. It breaks my heart."

Mel put his free hand on Colt's shoulder and squeezed, then laid Rose down in her cot. When he turned around, he noticed Colt had already taken his usual place at the table, making it easy for Mel to inform him on the day's events. While listening, Colt had kept his cool, but not for too long.

"Look, Mel, this is all Gus's doing. He's going out of his way to put the spotlight back on me. He knew I was going to tell you about that gun eventually, so he removed it. And don't even get me started on that Dr. Petersen. For all we know he's with the cartel, slinging drugs to housewives as we speak. But of course, *I'm* the one who looks crazy to everyone down at the LAPD or DEA or whatever. Please tell me you still believe me. I wouldn't blame you if you didn't. Man, I hate to be on the losing end all the fucking time."

Colt was pacing as he yelled, making Rose cry out in the middle of his rant.

"It's not about believing. We're following up on all the leads we've got. It's called due diligence."

"No, Mel. You're just falling for Gus's schemes. He's the one that led you right to that doctor's doorstep and you obeyed—just like I've been doing these past four years. Look where it landed me."

"What the hell, you guys? Can't you both keep it down? Our daughter is right there, for crying out loud," Kate said, walking in from the utility room.

Before she could head off upstairs with Rose clamped to her side, Mel stopped her, gently touching her forearm. "Wait. There's more. Kate, I need you to take Rose to your parents' house for a couple of days. Probably longer."

"What for?" Kate and Colt asked in unison.

When Mel explained everything about the incident with the black Rivian, silence flooded the house and was in no rush to leave.

When they pulled into the parking lot at the station the next day, Colt broke his silent streak with the suggestion Mel had been dreading ever since he had suggested it a few nights ago.

"Mel, I think it's time we pitched my idea to the Captain—or Chief, or whatever you people call that lady in charge."

"Jesus, Colt." He sighed and said, "It's too dangerous. Especially now."

"Hear me out. That's exactly why we should do it. Mel, I've been surviving for so long I don't remember what it's like to just live my life. This fear I should be drowned in right now is no different from when I was living in Holmby Hills, really. All I'm saying is, if I'm going to die before this case closes, I might as well do it trying to help. You may think keeping me by your side all the time will protect me, but I wouldn't be so sure. Look at me." He waited for Mel to do as he said, then continued, "I'm more worried about you. If bad comes to worse I don't think you'll handle my death well. You act all tough, but I think it would break you for good." Colt eyed him with a tiny smile.

Mel studied the Airbag sign on the wheel and breathed through the lump in his throat. He hated to admit it, but Colt was making a good point. "Fine. Let's go talk to her, then. But don't get your hopes up."

On walking through the staff entrance, Mel ran into Cam and told him he needed to speak to both him and the Chief together with Colt. Cam's appearance was a bad sign for the direction the major project was headed. With dark bags under his eyes, a shiny forehead and a slower gait than usual the man barely resembled Mel's eligible wingman from years ago.

"Okay, Mel and Colt. Tell me what was so incredibly important it couldn't wait while we're in the middle of this all-consuming investigation," the Chief said.

"Cam, Chief, I think you should hear Colt out. He's got a suggestion that could force Gustavo out of his shell. Trigger warning: it's quite unorthodox." Mel bit his fingernails again, not even caring anymore.

When Colt had finished explaining the details of his out-of-the-box plan both Cam and the Chief sat staring in front of them—the Chief working her jaw like it needed a tension-relieving pop. What astonished Mel was that they were actually considering it from the looks of it.

Cam inhaled sharply, "Well, truth be told, at this point

we're willing to try anything. The guys at Forensic IT downtown are having no luck finding anything worth our time on Gus's computers. The more they try to trace payments to that holding, the more back alleys they end up in. One transaction went through Liechtenstein, Venezuela, Barbados, The Caymans, San Marino and back before the trail ran cold. It's suspicious, but not enough to get him. It's barely enough to bring him in for more questioning, really."

"I like it," the Chief said, as though she hadn't listened to Cam at all. "Aside from it being incredibly dangerous for all staff involved we really need a breakthrough in this case. Colt, are you positive this is going to work?"

"One hundred percent. The only other thing that might enrage Gus in a similar way is talking about his mother. I know it's dangerous, but I'm asking you to trust me."

"Did you have someone in mind? Please don't say Mel," Cam asked, winking at Mel.

"I do. Oliver Ryder. He owes us, right, Chief? This would be a perfect way to redeem himself."

The Chief's eyebrows shot up with a suppressed smile—which looked all the more naughty with her burgundy lipstick. "All right, then. Is it horrible that I'm enjoying the thought of it too much?" With a hand in the air she added, "Careful, gentlemen. I'll deny having said that. Get him in here."

When Mel called out to Oliver and told him the Chief wanted him in her office, the guy's baby blue eyes went saucer-wide. Doing his best not to smile too much, Mel wondered what would happen to the guy's face when he heard about the plan. If talking to the Chief alone rattled him, there was no telling how he'd react to their plan. He signaled to Charlotte to come enjoy the show.

"Sit down, Officer Ryder—Oliver. Together with the DEA we've formulated a special secret mission for you," the Chief started. Mel had given up his chair for the guy, figuring it would be of more use to him in the next few moments. Oliver glanced at Colt standing next to Mel with a furrowed brow, like he knew on some level the request wasn't going to be of the everyday variant.

The Chief explained the details in her usual calm, yet commanding voice. Oliver nodded and hummed in agreement while he listened, eager to make a good impression. Mel remembered those days all too well. Without second-guessing the intricacies of the job, he would have said yes to the request himself in his rookie years. Was Oliver cut from the same cloth?

"All we're asking for is one passionate, believable kiss in public. Undercover agents are asked to do this all the time. Legally speaking, I can't even suggest this side mission to you, but I'm taking a chance on you. We could find someone else to do it, but it would take time—time Colt might not have, considering yesterday's events. Oliver, this next part is off the record. Remember that horrible night at Charlotte's place? You came in here the next day and told me the guilt was tearing you up on the inside. That you never should have let her assailants slip past you. This is how you make it right. You owe this to Colt and Charlotte—and to the station."

Oliver hunched forward, rested his elbows on his knees and dragged out a long exhale. After rubbing his brow he said, "Okay, I'll do it. But for the record, I am not gay."

"Then let's hope you're a good actor. Welcome to LA," Mel said.

"Great. Oliver, this truly means the world to us. Now, I suggest you go spend some time with Colt, so the two of you can figure out how to pull this act off. Find a way to make your interactions seem credible from the outside," the Chief said. Mel knew she was having too much fun, though she didn't show it.

Charlotte fished her phone out of her pocket and headed out the office. Mel had barely turned his focus back on Oliver and Colt when Charlotte called his name.

"Abby Fitzsimmons is here. She wants to talk to us."

Colt looked at him and said, "I'm coming with you."

"No, he can't be here," Abby said once Colt stepped inside the interrogation room. She had risen from her seat, breathing in heaves. Gorgeous as she would otherwise be with her lush blonde hair and delicate chin, her looks matched Cam's level of exhaustion. She may have driven all the way from Montana overnight.

"Abby, relax. This is not what you think it is. Colt here is a special victim just like you. We're keeping him safe because of threats against his life," Charlotte said.

Colt approached her slowly with his hands spread out as though he were afraid she might run off. "Abby, we're on the same side of this mess. Look." He lowered the waistband of his shorts and showed her his tattoo.

Abby gasped, covering her gaping mouth with her hand as the weight of the sign hit her in the stomach. "No, no, no. Not you, too. You can't go out there, do you hear me?" Abby took Colt's hand in hers and whispered something to him. They sat in the chairs on the opposite side of the table.

Mel leaned into Charlotte's ear, "Are you okay? If it gets to be too much, just say so and I'll take care of it."

"I'm fine. Thanks, Mel."

Abby Fitzsimmons had indeed driven twenty hours to get back to Los Angeles, though she couldn't recall any details from the drive except for a few coffee and gas stops. "I knew I had to get back here when Mark told me the truth. They can't keep doing this to people. They just can't."

Mark had told his wife the truth when the guilt had become too much to bear two nights ago. Their conversation with intermittent yelling had lasted through the small hours. Originally, her husband had agreed to drive to LA to come clean and hope for a plea deal with the DEA. However, when she woke up Mark had disappeared and left a note to apologize for his cowardice.

"The son of a bitch. Let's hope those crooks track him down. Anyway, I hope you're recording this, because here's what I know." Abby cleared her throat. "We didn't move to Hollywood because of Mark moving up in his accountancy company. It was a deal he had struck with the Cordelio cartel. One of his coworkers had been bragging about a cheap way to buy real estate in Hollywood with Carolino

Real Estate. Gullible and desperate as always, Mark had bought into the idea and set up a meeting with Gustavo and some other Latino guy. They offered him a ridiculously low price for our house in Holmby Hills in a contract that stated they needed—what they called—personal insurance and occasional services." She air-quoted the phrase. "The last part included drop-offs of certain amounts of cash all over LA, but he didn't tell me where. Personal insurance was the reason I got raped and branded." Abby started sobbing at the memory. Colt put a hand on her shoulder while Mel handed her a tissue. She got out the final stages of her story in often incoherent pieces.

"So, let me get this straight. They demand the spouses of their *associates* to be branded, so they know who to come after when they step out of line. Is that correct?" Charlotte asked.

Abby nodded. "If they don't get proof of the tattoo they'll take matters into their own hands. That's what happened to me. I thought it was stupid when Mark told me it's what he wanted for his birthday. A C-tattoo was the last thing I wanted on my body. We fought over it a lot. So much that I slept in the other room for a whole week. If I had known, I would have gone to the first parlor on Google Maps. Not telling the spouse was one of the rules, for obvious reasons. I'm so sorry, Colt."

"It's not your fault, Abby. I've been through worse. Do you remember that first dinner we had?" While Colt was telling Abby about how much of a monster Gus really was at home, Charlotte and Mel walked out to give them some privacy. As Charlotte went back to their office to make calls for a safe house for Abby, Mel walked outside to the parking lot to do some more vape-processing.

As prescribed in their team meeting that afternoon, Oliver would from then on stay under the same roof as Mel and Colt. Two cops body-guarding was better than one and it was the fastest way to break the ice between the two make-believe lovers. The DEA's preliminary forensics reports had declared the cause of death of both Rivian victims to be gunshot wounds to their heads. DNA and trace analysis would take more time, which made Colt's plan all the more palatable. The folks at IT confirmed the car had been operated remotely, but the trail had run cold. Abby's recorded statement had made the whole conference room so quiet Mel could hear the hairs on his neck rub against his shirt collar. It was a welcome emergence of a puzzle piece and fit beautifully with the rest of their observations and deductions about the cartel's inner workings so far.

Before she left for her parents' house with Rose, Kate had stocked their fridge to its maximum capacity. As Mel took out a bottle of beer, an idea popped into his head.

"Gentlemen, tonight I'm your chef. This will be your first rehearsal as a romantic couple having dinner in Hollywood. So get comfortable and, uhm, scoot a little closer for God's sake."

They did as he asked and started talking while Mel prepared his best version of spaghetti with hot dogs—like he used to make in college.

"So, Oliver, before we really start talking like lovers, are you sure you're straight?" Colt asked.

"I think I am. I had a girlfriend in New York until three months ago if you need proof. Met her parents and everything."

"Good. Are you at all bicurious?"

Mel suppressed a scoff and focused on weighing noodles.

"You mean, am I actively wondering what it would be like to kiss or fuck guys? No. Not that I'm aware of. Wait, was that the right answer?"

Good question.

"Yes, Oliver, it is. You wouldn't be the first allegedly straight guy to fall head over heels for me, trust me. Gus always says I'm the perfect bicurious bait. It's something about me being just a little effeminate—just enough to want to protect me on one hand and still be attracted to my trained body on the other."

"O-kay. I'll try my best not to fall in love with you. By the way, you should call me Ol. It's more intimate."

The Chief would have loved this.

"Right, Ol. Just so we're clear, this is not easy for me, either. I have a hard time trusting people, let alone allow them to get physically close. You can ask Mel. That said, I do have a unique amount of experience faking affection, so I don't think it's going to be an issue." Colt scooted closer so their knees were touching.

Mel looked over his shoulder a moment too long. The water in his pan had boiled over and was flooding all over the hub and onto the floor. As he was mopping and cursing when the hot liquid burned his fingers, he kept listening and heard Colt taking the lead.

"I'm going to hold your hand now, okay? You have a really handsome face. You've got that wolf-like combination of dark hair and icy eyes working for you. Are you part Italian or something?"

"Thanks. Yes, about an eighth, pretty much like everyone in New York. Then there's Irish, Polish and Albanian in my DNA. How about you?"

"No idea. My mom once joked about us being Swedish, but I don't think she was being serious. She might have been high, come to think of it." Colt paused, then said, "Ol, you're supposed to compliment me in return."

"Oh, right. I, uhm, like your voice. I could listen to you all night. Uhm, too far?"

Mel heard Colt hesitate and chuckled.

There you go.

By the time Mel had finished dinner and served both of them at the table, the two were past the awkward questions about their lives before moving to Los Angeles. While the three of them ate dinner, Colt and Ol had agreed to answer any question the other had, no matter how crazy.

"Am I correct in assuming you're a bottom?" Ol asked.

On hearing the bold question Mel swallowed wrong and needed to cough and beat his chest. Colt gave him a hard stare.

"You are, yes. Although you can never make assumptions like that. It's highly stereotypical and frowned upon in our community. You'd be surprised sometimes. All right. Morning sex or afternoon delight?"

"Afternoon delight. It feels naughtier knowing people are out there working. Now, what kind of men are you attracted to?"

"Interesting question. Don't judge, okay? Much as I hate it, I like dominant personalities with a sensitive side to them. I love a man who's protective, but needs me to take charge sometimes. It also helps when they like it a little rough in the sack, to be completely honest."

"Okay. How rough are we talking?"

Careful, Ol.

"Well, I used to think it was hot when a man hit me in the face during sex. But after having lived in Gus's prison, I've come to realize I like the threat more than the actual pain. I know it's what got me into this mess, but that loss of control and total surrender to someone's power still gets me going. But enough about my fetishes. What crazy stuff are you into?"

"Hmm. I've always wanted to try anal. Not with you, just to be clear." Ol touched his shoulder with a slight flush in his cheeks. Colt smiled and finished the last of his plate.

Mel looked at Colt with pride. There he was, sitting at his dinner table opening up to a stranger. Talking about his life with Gus as though it were a side story instead of an ongoing criminal case. A week ago Mel wouldn't have deemed the scene before him possible. He enjoyed thinking he had had something to do with Colt's transformation. At the same time he hoped their plan wouldn't blow up in their faces.

Mel's phone buzzed while he was stocking the dishwasher.

Cam: How are the lovebirds doing?

Mel: Better than expected, really. Oliver's a saint. This could all work out.

Cam: It'd better.

When Oliver had gone to the bathroom, Colt rose from his chair and joined Mel in the kitchen, leaning against the counter with his arms and ankles crossed.

"That seemed to have gone well, right?" Mel asked.

"Yes, surprisingly so. Our plan is going to work, I'm sure of it. He's very different from Gus, so that's good. From where Gus stands, it would make sense for me to go explore other options."

"You're probably right. Ol's a good guy for wanting to help us like this." Keeping Colt talking was always a challenge. It was the gentlest tug-of-war Mel had ever played.

"I just wish he weren't from New York." Colt let out a shaky breath. "To think him and Dave might have run into each other without realizing is just too much for me to handle right now, so I'm trying really hard not to think about it.

"There are so many things I wish I could have told him, Mel. About Gus, about Mom, about you helping me out. I know it's insane, seeing as we'd grown apart so much, but I really miss him. He was the one I looked up to as a child—before the system messed him up. When we finally got a chance to be brothers again he ran away, like he knew I was going to get him killed one day."

Colt had tears pearling down his cheeks, but avoided eye contact the way Mel had seen him do a few times.

Instead of trying to look for the right words, he handed Colt paper towels and another shoulder squeeze.

Ol was standing near the staircase. Without giving it too much thought, Mel signaled him over with a nod of his head. He got the hint and walked over to Colt's side. He pulled his hands out of his pockets and held out his arms with one upturned eyebrow. Colt eyed him for a moment, then uncrossed his arms. At first he seemed to stiffen against the level of intimacy, but seconds later he melted into Oliver's frame. From Mel's point of view it looked real enough to go straight to Awards season.

Chapter 22
Colt—Past

I can do this. I can take it. It will be over soon. Just give him what he wants. Whatever happens, don't talk back.

The last thing Colt wanted was a repeat performance of the choking collar Gus had put on him the week before. Giving Gus the satisfaction of watching him get close to passing out again was not going to happen if he could help it. The cuffs alone were bad enough, biting into his skin every time Gus pulled him closer—trying to get deeper inside him as usual. There were two pairs this time, fixing both of Colt's wrists to the bedposts on either side in complete submission.

As he looked into his husband's kryptonite eyes— maintaining eye contact while Gus fucked him on his back was essential to avoid violent escalations—he marveled at the sheer bliss spanning across his face. Three years into their fucked-up marriage, Gus was still lusting for Colt's body the way he had when they first hooked up. Like always, Gus was taking his time, making sure Colt orgasmed—or rather, succumbed—before stripping away all of his inhibitions and having his way with him.

Gus paused and leaned in for a slow kiss, then whispered, "I love you. I was close but I want it to last," with his signature boyish grin.

Sick bastard. Just punch me or something and get it over with.

Instead of speaking his mind, Colt came up with a scripted reply. "I love you too, honey. I'm not going anywhere."

With his enthusiasm soaring, Gus resumed his thrusts with a strong grip on Colt's hips in slow, rhythmic movements. Intending to go on for hours, Gus was edging, suspending his delayed orgasm every time he came close. When Gus finally did finish, he liberated a victorious groan from deep inside. He collapsed onto Colt's torso, his gleaming forehead touching Colt's chin. Gus's graying chest hair was damp with sweat and stuck to Colt's skin. Sadly, their combined musky scent was heavenly as ever—a cruel reminder of how well they matched despite everything.

While Gus's breathing slowed, all Colt could think was *untie me—now!*

"Our anniversary's coming up. Can you believe it's almost been three years? I know we had a, uhm, rocky start, Colt. But I'm so, so glad we've found a way to be together. You're my everything," Gus said as they were showering. He was massaging Colt's quaking thighs while he rested against the glass wall. Colt was sure he'd have trouble walking tomorrow morning. Sex marathons like the one he had just endured were taking a heavier toll on his body every time.

No, Gus. You're my *everything. You moved mountains to make sure it would be this way, remember?*

Three years of being married to Gustavo Carolino. Three years of violent, mind-fucking rape. Three years of *I love yous* and smiles that had made his stomach turn. Three years of looking in the eyes of the man he loved and knowing it could never be untainted again. Three years of beatings after having tiptoed outside the narrow path Gus had forced him on. He remembered every single one of those outbursts. The time he almost had Langdon send a letter to his mother. The time he had refused to go back to that sketchy therapist. And—proud as he still was—the time he had told Natalee Prescott to go fuck herself.

"Three years. It doesn't feel that long, does it?" Colt said, dutifully running soapy hands over Gus's back. It was funny how he knew exactly what spots would make his husband moan with delight, or pain.

Nope, it feels more like twenty.

After his morning workout, Colt walked into the kitchen to make himself a protein shake. As Sheryl Crow's *Ordinary Morning* was blasting through his earbuds, the sight of a stranger sitting at the kitchen island startled him. He pulled his earbuds out and took in the man's features.

"Alejandro? What are you doing here?"

"Good morning to you, too, Colt. I'm waiting for Gus. Your driver let me in." Alejandro barely resembled the man Colt had met years ago. His crew cut had grown into a mess of untamed black curls and his beard had become a haphazard food storage facility. In Colt's opinion there should always be a clear indication of where chest hair ended and facial hair began, but that wasn't the case with Alejandro anymore.

"Right. Good morning. So, how have you guys been? Are you still enjoying Beverly Hills?" Colt asked, fetching the vanilla whey powder container from a cabinet.

"Uhm, not really. I am, yes, but Jonathan isn't. We finalized our divorce last week, actually," Alejandro said, looking Colt in the eye with a thin smile that tried to say *it's all for the best.* There was something else in that look.

"I'm so sorry. I had no idea you guys were dealing with relationship troubles." *You should really ask Gus for advice. If one man knows how to keep your husband close, it's him.* After having scooped enough powder in his gym bottle, Colt filled it with tap water. "Coffee? Or something stronger?" he asked, shaking the bottle vigorously.

"Coffee's good, thanks. I don't really want to go into the details of our break-up, if that's okay with you, Colt. I'm trying to keep my mind distracted as I go."

Colt took out a new bag of single-origin Brazilian espresso beans and started feeding them to the machine. With every action he felt Alejandro's eyes on his skin. His yellow mesh tank top and matching shorts suddenly felt too revealing for this conversation. "Sure, whatever you need. I can't imagine what you must be going through."

Where the fuck do I sign up?

He took a swig from the gym bottle and put a tiny cup under the coffee machine's spout. Maybe the burr of the grinder was the reason he hadn't noticed Alejandro approaching him from behind.

Colt froze when Alejandro leaned into his back. One of his hands was dangerously close to his crotch while the other grabbed at his left pec. What made it even creepier was the *Shh* in his ear.

He elbowed Alejandro in his stomach and turned around, crying out for Gus. Coffee beans from the opened bag had spilled all over the floor, Colt tripped trying to get away from what was yet another predator in his life. He fell on his side, his forearm taking the full blow of the impact.

Alejandro took advantage of the moment and landed on top of him, pulling Colt's left wrist behind his back.

"It's okay, Colt. Gus told us all about how you like it rough. Let's see if he was right," he said, too close to Colt's ear. Barely having processed the danger he was in, he felt Alejandro pull down his waistband with his other hand. He called out Gus's name again, his voice cracking mid-scream.

"Colt! *Filho da mãe!*" Gus shouted with his rumbling voice, permeating the room with alpha-male rage.

Within seconds Gus had flung the man away from Colt and punched him three times with roaring grunts. Blood streaked down Alejandro's beard/chest hair. From the window, Colt watched Gus drag the guy along by the bloodied shirt collar and push him past the gate, spouting threats as the gate closed. When it had been done, Colt let out a long breath and sank onto a stool. He rubbed his wrist and realized the pain was still more Gus's fault than Alejandro's. The bar had become pretty high in that regard.

"Baby, are you okay?" Gus cupped his cheek and

scanned him from head to toe to check for marks of his intruder. Then he held Colt tightly, kissing the top of his head. He knew it was wrong and that the tenderness wouldn't last, but Colt took big gulps of it while he could.

"I think so, yes. Thanks for saving me. That guy always gives me the creeps, but I did *not* see that coming. What was he doing here, anyway?"

"We had a business meeting."

"Are they selling the house?"

"They're, uhm, thinking about it. I'm not sure what he wants this time. All I know is I don't like it. Not one bit." Gus sighed. "On the other hand, it's good business, so I'll have to invite him downtown and try to smooth things over."

Colt's jaw dropped. "Smooth things over? Are you kidding me? He assaults me one minute and the next you discuss business as usual? What the fuck, Gus?" Colt rose from his seat.

Gus grabbed his aching forearm. "Colt, there are things about my real estate business you don't understand. I'll do everything I can to keep him away from you, but I can't afford to lose him as a client. I expect you to come to terms with that, just like I will. Can you do that for me?"

"Gus," Colt breathed, waiting until Gus let go of his arm, "you know I have no choice. I never do. I appreciate you asking, but it makes no difference. At the end of the day I'll just have to find a way to suck it up and support your decision, like I've been doing for years. Now if you'll excuse me, I have to go wash that creep's hands off me."

Gus was staring in front of him when Colt started

walking to the stairs. The expected retort—with or without a touch of aggression—never came. When he had reached the first step Gus said, "I'm coming with you. Can't have you smelling of another man. I'll be gentle, I promise."

There was no way Colt could have turned his eyes back to Gus. As he focused on every individual step to the second floor, he sobbed quickly and quietly. Gus's compulsive jealousy had a way to dial his violent side to the max. He wondered what kind of man would want to fuck a guy who had just been sexually assaulted, and regretted knowing the answer all too well.

On the day of their third wedding anniversary Colt's hackles were raised every time he saw Gus tapping away on his phone. There had been a few mentions of a surprise in between the sparse conversations he and Gus had shared over the past two weeks. The incident with Alejandro had caused Gus to work much longer hours than before. At the dinner table he'd been having trouble maintaining their usual flow of topics. On mentioning it once, Gus had turned the blame on Colt himself for being the distant one, so he let it go and enjoyed the quiet moments—knowing they wouldn't last. Sex had been less elaborate too, so he considered it a win altogether.

Colt was standing outside, enjoying the view from the pool deck, where he did his best thinking. He was sure Gus's surprise, whatever it would be, couldn't be something he'd enjoy—not the way Gus himself would. It was going to require yet another round of supreme acting on his side, so he hoped standing in the sunlight would restore his mental strength. There was a way out of this claustrophobic existence. He was sure of it. Someday, somehow, Gus was going to loosen his leash—the literal or figurative one— enough for him to get away. Catching a waft of ocean air, Colt made a promise to himself. *One more year.* If by this time next year he hadn't found the way out, he vowed to make one for himself.

Gus had walked up from behind and held him at the waist. "Ready for your surprise? It's almost here," he said, kissing his temple.

Aaaaaand, action.

"I can't wait. You've been very cloak-and-dagger about this. It seems like you're more nervous than I am. You can relax, honey. Whatever it is, I'm sure it will be great."

Colt sensed Gus's phone buzz in the pocket of his jeans.

"It's here."

Inside, Gus held the door open for a woman anyone would have considered hard not to stare at. Apart from a colorful tattoo covering her left cheek, her purple braided hair was tied in a large bun on top of her head. It looked more like a messy ball of yarn in a fabrics store than a hairdo. The cat-eye makeup and nose ring reminded Colt of Amy Winehouse. She was dragging a silver trolley of the beautician variant into the living room.

What in the actual fuck did he get me?

"Welcome to our home. I'm Gus and this right here is my husband, Colt."

"Colt, nice to meet you. I'm Moon Light."

"Likewise."

Like that's your real name.

"So, uhm, what's my surprise?" he asked, unsure who to address.

Moon Light looked at Gus, who said, "You're getting a tattoo today, like you've always wanted. Isn't it great?"

Colt was speechless while he did the equation of the circumstances in his head.

A surprise tattoo plus a cartoon-character artist with an indistinct name, plus a home visit instead of a parlor appointment, multiplied by Gus's excitement equals…

A branding ritual, that's what this surprise was. Alejandro making a move on him was the final straw to have Gus's sanity go down the drain. He needed proof on Colt's body that he'd be forever his. Property of Gustavo Carolino. For him to use and shield from the dangers of the outside world. To snap his fingers at for his every desire. A mark that would take away the last figment of free will. Even if he'd have it removed one day, it would stay embedded in his brain for all eternity.

"Colt? Are you all right? Do you not like your surprise?"

Fuck.

He'd been silent for so long Gus's voice had taken on his blaming tone. "Oh, I do. It's just kind of overwhelming. What kind of, uhm, tattoo did you have in mind?" *Keep it together.*

Gus showed him his phone screen. "It's our shared initial. A circled c, as in Colt and Carolino. We are two of a kind, Colt, and this symbolizes that."

Colt sensed his acting skills plummeting. Try as he did,

he couldn't stop the tears. A lump the size of a jawbreaker was stuck in his throat. He feared Gus would notice and call him an ungrateful bitch or worse in a few moments.

"Oh, baby. You're all emotional. I love you so much. Come here. It's okay." Gus held him tight and pushed Colt's head against his chest. His grip was too strong to be sincere. Gus was only trying to avoid an ugly scene with the tattoo artist. The message was loud and clear: *pull yourself together, or else.*

The one good thing about the tattoo was its position. Placed on his right hip, the only two people in the world who would see it on a regular basis were Gus and himself. Gathering every last bit of his courage and determination to escape this life in the long run, he decided to look at this branding treatment as a small hiccup. Something as rudimentary as a tattoo in this day and age wasn't worth getting punished for. As was the case with all of his sacrifices, this one would buy him some time and relative peace of mind for at least a couple of days.

Colt took his shorts and underwear off and lay on the bed, covering himself with a towel. Moon Light inspected the area and took out a razor from her trolley's top drawer. After a few strokes she dabbed the spot with rubbing alcohol on a cotton wad. She stopped mid-swipe and locked eyes with Colt when she noticed the bruise on his side.

"Okay, let's get started. I'll hold your hand the entire time, baby. I love you," Gus said, grabbing Colt's hand. He had moved one of the armchairs to the bedside. Where it had the appearance of a dutiful husband, Gus's gesture was all about oversight and control.

Moon Light looked from Colt's eyes to Gus and back to the bruise. With a sharp inhale she dug into her trolley and got to business. She put a stencil with the intended C-mark on Colt's skin, rubbed her hand over it and stripped the paper away to leave an outline. Once the needle started buzzing like a dentist's drill Colt realized the painful part was about to start.

"The first few seconds are always the worst. Squeeze your husband's hand as hard as you can," Moon Light said with a wink.

The woman wasn't kidding, but she had no idea how much every touch of that needle hurt Colt's heart more than his skin. Gus was having him branded like cattle while holding him down. Like always, Gus got what he wanted without Colt's consent, which made this ritual just another type of rape. Just like Gus, Colt had now reached his final straw. He gritted his teeth every time the needle hit the thinner parts of skin on his hip. While doing so, he had an epiphany.

Colt's only shot at freedom, he decided, was killing Gus. In order to stop all the hurt, fear and humiliation at its source, he had to find a way out of the house and get hold of a weapon. It had to be a firearm of some sort, seeing as knives were conveniently sparse in the house—Hannah always brought her own collection in a locked briefcase. A potato peeler or bathroom razor wasn't going to do the trick, as they involved too many variables beyond his control. If—no, when he struck, it would have to be absolutely, fucking perfect.

Then he remembered the pawn shop down his old

street in Koreatown. Mr. Cho always had some type of gun on display, and wouldn't ask too many questions. If he could get there without Gus finding out, he'd be set. One more year. Plenty of time to hash out the details.

Chapter 23
Mel—Present

"Sanders and Chen, do you copy?" Cam asked through his headset.

"Loud and clear."

"Roger that."

"Okay. Initiate phase one. They should be here in ten. Break a leg you two."

As agreed, Colt and Oliver were taking a Lyft to the Guzman restaurant in Brentwood, tipping the driver more than enough to make sure they'd be on time. Only ten more minutes until the showdown at Gus's favorite restaurant in LA. Ten minutes of excruciating nerves in the case of Mel inside their *Los Angeles Devil's Upkeep* van.

"Mel, you either got to stop breathing like a thoroughbred or switch off your mic. It's going to be okay. Nothing bad can happen to them up there. That's what Sanders and Chen are there for."

Mel took off his headset and rested them on his shoulders. *"It's going to be okay.* That's probably what they told those guys on the beaches of Normandy on D-Day. Worked out great for them."

"Way to kill the mood. Speaking of moods, how's Kate holding up?"

"Her mother's driving her crazy. She can't get over the fact that we're not hiring a nanny. The woman's a nut job with a twisted world view. Oh, and her father's been pushing her to come back to work every waking minute. I give it forty-eight hours for her to cave. On the plus side, though, they're enjoying their time with their grandchild, so I should be focusing on that. Why are in-laws so tough to interact with? Parents in general freak me out."

"Thanks," Cam said with a chuckle.

"You know what I mean. So, how are things at *your* house nowadays?"

"Honestly? I wouldn't know for sure. Javi is doing so great in school he got to skip a grade, but he seems miserable. The twins are into all things pink and girly, so I'm no help at all in that area. One of these days they're going to dress me up like a princess for a tea party. You know, like you see on Instagram?" Cam shuddered at the thought. "Oh, and Mariana actually hired a part-time nanny two months ago. Lesley Anne. So, in short, I haven't been that much at home since taking on this Godzilla case, and now I'm paying for a white girl to look after my kids."

Mel's best friend hiring a nanny meant this case was close to consuming him completely. They used to laugh at people who paid strangers to deal with their rowdy offspring.

"Well, at least you know about the stuff that matters most."

"Yeah…it doesn't feel like it. How come no one ever

told us parenting is nothing more than an endless string of decisions while constantly feeling like you're making all the wrong ones?"

Nail on the head.

"Because it would stop procreation and end the human race?"

"Yeah, That's probably it," Cam said, downing his second RedBull. He nudged Mel's elbow and put his headset back on.

A dark gray Ford F150 truck drove up the parking lot at the bottom of the massive tower that housed the Guzman restaurant. Colt and Oliver got out and waved the driver off, holding hands. With his hair looking like a million dollars, red polo shirt and tailored black chinos, Colt stood out from the crowd without lifting a finger. To make him even more conspicuously inconspicuous, he was going to be wearing sunglasses all the way to their table—catching as much attention as possible along the way. Oliver was dressed in a black version of Colt's shirt to indicate how close they were in age—one more detail designed to add fuel to Gus's impending rage.

"Colt, kiss Ol on the cheek if you can hear me."

Colt looked around and did as he was told. He held onto Oliver a little longer, whispering in his earpiece, *"Cam, I could have just sneezed or something. This isn't Melrose Place."*

Mel stifled chuckles when he saw Cam roll his eyes. The two lovers entered the building. He detected a hint of elevator music and a ding when they got to the twelfth floor.

"Oh, baby, this is such a nice surprise. I used to come here all

the time. How did you know?" Colt asked in a louder, more cheery voice than usual.

"You like Brazilian food with a view. It doesn't take a genius to figure out you'd love this place. And remember, I'm buying. So go nuts with the order."

"You're the best."

Mel recognized the sound following Colt's last phrase. Together with Cam, Charlotte and the Chief, he had watched Colt and Oliver make out twice at the station that morning. They had gotten it right the second time—after flunking the first overly enthused attempt. It might have been the most awkward moment Mel had ever experienced at work. It almost reminded him of his first dating days with Kate way back when. Almost.

He heard Colt apologize to the maître d' for their display of passion.

"I hear the Santa Monica Pier is up for a remodel. Can you believe it?" Officer Kim Chen said—code for eyes on Colt and Oliver.

"I'm so glad we're doing this. You deserve good things in life, Colt. I love seeing you this happy."

A throat-clearing cough interrupted them.

"Bruno? Oh my God. Good to see you, man. It's been a while, hasn't it?"

"Likewise. Does, uhm, Gus know you're here?"

"I don't think so, no. We're kind of, uhm, taking some time apart for the moment. You know how it is."

"Are you? I'm sorry to hear it."

An awkward pause, then, *"Bruno, I want you to meet*

Jamie. The two of us go way back, actually. You know what they say. You can't make old friends. Are you here to take our order?"

Colt ordered a ridiculous amount of food and wine, all with names Mel had never heard of.

"They're holding hands the entire time. I think this might have done the trick already," Officer Ron Sanders whispered in between sipping sounds. Finding two officers unknown to Gus willing to have dinner on the DEA's tab was by far the easiest step leading up to this operation.

Cam took his headset off and turned to Mel, who did the same. "Colt really seems to have taken a liking to Ol. You think he's still acting?"

Mel nodded. "I know for a fact he is. His acting skills are what kept him from going insane the past four years. You won't be able to tell, but this is actually killing him on the inside. It's a fucking miracle he's not more damaged. You know, I've tried to imagine living the life he led with Gus. I don't think I could have done it. The sheer mental strength he must have shown day in, day out is a marvel on its own. It was probably a lot worse than how he's described it so far."

Cam leaned back and looked down at his crossed knees. "Kept you up at night, did it?"

"You know it did."

"Me too. But not just Colt's side of this case."

"Something's up," Officer Chen said. *"They're leaving their table. Both of them."*

"Colt, Ol, do you copy?" Cam said, fumbling with his microphone.

The other end of the line only provided them with giggling and shushing sounds.

Cam rose from his chair and repeated his question, but still got no answer other than giddy laughter.

"They're headed for the bathrooms," Officer Sanders said.

"Wait. Both of them? Why?"

"Unclear. They're being loud—drawing attention to themselves. At least half the faces in here have noticed. Want me to go after them?"

"Negative. What the fuck?" Cam's last phrase was more to himself than to the team. "Listen up everyone, if they're not out of there in ten we're aborting the whole thing." Cam threw his headset to the side. "Goddammit."

"Just wait, Cam. Colt must have his reasons to step out of line like this. They're in the spotlight. That's all that matters, right? They'll come out in a few minutes and make even more heads turn. It could be brilliant. Gus will have no choice but be pissed tomorrow."

"Brilliant? For someone who's been controlled for years he sure likes to color outside the lines, Mel."

They both sat in silence for a few minutes. Mel hoped he was right about this. He trusted Colt—had done for a while. Besides, Oliver was with him, and that guy had enough to prove as it was.

Come on out, you guys.

"They're back. FYI, the look on that Bruno guy's face is priceless. We'll catalog it as improv," Officer Chen said. Mel could hear her smile in the way she said it.

The rest of their night had passed without any further improvisation by Colt or Oliver, for which Mel was glad.

He wasn't sure his best friend could have taken more of that. Walking out of the building, Colt even acted a little tipsy, leaning on Oliver for his every step to their Lyft.

"Bruno is watching them from the windows. Let's give him an encore," Officer Chen said.

"Guys, you're being watched. Give it all you've got," Mel said. Oliver spun Colt against the side of the Cadillac Escalade and ravished him like he needed Colt's lungs to breathe. Through the windshield Mel saw Oliver pull up Colt's leg around his waist and kiss him one more time for good measure. The Chief's puppy really wanted to go home with an A+ to put on the fridge.

The next morning Mel drove back to the station with Oliver in the back and Colt in the front. An unspoken piece of information thickened the air inside Mel's Explorer. One that would cast shadows over Colt's face the minute Mel brought it up. Colt had taken a long shower after his performance last night and had refused to talk about it. Like Mel had expected, pretending to love a man and show affection in a public space had taken its toll over the years.

Oliver touched his shoulder from behind. "Hey, Mel. Could you turn that up? It's getting too quiet in here."

"Ol, there are rules in this car. One, no smoking. Two, the maximum volume on the radio is four. Three, no touching. Try not to break any more of them, because according to rule number four I'm responsible for passengers in the backseat," Colt said, smirking at Mel beneath his black sunglasses. He couldn't believe he remembered the rules verbatim.

"Despite his mocking tone, he's right, Ol," Mel said.

"All right."

Mel cleared his throat. "Colt, there's, uhm, something you need to know about today's planning. I didn't want to tell you this last night."

"Okay. Out with it." Colt took off the shades and showed a tiny crease in his forehead.

"Gus is coming in for questioning. Together with his lawyer. Don't worry, there's an entire precinct of officers and detectives between the two of you. He won't be able to get to you."

Colt scoffed. "You've got some nerve telling me not to worry, Mel. In case you forgot, Gus is always able to hurt me. I can't believe this." Colt shifted in his seat as his breathing turned into shallow heaves. "Let me out. Now. Pull over."

"Can't do that. Someone might see you."

"You want me to throw up all over your car floor? Pull. The fuck. Over," Colt yelled, holding the back of his hand over his mouth.

Mel did as instructed and pulled to the curb on Sawtelle Boulevard alongside the highway. Colt got out, took three steps and retched his breakfast onto the pavement. Oliver followed, resting his hand on Colt's back while scanning the area for onlookers. Through the opened door Mel watched Colt nod to Oliver and make his way back into the car.

"I'm sorry. It's just…I can't even picture it, being in the same building as him."

"Colt, Oliver and I will be by your side the entire time. Charlotte's taking the lead on the interrogation, together with Gene. Knowing her, she's probably prepared for this all night."

"Well, I guess it's a good thing you didn't tell me all this last night." Another good thing was Mel's increased tolerance for the concept of vomit as a new dad.

Fifteen minutes later Cam was raising his voice at Colt and Oliver after they had entered the main office space.

"You went off-script and endangered the whole operation. What the hell were you in there for anyway?"

"Cam, stop shouting," Mel said.

"Look, Cam," Colt said, "I had an idea that would piss off Gus even more. He once forced me to give him oral sex in a restaurant's bathroom. He had just found out one of our business dinner dates had once hooked up with me. Therefore he needed to make sure I knew who I belonged to. Last night I wanted to recreate that memory for him as payback. I'm 100% sure Bruno noticed. He was glued to his the phone for the rest of the night. Don't worry, we didn't actually—you know."

"Yeah, I didn't think you had, but thanks for putting that image in my head. You couldn't have told me all this through your earpiece?"

"And blow our cover? No way, Cam. Too many onlookers, which was the whole point."

"Where's Charlotte?" Mel asked.

"Interrogation room 2. Where else did you think she'd be?" Cam said.

With only fifteen more minutes to go, Mel ordered

Oliver and Colt to stay in the SV office until further notice. "We don't want to take any risks, so stay where you are at all times."

Then he headed on to Charlotte, who appeared to be in a trance inside the interrogation room. Her long soft curls were hanging free from their usual bun, framing her angular face like she'd finally found the confidence to loosen up. Watching her through the one-sided window, he could see her mouthing questions to herself. He hoped her mental strength had flooded back enough for her to be able to pull off this monstrous task. Like everyone in the building, she knew the stakes of this interview.

"Detectives, before we get started I'd like to bring something to your attention. On several occasions you told me you've been keeping Colt safe and hidden. Somehow he was spotted at a restaurant last night. I hear he wasn't alone, to make matters worse. So tell me. Did you let him get away? Are you guys that incompetent?" Gus asked. The man looked intimidating as ever. The pained grimaces and loungewear had now made room for a neatly trimmed graying beard and a dashing black three-piece suit with a bright yellow tie.

"Mr. Carolino. Can I call you Gustavo?" Gus nodded, so Charlotte continued, "Thank you for telling us. I know these must be trying times for you. You clearly love your husband very much. Are you sure your intel is correct? It's just that we haven't heard a thing about it."

"I'm positive. The owner of the Guzman told me so

himself. Apparently Colt and his alleged friend were having a really good time, too."

"Gustavo, how did that make you feel, hearing Colt was out there with another man? Hearing how great a time he was having?"

His gaze dropped to his lap. "Like getting shot all over again. I just don't understand it. This is not like him at all. I'm worried sick about what else he might do. You really need to keep a closer eye on him."

"Detective Weisz, what is the question here, really?" Silveira asked, mumbling something in Portuguese right after.

"Mr. Silveira, your client is the one who brought it up. I'm just trying to get the full picture for our investigation. Forgive us for being thorough."

Fucking brilliant. Mel liked this version of Charlotte. Together with Cam, he was watching from behind the glass in the space next to the interrogation room.

"Would you describe yourself as a violent man, Gustavo?" Gene asked. Him assisting Charlotte was the Chief's idea. Mel's partner was ready to fly solo, but not without a parachute.

"No. Not in the least. I'd rather label myself as passionate, like most Brazilians you'll come across out there."

"Your husband provided us with a rather aggressive image of you, Gustavo. You keep refuting his statements about your character, so I just have to ask. If you really are a passionate man instead of a violent individual, why would Colt lie to us about it?"

Gus squinted at Gene for a long beat. "Detectives, the thing you need to know about my husband is that he had a tough upbringing. Like I've said on previous accounts, he's got mental health issues stemming from a troubled childhood. Dead father, addict mother and brother, deranged stepfather, on-and-off foster care. Look, I wish I could tell you I completely understand why he's telling you those lies, but I can't. Maybe if I'd paid attention to his state of mind better I might have prevented him from shooting me in his manic state. Did you contact Dr. Petersen?"

Cam remained silent and rested his index finger on his lower lip. A lot depended on the outcome of this interrogation for him. Mel hated how good Gus was at playing the part of the concerned husband. Charlotte didn't let it get to her, however.

"We did, yes. It proved to be an interesting conversation. Anyway, for now it's your word against his, so let's talk about something else—the reason you're really here today. The joined forces of the DEA and LAPD have taken a deep dive into your real estate business's finances. It seems you specialize in a certain niche market, Gustavo. Can you explain which one that is?"

"You mean top-notch properties in the Platinum Triangle?" Gus crossed his arms and leaned back. This was the part his attorney had prepped him for, from the looks of it.

"You're hardly the only business covering that market, Gustavo," Gene said.

"That's right. Let's focus on a few of your recent sales."

Charlotte fanned out half a dozen documents of property sales.

"Now, you might not be able to tell right away, but there's a common denominator between these properties— one that confirms your specialty. You see, all of them were sold below market value after a family tragedy had taken place. This is where it gets fascinating. Every tragedy can be linked to the Cordelio drug cartel. Murder, sexual assault, things like that. And you just happened to be right there every single time, ready to work your realtor magic the minute they decided to sell. How would you explain that?"

"Don't answer that. Detective, this is all wild speculation. There's no hard evidence here of any involvement with something as preposterous as a Mexican drug cartel. I urge you to rephrase your question and stop wasting our time," Silveira said.

"Fair enough. How come these people sold their properties below market value? Did you advise them to?" Charlotte asked.

"I did no such thing. Like you said, these people had all gone through unspeakable trauma. What they wanted from me was a swift deal with zero attention from any neighborhood gossip squads. The best way to do that is to sell at a lower price than expected. By selling them that fast, these people were able to move out of town and start their healing process elsewhere."

"You're right. That was a very nice thing for you to do, Gustavo. You—" Charlotte cut Gene off by putting her hand on his wrist. To anyone else it might not have looked like an intimate gesture, but not to Mel. His breath caught the moment their eyes met. How had he been so blind all this time? And most of all, when had this thing between them started? Maybe Gene was the reason Charlotte had been keeping to herself before her assault. They'd been hiding it so well. Of course Gene needed to be in there right now. It all made sense.

"Gustavo, there's something else about these properties. All of them were purchased through a private holding. Our guys at IT were able to track the transactions to a certain degree, but most of them disappeared into a myriad of offshore accounts across the globe."

"Yes, Dahlia Rubia LTD. They show a lot of interest in top-notch properties in those neighborhoods. They see them as business opportunities to sell them at higher prices in the long run."

"What can you tell us about them? They're doing a great job at hiding their faces," Gene said.

"All I know is I deal with a man named Alejandro Suarez. They're one of my most trustworthy clients and decide quickly—within days. It's what everyone in this business dreams of."

"Yeah, here's the problem with that holding, Gustavo. Alejandro can't be the man's real name. There's one man with the same name in Folsom doing twenty-five to life for multiple homicide accounts. There's more. The manager of the holding is registered as Colt Whittaker." Charlotte pulled the document from her manila binder and shoved it under Gus's nose. He stared at Colt's signature with his mouth agape and a furrowed brow. Then he said something to Silveira in his native tongue, his tone anything but friendly.

"Detectives, my client and I need to discuss this matter further. Do you mind giving us the room? Five minutes is all we need. Ten, tops," Silveira said with his Hollywood smile in check.

Whether it was an act or not, Gus was getting more and more rattled. Chances of him stepping out of line were increasing by the minute.

As soon as Charlotte closed the door next to the one-sided window, Mel gave her a shoulder squeeze and a smile. "You did great."

"Mel? Colt's on his way here," Oliver said.

"What? You had one job, Ol."

"I tried to reason with him, but he's adamant to see Gus from behind the glass. You know how he gets."

Mel exhaled for a full five seconds with his hands gathered at the back of his head.

"Let him in," Cam said. "What's the worst that could happen? It could help the guy move forward for all we know. He deserves this after last night, Mel."

Charlotte agreed immediately, leaving Mel's concerns outnumbered.

Colt walked up to the glass as though every step he took could trigger a land mine. Mel saw his eyes mist over in his reflection. "God, he looks good. It's by far his best power outfit." After staring for a while, he said, "You want to hear something fucked-up? I still love him. Even right now, with all that has happened, I can sense him turning every fiber of my being toward him. I know it's not healthy and wrong on so many levels, but I can feel his pull all the same." Colt sighed, then continued, "We were so good together for a while. Those first six months were the best of my life."

Colt sniffled and wiped at his eyes with his index fingers. "Charlotte, whatever you discussed, he's clearly mad. Somehow Tommy is taking the grunt of it, so that's good. Whatever you're doing, it's working." He turned around. "Thank you for letting me see him. I needed that."

Colt walked away with Oliver on his tail. Even though they didn't need to act anymore, Oliver guided Colt out the room with a hand on his lower back. Ten minutes had passed, so Charlotte and Gene got back to it. Before Gene walked back in, Mel pulled at his forearm. "Be good to her, okay?"

Gene's eyebrows shot up as his eyes widened. He nodded and said, "I will," then went back inside.

"Gustavo, the next round of pictures might be upsetting so I'd like to warn you beforehand." Charlotte pulled out the photos of all the victims that highlighted the cartel's c-shaped tattoo or burn mark on each and every one of them. Mel knew this would be tough on her and had to remind himself to keep breathing.

"Colt has the same tattoo. Last time you claimed it to be an anniversary gift and led us to believe it was mostly Colt's idea to begin with. Are you sticking to your story or is there more to it? If so, I suggest you explain it right now."

"Detective, you can't be serious. I was under the impression that the LAPD was trying its best to resuscitate their dwindling image these days. I guess I was wrong, because otherwise they wouldn't have hired someone like you. Asked and answered. Move along," Silveira said, tugging at his tie. His forehead gleamed in the spotlight.

"Gustavo," Charlotte pointed to the most recent victims, "these last two victims were found in a car that drove on its own to our doorstep. Forensics determined they were both illegal Mexican citizens who had moved to the city a few months back. Ergo, they wouldn't be missed or chased by any relatives. Now, aside from the two dead bodies with those C-markings, the car also carried a direct threat to Colt's life." She pulled out the last picture featuring the threat written across Colt's photograph. "You love your husband, Gustavo. You don't want him to get killed, or do you? I'll ask again. What's the story behind Colt's tattoo?"

"All right, that's enough. We've been very cooperative despite the total lack of both competence and evidence. This is as far as we'll go. Unless you've got something else on my client, we'll be leaving now." Silveira mumbled more to Gus in Portuguese, but Gus remained seated for a while, rubbing his beard with his fingers. He was breathing hard through his nose. When he finally looked up from the picture of Colt he stared at the glass, almost directly to where Mel was standing, as though Gus knew he was there.

Gus's expression fell as soon as he got out in the hallway. He sniffed the air a few times and started looking around him with frantic movements.

"Colt? Colt?" he shouted with a deep, rumbling voice that ricocheted off the walls.

Mel walked out of the adjoining room and tried to calm him down. "Gustavo, Colt is not here."

"Bullshit. I can smell him. Amouage Interlude—I

highly doubt any of you would wear a fragrance like that. Colt! It's me. I love you."

Cam intervened, "Sir, you need to stop shouting this second or I'll have you dragged out of here. Do you understand?"

Gus coughed and wiped his knuckles at his welled-up eyes. He started following his attorney to the exit, but stopped and held his right index finger in the air three steps in. He turned on his heels and pulled a piece of paper out of his pocket.

"Detective Daniels? Could you give this to Colt for me? Feel free to read it. Please?"

Mel nodded and took the folded piece of legal pad paper from him.

"Thank you." As he watched the man leave with his long legs and menacing posture, Mel deliberated on whether to throw away the message altogether. Having had enough of Gus's games, he took a deep breath and folded it open.

Meet me outside, Detective. No recording devices.

Two steps outside the door were enough to spot Gus in the parking lot, waiting for him on the hood of his Bentley. Mel checked his surroundings for coworkers who might notice the illicit conversation he was about to have. Playing it cool, he pulled out his vape pen and started inhaling his cinnamon-flavored smoke like it was just another day at the office.

Gus immediately stood upright, making every inch of

his six feet four frame add to his intimidating aura. He was likely the kind of man that felt the need to establish his impressive height every chance he got. If the guy ever flew charter, he'd be first in line to claim the emergency exit seats.

Mel approached him, but kept a safe distance of about ten feet. "Gustavo. You wanted to see me?"

"Can I call you Melvin, Detective? It seems we're past formalities."

"Mel will do. No one calls me Melvin."

"Okay, Mel. Did you do as I said?"

Mel nodded.

"Recordings without consent are illegal anyway. Okay, here's the deal, Mel. You and that whole DEA and LAPD circle jerk you've got going in there want something from me, and I want something from you. Do you understand where I'm going with this?"

"I'm all ears."

Gus crossed his arms. "I can give you enough to bring them down. Not all of them, but enough big players to make them crumble from the inside out. You'll go down in history as the most successful anti-narcotics operation since Escobar's downfall. I'll hand everything over on one condition. You bring Colt home to me."

Never going to happen.

"What about your own indiscretions? If we don't come after you, the cartel will. You can't get out of this scat-free and you know it."

"I'm Brazilian, Mel. With my connections down there,

Colt and I will be gone long before you do your first round of arrests." He put on his shades, ready to leave.

No fucking way. He's insane.

Instead of doing the rational thing—like asking for immunity as an informant or proposing to wear a wire while meeting with the elusive Alejandro Suarez—he only wanted to get his prisoner back. Did he really think Mel was going to let it happen? Mel would rather take Colt's place in that house than allow the torture to go on for who knew how many years ahead.

Before Mel had time to react, Gus added, "You have twenty-four hours." He got in the car, closed the door and drove onto Butler Avenue heading north.

Chapter 24
Colt—Past

Please go. It's so much easier when you're not here.

Colt hadn't wanted to get out of bed, but Gus had—again—found a way to persuade him. Not that he was overly tired or hungover, no. Those days belonged to a different life entirely—where Colt's biggest worry was to make ends meet at the end of the month, not figuring out how not to get beaten to a pulp on a regular basis. This particular morning, various degrees of bruising and a burning sensation deep inside his lungs troubled his movements.

Colt noticed how Hannah had to look away when she laid eyes on him after he had stumbled downstairs. That's how he knew it was bad: when Hannah couldn't maintain eye contact anymore. He still thought of her and Langdon as awful human beings, but his anger had cooled enough for him to be civil again. Would he call an ambulance for either of them to save their lives? No, he wouldn't go that far. Co-existence was all they deserved.

"Okay, I'm off. Baby, that dishwasher guy is supposed to be here in an hour. Keep an eye on him and make sure he fixes it for good this time. I'm sorry I can't be here to do it myself, but these guys keep changing their schedules. You'd think by buying designer appliances maintenance would be a breeze, but no," Gus said. Then he kissed Colt on the lips and the forehead. He held Colt's head against his chest and whispered, "I'm sorry about last night. I love you. I'll make it up to you, promise." Then he was gone. Colt waited for him to drive through the gate before he collapsed in a sobbing fit, like he often did in those days.

Gus indeed had a lot to be sorry for, considering the night he had forced Colt to endure. In the last months, Gus's sexual tastes had entered the scary part of the BDSM spectrum. Nearing forty-nine years of age, Gus's body wasn't as cooperative as it had been when they met. The orange prescription bottles didn't lie: Gus was needing help in the blood circulation department. Erection problems led to a new source of frustration, which in its turn caused Gus to take it out on Colt. And when he did take it out on Colt, it solved said erection problems—after a while. It had become a vicious circle that focused all of its rage on Colt.

Colt had previously thought the beatings were the worst part of his imprisoned way of life, but that world of pain had segued back into their forced sex life. Last night he had taken repeated slaps in the face to get Gus's juices flowing. After the fifth one he noticed—to his horror—it wasn't working. Gus then cuffed his hands behind his back and positioned him on his knees. Still not satisfied with the sight of it, Gus opened the drawer of the nightstand and pulled out the black leather collar with its leash. Obedient as Gus had trained him to be, Colt pointed his chin up to make it easier for him to fasten the collar around his neck.

A few minutes in, Colt thought his head-giving efforts were working, although he got nothing but a half erection as a response. He received another set of blows when Gus told him he wasn't trying hard enough. He knew it was going to be one of those memorable nights the moment Gus pushed him back to the floor and said, "Follow me."

Unless people down in Santa Monica had been pointing a telescope directly at them, no one would have been able to watch the scene that had gone down on the pool deck. As Gus led him there butt-naked, collared and cuffed, he wished someone was watching their every move. Whatever Gus had planned for him, there was no doubt it was going to take time to recover from his wounds. Colt had seen that lopsided smile of anticipation and looming darkness in his eyes too many times to mistake it for anything else. Even though the temperature was still fairly warm outside, Colt was immune to it.

Please don't kill me. Please let it be quick.

Gus pointed to a place on the deck right at the water's edge. "On your back. Legs up."

He started prepping Colt's ass with his mouth and fingers. In between Colt's involuntary moans and shuddered exhales, Gus focused his licks on his balls and teased his cock. The contradictions between his mind's and his body's desires drove him crazy. At the same time he wanted to scream with delight, and punch Gus in the face for forcing his body to respond. By doing neither, he realized his mental scars would grow deeper once more.

"All right. We're getting somewhere."

Gus flipped him on his stomach and Gus pushed him dangerously close to the water with no place to rest his head.

Gus kissed his way from Colt's ass all the way up to his shoulders. Colt's neck muscles burned from trying to keep his head above the water. While Gus's lubed-up fingers entered him, Gus's other hand pushed his face under water. He held him there for over thirty seconds until he pulled him back up using the leash, all the while fucking him with two fingers. Colt gasped for air when he could, knowing it wouldn't last.

After the third round, Gus pushed him under again, this time inserting his cock into Colt in one go, making him choke on an underwater scream. When Gus pulled him up again he coughed and heaved with broken breaths. Gus was now thrusting in and out of him in a steady rhythm, making it even harder to collect oxygen.

"Please stop. Fuck me all you want, but please stop."

Colt winced as Gus pulled the leash back and moved his lips to his left ear. "Colt. I love you, but you know how this works. You just have to lie down and take it. I'll make it quick."

With his head back under water, Colt's panic got the better of him. He writhed against Gus's grip, but it was no use. In return, Gus only fucked him harder and faster. The process went on four more times, until finally Gus pulled out of him and laid him on his back. As Colt battled for air with burning lungs, Gus kneeled next to him and finished himself off with grunting strokes. The second he came, he pulled Colt closer with the leash and forced himself into his mouth. He had told Colt once that he enjoyed knowing his come would stay inside of him. Colt didn't struggle against the commands to swallow. By that time all he really cared about was that it was over. And that he had survived another aggressive tide in Gus's ocean of moods.

According to his personal deadline, Colt had two more months to come up with an escape plan. Positively uninterested in any more waterboarding sessions or other equally atrocious treatments, he realized time was running out. If Gus had entered the waterboarding realm, there was no telling what type of torture would be next. Sticking around to find out was not in Colt's plans—not if he could help it.

Step one of the getaway plot had already been taken care of months ago. When Gus had arrived back home one Tuesday afternoon, Colt had surprised him on the leather couch in the living room, wearing nothing but a jockstrap, a blindfold and handcuffs. In the aftermath, Colt had secured one of the electronic keys to the Land Rover Defender. It had taken a lot of stealth when Gus had asked about his car keys' whereabouts, but it had worked—the byproduct of years of abuse: stellar acting skills.

Now all he needed was a gun. With all of his digital activities closely monitored, googling *where to buy a gun without registration* wasn't an option. Neither was registering for a firearm officially. However, if he could call Mr. Cho at the pawn shop in Koreatown, he could drive there and trade it for his MacBook with no questions asked. Asking either Langdon or Hannah for a phone call was a risk he couldn't take—he had come too far for his plans to go up in smoke out of carelessness.

"Apologies, Mr. Carolino, but I need to make a quick drive to our warehouse in Beverly Hills. The blower's fried too, apparently. I'll be back in thirty. Sorry for the inconvenience," the dishwasher guy said. Apart from his blocky mustache the guy had a kind face below his graying curls and silver-blue eyes. The years of excessive carb intake had translated into a paunch filling out his overalls, but he didn't look like the kind of man that would obsess over it. Colt thought about how much easier the man's life must have been in comparison to his own.

He had almost walked out before Colt called after him. "Sir, your phone."

"Oh, you know what? Leave it here. It'll only slow me down, anyway. I could use some time not being connected to everyone and everything. Keeps the crazy at bay, if you ask me. Thank you for your concern, though. Appreciate it." He pointed to Colt, the way small-town people do as a token of affection, and walked down to his van.

Colt stared at the phone in his hand. It was a senior-like clamshell model without so much as a four-digit code to secure it. Without giving it too much thought, he dialed Mr. Cho's number from memory and hoped it hadn't changed. His one chance to get out of his personal hell hinged on two things: Mr. Cho picking up within the next thirty minutes and there being a gun for sale in his shop. Colt liked his odds and waited for an answer with a jackhammering heart. He pushed away the scary thought that this could all have been a set-up by Gus.

"Mr. Cho's Pawn Shop. This is Mr. Cho. How can I help you?"

"Mr. Cho, hi. This is Colt. Colt Whittaker. I used to live on your street together with Steve Blake. He used to sell you a lot of his collector items back in the day. Mostly old movie posters."

"Ah, yes. Colt and Steve. Those items were good business. Good to hear you after all this time. How have you been? You know, my wife still wears that Alien perfume you advised her. Changed her life."

Steve.

Colt blinked away a small tear. Hearing about his former life in his current circumstances was like floating in warm waves of nostalgia. How young and free Steve and him had been in the days they roamed Mr. Cho's shop. A cross between a laugh and a sob escaped his throat. "I'm glad to hear it. Listen, Mr. Cho, I'm sorry to ask this of you, but I'm in trouble and I need your help. I can't explain it right now, so I hope you don't mind."

"Son, the less I know in my business, the better. Plausible deniability's been my creed since opening this place. Tell me. What can I do?"

"I need a gun and some ammo. Without official registration. There can be no record tracing it back to me whatsoever. I'll trade you my MacBook for it and you can keep the change. Sound good?"

"Hmm. Well, I do have a good model for you. Don't be silly, I'm not keeping your change, Colt. You sound like you could use a friend, so let me be one. Now, uhm, that we've established us being friends, I just have to say this. I'm really sorry about Steve."

"Me too. Thank you, Mr. Cho. I really do need a friend." Colt could no longer keep his sobs down. He hadn't witnessed any kindness for over four years. It was a surreal experience that required an emotional outlet.

When he recovered he told Mr. Cho he'd be there the next morning, right before opening time. Gus was going to be scouting new properties with Natalee and Langdon all day, starting out with breakfast in Hollywood Hills. Who knew that feigning interest in Gus's shop talk over dinner—with the grace of an Academy Award Nominee—would finally pay off after all those years? One more day and he'd be out of Holmby Hills, never to look back. He'd break away from what would otherwise become a lifetime of slavery. And all he had to do was shoot and kill the love of his life—to aim a gun at Gus, look him in the eye and pull the trigger, all the while preventing the few happy memories from undermining his determination.

Chapter 25
Mel—Present

"Colt, please say something," Mel said, "anything."

After hearing about Gus's offer, he had turned semi-catatonic again—a coping mechanism that tended to take over once the mental distress got too high for him to handle.

"Oh God, Mel. Please tell me he isn't actually considering this suicidal deal. I'll lock him in my office if I have to—fuck, I didn't mean it like that," the Chief said. Together with Cam, Charlotte, Gene and Oliver they had all gathered in her office once again. Colt was staring into the distance with his elbows resting on his knees. The lines in his forehead assured Mel he was thinking at two hundred miles per hour.

"The truth is I don't know. He gets like this sometimes. It usually passes pretty quick—" Mel started.

Colt inhaled sharply, then said, "Okay. I'm sorry about that. It's just crazy how obsessed he is with wanting to control me. I mean, he's willing to blow up the entire cartel and go into hiding for a chance to get me back. It's all he cares about, and that scares me."

"Right. So, what are you thinking?" Mel asked.

"Well, just to be clear: there's no way I'm going back there. For all we know he'll drug me, have my name changed and move us to Brazil in under twenty-four hours. You'll never see me again—not alive at least. I suggest Ol and I go on another date or something. Give Gus a little more time to unravel. Jealousy is the one thing he really doesn't handle well. If he's willing to call it quits on those Cordelio guys now, he's bound to act up in other ways, too."

"I'm with Colt," Cam said. "We call his bluff and wait the bastard out. He's desperate, exactly the way we want him to be right now. Desperate men with power and money do the stupidest things to get themselves caught."

"Let's hope the cartel doesn't get to him first. If he's gathered as much intel as he's letting on, he might as well be their prime target as of now," Gene said, crossing his arms.

"You're right. I don't think he knew anything about Colt being the so-called manager of Dahlia Rubia LTD. It makes you wonder about what else they haven't told him," Charlotte said. Mel saw the exchange of quick glances between her and Gene in a different light now. The more he thought about it, the more the match made sense. It would explain the tension between Gene and Colt, for one, as he probably had been blaming Colt for Charlotte's assault all along.

Captain Perez took a big breath and pushed herself up with both hands on her massive desk. "All right, everyone. We can't do anything for at least one more day. Take this opportunity to get some rest. If anyone wants to talk some more, I'll be at the Mercury Well in an hour. We'll reconvene tomorrow. Oliver, would you mind staying at Mel's a little longer? We might need you to be Colt's date again soon."

"No problem, Chief," Oliver said. Mel admired the young officer's dedication to the operation, and didn't mind having an extra pair of eyes on Colt at home. With Gus stepping out of line, there was no telling how he was going to react to all of it. Tough as he had been acting all day, there was a chance of him turning into a bawling mess by nightfall. Colt's long healing process had only just begun, after all.

When Mel pulled up to his driveway at home he didn't kill the engine and handed his house key to Oliver. "I need to go see my family. I'll be back before dinner."

As soon as Colt had closed the passenger door, Mel addressed Oliver. "Hey, Ol. Keep an eye on him. It's been a tough day, so talk to him if he lets you. If he doesn't, stay close." Oliver nodded and followed Colt inside.

Somehow driving to his in-laws always made Mel feel as inadequate a son-in-law to them as a hammer was to a screw. The winding blacktop bringing his Explorer up to the Pacific Palisades contrastively sent his self-esteem plummeting as he drove on to the Summers' house. When he pictured living in his promised forever home as a foster kid he often imagined it just like this neighborhood: a modest-size house surrounded by as much greenery as LA could provide and neighbors that were just at the right distance—easy to avoid when needed. Thinking about how some people just fell into money and privilege backward filled him with resentment, no matter how hard he tried not to let it. Of course, Ronald—and especially Eleanor—didn't exactly make his mental stretching exercise any easier.

"Oh, Melvin, I really wish you could tell us all about this secret operation you've been working on. It sounds dangerous. Do you think you'll hit the evening news someday? Oh, that would just be great, wouldn't it, Ronald?" Eleanor rattled on. After meeting him in the entrance hall with its Bohemian crystal chandelier, they had moved into the living room with the cream-colored sofas and the rosewood coffee table. For an old house, it still managed to give off the air of certain wealth in every room. In this particular one, it was the black Baby Grand in front of the bay window in the corner.

"It would, I guess. It's been tough on everyone in our team, but I think we're getting somewhere." Mel took a sip from his coffee mug wishing it were Irish.

"Please tell me they're paying you extra for all the trouble you've put your family through." She clutched her hand against her chest and toyed with her pearl necklace. Mel had never seen the woman without it. There were probably indentations in her skin when she took them off, like Marge Simpson. Observations like these had become a survival instinct. It was either that or saying things out loud he'd regret.

"Eleanor, it's a state job. You know it doesn't work like that. Mel's doing this to make the city safer for Rose, and every one of us. So what if it doesn't pay extra for his personal sacrifices? I think it's admirable. I could never invest my time so selflessly. It takes a special kind of man to do so in this day and age," Ronald said.

Insult or praise? It was the perpetual question when his in-laws commented on his professional life.

"Mom, Dad, could you please sound a little more condescending? Mel has a decent job and actually helps a lot of people. I've seen it with my own eyes at home this time. He's spectacular at what he does, and that's all that matters. Now change the subject and behave, you two," Kate said after kissing him with a lingering brush of her lower lip against his. She was holding Rose to her chest. Mel kissed his daughter on the forehead and took her in his arm. Kate draped a moss green burp rag over his shoulder just in case.

"Fair enough, Kate. Why don't you tell Mel about your day?" Eleanor asked.

Alarm sounds were ringing in Mel's head as soon as he saw her face contort in a knowing smile. He wished Rose would throw up. "Tell me what?"

Kate sighed. "Okay. I went to the Dry Summers offices this morning to get a head start on all the things I've missed in my absence. Turned out there were a lot of those." She widened her eyes. Her red hair looked shinier and healthier than a few days before. Maybe it was a good thing for her to focus on something else for a little while.

"You did? It's only been two months." Mel shot a glance at Ronald, the unmistakable puppeteer of the day. Instead of recoiling, Kate's father crossed one knee over the other and pulled up the sleeves of his burgundy knit sweater—the one that looked about Mel's age. Wearing the same clothes for decades came with the territory of owning a successful state-wide dry-cleaning business, Mel figured. Just like Ronald himself, the sweater needed to retire soon.

"I know, but I have to say, it felt so good to be useful again. Among grownups. I know I shouldn't want to, but spending time away from Rose made me feel a better mother. Don't get me wrong, I missed her, and it was hard to walk out that door, but I love her even more because of it. It's hard to explain, really."

No, it's not. Daddy tricked you into it and Mommy handled the rest. He marveled at how blind Kate was to her parents' shenanigans. He took a deep breath through his nose—and noticed all too well why Rose had been silent and contented all this time.

"Funny you should say that, Kate, darling. It could always be like that, you know. It's only natural that you enjoy her presence more when you've had some distance. It's what we always did with you. And you turned out pretty great, now didn't you?" Eleanor said.

Sure. She works in the family company without any credentials. She can barely make a decision on her own and she's a perpetual people pleaser.

"Kate, I need your help changing Rose in the next room," he said, unable to stand the stench in the living room any longer—Rose had nothing to do with it this time.

"How's Colt?" Kate asked, ripping the dirty diaper's ends loose. She was so much better at it that they had reached a silent understanding: whenever Kate was near, she'd take over the diaper changes—mostly because she couldn't stand watching Mel make a mess.

"Okay, I guess. Our strategy seems to be working. He, uhm, saw his husband today through the one-sided window at the station."

"Oh my God. How did that go?" Kate's eyes went wide. She knew enough to figure out the answer herself.

"He was adamant about wanting to see him. It was tough, but I think it helped him."

"Closure can be very healing, but still. So, how long is this situation going to last?" Kate had just powdered Rose's butt cheeks and unwrapped a new diaper using her teeth.

"You mean: how much longer will you be your parents' hostage?"

They shared a glance and burst into chuckles. It felt good to laugh with her like that again. The mischievous dimple in her left cheek tugged right at his heartstrings. Only Kate could ever make him feel weak in the knees.

"It's not so bad. It's not particularly great, but at least they're getting to know their granddaughter."

"Right. Promise me they won't talk you into getting a live-in nanny. Your mother seems to be pulling out all the stops to make that happen."

"I promise." Kate fastened the last strap on Rose's diaper and held her in her arms. His daughter cooed softly when her eyes landed on his.

"She really missed you, you know. Me too," Kate said, looking down at her feet.

Mel pulled her in for a hug with Rose in between their bodies. Rose's baby head smell together with Kate's natural blueberry scent provided all the comfort he'd been seeking on this visit. He kissed the side of her head and whispered,

"You'll be home before you know it. I love you. You're amazing, you know that?"

Kate crinkled her nose. "Are you vaping again?"

Fuck.

He tried his best to hide the guilty hot flash surfing all over his face. "I, uhm…yes. Look, I've been under a lot of pressure with this case and…one moment of weakness later and there I was, vaping in the parking lot at work. I'm sorry, Kate. I promise I'll stop once the investigation's through."

Kate's eyes went cold as she stared at him. "We'll talk some more about this when I get home. Jesus, Mel." She shook her head. He cursed himself for his weakness. The look of disappointment flashing at him like a neon sign was all he could see in his mind's eye on the ride home.

Mel had made an executive decision and brought Chinese takeout home to Colt and Oliver. He was careful to bundle up the receipts in the glove compartment. The least the DEA and LAPD could do was cover the cost of feeding an additional pair of grown men in his house.

The lights being off in the downstairs rooms didn't surprise him that much when he stepped inside with the fragrant bags of sweet and sour foods. Colt had looked exhausted all afternoon, so he might have gone to bed early. Oliver was supposed to stay by his side at all times, meaning he'd be upstairs, too.

"Mel? Is that you?" The muffled call came from the utility room next to the garage.

"Ol? Where are you?"

"Utility room. Colt locked me in here." He banged twice on the door.

"He what?" Mel said, walking to Oliver as fast as he could. He unlocked the door and swung it open, cursing at all the baby-proofing he had put the house through.

"Thanks. He's got my phone. Half an hour ago I heard him get into someone's car. I think he ordered a Lyft with my account. Mel, you don't think he—"

"I'm afraid I do." Mel didn't dare to say it out loud. "Did he say anything?" he asked.

"Other than how sorry he was, he didn't tell me anything. I feel like an idiot."

"What was he doing with your phone?"

"He said he was going to try to call his mom again. Next thing I knew he shoved me in here and turned the key."

Back in the living room Mel noticed something he had missed in his strides. One of Kate's pink post-its stuck to the TV screen, reading:

Thank you for everything.
The Wayfaring Stranger.

"No. No, no, no. Everything we've worked for... How could he just throw that all away?"

"You know him. He probably wants to stop them from hurting more people, just like we do," Oliver said. "Fuck."

"Gus is not going to go easy on him, Ol. We have to stop him. Call the station."

"Bad idea. Look, Mel, we don't know for sure he's at Gus's house. I suggest we drive over there and check before we call anyone else. I don't want to share all about how Colt locked me up and got away if I don't need to, okay? The Chief just took me off her blacklist."

Mel thought it over. Sounding the alarms for nothing wouldn't be the best move, indeed. If Colt hadn't gone to Holmby Hills and police cars would show up at Gus's house anyway, then all chance of future negotiations with him would go up in flames. Besides, Gus wouldn't kill Colt. He thrived on owning and controlling him, like Colt always said. If Oliver and Mel drove up there on their own, it would at least be two to one if things went awry.

"You're right. Let's go," Mel said.

Before starting the engine of the Explorer he checked the magazine of his Glock and asked Oliver to reload it, who went to work fidgeting with spare bullets from a box in the glove compartment. He tried his best to keep his eyes on the road in the remaining purple-pink light, but every now and then Colt's statements about Gus's torturous ways came flooding back.

My husband has a very powerful grip. It'll make sense when you see him.

I screamed, cried, tried to fight him off, but it only made him beat me harder. It went on and on. And I just laid there and took it.

You don't know what it's like to have the world turn against you.

Chapter 26
Mel—Present

The black spired gate in the front was the only entrance to Gus's Holmby Hills mansion. Reaching up to about six feet six, it made it impossible for Mel and Oliver to tell whether Colt had already been inside or not. There was only one way to find out, and Mel was sure his companion wasn't going to like the idea very much.

"Mel, that's breaking and entering without probable cause."

"I know, but we've come this far. If he's not here we'll climb back over the gate and drive off like nothing happened. Besides," Mel paused and looked around to check what neighbors might have been watching, "I think I just heard a distress call. You too?"

Oliver rolled his eyes. "Fair enough," he said, holding up his palms.

Climbing over the gate was a two-man job, especially if neither one of them wished to become a shish kebab. Once on the other side—Mel panting far more than Oliver, to his disappointment—they both kept their heads down as they bypassed the LED footlights alongside the paved walkway to the house. Chances of spotting Colt were highest from either the back pool deck or the kitchen with its unobstructed window. Trimmed box hedges shielded the guest parking spots near the front lawn on three sides. Mel took the lead and moved closer to get a better look, crouching behind the hedge—the perfect vantage point.

At first Mel thought Gus was standing in the kitchen by himself, but two bare arms around his midsection confirmed a second presence.

Mel needed to be one hundred percent sure before he called for backup. After signaling for Oliver to stay put, he moved closer to the window, scurrying on his haunches in the sprinkled lawn. Darkness was his friend, or so he hoped. From his new point of view he still couldn't tell whether it was Colt. The arms pulled back from Gus's torso. What unfolded next before Mel's eyes was worse than he could have imagined. None of Colt's stories about his husband could have prepared his retinas for the violence they recorded. Gus grabbed his barely clothed husband by the throat, swung him around and forced his head against the wall of cupboards. Hovering over Colt's pained grimace, Gus appeared to be following it up by spewing more threats.

Mel moved back to the hedge to call for backup. He took his phone out of his pocket and told Rita what he needed her to hear as fast as he could. She told him to be careful and wait, as though it were at all in the cards. After the call he turned his phone on mute and locked eyes with Oliver. "Wait by the front door. I'll go around to the back deck. If things get worse, cause a distraction, okay?"

"What kind of distraction?"

"Anything. You'll think of something."

"Right. Be careful, Mel."

"You too, Ol."

Oliver nodded with a ghostly pale face, not exactly instilling Mel with much confidence.

Mel took the long way around to avoid drawing attention through the kitchen window. A few scratches on his forearms allowed him through the citrus shrubbery onto the wooden back deck, still hidden from view. The mansion's architects had angled the pool deck away from the kitchen area to the south, likely to catch as many sun rays as possible.

As he inched toward the opened French doors, Colt stumbled to the floor behind them. He was clutching his nose to stop it from bleeding.

Son of a bitch. He needed to be stopped. Mel tried to look at the situation from Gus's perspective. Colt needed to be taught several lessons that night. First of all, he deserved to be in pain for having tried to kill him. Second, because he had run away. Third, because he had told people about their special arrangement of a marriage, and fourth, there was the added bonus agony he deserved because of dating another man so publicly. A multitude of beatings and rape were on Colt's plate in the foreseeable future—enough to make the man break at long last.

"Come on, baby. You know this hurts me more than you. But if you want to go out there and tell people how I used to beat you up every night, then I at least get to know what it tastes like. Get back here and take it like a man," Gus said, approaching his prey.

"Please don't do this. I got back here on my own, didn't I? You got what you wanted. Can't that be enough?" Colt asked. He was shivering as he crawled backward and away from his husband. Blood caked his fingers and his lower face from his nose to his chin.

Gus caught up with him and went for his throat once more, pulling him to his face. "Listen to me. All I want is for you to love me as much as I do you. And you obviously can't do that without my help. So no, Colt. You being here is not enough. You need to be reeducated in the way this marriage works. I need to see it in your eyes that you can't live without me. Looking at you right now," he shook his head, "I just don't see it."

Mel unlocked the safety and aimed his Glock right at Gus's face before he announced his presence. "That's enough. Step away from him. Slowly."

Gus moved fast and put Colt in front of him as a human shield, crouching behind his husband. He pulled Colt's wrist behind his back and secured his head with his elbow.

Fuck.

"Mel, how nice of you to show up so fast. Are you here to pick up your end of our deal?"

"I'm here to get Colt to safety, as in away from you. Anything else you can give me would be just an extra at this point."

"Is it just you?"

Mel tilted his head to the side. "For now."

Gus thought for a moment, his eyes searching for something on the ground that wasn't there.

"All right. Let me get you those files you want. They're in my office." He started taking steps back together with Colt.

"Not until you let him go."

"Mel, come on. You're not going to shoot Colt." Gus sighed. "Okay, then. I'll let you look for them yourself. Follow me and I'll give you instructions as we go."

Mel hesitated. There was no way he could shoot Gus without the risk of hitting Colt instead.

"Do as he says, Mel," Colt coughed against the force of Gus's forearm on his throat.

Gus kissed him on the cheek. "Good job, baby. I think it worked." Colt closed his eyes and grit his teeth. The version of Gus Mel now witnessed barely resembled the one he first met in the hospital.

"Fine, back away to your office slowly. No sudden movements," Mel said.

"You're the boss. Let's go, baby." Gus took measured steps back toward his office around the corner to the left of the French doors to the pool deck. Mel followed at a safe distance and focused his attention on Colt.

"Hey Mel? I'm sorry about locking up Oliver. It wasn't his fault. Is he okay?"

"Oliver's fine."

Gus and Colt had entered the office and Mel was about to step inside as well. Gus moved to the wall of bookcases and started his instructions.

"Sit down behind my desk. It's easier to get to the secret drawer."

"Easier to get me distracted and run away, too."

Where the hell are Cam and his heavy duty team?

"Mel, this will only work if you trust me," Gus said in a singsong voice.

Mel let out a huff of air, rolled his eyes and took a seat at the glass-topped desk with its giant curved monitor. It was an attractive workplace with the smell of books from one side and the spectacular Santa Monica and ocean views on the other. Knowing all of Gus's wealth was tainted, none of it felt enviable.

"All right. Open the second drawer on your left, starting from the top." Gus paused for Mel to follow his order, then continued. Mel kept aiming the Glock in his direction. "Now put your hand in the drawer and peel the envelope off the bottom of the top drawer."

Mel had trouble finding the right angle. If he lowered his head too much he couldn't keep Gus at gunpoint. But if he didn't comply he wouldn't get the intel on the cartel. He ducked quickly to see if any of Gus's claims were real. He stopped rummaging through the drawers when he saw Gus move toward the door again.

"Wait, don't take one more—"

He watched Colt and Gus struggle until Gus decided he'd had enough. He shoved Colt to the side and ran off into the hallway. Mel heard Colt fall with a wince and beelined for him.

"Are you okay?"

Colt was out of breath, but grabbed hold of Mel's arm. "He's got a gun. It was all for show. Your fingerprints are all over his desk now. He'll claim self-defense after he kills you, or both of us. Whatever you do, be careful. Don't worry, I'll be fine."

Mel hurried after Gus, hiding behind every corner to be sure he wouldn't be walking into a one-man firing squad. To his surprise, he found Gus standing in front of the pool with his palms up.

"You win, Detective Daniels. I hereby turn myself over to you. You can take me to the station where I'll answer all of your questions about my connection with the Cordelio cartel. I'm tired of hiding and looking back over my shoulder three times an hour. You can read me my Miranda rights now. I won't be calling my attorney. He hasn't really been on my side anyway. Do I need to get on my knees, *daddy*?"

Mel took one step closer and started rolling his eyes over Gus's clothing to check for a gun. His loose loungewear pants didn't give away anything. Water lapping against the sides of the pool filled the silence. With the absence of moonlight, the pool's neon blue lighting offered the only source of brightness in the night.

"Okay. Have it your way. Not right now, though. We'll wait for the team to get here and have them do it. I'd like to watch you get manhandled, *sweetheart*."

A wide grin spread over Gus's face, making his eyes crinkle. He started shaking with laughter, yet the only sound escaping his mouth were sputtering exhales. Gus lowered his hands a little in the process and rubbed his nose.

Don't you dare.

"Hands where I can see them, Gus."

To Mel the following series of actions happened in

slow-motion. Gus put his hands back up, but took things one step further in his charade. He lowered to one knee first, then the other. Losing his balance, he caught himself with one palm on the ground and the other on his thigh. Gus looked right into Mel's eyes and cocked his head to the side with a closed smile. "You know what your problem is, Mel? You trust people too much."

Gus's hand lingered on his hip. Mel's heart felt like it bounced off his sternum like a fenced-in rodeo bull in Dallas. The second Gus's hand was behind his back one of his knees jerked back up.

Mel aimed for his chest and put his finger on the trigger, then closed his eyes at the loud bang that echoed off the wooden surface and windows all around. He could no longer hear the water.

With his eyes wide and his mouth a perfect circle Gus produced a guttural moan. He looked down at the red-rimmed hole in his chest, then back to Mel with a creased forehead, as though he failed to register what it meant. A vein at the side of his neck swelled. Mel started shaking all over as he watched the lights go out in Gus's bright green eyes. He fell backward into the pool, turning the water pink with smoky tendrils of his lifeblood.

That's when Mel finally breathed again. He remained in place as though his shoes were glued to the wood beneath them as he tried to make sense of what had happened. He stared at his gun for a while.

Did I...?

Mel removed the magazine from the Glock and checked for missing bullets.

One of them was.

As he sucked in big breaths he tried to maintain a rational line of thinking and revived his best deduction skills. He hadn't felt any recoil and didn't have any memory of actually squeezing the trigger. He could have sworn he hadn't fired a single shot. There was no trembling of his forearm muscles, other than what the horror of the moment had called for.

Bingo.

There would be no gunpowder residue on him. His chest fell with a long exhale. Forensics would be able to prove the absence of residue. It would take time, but they'd believe him. They had to. He vowed to explain everything calmly when they got there. But then again, if Mel himself hadn't shot and killed Gus, then who had?

He turned toward the French doors and peeked inside toward the kitchen, dining and living rooms. There was no one around, except for Colt in Gus's office, but the chances of him having found an extra gun to fire in his battered state were abysmal. He looked up to the second floor, holding his gun up just in case and scanned the window, taking a step back to get a better view.

Colt emerged at the French doors, still looking like a horror-flick extra. They stared at each other wordlessly for a long while. Colt's lips were pressed together into what looked like the slightest hint of a smile, though it was hard to tell with all the blood. Just like when they first met, Mel couldn't for the life of him tell what Colt was trying to convey.

That's when he heard the shouting.

"LAPD, drop the gun and move back. I will not say this again. On the ground. Hands where I can see them."

"No! You bastard! You fucking killed him! Gus!" Before Mel could register what was happening, Colt ran past him and dived after his husband. He shouted for help as soon as he got Gus's corpse to the edge. When he climbed out of the pool, he started wailing as he clung to his dead husband. Mel could still hear him when they guided him inside, cuffed like a real killer—which was exactly how he felt now.

Twenty minutes later Mel was sitting at the kitchen island, still restrained, opposite his best friend—who had taken it upon himself to interrogate him and try to make sense of the night's events. There was something about being handcuffed in this house that didn't feel right. It reminded him of Colt's first reaction to the concept at the station on the day they met.

"So, the post-it on your TV. What did it say exactly?" Cam asked.

"*Thank you for everything. The Wayfaring Stranger.*"

Cam furrowed his brow. "What is that supposed to mean?"

"It's a song he once sang to Rose one night to calm her."

Cam smoothed his palms over his face. "Mel, we can't find Oliver anywhere. Are you sure you told him to stay put near the front door?"

"Yes. Why? Are you saying I'm making this up, Cam?"

Cam held up one hand. "No one is accusing you of

anything. I'm trying to get a better picture of what happened here tonight. So far, it's not looking good, Mel."

"You think I don't know that?" He took as deep a breath as he could. "How's Colt doing?"

"Not great. He's getting medical attention as we speak, but he's not calming down. Needless to say, the DEA will be taking him off your hands and keep him safe from now on."

Mel thought about Colt's strange expression moments before the team had arrived. So many questions were running through his head, it was hard to single one out. "I understand. Can I at least talk to him?"

Cam shook his head. "He's being very eloquent about not wanting to see your face ever again."

"What?"

Cam closed the legal pad and shoved it aside. He was staring at the marble surface. "Mel, as your friend, I'm going to ask you one more time. Did you shoot Gus?"

"Fucking hell, Cam. I did not." Mel banged the cuffs on the stone.

"Colt seems to believe you did. Said he saw it happen."

"He did?" Mel shook his head. "Cam, listen to me. As my friend, I'm asking you to believe me. I did not kill Gus."

It was Cam's turn to bang his palm on the counter. "Then why the hell is there a bullet missing from your goddam Glock, huh?" Cam was yelling as spittle ejected to the counter's surface.

"I don't know. I had Oliver load it on our way here. I swear it's all just a horrible misunderstanding. Have them check my clothes for gunshot residue. That'll prove it more than anything, right?"

Cam wiped an angry tear away from his eye and coughed before he locked eyes with his best friend again. "I hope so, because the other thing we can't find is Gus's gun, or the one you claim he was carrying, at least. Do you know what that means, Mel? If you did fire that gun, you just shot and killed an unarmed citizen in his own backyard, after breaking and entering. With Oliver being MIA and Colt no longer on your side, there's no one to corroborate your justified entry to this house. You'd be fucking looking at time in prison, man. How the hell am I supposed to explain that to Kate, huh? This happened on my watch. I'm sorry, I can't even look at you right now."

Mel had never seen his best friend cry other than after the births of his children. Tough as it was to hear Cam's reasoning, he wasn't wrong about any of it.

Wait.

No. It can't be. Can it?

Unarmed individual. Colt was the one who had told him about Gus wearing a gun. Oliver had loaded his Glock and could have left one out on purpose. Mel sensed his mind balancing on the threshold of clarity for a few seconds, until it plunged right in.

Colt and Oliver. Oliver and Colt.

Have they been playing us all this time?

Cam's heavy footsteps on the tiles broke his train of thought. He slapped a beige manila binder on the counter right beneath his nose. "Looks like at least one part of your story is true. We found this in Gus's office. You're going to want to see what's inside."

Chapter 27
Colt—Present

When you watch a lot of crime TV shows and read a fair amount of mystery and suspense novels, you think you've gathered a pretty accurate idea of how to pull off a lie. In fact, those stories often confirm the same thing over and over again: they claim the key to a good lie is a heavy amount of details combined with a good memory, so that you could tell it all backward when asked. Well, I'm sorry to burst your bubble, because that's bullshit. Trying to memorize all of those fabricated figments is a sure-fire way to set yourself up for failure. The foundations being shaky at best in that case, your whole house is doomed to collapse sink-hole style before you can say *pants on fire*. In my experience, keeping the lie going requires two things: stamina and sacrifice.

To be able to fool the big swinging dicks of the LAPD and DEA in a big-budget city like Los Angeles the way I did, I had applied what I enjoy referring to as the Pluto method. Think of this. We don't call Pluto a planet anymore for two reasons. One, it orbits the sun in a different angle than all the other planets—probably reveling in its superiority throughout. Two, it doesn't clear space debris in its path—what an ego. However, for an impressive seventy-six years that sneaky rock had us all fooled, believing it was just another planet. Pluto's secret to success? Staying close enough to the truth so that no one would ever question its integrity for three quarters of a century. So, that's the path I chose—askew or not—when first targeting Mel. Bottom line, when you only alter or leave out a select amount of details in your story, there's not a question the LAPD detectives could come up with you won't be able to answer. A little advice on the sly: if you do find yourself in a tight spot because of some superhero-level detective coming at you, you simply shut down and blame it on emotional trauma.

Let's talk about Gus first. I used to devour men like him on a near-daily basis when I first got to Los Angeles. In the gay community we all know the type of top he was: high-strung, domineering, controlling, overprotective, jealous as shit and a downright insane work ethic for a high-end job—in line with his god complex. Now, the trick to getting a man of Gus's caliber to want you is making them believe they're the one in the driver seat. By setting up the illusion of complete power over my body and mind, I was the one calling all the shots the whole time without them even noticing. The second they think they're in a position of power is when you know you've got them by the throat. There's nothing they won't do to keep said illusion alive for as long as possible. I'm proud to admit I've consented to—and fully enjoyed—every single beating I've ever taken during sex. But here's the kicker. Every time it happened, the man on the other end always believed it was completely their own doing. Stupid, egotistic, single-minded fucks.

Gus was perfect in his own special way. Gorgeous, rich, extremely skilled in the sack and in cahoots with the biggest drug cartel in town. Boy, had I met my match with him in bed. It's pretty rare that you find a man who's willing to run that extra mile. Producing the needed scars for the detectives at the West LA station was super easy because of it. Okay, in all fairness, weeks of taking blood-thinners had also contributed to the bruising patterns. It's also why my nose bled so hard on the day Gus died.

The morning he first told me he loved me was when my masterplan really started to kick into gear. I almost laughed out loud when he proposed to me only an hour later. Telling him those lies about Steve Blake had tickled his jealous bone in all the right places—granted, the man was a total jerk—one I was more than happy to order a hit on—but not a bicurious one. I don't mean to gloat in this tell-all, but the next step of sabotaging my job at Sephora was a stroke of genius that sealed the deal of our engagement in record time. It's amazing how gullible men can be when they're head over heels.

Okay, I'd like to apologize for the monster of a husband I portrayed Gus to have been. Don't get me wrong, the man had many flaws. He was manipulative, possessive and often got too rough during sex—it wasn't technically rape at times, but he sure liked to push my boundaries every now and then. Also, he didn't much care for safe words—those parts were true. But was he in any way violent or abusive in the true sense of those words? If we forget about that angry scene in his last hour, no. Not once did he lay a hand on me other than per my instructions during foreplay. Truth be told, there were times I thought I could genuinely love Gus back—moments of weakness, if you will.

Then why go through all the trouble of having Mel kill him? you may wonder. Trust me—though I wouldn't advise you to—I'm getting there. As expected, I was never truly in love with Gustavo Carolino. He was outrageously sexy and lived a wealthy, enviable life and all, but my heart had already belonged to a different man long before Gus and I first hooked up. Jamie—not Oliver, as you know him—and I met when we were both twelve years old in our foster group home The Streets, just west of Topeka. It turned out the two of us shared a lot of scars. We both had lost one parent at a young age and were en route to losing the other to their cocaine habits. Furthermore, both his dad and my mom seemed to love the stuff more than they did us, and had made their decision painfully clear.

After our respective returns back home we kept seeing each other every chance we got. By the time we were fifteen we had kissed in the bathroom of the public library of Topeka and Shawnee county…and had started exploring more bases, growing closer and more in love with every milestone. I'll have you know that Jamie is the only man with the power to touch my heart just by looking at me. In my turn, I can identify all of his different glances from afar. It's the kind of connection you only read about in Colleen Hoover novels—with all the spice.

Except for having found a love that shined brighter than all the stars across the Kansas Plains, Jamie and I had nothing to show for our lives at nineteen. Not more than a combined few hundred dollars to our names and zero college or job prospects other than farming. Any money our parents had saved for our college tuitions had long disappeared up their deteriorating nostrils by that point. If one thing was clear, we needed to make our futures ourselves—not an easy thing to do for two gay kids in Kansas.

What we did have was a heavy amount of rage. Some targeted the foster system, some went straight to our parents, but the local drug rings got the lion's share. If they hadn't been dealing the shit in the first place, our parents would never have thrown the best years of their lives—and their kids—away because of it. Those low-life, bottom-feeding bastards owed us our futures. It was that kind of reasoning that had us pursuing a better life in LA. Before we left for good, I met Jamie every day to—among other activities—hash out all the last details of our masterplan to start taking back what was ours from the big drug cartels of Southern California. And that's why one night I targeted Gus on Grindr all the way up in Holmby Hills, where questionable morals permeated the thinning air.

All we really needed, except for Gus's unwavering devotion, was someone to be our fall guy when we killed him. My make-believe husband needed to die for two reasons. One, the Cordelio cartel needed to stop destroying lives the way they had done our parents'. It would have been a pain for them to do that without Carolino Real Estate's relentless financial influx. Two, by having Mel murder him instead of us—or rather, making it look that way—my inheritance as his widower would experience no pull-overs on its road to my bank account.

I do feel bad about Mel being our collateral damage, though. Telling his closest coworkers about how I'd seen him shoot my husband was the toughest part. Like the good father figure he is, he'd come by my heavily guarded DEA-assigned motel room almost every day, only to hear I wouldn't see him. Thank the powers that be, my inheritance came through within a month, so I could finally drop my act and follow Jamie. Poor Mel—he's one of those good guys in short supply you sometimes hear people talk about. But like I said, two things are needed in the construction of a good lie: stamina—I mean, four fucking years!—and sacrifice.

Chapter 28—Epilogue
Mel—Present

Ten months later

Mel's luck had really turned against him ever since he had Colt pull over on a similarly scorching morning in the South California sun. As was expected, the heat-trapping blacktop beneath his rubber soles and the dark LAPD uniform with its accompanying officer cap conspired to have him break out in a sweat. To make matters worse, the mandatory body cam device on his chest felt ready to combust.

They'll come and fix it soon. You'll be out of here before you know it. Just take it slow and breathe.

He was directing traffic on the crossing of Santa Monica Boulevard and Bundy Drive that morning. The exceptional heat—or some other malfunctioning oddity— had fried the traffic lights, meaning the Traffic Division was called to the scene, as in Officer Melvin Daniels. Just when his mind was traveling to the days of wearing blazers with Charlotte as his partner, the sight of an unusual vehicle caught his eye. More than that, it stopped right at his feet.

The shaded driver's window of the matte army-green

Defender rolled down. As soon as he saw the driver, Mel could breathe again. Where he had expected Colt behind the wheel against his better judgment, a Korean man with half-long hair stared back at him.

"Sir, I'm going to need you to keep driving."

"I know, and I'm sorry. But I need to pass a message to Officer Melvin Daniels. I suppose that's you." The man squinted at Mel's name tag.

"A message from whom?"

"They won't pay me if I tell you anything more than the message itself. So, listen. You need to meet the Wayfaring Stranger at noon. Alone." He handed Mel a pink Post-it.

Mel took off his sunglasses and wiped the sweat from his brow with his forearm as he squinted at the address scribbled on the Post-it. He then gestured for the man to drive off and wondered about how different his life would have been if he had never come across a Land Rover Defender.

When the technicians had fixed the red light, Mel decided to go on an early lunch break. He typed the address into his phone and failed to recognize the area's significance—a Mexican bar all the way up in Hollywood near Melrose Hill. If Colt wanted to see him, why there? There had to be a calculated reason behind it. To be able to pull off a scheme of deception the way Colt and Oliver—or whatever his real name was—had, Mel knew they had to be smarter than anyone had given them credit for.

Mel pulled into the parking lot of the Chimene's restaurant and bar two minutes before noon and scanned the perimeter to the best of his ability. Nothing in sight but a few acting schools, a small film studio and a car wash next to Sunset Boulevard's continual rush of cars. Biting his fingernails, he considered texting Kate, but quickly judged against it. After all, seeing how their marriage was still recovering from the fall-out of Gus's murder, he had no desire to revive all the resentment between the two of them. Besides, she'd be too busy bossing people around at Dry Summers, anyway.

Mel got out of his car, folded his sunglasses and hooked one if its arms into his shirt collar. After steeling himself with a deep breath, he walked through the entrance of the bar area, putting one foot in front of the other without overthinking it. The bartender waved him over before he could take in the details of the Mexican-themed establishment's colorful interior.

"Mel Daniels? The table by the window. I'm going to need your body cam, radio and phone. He'll be there with you soon." Mel gave the bartender a sideways glance, prompting him to elaborate. "The Wayfaring Stranger. Now hand them over."

After complying with his heart traveling up his throat, Mel walked over to the window and took one of the stools at a high table. For a Tuesday lunch break, only a handful of customers were enjoying either the food, the drinks or their company with Mariachi music in the background.

He looked over his shoulder and saw a man in full motorcycle gear heading over with a Corona bottle in each gloved hand. The yellow and black striping reminded him of the first *Kill Bill* movie, which felt like ages ago. The helmeted figure put down the bottles, one for Mel and sat beside him. He took his helmet off, making Mel inhale so sharply he had to cough the lump in his throat away. Those Pacific blue eyes staring right at him after all this time were almost too much. The nauseating betrayal from that one night came flooding back. He deliberated punching him in the face, but remembered that's what Colt liked—if any of that had been true, of course.

It seemed neither of them wanted to break the silent staring contest first. Colt's hair was now a chocolate brown instead of Hollywood blond—that, too, had been a prop in his play. Colt was the first to finally look away, facing the window. Mel, on the other hand, kept eyeing him with an array of emotions knotted together like a teenager's earbuds.

"Mel, please stop looking at me like that and say something."

"Looking at you like what? Like you destroyed my career and lied to my face every chance you got? Yeah, Colt, that's pretty hard to keep in check right now."

Colt sighed. "Mel, I'm not going to lie anymore. I don't feel sorry about the way things turned out, but believe me when I say I feel awful about the toll it has taken on you."

"Believe you? Are you being serious right now? Believing you is what got me in this mess in the first place, Colt." Mel was pointing at his uniform's badge reading Officer Daniels. "You played me like a—"

"Mel, stop it," Colt said between his teeth. "Keep your voice down. I'm here to give you some answers, but if you can't keep your cool, I'm going to have to get out of here and never come back again. This is your one chance. Am I making myself clear?"

Mel huffed out a breath and took a swig of the beer bottle after smelling it, just to be sure it wasn't another trick.

"Anyway. Do you want to know why we're here at this bar?"

Mel looked around again and said, "Mexican-owned, easy to bribe, quick exit and entrance possibilities, no significant means of surveillance… Am I getting close?"

"Not really. Those things are just extra perks. You really don't see it, do you?" Colt smiled at him like he was supposed to know what it all meant. "Fine, I'll open your eyes, then." Colt cleared his throat. "All I want to do is have a little fun before I die."

Mel recognized the phrase, but failed to put his finger on it. Then he looked across the street like Colt had been doing. That's when it hit him: the car wash, the beer bottles at noon on a Tuesday. Despite being scalding mad at Colt, Mel couldn't stop the smile the moment had called for. He turned to see the exact same smile painted across Colt's face.

"My name is not William. Or Billy," Mel said, taking another swig of beer.

Colt laughed. "I'm not sure this is the bar she was talking about, but it's the best my Google Maps skills allowed. I knew a little Sheryl Crow would break the ice. It goes to show that not all of it was a lie, Mel. In fact, most of the things I told you were true."

"It doesn't matter, Colt. You lied to me from the start, and I was stupid enough to fall for it."

"Don't do that, Mel. You're a lot of things, but stupid isn't one of them. Now, I don't have a lot of time, so you should start asking me questions." Colt looked at his phone, then turned it back to his pocket.

Mel didn't know where to start. He'd been dreaming of an opportunity like this for months. In every single one of his dreams the conversations played out differently. When he noticed Colt was staring, he started at the beginning.

"Did Gus ever abuse you in any way?"

Colt's eyebrows shot up. "Jumping right in. Okay, then. Yes, he did, but only on the day he died when you walked in on us. He was furious, which was understandable. All the other times I mentioned, he only hit me because I literally asked him during sex."

"Goddammit, Colt." Mel had started biting his nails and cursed himself for it. "Was me pulling you over an accident or not?"

"It wasn't. We singled you out months before, when Jamie—I mean, Oliver—started working at the station. You fit all the criteria. Steady career, trustworthy, foster kid… In short, a detective that fought for victims with unrelenting energy. Becoming a father had revved up your instincts just enough to believe me."

Mel buried his face in his palms and tried to make sense of it all. "All right, then. Colt, I need you to tell me what really happened with Charlotte."

Colt studied his hands on the table, like Mel had seen him do so many times before. He swallowed hard. "Jamie had made sure none of the safe houses would welcome me. I needed to be staying at your house, so that the two of us would become closer. When Charlotte volunteered to let me stay with her, we activated the emergency plan. Jamie was going to be on watch, so it was rather easy to get those hired guys in and out without trouble. I hadn't known anything about the details beforehand. That's what made the acting easier, because I was truly horrified at what they'd done—at what I'd done. Mel, Charlotte getting brutalized is the thing I regret most about my actions. She didn't deserve that at all. I'm sorry for allowing her to get hurt. If you want to punch me, please do."

Mel looked him in the eye and saw a tear springing from Colt's left eye. His jaw had been clenching so hard it hurt. His hands had turned into fists, but he wouldn't give into Colt's suggestion. "Please, Colt. We both know it would only turn you on."

Colt wiped the tear away and sniffed. "You're right. Keep going. Make the most of our time."

"How long have you known Oliver, or Jamie?"

Colt smiled—all the way to the wrinkles around his eyes. "We met in a group home when we were both twelve. Remember how I told you I used to sing *Wayfaring Stranger* to a kid with anxiety issues? That was Jamie. We fell in love somewhere around fifteen and we're still going strong, in spite of a four-year hiatus."

"Why did you guys do it? All of it, I mean?"

"It's rather simple, really. Jamie and I both lost a parent to an all-consuming drug addiction. Drug lords owed us for the crappy lives we had led in Kansas. So, we went looking for a way to make them pay us their debt. We actively targeted rich men with ties to a drug cartel. That's how Jamie found Gus through the grapevine of the escort world. Six months before our first Grindr hookup we started keeping an eye on him. It didn't require looking really hard to figure out he was besties with the Cordelio cartel. Then it was all a matter of finding out what made the man tick."

"And you thought by taking him out you'd hurt the cartel and get a big fat inheritance. Man, that's cold." Mel took a swig.

"Hey," Colt banged his bottle on the table, "he may not have been the monster I claimed him to be, but he was not a good man, Mel. He allowed those mobsters to terrorize innocent people for years in order to fill his pockets, and all of you LAPD or DEA lemmings had no clue where to even start dismantling their organization."

"Problem was, you couldn't do it yourself, so you tricked me into killing him for you. And then ended up doing it yourself. What was all that about?"

Colt took a sip from his beer, making his face contract in disgust. "The original plan was for you to shoot and kill Gus, but I decided to change it. After having spent time with you, I couldn't let you go to jail for trying to save me. So, we shot him ourselves using the exact same gun. We sowed enough doubt to cover our tracks and make it look like you shot him. I hate to mention this, but something tells me you would have pulled the trigger if we hadn't."

Mel had thought about those moments before he heard the gunshot many times, but rarely talked about it to anyone. What he remembered most was the rage he felt toward Gustavo as a violent individual. Hearing it from Colt now, he was sure he would have taken the shot if the scene had taken one second longer than it had. "Maybe."

Colt picked up his phone and typed a quick response to

a text. "Sorry, it's Jamie. He's nervous about this whole situation. Does anyone know you're here?"

"No. Sounds like he needs his song."

He cocked his head. "Don't I know it. I went from one high-maintenance man to the next." He frowned. "Sorry, too soon?"

"It's okay. Colt?" He waited for him to look up again from his phone. "What about your family?"

Colt observed the car wash while he talked. "My mom was in on it the whole time. Knowing she'd do anything for her next fix, she was incredibly easy to handle. I'll never see her again, and she knows it. Unless, of course, she decides to talk and needs an intervention. But I doubt anyone would believe her anyway. Dave, however, was a harder part of our plan. I mostly told you the truth about him, except for the fact that he'd turned his life around. That never happened for Dave. In a way, having him killed was an act of kindness. It was only a matter of time before someone would have found him frozen to death in some downtown alley. Just like Mom, his addictions had eclipsed his personality. Bottom line, they both might as well have died when I was sixteen. I know that sounds harsh, but it's the truth."

Mel now saw Colt in a way he had never seen him before. Sitting across from him in this dingy bar with its nervous music, he was not the abused, broken man he had met all those months ago. He was a child left all alone by everyone who had loved him except for Jamie. That gnawing feeling Mel often carried inside of never being good enough for anyone—not at his job, not at home as a husband and father, not among his friends—had to be at least ten times worse for Colt. It didn't justify the actions in his impressive scheme of lies, but Mel finally understood where it all came from: a dark hole in Colt's heart that had widened every time someone new had abandoned him. Instead of taking it out on anyone that dared to come close, all of the resentment in his young life had found its target in the Cordelio cartel. Despite all of the collateral damage, Colt and Jamie had indeed succeeded in something the DEA could only have dreamed of.

"Colt, are you happy?"

Colt eyed him with that same tiny crease in his forehead Mel had gotten used to. "You know, I really am. Mostly. I still feel bad about your demotion and Charlotte's assault, but other than that, I am happy, yes. Are you?"

Mel sucked in a slow breath before he answered. "I'm getting there. I'm trying to look past this, hoping to be a detective again one day. Oh, Kate's dad retired, so she's the new CEO of Dry Summers. And Rose is growing so big, you wouldn't believe it. I'd show you a picture, but it's on my phone behind the bar. We hired a live-in nanny, another battle I lost in this parenthood game, I guess."

"I wouldn't worry about that too much, Mel. If we allow ourselves to forget about your baby skills, you're the best dad any kid can hope for. I'm just going to say it, because I've lived with you and all: you're exactly the kind of father I wished I could have grown up with. Oh God, here I go." Colt stopped a tear from spilling over his cheek with his index finger. "Sorry, I didn't mean to do this to you. Mel, I can only imagine how much better I would have turned out if I'd had a dad like you." He sniffled, then coughed. "That's exactly why the next part is going to be so hard."

Through his tears, Colt waved at the bartender. The man got the hint and brought over a big brown envelope with Mel's name written across in black Sharpie. "Okay, before we say goodbye, I want you to have this. For the record, this is not me buying off my guilt—not entirely, at least." Colt handed him the envelope and gestured for him to open it.

Mel studied the document, but had to read it twice before it made any sense. "Is this a joke?"

"It's notarized and all. Look at the signatures and stamps. Gus's inheritance, together with all the funding I pulled from Dahlia Rubia LTD last-minute, will provide more than enough for Jamie and me to build a life elsewhere. If the memory of Gus's death is too painful, at least save it for Rose one day. With it being a murder house now it won't be selling for a reasonable price any time soon anyway."

"I don't want it. How would I even explain this at work? They'll start asking questions and making assumptions. Revive the investigation."

"Not if you play it smart and wait a few years. Just take it, Mel. Foster kids like us need to take care of our own. People never hand stray bullets like us anything but scraps and you know it. For once in your life, please accept this as a true gift. Jamie and I owe it to you. Also, your deadbeat parents fucking owe this to you. You deserve good things, Mel. Look around this town. Think about all those other children with rich parents handing them properties.

Nothing fair to it, right? Look at it that way. Think about Rose's future. But most of all, think of your own."

Swallowing hard, Mel turned the document back into the envelope and struck something hard and small inside it. When he fished it out he recognized it instantly. "What's on this?"

"Oh, right. That flash drive contains two things: the digital document of the deed and a recording for Rose—and yourself if you want to hear it. So, you're accepting the house?"

Mel nodded slowly, as though he were still trying to convince himself. "I am."

"You don't know how glad I am to hear you say that, Mel," Colt said, then got up from his seat. His leather pants squeaked. Their time had come to a close as the air filled with unsaid farewells.

"Mel, I… Please don't hate me, okay?" Colt's eyes were welling up again. "The one variable Jamie and I never took into account was me growing fond of you. I really wanted to be honest with you, but I couldn't. I hope you know that."

"I don't hate you, Colt. It was a shitty thing to put me through, but uhm…*at least you're being polite.*"

"Fucking hell. I can't believe you remember that. I really am sorry. Why did you have to be such a great guy?" Colt was sobbing, drawing the remaining handful of customers' attention. "Go enjoy your life, Mel. Whatever you do, I want you to be happy doing it. Oh, and tell Rose about me one day, will you?"

It was Mel's turn to wipe a tear from his cheek. "Absolutely, Colt. Say hi to Jamie for me. You be careful out there, okay? I don't want to see you hit the news—again."

Colt scoffed and smiled. He started swinging his helmet back over his head, but hesitated. Putting the thing back down, he closed the distance and put his arms around Mel. They hugged for a full minute, until Colt whispered, "I really need to go. Don't follow me. Goodbye, Mel."

Mel said it back and watched him put on his helmet. With a final nod, Colt walked back to the space behind the bar. Mel couldn't pull his eyes away until he was out of sight, out of his life for good. He took another swig from the beer bottle and smiled as he hummed Sheryl Crow's *All I Wanna Do*. Colt was right. Most of what he had told him had been true after all.

Mel got into his car, started the engine and plugged in the flash drive. Colt's voice roared through the speakers, singing *The Boxer* by Paul Simon. One verse stood out from the rest, filling Mel with a full-circle sensation in his chest. It was about how some people only heard the things they wanted to hear, and neglected all the rest. When it came to the story of Colt Whittaker, a foster kid just like himself, Mel could now admit he'd had more than one blind spot.

If there was one thing Mel knew for sure, listening to his favorite music would never be the same again.

THE END

Acknowledgements

I will never forget the look on my husband's face when I came downstairs one Sunday afternoon and he'd just read the first three chapters of this book. "Honey, do we need to talk?" It's safe to say his reaction was understandable, as this story was very much an experiment for me as a beginning writer. I had been running around with the idea for the first scene between Mel and Colt for a while, and then decided I'd put my mind to the test and see just how dark this story could go. By reaching this page, I'm sure you know the answer.

Dark as this book may be, if it hadn't been for the light of the wonderful people in my life, I never would have brought it this far.

First, I want to thank my kick-ass literary agents and authors, Mel Hartman and Sandra J. Paul from Hamley Books Publishing, for championing my stories across the globe. Your support in this crazy business means everything to me. Thank you, again, for believing in my work.

Second, buckets and buckets of praise go to the heartwarming team at Dreamsphere Books. Cali Kitsu, Craig Gibb and John Robin, you guys are so much fun to work with. In addition, I want to thank my assigned editor Margaret Larson for helping me with the final touches of my manuscript and all the aha moments that came with them.

Gwen and Guido, my mom and dad, deserve as many trophies as they can fit in their apartment. Thanks to them, I had the luxury of growing up in a house where my dreams were supported and expressing my feelings was not only allowed, but encouraged. Thank you so much for creating a home where taboos almost didn't exist. I truly believe it's the reason behind my confidence when it comes to writing spicy scenes today. I love you.

I will never stop expressing my gratitude for the existence of Martine V., the best beta reader a writer like me could have wished for. I remember sending her a long email in which I basically apologized for the 'filth' she was about to read in my manuscript. Undeterred, she took the binder from my hands and started reading that very same day. Thank you for willing to go on this epic journey with me, and for wanting to read all of my work with unrelenting enthusiasm. Your comments and suggestions have elevated my books to the next level. I'm 100% sure my editors have been grateful for your work, too, if unknowingly so.

My Saint Ursula support team of coworkers also deserves a cheer for riding along with the highs and lows of my writing days. Thank you, Anne V., Elise V., Thomas D., Leen G., Debby V., Lies H., Stefan V., Katleen D., Eef D., Lien M., Keshia V., Merel G., and so many others.

Special thanks to Detective Stijn B., for providing insights into the Special Victims Unit division of the Antwerp police department. The character of Mel Daniels wouldn't have been the same without your anecdotes and observations.

My father-in-law died the day before I got the call that the rights for this book were sold. Even though it was a dark and sad time, my in-laws found ways to be happy for me through it all. Lize V., Haiko P. and Helena B., thank you for showing such strength back then, and for always cheering me on. Lize V., I really hope this book teaches you things about male pleasure. You're welcome, Haiko P.

I also want to thank my friend Mark A., for giving me a confidence boost when it comes to my English proficiency as a second-language speaker.

It speaks for itself that the biggest thank you of them all goes to my husband Menno P. Strange glances and questions aside, I couldn't have done any of this without you. Thank you for supporting my career from the very start. For giving me space and time to pour my crazy ideas onto pages for hours on end. For reading my work, even though you don't really like reading at all. And most of all, for loving me just the way I am, warts and all. Looking back at our fifteen years together, I am confident when I say this: we make a damn good team, you and me.

And finally, thank you, dear reader, for choosing this book in an ocean of options. I hope you enjoyed it at least half as much as I did writing it.

About Jay Heron

Jay Heron is a gay Belgian author of young adult thrillers and adult MM romance novels. With a profound love for the English language, for twelve years he taught teenagers about the joy of reading English books. Nowadays he still handles IT and admin in his school. When he's not writing, editing, or working out, he's in his kitchen baking all kinds of delicacies (to his husband's endless delight).

More from Dreamsphere Books

Maybe It's You
Jay Heron

Work hard, get straight As, and do whatever it takes to get into a respectable college. It's a mantra all high school seniors are acquainted with. Although, most of them would never take it as literally as four students at the Saint Ursula Institute have. No, for aspiring architect Parker, nerdy athlete Eric, teacher's pet Shawna, and former cheerleader Addison, "whatever it takes" entails far more than they could have imagined.

The biggest obstacle on their roads to an Ivy League college is Mrs. Kaufmann, a mathematics teacher from hell. After failing her class repeatedly, the four students gather forces. They devise a plan to pull her out of the equation, buckle up, and do "whatever it takes". However, this comes with an emotional toll none of them are prepared for. It may even be worth it, if everything goes as planned…

One year later, anonymous threats start coming in. Someone knows what happened, and wants them to confess. Soon, the blackmailer shows they have no trouble following through with their violent threats. The four friends—the ones that are still alive—have a choice to make: turn themselves in, or put their fates in the hands of their tormentor.

Unless they find a way to turn this lose-lose situation around before it's too late…

More from Dreamsphere Books

The Unforgivable Crimes of Dana Cooper
P. Daniels

When Special Agent Jonathan Howard gets the call that serial sexual sadist Jeffrey Marks has been caught, he immediately travels to Rappaport, North Dakota, to confront the man. Jonathan has been on the Marks case for years with no breaks and a growing list of victims.

Entering the interrogation room, Jonathan is confused. It's not Jeffrey Marks he finds here…it's his recent victim, Dana Cooper.

Jonathan struggles to make sense of this twist in the case. Dana Cooper has murdered Jeffrey Marks in a fashion more brutal than anything Marks did to his victims, to an extreme that seems almost inexplicable. Before he can gather more information, Dana escapes custody and soon begins a preternatural vendetta, blazing a trail of death through several states, putting Jonathan in the last position he ever thought he'd be in.

He has to capture victim, instead of perpetrator, for unspeakable crimes that are more harrowing than anything he's seen before, and there's no predicting where she'll strike next…